Sweetwater Creek

Sweetwater Creek

A NOVEL

———

ANNE RIVERS SIDDONS

DOUBLEDAY LARGE PRINT HOME LIBRARY EDITION

HarperCollins*Publishers*

This Large Print Edition, prepared especially for Doubleday Large Print Home Library, contains the complete, unabridged text of the original Publisher's Edition.

SWEETWATER CREEK. Copyright © 2005 by Anne Rivers Siddons. All rights reserved. Printed in the United States of America. No part of this book may be used or reproduced in any manner whatsoever without written permission except in the case of brief quotations embodied in critical articles and reviews. For information, address HarperCollins Publishers, 10 East 53rd Street, New York, NY 10022.

ISBN: 0-7394-5762-4

Printed in the U.S.A.

Grateful acknowledgment is made for permission to reprint from the following works:

"The Wild Side of Life," by Arlie Carter and William Warrem © 1952 (renewed) EMI Unart Catalog Inc.; all rights reserved; used by permission.

"Last Night's Moon," "Skin Divers," and "The Hooded Hawk" from *Skin Divers*; "Memoriam," "Miner's Pond, Part I," and "What the Light Teaches" from *The Weight of Oranges/Miner's Pond*: all by Anne Michaels, all used by permission of McClelland & Stewart Ltd. and Alfred A. Knopf, a division of Random House, Inc.

This Large Print Book carries the
Seal of Approval of N.A.V.H.

*For Walter Mathews, who graced many lives,
mine among them,*

*and for Martha Gray, heartfriend,
who made so many of these books happen*

But one man loved the pilgrim soul in you,
And loved the sorrows of your changing face.

WILLIAM BUTLER YEATS
When You Are Old

PROLOGUE

In the Lowcountry of South Carolina, and only there in the world, a savage and beautiful ballet takes place twice a day. Usually in late summer and early fall, when the tidal creeks of the Lowcountry salt marshes are at their lowest, the fish and crabs who inhabit them cling nervously to the muddy banks, waiting for the tide to return and give them sanctuary in the tall spartina grass.

Suddenly, the dolphins come.

Pods of bottlenose dolphins, which have hunted these creeks and banks for generations and know every bend and mudflat, burst into the creek and begin to herd the fish, usually silver mullet, against the mudbanks. At a signal, perhaps a whistle or the echoing clicks from the out-riding scouts, the pods erupt, and with sonic blasts and perfect herding tactics, run the schools of mullet into a tight ball against the shore. In a thrashing rush that defies human ken, they create a great wave that washes the bait fish out of the water and up onto the mudflats. The dolphins, riding their own wave, follow them out of the water onto the banks, where they gorge on them until they are gone. The dolphins themselves come completely out of the water, lying side by side in a tight row, always turned on their right sides, as synchronized as the Rockettes. These salt-sea creatures come twice a day for two or three months, always to their pods' ancestral banks, and for a moment become completely creatures of earth and air. It is called strand feeding, and nobody really knows why or how it happens, only that it has probably happened this way since time out of mind. The waters they hunt are not fresh, but sweet in the way that only warm, salt-softened water can be.

This story is set on the banks of one of these creeks, and in the fields and woods around it. As long as anyone can remember, this ribbon of tidal water has been called Sweetwater Creek.

Sweetwater Creek

1

On a Thanksgiving eve, just before sunset, Emily and Elvis sat on the bank of a hummock where it slid down into Sweetwater Creek. Autumn in the Lowcountry of South Carolina is usually as slow and sweet as thick tawny port, and just as sleepily intoxicating. But this one had been born cold, with frosts searing late annuals in early October and chill nights so clear and still that the stars over the marshes and creeks bloomed like white chrysanthemums. Sweaters came out a full two months early, and furnaces rumbled dustily on in late September. Already Emily was shivering hard in her thin denim jacket, and had pulled Elvis closer for his body heat. In the morning, the spartina grass would be tinkling with a skin of ice and rime and the tidal creek would run as dark and clear as iced tea, the opaque, teeming strata of creek life having died out early or gone south with migratory birds. Emily missed the ribbons of birdsong you could usually hear well after Thanksgiving, but the whistle of quail and the blatting chorus of ducks and other waterfowl rang clearer, and the chuff and cough of deer come close. Emily loved the sounds of the winter animals; they said that life on the marsh would go on.

They sat on the bank overlooking the little sand beach where the river dolphins came to hurl themselves out of the water after the fish they had herded there. The dolphins were long gone to warmer seas, but at low tide the slide marks they wore into the sand were still distinct. They would not fade away until many more tides had washed them.

"There won't be any of them this late," Emily told Elvis. Elvis grinned up at her; he knew this. The dolphins were for heat and low tide. Girl and spaniel came almost every day in the summer and fall to watch them. Elvis's internal clock was better by far than the motley collection of timepieces back in the farmhouse.

They sat a while longer, as the gold and vermillion sunset dulled to gray-lavender. They would go back to the house soon, or be forced to stumble their way home in the swift, dense dark. Emily hadn't brought her flashlight. She had not thought they would be gone this long. But the prospect of the dim kitchen light and the thick smell of supper, and the even thicker silence, kept her on the marsh. This night would not be a happy one, even by Parmenter standards. Already words had been flung that could not be taken back, and furious tears shed, and the torturous wheel of Thanksgiving day loomed as large as a millstone. No, there would be silence now, each of them drowned in their own pools of it. The speaking was done. It was not the Parmenter way to go back and try to mitigate hurt and anger. By suppertime it would simply not exist anymore, except in Emily's roiling mind. Her father and brothers would be deep in their eating and drinking, and her Aunt Jenny would have gone quietly home to her own silent hearth. Tomorrow she and Emily and old Cleta would prepare the ritual dinner for the returning hunters. Weather or catastrophe, sickness or grinding grief, the

Thanksgiving hunt was sacrosanct. Walter Parmenter had instituted it long before Emily's birth.

"All the big plantations have them. It's an old sporting tradition," he said often, to anyone who might be listening. "We, of all the plantation families, should have one. We have the best hunting dogs in the Lowcountry, and some of the best bird land. The other planters talk about our dogs and our land. People tell me they hear about them all the time."

That there were now very few planters left on the huge river and tidal creek plantations around Charleston was, to Walter Parmenter, beside the point. He lived far back in his head, in the glory days of the family-oriented plantations. But most of the properties now were owned by northern sportsmen or hunting clubs, with managers to oversee day-to-day life. In this new millennium, they were largely weekend plantations. It was a point of immense pride to Walter that he had lived and worked Sweetwater Plantation almost his entire life. He scorned the holiday planters.

"Not one of them knows the woods and fields and marshes and the game and birds like I do. I could show them things about these parts that would pin their ears back. I could out-hunt the lot of them, too. Me and the boys and the dogs, we'll show them a thing or two about that one of these days."

Emily thought that unlikely; Walter had never been invited on the great Thanksgiving and Christmas hunts that were traditional with some of their landed neighbors. They visited only to look at and buy Sweetwater's famous Boykin spaniels. They would smile and speak admiringly of the Boykins, and usually go home with a pup or leave an order for the next litter, and then retreat to their fine old houses at the end of their long live oak allées. Her father was right about one thing, though. Sweetwater's Boykin spaniels were among the best in the Lowcountry, bred from strict breed standards and long lines of legendary hunters, and trained meticulously. If you took home a Sweetwater Boykin, whether started or broke, you had yourself a hunting dog that would be greatly admired in the field and house by every visitor who came. Elvis was one of them. Emily had trained him herself.

"You know I'm not going with you tomorrow," she said, only getting to her feet as the swift dark closed in. "I'm only your owner and trainer, and the best trainer this farm has. But Daddy and the boys are going to hunt you your first time because this rich muckety-muck wants to see a Boykin in action and Daddy knows you're the best we have, even if he won't admit it. He thinks this guy will watch you hunt and come back and order ten million Boykins, him and all his rich friends, and tell everybody what a fantastic breeder and trainer Walter Parmenter is. Nobody will ever know I trained you, because you can't have an eleven-year-old out-training the big expert. I think it stinks. I told him so, too. I said you were mine and I wouldn't let him take you anyway. He knows how I feel about hunting. And he said, every Boykin on this place has to pull his weight, no matter who he belongs to. And finally he yelled at me, and I yelled back, and . . . here we are."

Elvis wagged his stubby tail and cocked his head up at her. He knew, always, when she was angry or hurt. Emily often thought that no one else, except maybe Buddy, paid such exquisite attention to her or showed such uncomplicated pleasure in her company. Buddy had read aloud to her, during one of their afternoon reading binges, a passage from a man called Lord Byron, who, Buddy said, was a very great poet, though perhaps not quite so great as he thought. The passage went like this:

Near this spot are deposited the re-
mains of one who possessed Beauty
without Vanity, strength without inso-
lence, courage without ferocity, and all
the virtues of Man without his vices.
This praise, which would be unmeaning
flattery, if inscribed over human ashes,
is but a just tribute to the memory of
Boatswain, a dog.

Thinking of it now, Emily's eyes stung and filled. Lord Byron might have been talking about Elvis, except Elvis was alive. She shook the tears from her eyes. Buddy had told her that most tears were easy and cheap. Oh, Buddy. . . .

He had harbored the invading succubus that slowly sucked the life from his muscles and the breath from his lungs ever since she had known him, had recognized that he was an older, masculine part of her, a brother. Even though she had two other male siblings, younger by three years than Buddy but older by four than her, she thought of no one but Buddy by the word brother. The others were simply that: others. Other from her. Connected, but apart, like the man who wore the word "Father." They were all large, at least to her, and massive, and their eyes, though they saw her not unkindly as the small, wild-haired creature who haunted the corners and passageways of their world, soon slid over and past her to the outside, where the lush sun and the thick, still air and the limitless spaces of marsh and creek and woods and fields lay. And the dogs. Always the dogs.

Buddy did not go out into the air of that world, except in his wheelchair on the way to see his Charleston doctor. Emily thought she could remember, barely, a time that he walked; in her mind she saw a cane, and the thin, wiry figure of Morris, Cleta's husband, supporting Buddy as he shuffled from the front steps to the big black car that never seemed to change over the years. But the scene was misted and flickering, like the one in which her mother had stood when Emily last saw her. The reality of Buddy was the chair, and his quick, wry smile, and his

blanket that covered his wasted legs. And
his voice. The sweet, deep, slow voice that
told her ten thousand wonderful things and
taught her where to find them herself, in the
piles of books that were always strewn
around his big, cave-dim room.

Even with the chair and the oxygen tanks
and the other paraphernalia of chronic illness, she never thought of Buddy as "sick."
It always took her by surprise when visitors
to the farm, almost always dog people,
spoke to her father in hushed tones about
his poor, damaged, oldest son. Once she
had heard a large, leathery-tanned woman
in a shapeless tweedy poncho-like thing,
say to Walter Parmenter that she had been
praying that the terrible burden under which
his family staggered would be lifted. Walter
had nodded gravely and thanked her.

"Have we got a burden?" Emily asked
Cleta, who was rolling out biscuits in the
big, shabby old farm kitchen. "Some big old
lady said she was praying our burden would
be lifted."

"I guess she mean po' Buddy," Cleta
said, slapping her rolling pin down on the
dough on the old marble pastry slab.

" 'Cept it always seem to me like he more an angel for this family than a burden."

"Maybe she means me," Emily said. She had known since she was very small that she was a dark thread in the fabric of this family, though at that time she did not know the nature of it.

"You ain't no burden, Emily," Cleta said smiling. "They's two angels in this house. You the other one."

Each Parmenter child was allowed to choose a pup when he reached his tenth birthday. Walt Junior's was Avenger, and Carter's was Sumter, after the Union fort in Charleston Harbor that the Confederates fired upon, thus starting the Civil War—or simply The War, as many Lowcountry denizens called it. That the aggressive, jingoistic names were totally unsuited to the sweet-tempered, eager-to-please Boykins did not cross her brothers' minds. If the dog was yours, you got to name him. Buddy's was Aengus, after the beauty-possessed wanderer in William Butler Yeats's poem "The Song of Wandering Aengus." Since the name was pronounced Angus, most people simply assumed that Buddy was honoring his Scots forebears, and he did not explain.

Oddly, Emily thought now, she and Buddy seldom talked about the real furniture of their world: the farm, the dogs, their father, his disease, her school. They lived largely inside themselves, and spoke of that. Only once had they talked about their mother. Emily had been quite small when that happened. Of her mother she remembered only low ivory light and warmth, and the softness of her arms, and the smell of gardenias.

And then all those things were gone. No one spoke of her mother to her, but she saw some of the adults look quickly at her and shake their heads when the name Caroline was mentioned. Emily quickly learned two things: that Caroline was her mother and that she herself was not to know anything about her. In the way of a child, she did not ask. The shaken heads meant pain, trouble, unknowably terrible things. Very early on, though, Emily had learned to read faces. Theirs all said that she was part and parcel of the pain. Better by far not to ask.

But she did ask Buddy, just once, "Where is our mother?"

He turned his back to her and looked out the long windows of his room onto the unkempt circular gravel drive.

"I don't know," he said.

"Well, is she dead?"

"Why do you ask that?"

"I thought she'd come back unless she was dead."

"No," he said in a flat voice, without resonance. "I don't think she's dead or sick or hurt or anything. She always took very good care of herself."

"Do you remember her?" Emily asked. It seemed a question of great import. It brought life to her mother.

"Of course. Do you?"

"I remember that there was never much light and she sang to me sometimes, and she smelled like flowers."

"Nice memories," Buddy said. "Don't push it any further, Emmy. Maybe I'll tell you about it later, but right now the most important things are the reading and the being together. You remember that."

And so they read and read in his lair, and laughed, and ate sweets pillaged from Cleta's kitchen, and there seemed to Emily virtually no distance between her older brother's mind and her own.

One winter afternoon when rain streaked the windows of his room and the fire in the hearth hissed damply and snakily, he read a poem to Emily.

"Listen, Emmy," he said, "and you'll hear four of the most beautiful lines in the English language."

Emily, sprawled on the hearth rug, leaned her head against Aengus's sleeping flank, and closed her eyes. She was eight at the time, and attended the little stained cinderblock consolidated elementary school on James Island, where the only poetry you were likely to encounter was scrawled on the walls of the girls' bathroom. Emily had made no friends there. Most of her classmates, from working-class and frankly impoverished families, thought it was because she lived on a vast plantation and was stuck up, but in reality, Emily needed no other friend but Buddy. He had never, in the years she had known him, patronized her. He was perhaps the only person in her world besides Cleta who did not. She was small and neatly curved, and only the burning tangle of hair branded her a girl child. It was all too easy to treat her like a doll.

Buddy began to read: "I went out to the hazel wood / Because a fire was in my head . . ."

Emily's very skin burned with recognition. She breathed in tremulously. A fire in your head . . . yes.

And then he read, "And pluck, till time and times are done / The silver apples of the moon, / The golden apples of the sun."

Emily began to cry.

"I want to see that," she sobbed. "I want to see the silver and gold apples."

"You do, every day and every night," Buddy said. "This just gives you a different way to think about them. You'll think of this poem whenever you see the sun, or the moon. I did after I first read it."

And Emily had.

Two years later, when he was seventeen and Emily was ten, Buddy wet himself in his chair. Emily looked on in horror and sympathy as the pale urine dripped from the seat and soaked into the rug.

"I'll clean it up before anybody sees it," she said, and got up to scurry for towels and a mop.

Buddy did not answer. In his late teens his features had grown chiseled and high-planed like his father's, and crowned with the same thick wheat hair. Now his face was white and blank as he stared straight ahead.

"Get out of here, Emily," he said, without looking at her. Emily got.

The next day, while Emily was at school and the men out with the dogs, Buddy somehow managed to shoot himself in the head with the antique Purdey shotgun Walter had given him on his sixteenth birthday. It was a legendary gun, Walter said, made in England just after the turn of the nineteenth century, for an unremembered Englishman named Carter, and had belonged to the oldest son in the Carter line ever since, passed on down over the years. Her father had coveted the gun, Emily saw, caressing and polishing it, hefting it to his shoulder, tracing with his fingers the intricate, age-smoothed design of ducks and swans and graceful reeds carved into the silver stock.

Buddy cared nothing for it. After perfunctory thanks, he had put the gun away somewhere, and Emily had not seen it again. But he had obviously kept it at hand, for with it Buddy charged his old foe and cheated it.

He left one note for his father and the boys, and since no one ever spoke of it, Emily never knew what he had said. He had left her one, too. In it were lines from another poem he had once read her, one by John Donne, that he said was the bravest and most gloriously human poem ever written.

It read, in part,

> *Death be not proud, though some have called thee*
> *Mighty and dreadful, for thou art not so,*
> *For those whom thou think'st thou dost overthrow,*
> *Die not, poor death, nor yet canst thou kill me.*
> *. . .*
> *One short sleep past, we wake eternally,*
> *And death shall be no more; death, thou shalt die.*

At the bottom he had scrawled, "I got him, Emily."

After his funeral service, which Emily remembered none of forever after, her father and brothers took him to the old Carter family graveyard, in a grove of moss-scarred live oaks on a hummock in the far marsh. Emily took Aengus to her room and into her bed and held him through the afternoon and night and into the next day while he shivered and whined. Emily herself did not cry for Buddy; she never did. She simply stopped reading.

That evening Walter took the legendary Purdey down to the great curve where Sweetwater Creek ran deep and dark, and threw it in.

After that, Emily haunted the big, shabby house looking for a place to be. She went once or twice into Buddy's room, but Cleta, weeping, had cleaned it antiseptically and put all Buddy's personal things away, and there was nothing of him there, and consequently, nothing of her. The still, silent room and dead hearth frightened her. She began to spend all her time, except for family meals, with the dogs.

Sweetwater Plantation bred and trained exceptionally fine Boykins descended from the original stock founded in Boykin, South

Carolina. Walter had grown up there, working furiously to lever himself out of the hard-
scrabble farm existence his family led, and
much of his work was in the homes and gardens and fields of people who bred and
raised the chunky little bronze dogs. He
came to know the myths and the realities of
the dog: that it had originated with a stray
puppy who followed a prominent citizen
home from church one day; that it had been
bred and interbred specifically to serve the
needs of the Lowcountry waterfowl hunters.
It was large enough and had enough stam-
ina to retrieve for hours in icy water, small
enough to fit neatly into a small boat, often
with a blind attached. "The dog that won't
rock the boat," was the dog's unofficial slo-
gan.

The little dog had touches of this and that
in his ancestry: Chesapeake Bay retriever,
American water spaniel, cocker and
springer. It turned out that the new breed
was naturally affectionate in the house and
joyfully enthusiastic in the fields and
marshes. His dense, curly coat protected
him from icy waters, his autumn-brown
color effectively camouflaged him, and his
stub of a tail did not disturb undergrowth

and give away the position of the blind-hidden boats. He was equally at home flushing small waterfowl and upland birds: doves, turkeys, and ducks. He was even proficient at flushing deer. By the time Walter Parmenter met the Boykin spaniel, the dog had become a favorite with sportsmen up and down the eastern seaboard.

Walter was enchanted with the little dogs, and watched and listened and learned. He mucked out kennels, fed and watered, exercised, and soon was allowed to help train the spaniels. When he went away on scholarship to a small agricultural college upstate he took his own Boykin, given to him by a grateful breeder, and he studied a great deal about animal husbandry and care. He entered field trials and hunt tests all over the South, with his own carefully trained spaniel. What time he had left over he and his Boykin hunted. By the time he met and married Caroline Rutledge Carter of Sweetwater Plantation, he was determined to be a breeder and trainer of extraordinary Boykin spaniels, and over the years he had become just that. He was at heart a simple and single-minded man, and he put all the focus and energy he had into the dogs. They flour-ished, bringing a steady, barely adequate income to the farm. Walter's family, keenly aware that they were second fiddle at all times to a little brown spaniel, did not.

When Emily came among the field Boykins, in flight from the dead house, Walter had a number of breeding bitches and sires, a constant supply of new puppies, well-built and well-kept kennels and runs, carefully groomed field facilities, and part-time workers and trainers. Emily had always loved the small puppies and the beautiful mothers and sires, but she had not been allowed to make pets of the kennel dogs lest it spoil their hunting temperaments. Avenger and Sumter were devoted only to her older brothers; they wagged their stumpy tails at Emily when she petted them, and sometimes licked her face. But there was no question that their hearts belonged to Daddy. Aengus was the most she knew of Boykins, and when Buddy died Aengus went to the family of a breeder in North Carolina who was seeking to improve his stock.

Buddy had not allowed his dog to be trained for hunting, but Aengus came from magnificent hunting stock and was as close to breed standard as Sweetwater had. Walter got a princely sum for him. Emily and Aengus both cried when the North Carolina truck took him away, but her father had assured Emily impatiently that Aengus was going to the best dog's life imaginable.

"No, he isn't," Emily said under her breath. "He's already had that."

She had been spending her afternoons exclusively with the kennel dogs and puppies for three weeks before Walter took notice of her. The day he saw her in the little fenced training paddock with a small puppy, he went out to chide her for making pets of pups that were destined to be gundogs and that only. And then stopped still by the fence to watch her.

She was sitting on the dried grass with Ginger, a twelve-week-old of particularly opinionated temperament. Walter had been planning to start her on the basics the following week, and was rather dreading it; he anticipated a long struggle with the beautiful puppy over who was going to obey whom about what. The first thing a hunting puppy learns is to sit on command, and in Walter's way this entailed a good bit of pushing the baby's behind to the ground while saying firmly, "Hup!" and then repeating the process over and over.

Emily, however, sat still on the ground and leaned her head close to that of the attentive puppy. She did not move, nor, for a long time, did Ginger. Girl and dog simply looked at each other out of hazel and golden eyes, respectively.

Then Emily stood, and Ginger got up also, and stood attentively in front of her. Emily nodded. Ginger sat down. And did not get up.

Finally Emily nodded and Ginger stood, waiting quietly in front of Emily. Emily nodded again, and again Ginger sat down and waited.

Walter walked over to his daughter as casually as he could and said, "Can you do that again?"

"I think so," said Emily, and turned to the puppy once more, and nodded.

Ginger stood up.

"So . . . have you been working with Ginger for long?" her father said. "Because you know our Boykins are trained our own way. You ought not be meddling with their first lessons."

"Just today," Emily said, looking at her

feet. Her father's impatience with her was worse, on the whole, than his indifference.

"What are you saying to her? Are you whispering?" Walter said.

"Nothing," Emily mumbled.

"Well, then, how do you get her to sit and stay like that?"

"I just think it at her," Emily said. "And I listen to see if she understands. And then I think at her what she should do. Ginger is real good at it. I don't have to think it more than once, usually. She didn't want much to stay, but it was because it bored her. I told her I really, really wanted her to do it. And she did. She's a nice dog."

"Emily, that's just wishful thinking, or something," Walter said nervously. "It's co-incidence. You can't think a dog into learn-ing anything. You have to show them, over and over, and you have to do it firmly. Gin-ger just happened to want to sit down."

"No, she didn't," Emily said stubbornly. "I told you. It really bored her at first."

Her father looked at her silently.

"Would you like to help me train Ginger?" he said. "We could start with walking to heel, since she seems to have caught on to sitting and staying. We could do a little bit tomorrow; I could show you how, and then maybe you could carry on with it by yourself."

"Yes," Emily said, looking hard at him to see if he meant it.

The next afternoon Emily and Ginger were waiting when Walter came into the paddock carrying a slip-cord leash, a choke chain, and a whistle.

"What's all that stuff for?" Emily said suspiciously.

"Walking to heel is complicated. It takes a lot of repetition, especially with a dog like Ginger. Let's see which of the collars she'll work best with, and then I'll start, and you can watch."

"Can I think with her a little while first?" Emily said. "She doesn't like all that stuff you've got, and I don't think she's going to let you put it on her."

Walter stared at his daughter and the stiffly erect puppy, and then gestured helplessly.

"By all means. Think away," he said.

Again Emily sat down in front of Ginger, and Ginger sat still and looked at her, head cocked. Presently Emily stood up and turned her back on Ginger and nodded. She walked away. Ginger got up agreeably and trotted along just behind her left heel. Emily turned to the right and left; Ginger turned, too. They made small circles in the paddock, then they turned and came back to Walter. Emily nodded. Ginger sat.

By her tenth birthday Emily was regularly starting the Sweetwater Boykins off, and even taking a few of them through some of the more difficult steps: introduction to gunfire (with a cap pistol), single marked retrieves, double retrieves, water work. "But I won't do birds, live or dead," Emily said. "I won't teach them to hunt."

"We'll take them from there. You've given them a nice start," Walter said, and it was as near praise from him as Emily had ever gotten. Emily's part in the education of the Sweetwater Boykins was not mentioned outside the house. Her father continued to smile modestly at the compliments his impeccably bred and trained spaniels received, and sold them like hotcakes.

On her tenth birthday, Emily went out to the bitches' kennels to select her puppy. The newest litter was just three weeks old, and her mind and heart were made up instantly when a scrawny, ill-favored puppy tumbled out of the nest and toddled over to her and sat on her foot.

"That's no hunting spaniel," her brothers jeered. "That's a hound dog."

So Emily named him Elvis, and took the puppy to her room, and fell as irretrievably in love as she ever would in her life. Girl and dog were two halves of a whole, two chambers of one heart. The swirling black abyss that Buddy had left was almost filled. But only almost.

He still spoke to her sometimes. Not audibly, but through the words of poets she had pushed far down and slammed a door on when he died. Sometimes they broke through, and then Emily knew that Buddy was with her.

On this night the fast-falling dark caught them, and the moon was riding high and white when Emily turned to leave the creek bank and hummock. She stood in the darkness of the live oak grove for a moment, to watch the tapestry of silver tidal creeks and icy, gilded marsh. The bank down to the little beach where the dolphins slid was pure vermeil, every oyster clump and cypress stump and bleached shell inked in black.

"How sweet the moonlight sleeps upon

this bank." The words slid whole and perfect into her mind. She smiled slightly, a smile tightened with pain and softened with love.

"Show-off," she whispered, and turned to leave the hummock for the narrow path through the reeds and fields toward home.

Elvis had gone ahead of her, and stood in the moonlight on the path, motionless and waiting. The wash of moonlight turned his chestnut curls to fire. Love smote Emily, pierced through her so quickly that it almost brought her to her knees. Love for the amber eyes on hers. Love for the tumbled curls. Pure love.

"I love you, dog!" she called, and he wagged his nubbin of a tail, and girl and dog started for home.

In point of fact, Elvis's curls in the moonlight were the exact color of her mother's as she stood in the dim light of the overhead globe in the farmhouse foyer, the last time Emmy ever saw her. But it was a long time before she realized that.

2

There was an oil painting at Sweetwater Plantation over the dusty carved and gouged mantelpiece in the dining room. It was dark and brooding, and romantic in the extreme, Emily always thought. A pale, radiant orb that must have been the moon sailed high over the shallow-hipped roof, and beyond it the Wadmalaw River shimmered like quicksilver. Groups of graceful black men and women strolled about on the circular front drive, arm in arm, their mouths open, faces lifted up to a second-floor balcony, where a man and woman in eighteenth-century dress stood. Obviously, the black people were happy slaves, singing in the twilight to their master and mistress. Small black children tumbled and rolled in the smooth grass. Gigantic roses glowed palely in the twilight. The Spanish moss in the live oaks in the great allée were ghostly under the high moon.

"It must be very old. It's a real primitive," Emily said on Thanksgiving afternoon, as she was dusting the heavy gold frame. Buddy had told her about the early primitive limners who came to Charleston in the late 1600s to paint the houses and families of the rich planters. She liked showing off her knowledge.

She only dusted the painting twice a year, at Thanksgiving and Christmas. The Parmenters took virtually all their meals in the small breakfast room off the cavernous kitchen. It had once been a ladies' morning room, Walter had told her, but no ladies had morninged in it for a very long time. Still, Emily loved the name and called it the morning room when there was no one around to correct her. The Sweetwater Plantation she lived in now had only a cluttered breakfast room in need of paint, but the Sweetwater of the painting undoubtedly had a morning room.

"I've always loved Sweetwater best at twilight," Emily said to her aunt Jenny, who was polishing the silver service she had brought from her own house for the feast. It was, in fact, 1847 Rogers Brothers silver plate, and her aunt had bought it for herself after she divorced her feckless, philandering husband Truman, but Emily did not know that. She loved the sight of the ornate silver, gleaming in the light of the tall white tapers at Thanksgiving and Christmas dinners. It spoke of a birthright that was, perhaps, only temporarily lost.

Walter Parmenter loved it, too; he never failed to say at these holiday dinners that the Carter girls had always known how to set a fine table, and he had always meant to replace the family silver before Emily grew up. Everyone would nod pleasantly but no one spoke; they all knew that Caroline Carter Parmenter had taken the scant store of silver with her when she left. Emily did not even remember it. She did not want the silver replaced; she had no intention of presiding over a fine table with just-bought silver. Silver should come with the house and be as old as the family name.

"That's not twilight," her aunt said acidly. "It's years and years of smoke from the blasted chimney. The painting is of the house in bright sunlight, and it never had one single rose. My crazy aunt Harriet painted it in 1950. Your great aunt. The only other thing she ever painted was a pitcher of buttermilk with a zinnia stuck in it."

Emily did not look at Jenny Raiford. She knew that it was not an early limner's work, nor twilight, nor any of the other things that she kept in her head and heart. The knowledge did not stop the needing, though. Emily needed Sweetwater to be as it was in the painting.

"It could have been, though," she muttered stubbornly. "It could have, sometime before we had it. Daddy said it was a great rice plantation once, and then a sea island cotton plantation. He said we have the best river access on this island. You can ship anything anywhere from our landing. I bet . . ."

"Emily," her aunt said more softly. "You know it was never a great plantation. You know that. Maybe it could have been once, but the people who built it managed to sink everything into rice just when cotton was coming in, and then the next crowd forgot about the old rice gates and flooded the cotton crop and left, and the next crowd—

the Olivers, I think—just let it sit fallow except for a kitchen garden and a cow pasture, until Grandaddy Carter bought it in 1925. Planted it in soybeans for a cash crop and put in the barns and stables. He was going to make it into one of the great horse farms in the Lowcountry. Of course, he didn't figure on 1929. I guess nobody down here did. It's been the way it is now ever since, except for the dogs, of course. Why do you keep on with this great plantation business?"

Emily did turn to look at her aunt then. She smiled unwillingly in answer to Jenny Raiford's own soft smile.

"I just want something to be special," she said.

Jenny came to her and hugged her. Emily felt the sparrowlike ribs and the sharp shoulder blades. Unlike the other female Carters, her aunt was not round and small and vivid. She was tall, as tall as Walter Parmenter and taller than the boys, except for Buddy. Emily knew this because there was a yellowing photograph of her and her father and her aunt and all the boys in the living room, taken when Buddy could still manage to stand erect for a short time.

She had the flaming Carter hair, though, except that on her narrow head it had dulled down to a tarnished copper and was threaded with gray. She had a thin, pure face that reminded Emily of a John Singer Sargent painting, dusted with faint freckles on her nose and cheekbones. Her neck was long and her hands and feet were thin and beautiful. Her eyes were the light-spilling hazel of Emily's own—chatoyant, Buddy had called them once. Buddy had thought Aunt Jenny was beautiful. "Elegant," he always said.

Her aunt had been stricken mute when Buddy died, just as Emily had been.

"You're all the special this place needs," she said.

Emily let her face burrow into Jenny's clean-cotton-smelling shoulder before she stepped back.

"No, I'm not," she said. "I'm the least special thing on this whole plantation."

Her aunt held her shoulders and looked down at her.

"Whoever on earth told you that?" she whispered.

"I don't know. Somebody did, though," Emily said. And this was true. The words shivered deep in her stomach sometimes, or woke her sweating from sleep. Whoever had spoken them was lost to Emily, but the words themselves were as solid and real as earth or flesh.

"Well, somebody was full of horse hockey," Jenny said, and gave her a smart slap on the fanny before she let her go. Emily laughed, unwillingly. The whole family laughed at Aunt Jenny's attempts to swear. She always started out fine and ended up as archaic as a Victorian boy's novel.

Cleta came through the swinging door from the kitchen, wreathed in great, fragrant clouds of steam. Her hands were floury up to her elbows.

"Ain't y'all done in here yet?" she said. "Everything's ready to go in the oven but them benné seed things Mist' Parmenter wants. Jenny, you was going to make them, remember? And did you remember to bring any sherry with you?"

"I got the only thing they had at the Bi-Lo," Jenny said. "I don't think it's what Walter had in mind, but you can't get 1949 amontillado around here, I don't think. Okay, I'll start the benné seed biscuits, though

why on earth he wants them, I don't
know . . ."

Emily knew. The night before she and the
boys had sat long at the supper table, while
Walter, his anger at Emily past, spun his
gleaming visions out into the smoky air. He
did this often, and they always listened as
silently and intently as they had done last
night. Emily did not know what went through
the dark blond heads of her twin brothers
during these grandiose monologues, but
her own swam with exasperation and secret
laughter and sheer boredom. Walter Parmenter's suppertime rhapsodies rarely altered, either in content or in tempo. They
were the only occasions that Emily ever saw
him animated and grandiose. Most of the
time he was close-faced and quiet, with the
look of great distances in his eyes.

He talked of the not-too-far-off days
when the aristocratic buyers of his Boykins
would see in Walter a kind of rustic patrician
kinsman, and would be visitors in his house
as often as he visited theirs. They would be
an entity apart, the river plantation aristoc-
racy that still bloomed, whole and perfect,
in his mind. His sons would ride and hunt

with the sons of these men, and dance with their daughters at the great hunt balls, and follow their peers into the Citadel or, perhaps, Clemson. Emily would move gracefully into some small, select girls' school, possibly Charlotte Hall, and would come out at the Christmas season with her beautiful young friends, and marry, eventually, a young man whose family name was to be seen on street signs and public buildings and the myriad, tasteful bronze plaques on the old doors along Broad Street. He himself would sit in clubs and drawing rooms with the fathers of these gilded young, and his knowledge of hunting and hunting dogs would hold them all in thrall. His Boykins would be prized in the entire sporting world.

"Sweetwater Boykins?" sportsmen would say from Grosse Point to Sea Island. "Best hunting dogs in the world. I got mine early, before every fool with a shotgun found out about them. You'd have to go some to get one now. Parmenter's got a waiting list for pups a mile long. And if they've been started and broke at Sweetwater, you'll never want another dog again in your life. Good man, too, Parmenter. Knows what's important. And that place of his is the best natural hunting land I've ever seen. Deep-water docking, open marsh and wood marsh, deep woods, and open fields for quail."

But last night's fugue had been rococo even for him. In the candlelight he insisted on at supper, his sharp-planed face had glowed with more than sun, and his long, slanted blue eyes shone like mica. The hectic flush was not from liquor, Emily knew; her father allowed himself one small glass of single-malt scotch each evening before dinner. He never drank less or more. It seemed to be a part of the ritual of their evening meal, like the absurd candles teetering on the scarred wooden table, and the clean shirt he insisted on for himself and the twins. Even the glass he drank from was the same each evening: a heavy, cut-crystal tumbler, the only one remaining of a set that included a large, ornate decanter. He had told them at one early supper that the glass had come from England with the first of the Carters, though no one seemed to know precisely when that was.

"Baccarat," he had said when he told them about the tumbler and decanter. "Best crystal in the world. Only thing worthy of a fine single malt."

Walter used the word "fine" a lot. It was a ritual, too. Walter Parmenter sometimes seemed to his daughter a restless subterranean force held together by rituals.

His euphoria last night had, for once, a tangible thread in it. He and the boys had a guest on the Thanksgiving hunt, a neighboring planter with homes in Idaho and Long Island and even Hungary, where, her father said, the hunting was the best in the world.

Townsend Chappelle had both inherited money and made it, managing the network of supermarket newspapers about this Hollywood star's anorexia and that one's secret marriage at thirteen to a male exotic dancer at Chippendale's. It had been the family business for decades. By now he had an unimaginable amount of money. Hunting was his life, and he had made Spartina, his great plantation on Wadmalaw Sound, into a sportsman's paradise. Friends came from all over the world to hunt there, among them celebrities of every persuasion, whose post-hunt antics made the rounds of Charleston, usually in whispers. An invitation to hunt at Spartina was tantamount to one to hunt at

Bernard Baruch's fabled Hobcaw Barony in its halcyon days. The mere name Spartina shrouded the guest in privilege and singularity.

And he was joining the Parmenters on Thanksgiving morning because he wanted to see a good Boykin in action and he had heard that Sweetwater had exceptional ones. His own prize Labradors were too large for the stubby little boats that slipped into duck blinds, and his own flushing spaniels were too small to sustain long runs in extreme heat or swims in icy water. He wanted to start his own kennel of perfect waterfowl spaniels. Friends had referred him to Walter.

"Who are you taking besides Elvis, Dad?" Walt Junior said.

"No others, this time. Elvis is the best we're ever likely to have. I'm going to let him go after a quail or two, too, and if we're lucky he can flush a deer for us."

"Don't you think that's kind of risky?" Carter said. "Elvis has never actually hunted. Maybe you ought to have some backup."

"Don't need it. Dog can do anything you tell him to," their father said. "He's done everything but go in the water after a shot game bird; he's a beautiful sight in the water with the dummies. Sails right in like a dolphin."

"You going to take Emily?" Walt Junior said, looking sidewise at her out of his father's narrow blue eyes. Emily did not raise her head or speak.

"Not this time. Might put ol' Townsend off, to have a little girl underfoot petting the dog."

Still, Emily said nothing. Did he truly not remember who had trained at least half of last year's Boykins?

The silence spun out awkwardly. Walter jerked around to look at her, suddenly, as if remembering she was there.

"I'll let her come down and put a bug in Elvis's ear before we leave," he said jovially. "That way he'll have it on good authority what he's supposed to do. By the time we get back Chappelle will order every pup we've got coming along for the next fifty years, and let us train them, too. The whole Lowcountry will follow on his heels, just like water when you pull the stopper out."

He looked as if he might actually levitate into the murky air of the breakfast room.

Emily excused herself and got up to go to bed. She thought her heart would burst with rage and a sneaking, childish sorrow.

"Wait a minute, Emily," her father called after her. She stopped but did not turn.

"Tell Cleta and your aunt Jenny that I want somebody to make up some of those benné seed things they have at Charleston cocktail parties, and get a good bottle of sherry in here, and polish up the library and have a fire going in there about sunset. I expect Mr. Townsend Chappelle would be glad of a drink and a bite in front of the fire while we're finishing our business up. It's only hospitable to offer."

Emily nodded but did not turn, and went out of the breakfast room. Behind her, she heard one of the twins say, "Where's the library? You mean the office? Dad, it looks like a hundred-year-old kennel in there."

Emily heard her father's voice in response, but she did not hear what he said. Whatever it was, it did not matter.

Her father had decreed that Elvis sleep that night in the kennels with the other dogs so that his guest would not see him coming out of the house. It was not seemly for a champion flushing spaniel to be a house pet. Emily had taken him out to the kennels and settled him into a big one, warm with deep fresh straw, and told him to be quiet for a little while. He was; he watched her anxiously from behind the cage bars when she left, but he did not fuss. When the house was finally dark and quiet she slipped down the fine old spiral staircase, flaking paint now, and out to the kennels where she released him.

"Shhh," she whispered. He wagged his stumpy tail and padded silently beside her left heel into the house and up the stairs to her bedroom. Girl and spaniel slept that night as they always had, so deeply curled into each other that they might have been conjoined.

It was only five hours later that she woke him and took him back to the kennels. She sat down on the straw with him and put her arms around him.

"You're going out with Daddy and a real big shot today. Daddy wants to show you off. I won't be there, but you know how to do everything he'll ask you."

She stopped, seeing in her mind endless cold, dark mornings, with Elvis being loaded into the trailer and taken out to the freezing marsh to bring back to the blind the warm, now-limp ducks who wintered there. She saw him scrambling out of the water with a wood duck in his mouth, wagging his tail and taking it straight to a grinning Walter Parmenter. Emily thought wood ducks the most beautiful birds she had ever seen. Her eyes filled with tears.

"You just do what you think is right," she said. He wagged his tail and grinned at her, his yellow eyes full of trust and love. By the time Emily was back in bed a cold red dawn was breaking over the steely river outside her window. Soon she heard the growling of a powerful engine, and her father's jovial voice welcoming the incoming supermarket tabloid king, who replied in a clipped New England accent.

She crept to the landing window and looked out. In the chill fog off the river she saw the dim outlines of her father and two brothers standing beside a huge custom hunting vehicle shaking hands with the visitor. Her father's voice was hearty and booming, not level and almost toneless as it usually was. She cringed in embarrassment. Her brothers faded into the fog and came back with Elvis on a chain lead. The old two-dog aluminum crate already sat in the bed of her father's Dodge pickup. Just before one of the twins hoisted him up into the crate, Elvis looked up in Emily's direction and wagged his tail. Emily ran back to her bed and pulled the covers over her head and wept. She did not hear the hunting party move out.

By two o'clock that afternoon most of the dinner preparations were done and the table set. Cleta shoved the enormous wild turkey that Carter had shot and dressed into the oven. The black iron pan of corn bread-and-oyster dressing was ready to be put in an hour before dinnertime. Two pecan pies sat cooling on the oilcloth-covered kitchen table.

Cleta put on her outsized down-filled jacket and prepared to go home. Emily knew that she would begin cooking for her own household when she got there. She had said there would be roughly eighteen for dinner. Cleta had kin all over the Lowcountry.

"It doesn't seem right that you should spend practically a whole day cooking for just us when you've got all those folks to feed at home," Emily had said to her once.

"Shoot, I'm glad to get home this late," Cleta said. "Bertha and the girls will be so hungry they'll have made up the dressin' just so they can cook some extra and gobble it, an' all the men will have been into the shine since noon. Nobody be 'specially hungry, and half of 'em be too drunk to care if I'm late. Works out real good."

Now she said, "Y'all have a happy Thanksgiving. I sho' do hope things work out for Mr. Walter."

Her expression said that she had her doubts on this matter.

Emily and Jenny took rags and brooms and silver polish and the bulbous old Hoover and went down the hall to the small room that served as office, trophy room, refuge, and sometime puppy pen for Walter Parmenter. Emily was seldom invited into it. Walt Junior and Carter sometimes closed themselves in with their father, but usually it was Walter's domain alone. Cleta dusted and Hoovered occasionally, but was not allowed to touch anything else.

"My God, it looks like the stock room in a feed store," Jenny Raiford said. "If Mr.

Gotrocks comes in here he'll choke to death."

Dust swirled in the dim light, puffed up from the wrinkled oriental throw rugs, and poured like smoke from the heavy, faded damask draperies that were pulled shut over the tall french doors onto the porch. The mahogany paneling and shelving, once thought unrivaled in quality among the river plantations, were now felted with dust. Doors, window frames, and mantel, all carved with sunbursts, fans, and Chippendale gougework, were a uniform smoky gray from years of fires in the small grate. The floor of the fireplace itself was completely buried under a sooty black and silvery gray drift of ash. The shelves were jammed with tarnished trophies and faded ribbons and photographs of grime-dimmed spaniels. Sacks of dog food and cedar bedding and boxes that had held whelping bitches covered most of the wide-planked cypress floor. Dusty scrapbooks were piled on the twin leather Morris chairs beside the fireplace. Walter's desk, under the tall windows, was piled chin-high with account books, legal pads, ancient hunting magazines, and yellowing newspapers. A roll of toilet paper sat on top of the heap.

"Where should we put the silver tray of benné seed biscuits and the sherry? On his desk beside the toilet paper or over there on that fifty-pound sack of Eukanuba?" Emily said, beginning to laugh helplessly.

"I could tell him where to put it," Jenny said, beginning to laugh too. It was impossible not to.

Two hours later the shelves were cleared out, the sack of dog food was moved to the back porch, the rugs and furniture and drapes were Hoovered, Walter's desk was cleared and polished, the fireplace was clean, and a fire had been freshly laid and ready to light. Jenny brought in a large copper vase of bittersweet berries, and Emily was finishing up the silver frames of the photographs on the mantelpiece.

She picked up the last one, a large photo of a beautiful, unremembered Boykin, and the photo slipped out onto the floor, revealing another behind it. Emily took it over to the now-sparkling windows and stared at it. It, too, was badly yellowed, but she could make out the figure of a stocky man with ginger hair and a slender, erect blond man with a barrel trunk, short legs, a fine chest and shoulders, and a large head. He wore a V-neck sweater over a button-down white shirt and was almost movie-star handsome. Between them stood a willowy girl almost as tall as them, with long, perfectly straight auburn hair and slender, pretty legs under a miniskirt. Both men had their arms around the girl, and she was smiling with unmistakable delight. Both men were squinting solemnly into the sun.

She looked at it a long time and then turned to her aunt.

"Why, this is you! Isn't it? Just look at that skirt . . . and Lordy, this is *Daddy*! And I guess this is Grandaddy Carter. Aunt Jenny, Daddy looks just exactly like he did then. And you look—really, really pretty . . ."

Jenny Raiford came over into the light and took the photo from Emily. She looked at it for a long time, her head bent over it.

"Yes," she said, raising it to look at Emily. There was a sort of pinched look around her nostrils that Emily associated with sick people.

"That's us, all right. I haven't seen this since . . . I guess right after it was taken.

What would it be . . . 1969? 1970? Where did you find it?"

"Stuck behind this dog picture on the mantel," Emily said. "I wonder why? It's a great picture of you and Daddy . . ."

"I wonder why, too," Jenny said. "Well, come on, let's get these trophies polished and go have a cup of tea or a Coke. I feel like I've swallowed a bale of cotton."

She set the picture smartly down on Walter's desk and went out of the room. In the kitchen, Emily stared at her. Her aunt moved quickly and with sharp movements, not at all with her usual lazy, flat-footed grace. Emily remembered that Jennifer Carter had studied ballet at the College of Charleston. Jenny kept her face turned away.

"Who took the picture?" Emily said. "Did . . . my mother take it?"

"No," her aunt said. "She was still at Converse. I don't even think she'd met your dad yet. Our daddy brought him home from a field trial the day it was taken. I'd just met him."

Emily could hear unsaid words. She came sometimes to know, usually unwillingly, the thoughts of others. Her place in the world depended on it; her father and brothers made almost none for her. She looked at her aunt's straight back and thought, "She was in love with him. He was her beau first. You can see it on her face in the picture. How did it get to be my mother he married?"

But she knew the answer. Caroline Carter had come home from school with her curls and curves and lilting laughter and set her great hazel-gold eyes on Walter Parmenter, and that was that.

"I guess she married ol' Truman Raiford on the rebound," Emily thought. "What a mistake *that* was. I don't think . . . I wish my mother hadn't done that."

"But then where would I be? And where would Walt Junior and Carter be? Would there ever have been Buddy?" She opened her mouth to ask more questions, and Jenny said, still not looking at her, "Let it alone, Emily. It was a long time ago."

Emily might have persisted but for the rattling sound of the Dodge pickup in the front drive. Car doors slammed and men's voices spun briefly out into the cold, pale air, and then there was the sound of a heavy, expensive SUV purring to life and retreating down the driveway, and then silence. A long silence.

"What on earth are they doing home so early? I thought your dad said sundown . . ." Jenny said.

A lump of ice began to form in Emily's chest. She stood still and silent.

The front door flew open and she heard her father's heavy footsteps come into the foyer. They did not stop at the kitchen, but went straight up the stairs. A door slammed, and then there was silence again.

In a moment Walt Junior and Carter came into the kitchen. Their faces were raw with cold, and they did not have the look of happy hunters home from the hill. Behind them, on Carter's left heel, Elvis padded obediently. He looked up at her. There was no life in his golden eyes, and his stumpy tail did not wag. He merely sat down quietly in front of the boys. He would not look up at Emily. The silence spun out again, as palpable as the dust motes in the slanting afternoon sunshine.

"What happened?" Emily whispered finally, around the lump of ice in her chest. "Where's Mr. Thing?"

"Mr. Thing has gone home to quote, think it over," Carter said. "You ought to put that stuff somewhere out of sight." He gestured at the shining decanter of sherry and pierced silver platter of warm benné biscuits. "I don't think Dad's going to want to see it."

"Carter . . ." Emily began, desperately.

"Elvis wouldn't hunt," her brother said briefly. The muscles beside his mouth twitched. "He did it all perfectly. He was beautiful. Mr. Thing, as you call him, was knocked out with him. And then he shot a mallard and Elvis got right up to the water and crouched down to jump . . . and then he looked around at us and grinned, and wagged his tail, and wouldn't move. Nothing Dad did could make him. Nothing. We finally just came on back. If I was you I'd get that dog out of sight for a while. I think Daddy might kill him."

Trembling, Emily knelt down and put her arms around Elvis. She could feel a fine shivering and twitching muscles under his damp, curly coat.

"Did anybody yell at him—or hit him?" she whispered. Elvis put his head under her arm and burrowed against her.

"Oh, shit, no, of course not," Walt Junior said impatiently. "You know Daddy wouldn't mistreat a dog. He just didn't . . . talk to him anymore. Bundled him into the crate and stuck him in the back of the truck and brought him home. He was out of it and up the steps before Carter and I could open our door. We got the crate down and let Elvis out. He knows he did a bad thing, though. Look at him."

Emily gathered the dog up in her arms and stood, holding him close against her.

"He did not do a bad thing. He's never done a bad thing in his life!" she spat, feeling her face whiten as the blood rushed from it. "The only bad thing anybody did today was to take him out there and show him off like a . . . a prize steer! I hope he never hunts! I hope he won't hunt for anybody else on this place ever again!"

She turned to start up the stairs to her bedroom with Elvis. Her father's bedroom door flew open, and he stood at the top of the landing looking down at her. She stopped still. His face was tight and white, and there was wildfire in his eyes.

"*What the hell did you tell that dog?*" he shouted at Emily.

She was up the stairs with the dog and past him and in her room before she heard her aunt Jenny say, in a hushed, furious voice, "What are you talking about, Walter Parmenter? Are you crazy? Just listen to yourself. Don't you speak like that to Emily ever again in my . . ."

Emily slammed her door and, for the first time she could remember, locked it. It was a very long time before she opened it again. When she did, nothing and everything had changed.

3

Deep into Thanksgiving night Emily dreamed.

She dreamed of a crystalline white mist rolling in from the river, much like the usual fall and winter mists and yet not. This mist was palpable. It had form. It spread itself in a layer over the house and the river and the marsh, over all the plantation land, from Toogoodoo Creek upland almost to Hollywood, back down to Yonges Island on the Wadmalaw River, to the mouth of the North Edisto.

Somehow she was riding on the mist, sitting cross-legged atop it. Soft sweet sun spilled down over her. Fresh wind teased her hair. She was looking down on the plantation that she should not have been able to see through the carved-marble white mist.

For a long time she simply sat on the mist and looked, and was happier than she could remember being in her life.

She was directly over the house, and she could see it as clearly as if in ordinary daylight. The simple Greek Revival architecture was the same, with the two-story main house and the wings spreading out from it, and the encircling wooden porch and the four plain white wooden columns. It still sat on its arched brick foundation, raised to catch the breezes from the broad Wadmalaw behind it. Sweetwater had never been an ornate, manorial plantation like those of the Ashley and Cooper and the Peedee Rivers. But it had a kind of pared-down symmetry that seemed a part of the river light and the wide skies over it, and in the dream it gave off its own light, soft and radiant, like an August moon.

It was morning in the dream, a spring morning, and the new gold-green of the marshes and the shining fresh-paint green of live oak groves that had never been there glistened like vermeil. Wildflowers rioted on the higher ground behind and to the north of the house, where on other days there was only broom sedge and scrubby low trees and brush and ditches, all rimmed with the dark, encroaching forest. Quail land, Emily had come to think of it. A garden more beautiful than anything Emily had ever seen in a book surrounded the house: roses, daylilies, iris, azaleas, camellias, annuals in a riot of improbable colors; velvety, perfectly trimmed boxwood hedges. Off in the marsh and on the hummocks, live oaks spilled curtains of silvery moss onto the high grass, and resurrection ferns burned primal green. At the marshes' edges the spartina danced in a light wind that smelled so densely of the clean, fishy river and the sea far beyond it that you could get drunk on it. A hundred bird songs haunted the shimmering air. Over it all arched the great tender, washed-blue skies of spring.

Emily felt drunk—drunk with happiness and a sense of safety and cherishing, drunk with sheer possibility. She found that she could move the mist by leaning this way or that, and she sent herself sailing placidly down to the river, which danced and shone like spilled mercury.

From above the wooden walkway and dock, which stretched far over the marsh out to where the river ran swift and deep, she heard music, and she saw people and animals and boats. The boats made a long line from the dock back practically to the great turn into Toogoodoo Creek. Beyond the turn you would need only to drift past Bears Bluff to be in the great North Edisto, which ran directly into the open Atlantic between Edisto and Seabrook Islands. The boats were beautiful, towering three-masted schooners with their sails furled, wallowing gently on the morning tide. Their decks were crowded with people she could not see clearly. None of this surprised Emily. The boats were stitched unalterably into the fabric of the day.

The music came at her in bursts and sweeps: a skirl of Pachelbel, a ribbon of Bach—"Jesu, Joy of Man's Desiring" she thought; Buddy had loved it—a joyous, rhythmic shout of song rising over strange old drums and tambourines, surely a Gullah praise song; a thread of the Shirelles singing "Foolish Little Girl," Carolina beach music at its best; a soaring snatch of the Fifth Dimension singing "The Age of Aquarius"—who was it who had loved that song? Emily could not remember, but the song made glee rise and catch in her throat. The music was not incongruous. Emily thought how empty this magical air would be without it.

The people who stood on the dock beside the first ship, unlike those on the boat's deck, were as clear as if they had been outlined in light. There was her father, his tanned face lifted to the sun, laughing. Aunt Jenny stood beside him, dressed in something long and flowery, its skirts and her unbound hair blowing in the wind. She was smiling up at Walter Parmenter. The twins were there, in their beloved, disreputable old camouflage hunting clothes, grinning and shoving each other amiably. Behind them, alone in a wagging, grinning turmoil of beautiful, red-burning Boykins, stood Buddy.

Emily could hardly suppress a shout of joy, but she knew in the dream that to speak would rupture it. Buddy stood tall and lanky, taller than anyone else on the deck, hands in the pockets of madras walking shorts, a blue oxford cloth shirt rolled up over his brown wrists and arms. He had sunglasses pushed up into the thick dark blond hair that was his father's, and every now and then he reached a sockless boat shoe out to tap a fractious spaniel. Emily knew she was seeing Buddy not as he had been, but as he might have been if he had lived to college age. He had wanted to study poetry and drama at Yale.

A ship's long hoot sounded, and the jib on the leading schooner spilled out into the air and caught the little wind. The people on the dock all smiled up at her and filed aboard. They stood staring out over the bow, watching the swirl of the water. They did not look up at her again. Ever so gently the ship moved off into the broad river. In a moment another of the great sails bloomed.

Emily leaned forward to follow on her ledge of mist, but it would not move. She tried again and again: nothing. By the time the ship reached the Bears Bluff its suit of sail was full and proud, and it was moving fast on the current in a following wind.

She opened her mouth to call, "Wait! Come back! You've left me!" but she could not get words out. There seemed to be cotton in her throat. Her heart was hammering with fear and loss, and by the time she produced a small shriek, the ship was gone around the point into the Edisto and out of sight.

Emily sobbed once, a great, hiccuping

shudder of pure aloneness. She leaned this way and that, trying to make the mist move, but it might have been stone. And then it began to move of itself, swirling around over the river and flowing off directly across the island, over the marsh and forest, faster and faster, until she could see nothing below, and feel only wind and sun. Both now felt cold.

She was hunched over on her side, hugging her knees and attempting to burrow into the mist for safety, when it slowed and stopped. Once again, she could see through it clearly, to the earth below. She was over Sweetwater Creek, where it ran into the Toogoodoo, the exact place where the dolphins came in the summers. She could even see the grooves of last summer's slides. Her fear slid slowly into the comfort of familiarity. She felt a sudden surety that the mist was not, after all, going to float her off the edge of the world. For a long time she simply sat still, looking down as the ribbon of tidal water swept in to fill the high-banked, corrugated creek bed. The tiny rivulet that it was at low tide would scarcely accommodate a shrimp. But at full tide it would be wide and deep and the blue-black of the reflected sky, and alive with tiny transparent and incandescent creatures and other life, on up the spectrum to the splashing mullet in the mullet holes, and big, thick-tailed, sluggish gators. On either side the cordgrass swept away, a waving meadow of a million greens.

Emily looked over it to the hummock directly across Sweetwater Creek, where she often saw the flashing white ensigns of deer, and on several occasions a small, wind-bent oak so thickly packed with nesting white herons that it looked like a tree in a Currier and Ives winter print. Under the great oak that was the centerpiece of the hummock little sunlight reached the ground, but Emily had seen wood ibises clustered there, pecking away at the earth, and once a doe and fawn sheltering from the rain.

Today, a woman in something fluid and shining and peach-colored sat on the rich grass, her legs folded out to the side. A winking ray of sun caught her hair, which crackled with red life, and dappled the pearled white of her shoulders and neck. Creamy pearls glowed against her throat, and, though it did not seem possible, her scent of tuberoses and fresh rain was strong and warm in Emily's nostrils. Beside her, in the circle of her white arm, sat Elvis.

"That's my mother," Emily said aloud, her chest constricted with joy and longing. "I remember that nightgown and those pearls. I remember the way she smelled when she leaned over me at night. I'd know her anywhere! Why did I ever think I couldn't remember her?"

She leaned into the mist hoping it would take her over the marsh to the hummock, and it did move a little way before it stopped again. It was close enough now that she could see her mother's face, and the little V-shaped kitten's smile on her lips, and the tangle of curls over her forehead. In the nest of her arm, Elvis wriggled happily and looked up at her. He was, indeed, the same color as her mother's hair. He smiled his doggy smile.

"Mama! I want to come over there," Emily called. "Please don't leave! Hold on to Elvis! I've been looking for you such a long time . . ."

She gave a mighty lunge forward and the mist began to move again, slowly and jerkily. For some reason, Emily felt herself sink-ing slightly into it. Below its surface it was wet and thick and cold.

Her mother sat upright and held Elvis close to her. She was shaking her head, and making pushing-away movements with her other hand. Elvis began to bark. It was his warning bark.

"Go back! Go back!" her mother called. "You can't come here! This is not for you! Go back . . ."

"It *is* for me! I *am* coming there!" Emily cried in terror and sorrow. She struggled to stand in the mist, to pull it forcibly behind her, to dive into and through it. Suddenly there was nothing around her but cold, white mist, mist that put sticky fingers into her nose and mouth and drenched her hair, mist that blinded her and filled her throat and lay wet and icy on her face. She struggled and flailed against it, fought against the suffocating, drowning whiteness . . . and woke up deep under the covers of her bed, struggling to breathe, her face wet with tears and the anxious ministrations of Elvis's tongue. She could hear a small, unhappy whining in his throat. She took a great rattling breath, put her arms around him, and sat up in bed.

Even after her heart had stopped its sick thudding, and her tears had dried, Emily did not move. She sat in the middle of her bedraggled covers, breathing slowly so as not to make noise, holding Elvis warm against her frozen chest and shoulders. Her pajamas were wet, too, and the sheet around her. Cold and wet, as if they had just been pulled from chilly brackish water. It was not until her eyes acclimated to the dark and she could see the faint gray of dawn around the curtains and the pale light that outlined her closed door, that she got up out of bed and found fresh, warm flannel pajamas and a dry top sheet, and jumped back into her bed with Elvis. They lay close together for a long time. She did not think about the dream, and she did not think about anything else, either. Warmth and dog were the only things that had substance.

It was not until Elvis began to wriggle restlessly, and to whine, that she realized that it must be the middle of the night, and both of them had been locked in this room for a long time. He was undoubtedly hungry, and needed to be taken out.

"Good boy," she whispered, getting up and wrapping herself in her too-small fleece

bathrobe and slipping on her wooly slippers. "Good boy. You didn't make a sound
until you just couldn't stand it, did you?
Come on. We'll go out now, and we'll get
something to eat."

Girl and dog moved soundlessly down
the dim hall, past her father and brothers'
bedrooms, which were dark and closed,
and down the great sweep of staircase.
Emily had long known which stairs
squeaked, and avoided them. Elvis did, too.
She slowly opened the back door onto the
porch and he trotted out and down the
steps to the grass, did his business, and
came directly back. Emily knew that if she
had looked up she would have seen the incredible, extravagant pageant of winter
stars over the river, and perhaps the running
black shape of something whose purview
was night and wildness, but she did not
look. She was afraid she would see, forming
over the quiet river, the curling edges of mist
reaching out to the shore.

The afternoon before, both her aunt and
Cleta had come to her door and knocked
softly, coaxing her to come down and eat
her Thanksgiving dinner, telling her the
coast was clear; her father and the boys

were shut up in the small, glass-enclosed section of the porch they used for a TV room, lost in the football games, unlikely to come out or hear anything until much later.

Emily had not answered, and finally her aunt had called, "I have to go now, sweetie, but I'll talk to you tomorrow or the next day. Tell you all about Columbia. Maybe you can go with me next time."

She heard her aunt's steps going away. Presently Cleta called out.

"I gotta go on home for a little while, but I'm leaving you a plate at your door. You call me if you need me. I just be at home. Don't worry, baby, he don't mean nothing he say half the time. Probably done forgot all about it. They in there lisenin' to that football game and eatin' pie."

Cleta's heavier tread went away down the stairs, and then there was silence. Utter silence. Emily knew she did not sleep until much later, but she did not hear her father and brothers come up to bed. And no one stirred now, as she and Elvis crawled deeply back under the piled covers of her bed. She had been afraid that the sheer awfulness of the dream would keep her awake, but it did not. Both girl and dog slid into sleep before the covers had settled.

When she woke, it was late, toward noon. She could tell by the rectangle of light on her bedroom floor, let in by the place where the curtains would never quite close. From hundreds of mornings gauging how long she might linger in bed by the position of the oblong, Emily knew that it was near noon.

She swung out of bed and padded to the bathroom, followed by Elvis, his claws clicking on the tile. She washed her face and brushed her teeth and dressed in corduroy pants and an old sweater of Buddy's that still smelled faintly of him. She could tell without looking out that it was cold. The floor was frigid, and the bathroom mirror had had a cloud of icy breath on it. She listened, but did not hear the faint subterranean rumble of the old furnace. She added heavy socks and high-topped tennis shoes and went out into the hall, tentatively, lest she run headlong into her father.

Once out in the hall, she knew that she would not encounter him or anyone else. An empty house has its own special silence. It is like a great held breath. There is no sense that somewhere within it someone will break the silence with footsteps, or a slammed door, or a rattling of pans in the kitchen. Emily stood letting the quiet wash over her, and then went silently and uneasily down the stairs. She did not know why she found it necessary to tiptoe. Even Elvis, at her heel, moved silently, with no jingle of collar or tick of toenails.

Downstairs there was no light except natural daylight. Not that it was needed; Sweetwater had lovely natural light from the river, and large windows. But a lighted lamp would have been welcome this morning. Emily crept from room to room: the kitchen was empty and spotless, but where was Cleta? The living and dining rooms, her father's office, still glistening with its polishing, all were empty. The glassed-in television room was empty, though strewn with newspapers and empty glasses and candy wrappers from last night's football orgy. Even as she had passed them, she had known that her father's and brothers' bedrooms were empty. You could smell the emptiness.

She went out onto the back porch and looked toward the river. It was the kind of

winter day she liked least, vast and shadowless and so bright there was no succoring pool of shade for the eye to light in anywhere. It was a merciless kind of day, as if
the great skies and the cold earth and water
had turned alien, indifferent to man, absorbed in some elemental and unstoppable
cosmic business of their own that did not
take into account anything that breathed air.
Emily found it was easy to stay inside on
this kind of day.

Nevertheless, she and Elvis walked away
from the steely river and around to the side
of the house where, deep in a grove of
pecan trees, her grandfather had built the
never-to-be stables and corrals that would
have housed his thoroughbreds. They were
used now for the dogs. Emily walked slowly
down to the kennels. Her father's truck was
gone, and the battered old Volvo station
wagon that the whole family shared. She
did not see the twins' shared, shambling
Mustang, either.

"Nobody home," she said aloud to Elvis,
simply to hear the sound of a voice. Then
she saw a movement over behind the kennels and Kenny Rouse came around the
side, carrying a huge sack of dog food.

Kenny was Emily's least favorite of the helpers her father employed to do the heavy, tedious work around the kennels. The count varied, but there were usually three or four young men, none of whom were in school for one reason or another. Emily doubted her father ever asked why. Kennel helpers were hard to come by. Walter treated his workers well, if abstractedly. Kenny was the only one who never talked or stopped to pass the time of day. He seldom met anyone's eyes. He was short and bull-necked with the skinned head of a marine recruit, and his small eyes and mouth seemed to be set too closely into the middle of his face. He wore a ring in one nostril and two in one ear. Emily knew her father disapproved of that, but knew also that he would not task Kenny with it. Kenny could, if he chose, do the work of two others.

He stopped when he saw her and put down the dog food.

Emily could not gracefully retreat, so she stopped, too, and smiled at him, a silly, prissy little smile. He looked at her as he always did, which meant all over her. Emily hated the weight of those little pig eyes on her. They always made her want to wipe her feet and wash her hands. This day they out-and-out frightened her.

"Hey, Kenny," she said.

"Hey, Emily," he mumbled. His eyes roamed, probed, measured.

"Where is everybody?" Emily said in a crazy lilt.

"They gone to that field trial up in Santee," he said. "Didn't nobody tell you? Gon' be gone all today and tonight and maybe tomorrow night, too. I know I got to feed the hounds till day after tomorrow. I didn't know nobody was here."

There was a slight pause, and he took a step toward her. Emily, whose hand was lying lightly on Elvis's back, felt a fine, soundless growling start up in him. She stood stiff and straight.

"You all by yourself, Emily?" Kenny Rouse said. His voice was softer, almost a whisper.

"Oh, goodness, no," Emily burbled. "Cleta's here."

"Didn't see that ol' car of hers."

"Her son brought her. We're just waiting for my aunt. She and her boyfriend are coming over." Emily's voice sounded quite mad in her own ears.

"Do tell. Well, y'all enjoy your day," Kenny

grinned. He looked, Emily thought, like a Halloween jack-o'-lantern. Not one of the cute kind.

"I'll be around for a while," he said lazily. "Might come beggin' a piece of pie, who knows?"

"It's wonderful," Emily said. "We'll save you some. Well, bye, Kenny."

"Bye, Emily."

She ambled back to the house, trying desperately not to break into a run. She could feel his eyes on her back; they felt as if they would leave smoking craters. Behind her, Elvis marched stiff-legged. She could hear, now, the tiny, high growling. When she reached the house she locked all the doors and the french windows, and put on all the lights in the kitchen, and turned the radio up as high as it would go. She did not realize until she sat down at the kitchen table that she was trembling all over, a shivering as fine as Elvis's. She did not see Kenny Rouse again, but from the corner of the kitchen window she could see that his old pickup was still there. It was there every time she looked out.

Cleta did not come and did not come.

By four o'clock the brightness was fading

from the cold sky, leaving it the opaque white of a lidless eye. The dark would fall down suddenly. Emily let Elvis out the front of the house, the side that faced the driveway, not the kennels and the river. He trotted a short way into the browning grass, relieved himself, and shot back into the house as if Emily's need for speed and silence was his own. She locked the door behind him and did not go into the front of the house again.

She wandered around the too-large, too-quiet kitchen, foraging for food for herself and Elvis. She found cold turkey and dressing, milk, and the untasted benné seed biscuits Jenny had made. She thought to take them upstairs to her bedroom to eat, and to light her lamps and listen to her radio and lock her door. Surely by then Cleta would have come. . . .

She lingered by the refrigerator and scanned the calendar that hung on a magnet on its door. If was, of course, a dog calendar, sent courtesy of a brand of dog food they never used. This one was puppies. She found yesterday's square, and saw her aunt's slanted black handwriting saying, Thanksgiving w. Parmenters. The square after that, today's, read, Columbia, symph. w/Althea/Evelyn/Lana.

Emily knew that for years her aunt had gone on a Thanksgiving excursion to Columbia, to hear a visiting symphony orchestra and stay in a large, square white Radisson Hotel, and spend the next day shopping. All of a sudden it seemed a pitiful thing to do, such a scanty pleasure. Her eyes filled thinking of her aunt's life. She had known the story since early childhood; it must have been Buddy who told her. Jenny Carter had indeed married handsome, good-for-nothing Truman Raiford a scant two months after her sister had swept Walter Parmenter into marriage, and they lived first in a small apartment in Ravenel, where Truman was a sometime general contractor. Jenny had been teaching at the consolidated elementary school there. They had high hopes, as her father had promised both girls large land inheritances, and by that time it was clear his diabetes wasn't going to give him much more time.

Her father died the next Christmas, and left the plantation and all its holdings to Caroline and Walter. To Jenny and Truman he left a large working farm on John's Island, complete with a neat, if not at all pretentious, farmhouse and land so fertile that tomatoes and other vegetables seemed to leap out of it. Truman sold his ragtag business to a casual friend and became a gentleman farmer. It did not take him long to persuade Jenny to sign her ownership over to him "for tax purposes," and only a year or so longer to run the farm almost into the ground. Truman took the deed to the farm and a nineteen-year-old Rantowles blonde, an acrylic nail technician by trade, and disappeared into the great Midwest. Walter tried halfheartedly to track him down for Jenny, but nothing came of it. Walter was busy building his own empire on the curvy backs of his Boykins. Caroline was busy becoming a planter's lady. She offered Jenny a room at Sweetwater, but Jenny refused politely and moved back to another apartment in Ravenel. She was a good teacher and quickly found a position teaching third grade at the same school in which she had started out. She had been there ever since. Her children loved her. Emily wondered if she missed having children of her own.

It seemed to Emily, standing in the chilly kitchen and seeing whole, for the first time, her aunt's life, a bad bargain in the extreme. She knew that Jenny would have loved living at Sweetwater with Walter. Now, she was gone into sensibly shod early middle age, and he was gone into his bitterness and his Boykins. Too late. She thought of the dream. Was everything always too late?

She carried her plate past the tall french doors out onto the porch and saw that Kenny Rouse's truck was still there. Kenny himself sat on its front fender, arms folded. He sat very still, staring at the house. When Emily passed the window he gave her a jaunty wave and a smile that seemed to have the jumbled teeth of a shark. Elvis froze and slid into perfect point, something spaniels seldom did. The growling began again. Emily dashed up the stairs and into her room, the steps seeming endless, and locked herself and Elvis in. She scrambled about in the mess on her desk for the pink cell phone Jenny had given her last Christmas, and punched in Cleta's number, one of the few she knew by heart. It seemed to her that in the space between the dialing and Cleta's answering voice, she did not breathe.

"Cleta?" Emily said in a tiny voice with no breath behind it. "Is that you?"

"Yeah. This me. Who this? Emily? Is that you?"

"Yeah, it's me. I, ah . . . I was just wondering when you were going to get here."

There was a long pause, then Cleta said, "I'm taking today off, Emily. Tijuan got in a bad way yesterday morning and Robert had to take her to detox. I got the babies with me. I told Mr. Walter I takin' a day off. Where's Jenny?"

"Well, you know, she's gone up to Columbia with her friends to hear that orchestra thing. She goes away after Thanksgiving. I don't think she's coming back till tomorrow or Sunday."

"You by yourself?" Cleta said sharply. "Yo' voice sound funny."

"Yeah," Emily said, trying to whip strength into her wobbling voice. "Daddy and the boys have gone to some field trial upstate. I think they'll be gone till tomorrow."

"Lord, God, he didn't say one word to me about no field trial," Cleta said. Her voice was an octave higher. "I'd of got somebody to come over there, or asked Jenny. You know she'd be glad to stay home with you."

"I guess he forgot," Emily said.

"He ain't gon' forget again after I get hold of him," Cleta said hotly. "You scared over there, baby? I really think you be all right, with them security lights and the dogs. I be over there first thing in the morning. Tijuan's cousin Esther comin' to get the babies and take 'em home with her. Don't nobody know how long Tijuan gon' be in there this time."

"Oh, well, no, I'm not scared," Emily said. "Only ol' Kenny Rouse is over here sittin' on his truck and he won't go home, and he's been here since noon. I think he knows I'm by myself."

There was an indrawn breath and a pause, and then Cleta said in a calm, no-nonsense voice: "You stay right where you is and lock them doors, Emily. Pack you a little bag and wait. I'm gon' send GW over there to get you and bring you over here. He be there in fifteen minutes. He blow his horn; don't you come out till you hear it. I've told Mr. Walter and told him that ol' Kenny Rouse is sorry as gully dirt. He try to get in before GW get there, you just call the police. You got Elvis with you?"

"Yeah . . ."

"You be all right, then. Bring him with you.

I got fried chicken and collards and corn bread and a Coca-Cola cake. We have us a feast."

Emily hung up the phone and sat down on the edge of her bed to wait. She shut off the radio when it occurred to her that she could not hear the sound of the door being tried over it, or soft footfalls on the stairs. By the time she heard the cranky soprano squall of GW's old truck, she had worked herself up into such a state that she was hyperventilating and could scarcely stand. She was halfway out the back door before her heart began to slow its crazy hammering. A sidewise glance revealed that Kenny and his truck were gone. She had not heard him leave. Disgust with herself had replaced the frozen terror by the time she opened the door to GW's truck.

"I had him turned into the devil," she said under her breath, "and all the time it was just old white-trash Kenny Rouse."

Realizing what Buddy would have replied to that, she blushed and crawled into the stuffy cab. GW gave her his wide, sweet white grin.

"Hey, Emily," he said. His voice was clear and tenor and beautiful. Emily knew that he

sang in the Goshen African Methodist Epis-
copal Church. All of Cleta's brood went
there.

"Hey, GW," she said. Beside her, Elvis
wiggled his red behind and licked GW's
knuckles on the steering wheel. Everyone,
human or dog, loved GW Pringle.

"Did you happen to see anybody when
you came in?" Emily asked him.

"Nobody but that ol' Kenny Rouse," GW
said serenely. "He jump in that truck and
take off like a bat out of torment when he
seen me. Scratch out of the driveway like he
was Dale Earnhardt. Who was you lookin'
for?"

"Nobody," Emily said. "I just wondered."

They drove through the dusk, smeared
now with river mist, sunk into comfortable
silence. GW was a hulking coffee-colored
boy of sixteen with the mental capacity of
an eight- or nine-year-old. School had long
since proved beyond him, so he stayed with
his mother and worked around the house,
and did chores and heavy work all through
the neighborhood, and pumped gas for
Besson's service station up on Highway
162. He also picked tomatoes in the big
truck farm fields, and was the weekend sex-

ton at his church, and was usually available for baby-sitting on short notice in the neighborhood. GW loved almost everything he encountered, but the three things he loved most were children, stars, and singing. Sometimes he took his small charges out to the creek banks, especially during meteor showers, to watch the burning, wheeling stars, and when he did, he would sing to them, strange, haunting songs that Emily could not understand. Cleta told her they were very old, and came from Africa with the first of the captured slaves. Gullah, the language was called, possibly from the place named Angola, in West Africa, where many of the slaves came from.

Emily had known GW since she was a small child. She had been one of his baby-sitting charges. They were totally comfortable with each other and did not need to talk. It was good, she thought, just to sit in the rattling cab with her head back against the gut-spilling headrest, feeling the blast of the faltering heater on her feet and hearing the drone of the engine in her ears. By the time they reached Cleta's small house at the end of a muddy, moss-haunted lane deep in the marshy wood near Pleasant Point, she was dozing, and Elvis slept soundly, twitching a bit in dreams of wildness.

Cleta was standing at the front door when they arrived, beaming, with a small sleeping black baby over one shoulder and a wooden spoon in the other hand.

"Now we got you all safe and sound, we gon' feed the both of you till you hollers uncle," she said.

"Cleta, you've painted your door blue. When did you do that?" Emily said, noticing. "It's pretty."

"Keeps the haints and plateyes out," GW said happily. "I painted it myself, just before Thanksgiving."

Cleta looked at him and smiled.

"It a Gullah charm to keep out bad spirits and bad luck," she said. "I can remember when half the houses on this island was blue. I don't say I believes, but it don't hurt, just the same. We got us a crack house down to the end of the road since early fall, and the police don't do nothin' about it. Seems like them people gets louder and meaner every day. I've heard gunshots down there. I'm pretty sure that's where Tijuan got hold of her stuff this time. If a little blue paint will help, I says go to it."

Inside, the little house was clean-scrubbed and warm with firelight, and a red-glowing kerosene heater had pride of place in the middle of the front room. It was a pieced-together, patchwork room, with newspapers and magazines substituting in places for wallpaper, and the small-paned windows had a few cardboard panes. None of the chairs and tables and sofas matched, and many were covered with old shawls and rugs, some quite beautiful. Emily recognized the old sofa that used to sit in their kitchen, and a leather chair that was ripped and mended with duct tape. It had, she thought, lived in her father's office for a time. By the fire sat an ornate wicker rocking chair with holes in the woven seat and back. It was painted a cheerful yellow, and looking at it made Emily feel oddly warm and cosseted.

"Yeah," Cleta said, following Emily's eyes and smiling. "It was yours. Your mama and I both used to rock you for hours in it, trying to get you to hush up and go to sleep. Mr. Walter gave it to me when . . . a few years ago. These babies love it."

"May I?" Emily said, looking at the rocker

and then at the blanket-wrapped, puppy-sized baby Cleta held.

Cleta smiled.

"Set down in that rocker an' I hand him to you. I think he sleep for another hour or two. This here Robert Jr. He the sleepin' one. Wanda, she the wigglin' one. She 'bout ready to get up from her nap, an then it'll be Katie bar the door."

Emily pulled the old rocker up to the fire and sat down in it. It seemed to begin to rock of itself, a primal, old-as-the-world rocking, a wooden womb. Cleta put a clean towel down over Emily's shoulder and then draped the sleeping baby over it. Emily's arms rose up to cup him as if they had been doing it for eons. She put her face down into the warm-baby, talcum-powder smell of him, took a deep breath, and began to rock. Robert made a small mewling sound and formed a bubble with his pursed pink lips, then settled back into sleep.

"Did you know that babies smell like new puppies' stomachs?" Emily said.

The flickering light and warmth of the fire, the smell of sweet wood burning and collards simmering and milky, powdery baby lulled Emily into a fugue state. In it fires burned in forests and people sang softly over the beat of quiet little drums . . . all of them, she knew, somehow, family . . . and outside the circle of the leaping fire wondrous magical things walked softly. Emily smiled slightly and snuggled her cheek into the baby. Home. She had never felt such a powerful sense of home.

Behind her, on one of the old sofas, GW began to sing, softly,

> *"Honey in the rock, got to feed*
> *   God's children,*
> *Honey in the rock, honey in the rock.*
> *Honey in the rock, got to feed God's*
> *   children,*
> *Feed every child of God."*

When she jerked awake, Cleta had taken the baby from her and was plopping him into a little basket on a sofa in the corner of the room. He was beginning to fuss and whimper. Again, Emily thought of puppies.

"I can see why people want to have them," she thought. "If they just didn't get any bigger."

At supper she turned to GW.

"What was that you were singing? It was you, wasn't it?" she said.

"Yeah. I don't really know what it means. Ol' man Gilley from down the road taught it to me. I just likes it."

"It's Gullah," Cleta said. "It's a song of blessing and safekeeping."

"Did Mr. Gilley teach it to you, too?" Emily said.

"No. I always knowed it. The old folks down in Frogmore where I was born all used to speak it, and sing and shout. Dance too, sometime. Now that's a sight. I can still remember jumpin' over that fire . . ."

Emily had a sudden and powerful sense of Cleta belonging to another world entirely, a huge, ancient one, as much of air and fire as earth, a world where the blessing and keeping of families was the primary thread in its fabric. It seemed, for a moment, as if she was someone Emily had never known, that the woman who had been coming to her home since as long as she could remember was merely a borrowed woman, someone who chose to spend her days with them because, perhaps, they needed blessings and safekeeping as much as she needed the salary Walter Parmenter paid her. She felt as tongue-tied, there in the light of the kerosene lantern, as if she had found herself dining with an oracle from another planet.

Finally she said, "That was pretty. I'd like to know some of those songs and stuff."

"GW and I teach you some, sometime," Cleta said.

Emily slept that night on a white-painted iron bed that served as a sofa, pulled up to the banked fire and covered with beautiful, strangely marked old quilts that smelled of mothballs and wood smoke. Elvis curled beside her, his nose to the fire, and slept peacefully and heavily, with no twitching dreams and no jerking awake. When it was time for them to leave and go back to Sweetwater the next morning, Emily felt near tears.

"I wish I could live here," she said.

"You got a beautiful home," Cleta said.

"It's not a home," Emily murmured.

"It be one day," Cleta said softly. "It need you there to make it one."

Climbing the stairs to her room in the cold noon sunlight, with Elvis padding behind her, Emily never felt less like this house needed her, or ever would.

She was still lying on her bed watching the little black-and-white TV Buddy had given her for her birthday the year that he died, when her father and the boys came home. Over the opening of *Star Trek,* which always thrilled Emily—"to boldly go where no man has gone before"—she heard the slamming of the front door and the sound of heavy boots and men's voices. When had the twins' voices become those of her father? Maybe, Emily thought, it happened at the hunt yesterday. Or at the field trial. Maybe one of the events was the turning of boys into men. She did not figure she would ever know, since as far as she knew, girls and women did not go to field trials. The twins had told her that when she was small, and cried to tag along.

She turned off *Star Trek* to listen. She heard Cleta call out sharply to her father, and heard the kitchen door close. She heard the boys' feet stop outside the closed door as if they were listening, and then go on down the hall to the TV room. She heard the idiotic bray of *Cops* come on. And she heard Cleta's voice, tearing into her father. She heard no answer from him.

Much later he came to her door and

tapped, and called out, "Emily, may I come in? I think we need to talk."

"Yes," she called back, her heart beating in great, dragging thuds. Beside her, Elvis lifted his head and whined.

Her father came into her room and stood there in his field trial clothes, a battered old waxed-cotton jacket and high rubber field boots, and looked at the floor for a long moment, as if examining the rug. Emily had brought the old oriental that had always been before the fireplace in Buddy's room into her own, and her father seemed to be studying it. Then he lifted his head and looked at her. Emily seemed to see him freshly all at once, as you sometimes do someone whom you see every day. Her heart squeezed. Buddy looked back at her—a Buddy whose face someone or something had closed down, whose eyes saw little but middle distance and tomorrow's dreams.

"He is so handsome," she thought. "I wonder why I never really saw that before? I wonder if he ever really sees me?"

"I'm sorry you were left alone," her father said. "I wish you hadn't hidden up here all that time. I'd have remembered if I'd seen you."

Emily was silent with the sheer idiocy of that. Did she have to be in view to be remembered?

"We'll make sure it won't happen again," he said. "Now. I think the time has come to make a few little rules, just so we'll always know where we stand."

He moved his eyes from her and looked out her window to the river in the distance. Slate-gray mist was coiling in.

"First, about Elvis. He's a fine dog, and I know you're proud of him, but any Boykin who won't hunt is not an asset to the plantation. In fact, he's a liability. I don't want anyone coming here to buy Boykins to see him. He just looks too good; they're going to want to see him in action, and we can't have that. So when people are coming, I want you to take him to your room and keep him there. If they drop in unexpectedly, I'm going to lock him in the back barn if you're not around. I don't think this is unreasonable, but if you can't comply with it, we'll have to find him another home."

In the silence that followed, Emily felt as if she had been too close to a gunshot. Her ears rang and her face tingled. Elvis whined again. Her father was still studying the river.

"Can you do that?" he said. Still, he did not look at her.

"Yes, sir," she said.

"All right. Now. I don't think it looks good for you to spend much time at Cleta's house, and especially not with GW. I know this was a special occasion, but it's not a habit I want you to get into. Surely there are some little girls at school who could come visit you on weekends, or you could visit them. I know you like working with the dogs, but weekday afternoons are enough. You're getting to be a young lady. You need to act like one."

"Yes," Emily said numbly. She was talking to the side of his head. He was studying the marsh and hummocks on the other side of the river now, and the deep, wet-glistening woods.

He was silent for a minute more. Then he looked at her again and said, "I'm glad you agree. I don't want to have to worry about you all the time."

"When did you ever at all?" she thought furiously, tears beginning to sting in her throat. She wanted to hide her face so that he would not see, but she could not seem to look away from him.

"Okay, then," he said, and turned away, and went out of her room, closing the door behind him. There was a pause, and then from the other side he called, "I'm sorry I yelled at you about Elvis the other day."

She did not answer, and presently she heard his footsteps going downstairs.

She did not, after all, cry. She simply sat on the floor, holding Elvis against her. *Star Trek* slid into *The Twilight Zone* and then *The X-Files.* It seemed much later when Cleta knocked softly on the door, but the sun had not yet set.

"I made you some tea cakes; they still warm. You eat 'em now with this glass of milk. You ain't had no lunch, and it's been a long time since breakfast. Can I come on in?"

Emily thought of breakfast that morning at Cleta's house: crowing babies, crackling fire, fresh corn pone and syrup, eggs scrambled endlessly high and golden, homemade sausage sizzling from a cast-iron skillet, and coffee lightened with cream. Warm, all of it, everything, warm.

"Come in," she said. She did not get up from the floor.

Cleta set the tray on her desk and stood looking at her, hands on hips.

"Yo' Daddy say he gon' have a little talk with you. I let him know right off what I thought of him goin' off and leavin' you here. I reckon it didn't go so good, huh?"

"Oh, it went great," Emily said savagely. "He's made a few rules so we'll all know where we stand. For one thing, I can't let anybody from outside the farm see Elvis. Ever. I've got to keep him hidden when we've got customers here. Either that, or Daddy will find him a good home. Then, I'm supposed to have my little friends visit me on weekends, or go and visit them. I wonder what would happen if I brought some of my little friends home? They've all got nose rings or belly rings, and they wear blouses that their bras show through—if they bother with bras. They cuss every other word. And some of them are already doing the dirty deed. They use a trailer in that old burned-out park outside Meggett.

"And, I don't work with the dogs on weekends. I'm getting to be, quote, a young lady, and I need to act like one. Like he knows what a young lady acts like . . ."

She stopped, breathing hard. Something was filling her chest up like wet cement. She did not tell Cleta about not being allowed to go to her house anymore. She sat, hugging Elvis, struggling to control her breathing.

"That man ain't hear a word I said," Cleta muttered.

"Oh, Cleta, he wouldn't even look at me! He never did the whole time! He looked off at the river and the woods, but not at me! I didn't realize he couldn't stand to look at me!"

The words burst out on a geyser of tears. She buried her head in Elvis's curly coat. Cleta knelt awkwardly and put her arms around both of them. After a while Emily's tears slowed and stopped. But the paralyzing hurt did not.

"Emily," Cleta said presently, "I want you to get up and go look at yourself in that floor mirror. Go on now."

Unwillingly, Emily did.

"What do you see?" Cleta said.

Emily looked closer. She saw a tear-smeared, red-nosed small figure with a tangle of blazing curls over her face and large, brimming hazel eyes. And she saw, as if for the first time, curves. The swell of hips. The circle of waist. Breasts. Distinct small mounds under the too-tight old T-shirt that said BOYKIN SPANIELS—THE DOGS THAT WON'T ROCK THE BOAT. Her nipples showed distinctly through the *e* in "Spaniels" and the *w* in "Won't." She stared at her image, aghast. When had all this happened? Why had she not noticed? A miniature woman looked back at her. Emily hated her on sight.

She looked up at Cleta.

"Yeah," Cleta said. "All of a sudden you ain't little Emily anymore. That bother your daddy. But what bothers him most is that you look exactly like yo' mama, when he first married her. I been thinkin' for a long time that you did. I wondered when he'd see it. I knew you wouldn't, because there ain't no pictures of her like she was back then around here. But there you are. Miss Caroline in the flesh. He must have just seed it today."

"If he loved her so much, why wouldn't he want me to look like her?" Emily sniffled.

Cleta said softly, "He like to die when she take off. He ain't even say her name, from that time to this. I 'spect it just plain hurts him too much to look at you right now. He get over it, you'll see."

I don't see how he can, Emily thought, if I look more and more like her the older I get. Maybe pretty soon we'll just pass notes to each other.

"You eat them cakes, now," Cleta said. "I brought Elvis some bacon, too. I got to go get y'all's supper, and then get on home. You needs to come down to supper, Emily. Right now ain't a good time to buck yo' daddy."

When she had gone, Emily sat munching vanilla tea cakes and feeding Elvis strips of thick bacon and feeling the import of this day. It would, she knew instinctively, divide time. Forever after she would have to think of her father in an entirely new way, a nearly mortally wounded man trying to live around his pain. She was not ready to forgive him, but she knew that she could never see him the same way again. She did not know what she would ultimately see. Whether or not pity would ever come creeping in, she did not know.

She got up slowly and went to the mirror and peered at her new self through splayed fingers. This was a far more profound shift of perception than she was asked to make toward her father. This was a seismic shudder. She could not and would not be that changeling woman in the mirror. Not now. Maybe not ever. The very thought made her nearly ill with fear.

When Emily went down to supper that evening she wore an oversized flannel shirt over her jeans. She had scrubbed her face and pulled her wild hair straight back into a tight ponytail. She did not look at herself, either in the flesh or in the mirror, when she bathed and changed her clothes. And before she went to school the following Monday morning, she bound her small breasts absolutely flat with adhesive tape. Getting it off at night was painful. Going without it would be agony.

The conventional wisdom in the Lowcountry was that an unusually cold autumn meant an unusually early and warm spring. But in early January, when the forsythias and camellias should have been softening garden beds and the marshes beginning ever so faintly to green up, the bitter cold bit deeper and hung on.

"Never seen another winter quite like it,"
people at school and around the drugstore
and Bi-Lo said.

"Shoot, there've been worse," the old-
timers around the mom-and-pop grocery
and gas stores in Meggett and Hollywood
and Adams Run said. "I remember one time
it snowed in April. Think it was '37. You
don't see it much now, though. All that
space stuff's heating the planet up."

It was bad hunting weather for the few remaining birds and animals whose seasons
lasted into early spring. And it was not good
training weather for the Boykins who had
graduated from the paddock to the field and
the watery marshes. A sort of stasis, an in-
drawing that might have been the hallmark
of a far northern winter shrouded Sweetwater. The boys stayed late at school, pleading
athletic practices, and came home smelling,
sometimes, of drugstore perfume or beer
and, oddly, oregano. Emily and every other
child in the rural Lowcountry over the age of
ten knew what the smell meant, but Walter
Parmenter did not, and so did not task them
with it. Walter himself spent longer hours
shut up in his office, poring over wildlife
magazines and sporting newspapers. The

boys had given him a second-hand computer for Christmas, knowing that the wealth of obscure information about hunting and dogs available on the Internet would please him, but he had tossed a macintosh over it in late December and had not looked at it since.

Emily confined her training to the big barn and sometimes, if the wind was down, the front paddock, and kept the heaters in the kennels and runs going, and curled up with Elvis and *Stargate SG-1* in the long dark. Somehow, going outside without a purpose did not occur to her. Running to and from the bus at school she kept her head down and her coat collar up. She might have been the only person within shouting distance of Sweetwater Plantation who did not mind— even welcomed—the dark cage of winter. It made her feel as if nothing had to be dealt with yet. Anything troublesome could wait until the great cold broke. Deep under their layers of quilts, Emily and Elvis slept in the long nights like dreaming plants dormant under snow, and felt no tug of spring.

4

In the pre-dawn hours of a day in late March, winter tore its talons out of the Low-country earth and lumbered away on its great, dirty-ice wings. It happened suddenly: if you were awake, as many country-men were, you could have smelled in one breath the stale dank scent of dead marsh and river, and in the next a small, soft puff of warm wind, heavy with briny life and the smell of faraway flowers and above all the sea. You could lift your face to it, knowing in your viscera that the season had turned at last. Animals who slumbered deep in straw or made moss nests for themselves on the hummocks raised their heads and lifted their noses. Ears pricked with the promise of what was coming.

Even if you were asleep, as Emily and Elvis were, drowned in their quilts, the deepest part of you would have felt the impending transition. Emily had known for weeks that a great change was coming, though she didn't know precisely what it was. It followed at her heels, and sometimes she could feel the earth shake under its tread. It felt like more than spring. It felt like a formless, limitless kind of *knowing.* Emily felt, though she did not think it, that after the knowing overtook her she would be a different person altogether: somehow more finished, more substantial, worthy at last of the world's notice now, because she would know the nameless thing that children do not know.

Deep in her sleep, Buddy whispered to her: *"And what rough beast, its hour come round at last, / Slouches toward Bethlehem to be born?"*

"Showoff," her heart whispered again, though her sleeping mind did not.

Presently she turned over restlessly, and tossed the heavy covers away without waking, and lay flat on her back, arms and legs outstretched, waiting to receive the gift that came on the warm wind. Elvis came awake

suddenly and fully and sat up, looking intently into her sleeping face. Emily smiled,
very slightly. Elvis whined.

Another dream came. This one was not
ethereal and mist-borne like the first of the
great dreams. This one had the itching par-
ticularity of real life. It was not a child's
dream. Emily felt grit under her bare feet
and looked down at the sisal carpet that
had lain on the foyer floor when she was a
small child. She smelled chicken frying in
the kitchen, tasted the stinking sweetness
of pluff mud on the back of her tongue.

When she looked about her she saw that
she was crouched in the dark alcove under
the curving front stairs, where the telephone
table and chair sat. It was seldom used for
telephoning, since you could not read the
numbers in the murky gloom there, but it
had long been Emily's special place. It was
the cave from which, in safety, she eaves-
dropped on the grown-ups of Sweetwater,
trying to assess the precise tenor of her
world at the moment. She was alone. She
knew, as you do in that sort of dream, that
there was a dog named Elvis who was half
of her heart, but had not yet been born.

She did not often look out into the foyer

to spy on the adults. Things came to her more clearly when they were only heard. Emily could read voices even before she could read faces. She thought perhaps she had been born knowing how.

She heard her mother and father's voices, but they were too low for her to make out the words. They were angry, though. Emily's heart pounded sickly. She had never heard her mother's voice raised in anger. She had only heard her father's anger in connection with mismanagement of the dogs, and then it was a flat, level tone that chilled rather than burned. For a long moment she was afraid to look out into the foyer, and then she did.

Her mother and father stood beneath the big chandelier that had always hung there, fine but chipped and clouded now. Its light was foggy and pale, but it was sufficient to set her mother's tumbled curls blazing, and to sit shallowly on the sharp planes of her father's face. His narrow blue eyes sparked in a way Emily had never seen, and incredibly, his face was streaked with tears. This frightened Emily far more than the anger. That her father could weep was simply not a part of her small universe.

Her mother was wearing a drifting silk dress the color of candlelight; Emily had seen it before, and loved it. It was a dress for a princess. Even though her mother's back was to her, Emily knew how she looked in it from the front. It had a shallow scooped neck that showed her mother's luminous skin, and pearls the same color as the dress would swing down as she leaned over Emily in her small bed to kiss her good night. Emily sniffed instinctively, wanting the scents of tuberoses and lemons that were her mother's. She craned her neck around the stair, to see her mother's face. She knew that there would be a soft, slightly mischievous smile on it, and coppery lipstick. Her mother would brush her cheek with her glossy lips, and sometimes leave a soft, tawny imprint there. Emily never wiped it off. It was a part of her mother that stayed with her when her mother went out into the night.

"Sleep tight, my little bedbug," her mother would say softly. "I'll bring you something fancy from the party."

And Emily would slide into sleep on a warm wave of perfect safety. Usually in the morning there would be, on her pillow, a bit of cake, or a tart, or a scrolled and swirled canapé tasting of creek shrimp.

In the dream, though, Emily did not want her mother to turn toward her. She knew instinctively that the face would not be one that she knew. It would be a face whitened with anger, and the mouth would be slitted with the hissing of it. Emily tried desperately to wake herself up, knowing in some small part of her heart that this was a dream. But in the way of truly terrible dreams, she could not move, no matter how hard she tried.

And then her mother said clearly, "There is absolutely nothing in this place for me anymore," and picked up her small crocodile overnight bag from where it sat on the rug beside her, and walked past Walter Parmenter through the open door—for it was high summer in the dream—and banged the screened door behind her. The last Emily saw of her was a flare of the ivory silk skirt as she went down the steps into the darkness. After that the dream went abruptly and totally dark, and Emily stood in a black, featureless place where no living being was, or would be again.

She woke herself with her strangled scream. Even sleep-stunned, she could tell that it was the scream of a small child. Elvis brought her all the way awake by franticly licking her face, and she heard Cleta clanging around in the kitchen. She saw the pale sunlight and the blood at the same time. The blood stained the back of her pajamas and smeared on her hands when she reached down to touch it. It was warm and thick and came, she knew, from the sharp stiletto that was turning in the pit of her stomach. In that first moment Emily thought quite clearly that the dream had killed her.

In an instant she was out of bed and down the stairs and into the kitchen, where she threw herself into Cleta's floury arms. She was strangling on her tears, and could not get words out. Cleta held her hard and rocked her back and forth, back and forth, as if she were a toddler, and breathed a wordless crooning into Emily's tangled hair. Emily held onto her with all the furious strength in her arms. If she let go, she would surely fall off the face of the earth.

Presently Cleta disentangled her arms and pushed her away slightly to look at her.

"What on earth's the matter, lovey?" she said. And then, looking down, "Oh, honey. That ain't anything to cry about. You just got your flowering. I thought it about time for that."

"No, no, it's not that," Emily sobbed. "I know about that, that just means you can get pregnant if you do it. A lot of the kids at school spend half their time moaning if they get it and the rest moaning if they don't. You'd think the Kotex machine was the Holy Grail! This is different; this is . . . Cleta, I had this awful, awful dream, and I think this is . . . it's, killing me! It feels like a knife in my stomach!"

Cleta shook her lightly. "You listen to me, Emily. Ain't no dream ever got dreamed that can kill you, no matter how bad it is. The flowering hurts when it first happens. We can fix that. Now let's get you upstairs and into a hot bath, and I fix you up a little, and then you tell me about this dream. Go on, now. Yo' daddy and the boys be down for breakfast pretty soon."

There were three modern bathrooms in the house, with showers and built-in shelving and white tile. Her father and the boys claimed two of them, and the other adjoined Buddy's room and was never used. Emily had the original bathroom, built in 1936 and looking every inch its age. It was high-ceilinged and cavernous—you could have skated on its vast expanse of pitted, mossy green linoleum. All the accoutrements— bathtub, washstand, toilet—were tucked into the corners, and the only lighting was a dim overhead fixture and a little lamp with a pull chain over the washstand. The walls were green, like the linoleum, and in the early morning or at twilight, it seemed like an underwater chamber, aqueous and shimmering. Even the air seemed to shimmer because the old washstand mirror was speckled where the silver coating had worn off, and the windows were the original nineteenth-century wavy glass. It had no central heating, because Walter Parmenter thought that heating a room of its size just to use the toilet or have a quick bath was absurd. A tall, bulbous blue kerosene heater sat in the middle of the floor, and whoever wanted to use the bath in winter had to creep in and turn the little knob and wait until the belly of the stove glowed dull red. Emily loved the room with all her heart. From the time Buddy had told her about Atlantis, she had imagined it to be a princess's chamber there.

She huddled in bed in her thick bathrobe

while Cleta lit the heater and drew a bath, and then, when Cleta called out, she ran into the bathroom and turned her back to Cleta and dropped the robe, and practically dove into the tub. It was huge and claw-footed and deep, and it was filled now with steaming water. Emily shrank into it up to her neck and put her head back and closed her eyes. The hot water seemed to be leaching some of the pain from her abdomen, and a small margin of the dream's desolation shrank back. Beside her, on the bathmat, Elvis snorted as he pursued a flea. For just this moment, she felt safe.

She did not open her eyes until Cleta said sharply, "Emily, what them marks on yo' chest?" and she looked down and saw that the tape had left pinched red pleats and folds over her breasts and ribs. She grabbed for a washcloth, but it was too late. Cleta pulled it firmly away and studied her torso. Then she lifted her head and looked into Emily's face. Her own was soft with pity.

"You been tapin' yo' breasts down, ain't you?" she murmured. "Oh, Emily. What we gon' do with you? You knows as well as I does you can't stop the woman comin' out in you with no tape."

"Well, I will," Emily said, beginning to cry once more, wearily. "I will not grow up to be some simpering fool who waves her . . . bust . . . at every man who comes within fifty miles of her, and I will not hang around the Kotex machine and the trailer park. It's *my* body. I'll tape it from my neck to my knees if I want to!"

Cleta reached out and brushed a wet strand of hair off her face.

"They's lots of other ways to be a woman," she said. "Good ways. I reckon you don't know much about 'em because you don't see no women very often. You never did. I worry lots about that."

"You're a woman."

"Emily, the kind of stuff you need to learn now, I just can't teach you. I'm just plain too ignorant. I don't know nothing about the places you gon' be goin'. I can love you all your life, but I can't be much help to you right now. I got to think a spell about this. Git on out, now, and I get you a clean towel and a cup of hot tea and an aspirin, and you can sleep some more. I ain't lettin' you go to school today."

As she climbed out of the water, Emily saw that her blood had curled stringily out into it, and made little whorls. She fled into her room into bed. Presently, in clean underpants and the small, folded towel Cleta had brought, she drank steaming tea.

"This has got liquor in it," she said to Cleta.

"Got gin," Cleta said. "Best way to water the flowering. You won't be hurtin' much for a while. I'm gon' call Miss Jenny after school and get her to bring you what you need over here. Then we gon' have a talk."

"I don't want you to tell Aunt Jenny, or Daddy, or anybody," Emily said thickly. The gin and the aspirin and the warmth of the bedcovers were putting the pain and the rest of the world at a remove. Emily wanted to lie suspended here forever.

"I ain't gon' tell yo' daddy or the boys, certainly. Scare 'em right out of their britches. But yo' aunt got to know. Ain't nobody else can help you much right now."

"My mother could have," Emily murmured. She realized with foggy surprise that it was the first time she had spoken of her mother to anyone but Buddy.

"Yeah, but she ain't here, is she?"

Cleta's voice was sharp and grim. Suddenly, the dream came scalding back, as palpable and present as breath.

"I dreamed about her last night," she said. "It was the worst dream I ever had. I just know it started . . . all this."

"Tell me about that dream," Cleta said, sitting down on the edge of Emily's bed.

And Emily did. By the time she had finished, she was gasping deeply, drowning in grief, struggling once again to break the dream's murderous hold. When she began to retch silently and claw the air for breath, Cleta turned her over in bed and gave her a mighty slap between the shoulder blades. Emily jackknifed, and then gave a great gulp, and air came flooding back into her lungs. But it was a long time before the tortured rasping stopped. Beside the bed Elvis whined and tried to jump in with her until Cleta put him out in the hall and shut the door. He cried and scratched, but Cleta was adamant.

When Emily's breathing slowed, Cleta brought the bottle of Gilbey's over to the bed and pressed it matter-of-factly to Emily's lips.

"Swallow," she said.

Emily did, and choked, and spat the stinging liquid onto her quilt.

"Again," Cleta said inexorably, and this time Emily kept the gin down. In a few seconds warmth curled out from her stomach all over her, and the dream withdrew silently, like a wild animal. It muttered at her from the edges of the room, though. Emily kept turning her head to look into the corners, as if she could actually see the great inky shape of it.

"Now," Cleta said. "We needs to talk about that dream."

"No," Emily whimpered, shrinking back into the pillows. "What if I have it again? Oh, Cleta, what if it comes back, and back . . ."

"Ain't gon' come back," Cleta said, looking far away into some distance of her own.

"How do you know?"

" 'Cause it ain't no dream. I the last person in the world ought to be tellin' you this, Emily, but it's past time and I reckon the only other one who knows about it ain't ever gon' speak. An' you got to know, because it ride you like a hag all your life if you don't. You ain't gon' know what it is, but you'll feel it behind you, and you be wonderin' all the time when it gon' catch up with you."

"I've already felt that," Emily quavered. "For a week now, at least. How did you know about it?"

"We all knows," Cleta said. "Some people call it a haint and some says it's a plateye. But we all knows down deep that it ain't nothin' but a big truth tryin' to catch up with you. You run, and it run harder. You turn and stare it down and it go slinkin' off like some ol' sissy. I seen it happen a lot of times."

"You mean—that dream is the *truth*?"

"Yeah, it is. I wondered if you'd remember it on your own. Lots of chirrun never do. It'll hurt you a lot right at first, but it won't ever chase you through the nights no more. God knows this ain't the time for it, but yo' insides knows it already, an' it tryin' to come out now. We needs to help it on out."

Emily closed her eyes and leaned back. The whole world seemed warm and enveloping. She felt swaddled, cocooned. What could possibly touch her? Elvis's cries sounded like those of a dog in a far-off TV program.

"You can tell me now," she said, and smiled. She could feel its foolishness on her mouth. The smile became an even more ludicrous giggle. "All I've got to do is keep drinking gin."

"It don't hardly never help none, but there's times it's a right good friend," Cleta said. "This is one of them. All right. You be quiet and listen till I'm through, and then we see what we need to do next."

Emily looked at her silently. Gin or not, this was going to be a bad thing. She could see its dense shadow advancing before it. But it was abstract, unreal.

"What you dreamed happened one night when you was about three," Cleta said. Her rich voice turned suddenly flat and hard-edged. "Yo' mama and daddy thought I'd gon' home, I reckon, but I was still in the kitchen, ironin'. First I just heard their voices real loud and mean, like I ain't never heard before, and then I could hear what they sayin'. An' after a while, Jesus help me, I opened the door a little ways and watched. It was wrong, but I ain't sorry."

"What . . ."

Cleta held up her hand. "I reckon they'd been fightin' for a long time; I knew yo' mama lose her temper sometime, an' bang things around when she don't get what she want. Her daddy spoil her bad. But until that night, they kept it upstairs. The help usually knows, but I didn't. They standin' there in the foyer under that chandelier, and she got on that pretty silk dress she got up in Atlanta for that big weddin' in Charleston, and her little suitcase was sittin' there on the flo' beside her. She right up in yo' daddy's face, and she hollerin'. He just standin' there like a statue, an' he got tears rollin' down his face. But he mad, too; I could tell. He say somethin' like, 'Don't you care about nothin?' and she say, clear as day, 'There ain't nothin' in this house for me to care about.' That's when I saw you. You was standin' there by that telephone place in yo' nightgown, an' you look like somebody done strike you dead. White as a sheet. I wanted so bad to go get you I couldn't get a deep breath, but you turn around then, and scoot back upstairs like a little rabbit, so quick and quiet.

"Then he say, 'You jus' gon' leave yo' chirrun? Just like that? You mean they ain't nothin' to you?'

"And she say, 'The twins got each other. They always did. An' they got you. They ain't paid me no mind for a long time. Emily ain't old enough to even remember me.

You'll find somebody to take care of her. Jenny, maybe. I bet my long-sufferin' sister would just love to git in this house one way or another. And Buddy . . . I'm coming back for Buddy. I'm not leaving him alone in this awful dead place where nobody cares about nothing but dogs and shootin' birds. He's goin' with me. He's sensitive like me; he needs people and music and art and . . . and *grace.* There ain't no grace in this house. You tell him I'll be back for him before he knows it.'

"An' she pick up that suitcase and walk out that do', and that the last this house ever see of her. Yo' daddy just stand there for a long time, and then he go down the hall to his study and shut himself in. An' I go on home, and worries all night about how to fix things for you. But besides askin' yo' daddy where yo' mama was the next mornin', an' he say she gone on a trip, you never talk about her again, that I knows of. It was like it never happened. For a long time I hoped to God you weren't never gon' remember it, but all the time I knows in my heart you would, an' I hoped somebody got the sense to tell you about it before you did. Otherwise I knowed it gon' chase you down jus' like it did. But you knows now, and it ain't gon' chase you no more."

Emily felt a great, dead coldness like an iceberg, so deep in her stomach that she knew it would never melt. But it did not flay and cut her like the dream had done. It simply sat immobile, slowly freezing the life out of her.

"It was because of me, wasn't it?" she whispered. "I always sort of knew it was. Everybody would look at me when somebody mentioned her. I was the nothing, wasn't I? If I'd been something, she wouldn't have left."

"No. It wasn't you. It wasn't ever you. She got nothin' inside her to care about anybody else with, an' so she think she gon' find somethin' wonderful if she go out lookin' for it."

"But I remember her . . . leaning over me, and kissing me, and sometimes she sang to me, and she always brought me stuff from parties . . ."

"It ain't that she didn't love you. Who could not love you? It just that she can't love nobody enough to hold her anywhere long. Well, wherever she is, I hopes she find

it. No. No, I hope she don't. She don't deserve it."

Emily heard real anger in Cleta's voice,
where there had never been anger before.

"You . . . you don't know where she is,
then?"

"Don't nobody know, I don't reckon, 'cept
maybe yo' daddy, and he ain't sayin'. It's
like she died that night. But at least we'd
know if she was dead."

"You don't think she . . . she's sick, or
anything?"

"No. I don't think that."

"Buddy didn't either. He said once he
thought she could take care of herself real
well."

"You all talk about her, you an' Buddy?"

"Just that once. He always changed the
subject."

"I reckon he did, after what she do to
him."

"What? I know she must never have
come back for him, because there he was.
Is that what you mean by what she did to
him?"

"Yeah," Cleta said slowly. "I think she
must have tol' him she was gon' but she be
back for him. He love his mama somethin'

mighty, and she make over him all the time, about how handsome he is, and how smart, and how proud he gon' make her one day when she git him away from this place . . ."

"But she didn't come back."

"No. Right before she left, Buddy start stumblin', an' fallin' down in public. I guess she think he slow her up or somethin'. He ain't never said nothin' to me about her, but it must of hurt him bad. He know somethin' ugly and bad was wrong with him from the beginning. He a smart boy. He know why she ain't come back."

Oh, Buddy. The words felt as if they were etched in acid on the surface of the iceberg inside her. Oh, Buddy . . .

Emily felt tired tears well up, but she did not think her sore eyes could shed them. Too big, it was all too big. She knew that if she tried to process it, it would, after all, kill her. Murder her. She kept her mind white and blank.

"And nobody ever said anything about her again?" she said, faintly, as if beneath a bell of glass.

"Not that I hears," Cleta said. "Yo' daddy got them boys, and them dogs, and this ol' place, that he think he gon' turn into one of them fancy river plantations somehow or other. He gon' show everybody, yessir. He show 'em he can do it without her, all by himself. He been killin' himself tryin' to do it ever since that night."

"I could help him," she whispered.

"He see that one day," Cleta said.

She opened the door and Elvis came bounding in and dived under the covers, as close beside Emily as he could get. He did not sleep, only kept his golden eyes on her face.

Cleta stayed until Emily fell asleep. She did not think that she would ever sleep again, but she did, abruptly and so deeply that she did not stir until twilight, when her aunt Jenny came tiptoeing in and shook her gently. She had not, after all, had the assassin dream again, and after that day, she never did.

Aunt Jenny moved in that weekend. Emily was only vaguely aware of it until she woke, fully and finally, on Sunday night. She had slept like a dormant animal for three days, bobbling up from the depths of sleep occasionally to eat the soft foods Cleta brought for her, go to the bathroom and change the sanitary pads that her aunt had brought, and scrub her face and spiral down into sleep again. She was dimly aware that Elvis was beside her, licking her face gently whenever she woke. It was only later that Aunt Jenny told her that he had refused to leave her side for the entire three days, except to dash outside to relieve himself, and had burrowed almost under her, still as a statue. They brought his food and water into Emily's bedroom, and he ate and drank there.

"You have a real friend here," Emily remembered her aunt saying during one of her tenuous excursions into wakefulness.

"I know," Emily mumbled. "He's my best friend. He's probably my only friend."

"You have lots of friends, Emily," her aunt answered. "You just haven't met most of them yet."

When she woke on Sunday night, she knew instinctively that she would not be permitted to hide in sleep anymore. For the moment, sleep was gone, and all her senses were almost preternaturally sharp. The pale green spring twilight glowed iridescently outside her window. The breeze that came in was like a blessing on her face. Emily heard dogs barking off in the kennels, the TV downstairs squalling, Elvis breathing contentedly beside her, hollow footsteps in the hall and on the stairs, pans rattling in the kitchen. Far away in the marshes she heard the plinking of the spring peepers. She smelled vegetable soup cooking, pluff mud, the sweet, funky odor of warm dog, her own unwashed body, and the light, green-smelling perfume her aunt always wore. She tasted cold artesian well water and the cottony inside of her own long-closed mouth.

She saw, as if limned in light, her shadowy bedroom and the face of her aunt leaning over her. She could even see Aunt Jenny's pores, and the tiny sun wrinkles fanning out from her eyes.

"Hey," she said, and cleared her throat around the unaccustomed effort of speaking. "How long have you been here?"

"A while," her aunt said. "It's been some fun, watching you and Elvis sleep."

"How long have I slept?"

"Almost three days, off and on. It was good for you, I think. You look a lot better than when I got here. You've got some color in your cheeks, and your eyes are at least focused. How do you feel?"

"Okay, I guess," Emily said, and then memory flooded in and she closed her eyes and waited. Her stomach gave a snakelike twist, but the deep, grinding pain didn't awaken.

"Aunt Jenny, all this stuff . . . did Cleta tell you? She said she was going to. It was—it was just awful. It was terrible. I don't know what to do about it."

"You don't have to do anything about it," her aunt said. "You've done exactly what you ought to do, and that's sleep. Poor baby, you had a triple whammy, didn't you?"

"Triple whammy . . ."

"Yes. The dream, the curse, and—the truth. I'd have slept for ten days, myself."

"You know about the dream and the . . . what I remembered?"

"Cleta told me. I needed to know. We didn't tell anybody else, though. That's for you to do, if you ever want to, or not."

"Did you know about . . . her leaving like that?"

"I knew she left suddenly. I never knew exactly how it happened until now. Your father never spoke of it to me, and none of the boys did either. I really thought you couldn't remember."

"I couldn't, for a long time. Till now. Did anybody try to find her, to bring her back or anything?"

"I don't know. Your mother and I weren't very close by then. If your dad tried, I never knew about it."

"And nobody knows where she is?"

"Not that I've heard, baby."

Aunt Jenny pushed Emily's tangled hair out of her eyes. People were always doing that.

"But . . . how could she live? I mean, did she take some money with her, or what? I don't think she could get a job; she didn't know how to do much . . ."

Jenny Raiford smiled. It was not a soft smile.

"She knew how to do what was necessary. Don't you worry about that. I doubt she went without money for a single day."

"But . . ."

"That's enough for now. Maybe we'll know more about it later. Right now it's time for you to take a bath and get dressed and have some supper with me. Your dad and the boys ate early and went over to John's Island to look at some fencing for the runs. It'll be a while before they're back."

"I don't want to see my father right now."

"You don't have to tonight, but I want you to have supper with us tomorrow night. You need to get back to normal."

"Are you coming to supper tomorrow night?" Emily said.

"Emily, I'm going to be staying here for a while. Maybe for a year or two. Will you mind that?"

"No. Oh, gosh, no! But why?"

"Cleta and I had a real girl-to-girl the night all this happened, and then we went and talked to your father. There's no doubt you need another woman in the house. You're outnumbered three to one, and Cleta is getting old; she's tired. The deal is that I'll take over after I get home from school, and make dinner and all that, and be here all weekend. She'll keep on coming mornings to do everything she used to do except cook at night. I'm not bad at that, even if I don't fry chicken in lard."

"What did you tell my father?" Emily was dumbstruck. Change, too much change.

"Just that you were growing up now, and

you needed somebody to sort of help you on the way, and be with you."

"What did he say?"

"He looked like somebody had lifted a cotton bale off his shoulders, and said he'd pay me anything I asked if I'd do it."

"He's going to *pay* you?"

"Of course not. I don't want money to be with you; you're a treat. And this was my home first, after all. I grew up here, lived here even longer than you all have been here. I don't need to be paid for coming home."

"Will you miss your apartment?"

"Not for a minute. Who could miss that? I've missed this place a lot, though."

She left to get Emily's supper, and Emily went into the underwater bathroom and stared at her face in the greenish mirror. She looked just the same. How could that be?

Presently she lay in deep, hot water, Elvis beside the tub on the bathmat, and let herself think a little about the last three days. She thought that it would be all right to begin to do so now, with her aunt in the house. What she thought was that she could never again see her father and her aunt as she had seen them before. From now on, whenever she looked at her father, she would see, as if in pentimento, the wounded young man who had watched his wife walk away. And when she looked at her collected, efficient aunt, she would see the girl child playing in the sunlight all over the plantation, perhaps in the very places she and Elvis went. She would see her watching the dolphins slide at Sweetwater Creek, reading in the deep shade of a live oak off on a hummock, dangling her feet in the glittering water of the river from the dock, the tide creaming in.

She would see her leaving this house and moving into an apartment when her sister brought her new husband home to the house that had become hers alone.

Emily felt a new emotion that she knew she must now work into the fabric of her knowing. It was pity. It seemed impossible to do. She hated it. She would not do it. Change . . .

She scrubbed herself nearly raw and put on clean clothes, and went down the stairs to have the first of many suppers with her aunt.

And after all, it had worked well. Before long her aunt Jenny was as natural a part of life at Sweetwater as her father, the boys, the dogs, and the river. By the time a month or so had passed Emily found it hard to remember when she had not been there.

On the first night she ate supper with the whole family, her father had welcomed her back solemnly and formally, and said he hoped she was over the flu bug—Emily shot a grateful glance at her aunt—and that the new arrangement was just what the doctor ordered. Cleta would get some well-earned rest, Jenny was gracious enough to say that she would enjoy being here, and she, Emily, would learn how to be a real young lady. He seemed very pleased, almost hearty, and ate two helpings of the pasta puttanesca Jenny had made.

"Very tasty," he said, rising.

"Good macaroni, Aunt Jenny," the twins said, and melted away toward the TV room.

Walter stood there, and then drew a piece of folded paper from his pocket.

"I've made a list of things Emily ought to learn to do," he said. "Of course she can't do them all at once; she can take them one at a time. I believe you know how to do most of them, Jenny, but I'm sure you can find someone to teach her the things you don't know. I've arranged them in order of priority. You can look them over after supper, and we can talk about them tomorrow night."

And he, too, faded away toward the TV room, drawn there by flickering light and male pheromones like a moth.

Emily and her aunt looked at each other, and then took the list upstairs to Emily's bedroom to peruse it. Her aunt read it first and then handed it to Emily, the corners of her mouth twitching. She said nothing, though. Emily read through it:

1. *Learn to dress like a young lady. Skirts for school and special occasions. No makeup or high heels yet, and no more short shorts. I will set a suitable budget for her clothes, and I won't need to okay them. I trust your taste, Jenny.*

2. *Learn to do some simple company cooking. Soufflés, little sandwiches, crab cakes, chafing dishes, shrimp*

and rice, desserts. Your benné seed biscuits would be good, Jenny.

3. Learn to carry on intelligent conversation with guests. No more hiding upstairs with the dog. No more running off to the kennels.

4. Learn to play an instrument. I always enjoyed ladies playing the piano after dinner. I will set a budget for this, too.

5. Learn a lady's sport, and some social games of some sort. Tennis would be good, or golf. On second thought, golf is awfully expensive. Let's make it tennis. Needless to say, I've budgeted for this also. And bridge, certainly. I believe you play, don't you, Jenny? And, of course, dancing. I know there is a class the young women in Charleston take when they're about thirteen. Please find out about this.

6. Get some catalogs from the private schools around Charleston and study them. I think Charlotte Hall would be suitable. I would like Emily to familiarize herself with this school by the time she is thirteen.

And he signed it Walter L. Parmenter.

Emily and her aunt looked at each other for a long moment, and then collapsed in laughter. They laughed so hard that they rolled onto Emily's bed. Elvis joined them, frisking and barking joyfully.

When they could speak, Emily said, "But we're really not, are we? All that, I mean? Skirts at school, dancing classes . . ."

"Oh, of course not," her aunt snorted, still laughing. "It sounds like a blueprint for a south of Broad debutante. Of course, if you'd like to do that . . ."

"I'd rather die."

"Me too. We'll learn some things together, and it will be fun, and we can tell him you're making good progress. As long as you wear a dress to dinner occasionally, and say three words to whoever is visiting, he'll probably forget about the rest. But some of these things are fun, you know. Dancing is. Tennis is. And some new clothes carefully chosen by you and me will not be amiss, either. Starting, my dear, with a good bra. And cooking is a dirt-road cinch. We can do that together. We've got all weekends."

"He didn't say I had to quit training the dogs."

"No," her aunt said. "I think he knows what side his bread is buttered on."

"What do you mean?"

But her aunt would say no more, and the days turned into weeks and time spun on. The changes Jenny Raiford made were gradual and pleasant, and did not feel at all like changes after a while. They felt as if the Parmenter family had always done them. They ate dinner together, at a leisurely pace. Jenny insisted that everyone share a little of his or her day, and soon they did, even though the words were mumbled and eyes rolled. Still, it was dinnertime conversation, and Walter Parmenter beamed to hear it.

They watched TV together. Emily thought it was a gargantuan achievement.

"It's barbaric, the way you three sneak off down there and let that thing blare all over the house without a word to Emily or me," Jenny said. "You might as well be living in a log cabin in the Yukon. What good does it do Emily to learn to be a young lady if she has to bring her friends home to that?"

And soon they all gathered for an hour or so, and compromised on CNN, and then Emily and Jenny went up to their rooms— Jenny had Buddy's—and chatted or maybe watched Emily's little TV, and went to bed early. If her aunt was sad or homesick for her previous life, if she staggered under the burden of this new family, or wept for the one in this house that she had never had, Emily never heard it. The rooms were too far apart.

The images of her mother, leaving, faded.

The specter of change shrank back under the weight of the pleasant, nearly identical, altogether ordinary spring days. Emily floated on the sameness and ordinariness, and was soothed.

On an early May Saturday afternoon she and her aunt sat on the old silver-gray wooden benches at the end of the long dock out over the Wadmalaw, sipping lemonade from a thermos and stretching their legs to the young sun. The marsh was almost totally green now, and alive with its teeming, gliding, scuttling, splashing denizens, and the smaller creeks cutting it ran full. It was nearly high tide. Behind Emily's closed eyelids the sun made red whorls and pinwheels, and was tender on her face.

Jenny took a deep breath and exhaled.

"Smell that?" she murmured sleepily.

"Wisteria and honeysuckle. Summer's coming. You can smell the change."

But what came, on the new wings of summer, was Lulu Foxworth, as glistening and beautiful and vulnerable as a beached Portuguese man-o-war, and just as dangerous. And for everyone at Sweetwater everything changed, and nothing ever went back to the way it was before.

5

People who live beside moving water have been given the gift of living light, and even if they never come to recognize it as such, any other light, no matter how clear or brilliant, is pale and static to them, leaving them with a sense of loss, of vulnerability, as if they have suddenly found themselves without clothes.

"I have to be near the water," they will say. "I can't live away from the ocean" . . . or the river or the creek, or whatever water throws back to them the sun, or the boiling storm clouds, or the pearl of moving fog, or the wash of sunset.

But what most of them are really saying, without knowing it, is, "I can't live without that light that dances with me. I wear it like a living skin. Without it I am incomplete."

This epidermis of light is what keeps the waterman, the shrimper, the lobsterman at his work long after his home waters are fished out, dead. You see them sometimes, sunburnt old men sitting on benches at the end of docks, indigent now, but unable to leave and go inland because it would be to live without skin.

Emily felt the absence of waterlight deeply and miserably when she was away from the river. Once, on a school trip to Washington, she lost herself from her group and stayed behind beside the fast-moving Potomac while her class went on to the Air and Space Museum. She could never explain why. And the only time she was sent to camp in the North Carolina mountains, when she was seven, the deep, still, opaque lake that threw her back no connecting spark haunted her days and nights until she wept inconsolably and had to be brought home five days early. Her father thought she was homesick, and was impatient with such childishness. Emily knew her grief was not homesickness, but she did not know what it was, so she was silent on the trip home.

But when she got to Sweetwater, the Wadmalaw, running deep in full tide, wrapped her in trembling waterlight, and she felt full and healed. For a long time after that, she refused to leave the river except for such routine trips as school and doctors and dentists, and even then she knew in her heart the number of miles and minutes it took to get back.

When she was older, she told Buddy about that panicky feeling of grief and loss she had had when she left the river for camp, and he had said, "You don't have to be afraid of leaving people and places. You take them with you somewhere inside you."

"You mean, like in your heart?"

"Or your liver or your spleen, or your medulla oblongata. Who knows? Everybody has a different place inside he stuffs things he needs to keep."

Emily thought perhaps her own place was in the pit of her stomach. Everything that hurt or frightened her settled there indelibly, and often she first felt joy there, too.

"My stomach leaps with joy," she said to Elvis. "It could be worse, though. What if I had to say, 'My colon leaps with joy?' "

On a Saturday morning in early June the

dancing stipple of light off the river woke her, and she lay looking at it play on the ceiling and walls of her room, and stretched her arms and legs as far as they would go, and smelled, through her open window, perhaps the very last of the cool, sweet, fresh mornings of early summer. Wet punishing heat hung like a fog bank in the distance, waiting to stun the Lowcountry into somnolence. It would soon be here. Everything would be full, ripe. What you would smell for the rest of the summer through your window would be rich, fecund marsh and the amniotic sweat of the summer river.

She was usually up with the light, not for chores, just to be in the world. But on a few mornings like this, she lingered half-asleep in bed, stroking Elvis and thinking dreamy, abstracted thoughts that never occurred to her any other time or place.

"If you've been with somebody for a long time and then they leave, are you the same person alone as you were with them?"

"Does the furniture freeze in the Antarctic? Do sofas freeze?"

"Has anybody ever stopped growing up just because they wanted to bad enough?"

"Is it all right to pray if you don't believe in God?"

She had asked Buddy this once. He had considered it, and said, yes, he thought it was both all right and a good thing. People might not believe in their heads, but their hearts knew there simply had to be something bigger and more powerful than they were, otherwise, everybody would be scared to death all the time, and it was *that* that they talked to in prayer. Or whatever you wanted to call it.

"Then, do dogs pray to us?"

"Could be. Makes sense, doesn't it?"

The dapple of light on her ceiling had moved to the wall. She stretched again. This day had promise. Her father and the twins had probably already left for North Charleston, where a regional Boykin Spaniel Council was meeting in yet another of the endless attempts to get the high-nosed American Kennel Club to recognize Boykins as a breed. Since the South Carolina Boykin breeders and owners stubbornly refused to accept any of the AKC's tenets and restrictions ("No goddamned New Yorker is going to tell me how to raise my spaniels, by God"), Boykin recognition seemed about as attainable as Saturn. The need to fight the marauding Yankees never quite died in the Lowcountry. But the meetings went on.

Emily was going to love this day. She could work unhampered with the starters and begin training a beautiful new Boykin bitch puppy someone had brought to be polished, and there was a new litter of milky-sweet, mewling babies in Gloria's box in the kennels. Later she was going to show her aunt the dolphin slide over at Sweetwater Creek, and then they were going to pack a picnic lunch and take the whaler far down the Wadmalaw, almost to Bears Bluff, and see if it was warm enough to swim. Probably not; in early June the deepest rivers were warm and seductive on their surfaces, but an electric chill like frozen ginger ale lurked just below. It didn't matter. It would be a sweet day.

It was near ten when she emerged to sit on the front steps with a cup of milky coffee and a doughnut, simply looking at the morning. Aunt Jenny came and sat beside her, shelling new peas, and Elvis lolled at her feet.

"Don't you need to get going?" Jenny said. "You'll spend at least two hours with those dogs, and by the time we get down river we'll be starving to death."

"Yeah," Emily said, not moving.

They sat in another small silence.

Beside her, Elvis lifted his head and swung it sharply toward the door behind them. A second later they heard Walter Parmenter's brisk steps and the twang-thud of the screen door, and he was with them on the steps, military-crisp in pressed khakis and a blue oxford cloth shirt, his face shining from its close shave and his thick hair still showing damp comb tracks.

"Morning," Jenny said. "I thought you'd be halfway through your meeting by now."

"Morning, Daddy," Emily mumbled.

"Ladies," her father said. "We're in for a real treat this morning. And a real shot at the brass ring. Rhett Foxworth called last night after you'd both gone to bed and said he was looking to buy a Boykin, and Towny Chappelle told him ours were the best in South Carolina. I guess something good came of that Thanksgiving business after all. Foxworth is coming out about noon to look at the pups and see some of the older dogs work. He's bringing his wife and daughter with him, and I want us all to make a good impression. Jenny, maybe you could make some mint iced tea. Emily, I'm going to let you work the dogs this morning, but not in shorts and a shirt like that. A dress or skirt, please, and Elvis goes to your room."

"Who is Rhett Foxworth?" Emily muttered, already disliking the man and all his family, past and future.

"Rhett Foxworth *is* Charleston," her father said. "One of the oldest families, most money, biggest plantation south of Hobcaw, house in town on the National Register. If the word gets out he's bought dogs from us, we'll be in solid with the Hunt Club crowd, and there's no other place I'd rather be. Emily, after you've done the dogs, I want you to take his daughter and show her around, get to know her. I happen to know her mother's on the board of Charlotte Hall."

"Whoop-de-do," Emily said under her breath.

"How old is this daughter?" she said aloud. "I'm not very good at baby-sitting."

"She's older than that," her father replied. "I think her mother said she was out of school for the summer. Who knows, you might make a new friend. Now, run and change."

"Daddy," Emily began desperately, but her aunt cut in.

"Not a skirt on a June morning in the country, Walter. Maybe some nice pants and a matching shirt."

"Whatever," her father said, moving down the steps toward the kennels. "Just not those ragged blue jeans. And *not* that shirt. Oh, and comb your hair."

Emily looked down at her chest. Her T-shirt had GOD IS DOG SPELLED BACKWARD written on it. It was obviously too tight.

"I'll take the bone out of my nose, too," she said resentfully as she stood up to go into the house.

"Go easy on him, Emily," her aunt said. "This is a big deal for him. And he's just now learning to think of you as a young woman. He's not exactly the quickest study, you know. But he wants you to show the dogs, and that's his way of saying he knows you're better at it than he is."

"He could just come right out and say it."

"No," her aunt said, "I don't think he could. Not yet."

The stipple of light was gone from her room when Emily came into it to change her clothes. Out the window the river shimmered, crumpled foil. "Glitter water," Emily had called it when she was small. It had stuck.

She shucked off the jeans and T-shirt and, without looking at herself in the mirror, pulled on the cropped pink cotton pants and peasant blouse her aunt had bought her. She had never worn them; they did not seem to fit anywhere in her small arena. But they'd probably be right at home in the Foxworths'. She slid her feet into white sandals and combed her unruly red-gold hair straight back, and tied it with a shoelace. She thrust her face close to the watery mirror in the bathroom and winced. This girl would be far more at home shopping on King Street than working spaniels.

"You know you'll have to stay here for a little while," she said to Elvis. "Daddy's doing the big dog breeder thing for some rich guy. I'll let you out the minute they're gone. It shouldn't be long."

At the door she turned and looked at him. He was already settled resignedly on the quilt at the foot of her bed.

"You won't cry or bark, will you?"

He sighed and put his head down on his

crossed front paws. She knew that he wouldn't.

The family was assembled at the front door by a quarter to twelve. Aunt Jenny had changed into a long flowered skirt and sleeveless blue T-shirt; she looked young and pretty. Walt and Carter were echoes of their father in clean khakis and polo shirts.

"Ten-SHUN!" Emily whispered to her aunt, and Jenny grinned.

At noon exactly a mud-spattered Land Rover crunched up on the circular drive and stopped.

"If he's that rich, why can't he get his car washed?" Emily said under her breath to Jenny.

"I think it's called shabby-chic," her aunt whispered back.

Walter went down the steps to meet the Foxworths, who were getting out of the Rover.

"Welcome to Sweetwater," he said jovially. "It's good to have you here."

"Thank you," said a huge, sunburnt man with thinning black hair and a boy's smooth pug face. "Walter Parmenter, isn't it? Rhett Foxworth. Call me Rhett."

He gestured at the two women standing

behind him. "This is my wife Maybelle, and my daughter, Lulu. We've forgotten her real name."

Everyone laughed and moved together and shook hands and bobbed heads and murmured greetings. Emily hung back and looked at the fabulous Foxworths, who *were* Charleston.

Maybelle Foxworth came forward with her hands outstretched to Walter Parmenter, smiling brilliantly with large Chiclet teeth and teetering just a bit on the rolling gravel of the driveway. Her yellow glacé flats, Emily thought, would last about two minutes in the dog ring. Maybelle was short and voluptuous and tanned to an impossible, silky cappuccino tan. Her silvery blond hair was held off her round face with a black velvet headband, and her flowered wrap skirt and yellow blouse matched the shoes and showed a trim waist and startling cleavage. Her blue eyes had smile and sun crinkles fanning out from their corners, and except for a certain crepey skin on her chest and neck, she might have been a much younger woman, far too young to have a grown daughter. Later, Jenny told Emily, with just a hint of laughter in her voice, that some women simply got stuck in the best time of their youth, and would do whatever it took to remain there. Maybelle Foxworth's was obviously the Lilly Pulitzer era. Emily thought she had done a good job, all told.

"I have heard *so* much about you," she trilled to Walter Parmenter. "Towny talks about nothing but your beautiful dogs, and said that your house was a fine specimen of the earliest river plantations, the modest, plain ones that had fine lines and almost always beautiful river views. I can see he was right!"

Walter took her outstretched hands in his own, and looked fleetingly and with puzzlement at his fine-lined modest plantation house, and almost stammered. Maybelle Foxworth often had that effect on people. Meeting her for the first time was rather like meeting a beautiful creature from a Disney theme park: vividly colored, animated, displacing too much air.

"We're glad you could come," Emily's father said. "Towny Chappelle talked a lot about you."

He hadn't, Emily would have been willing to bet, but she was quiet, studying, absorbing. So this was how it was done.

"Nothing bad, I hope," Maybelle Fox-worth giggled. "Towny is so *naughty*! I'm going to have to get after him one of these days."

"Oh, all good," Walter said, nodding his head vigorously.

"Well, meet my daughter," Maybelle said, and stepped aside so that they could see the young woman who had stood perfectly still and silent while her mother trilled and her father grinned his fierce baby's grin.

She did not look up at first, and all Emily could see was the top of her silvery blond hair, so like her mother's that she thought perhaps Maybelle did not bleach hers after all. Her daughter's was skinned back into a careless ponytail.

"This is my daughter, Lulu. Or Louisa, but I always have to check her birth certificate to remember," her mother said.

The assorted Parmenters murmured hello. There was something almost eerie in the young woman's stillness. The word "taboo" popped idiotically into Emily's mind.

Lulu Foxworth lifted her head to them then, and Emily felt a tiny frisson of . . . was it shock? The first thing that went through

her head, also idiotically, was that Lulu Foxworth was dead, mummified. Her face and
arms and neck were so pure and carved
that she might have been an effigy on a medieval tomb, or a marble saint. She was all-
over tan, a matte bisque with no tonal gra-
dations and almost no shadows, as if
someone had carefully and lovingly painted
her. Only her eyes were alive, but they made
up in living flame for the rest of her. They
were her mother's blue, but in her face they
blazed out like leaping fire, sparking blue.
There was a very small sound as if a little
wind had come up and then danced on by.
Emily knew that it was the indrawn breath of
the Parmenters. Those eyes made of Saint
Lulu Foxworth something else altogether.

"I'm pleased to meet you," she murmured, looking back down at her feet. They
were narrow and tanned in glove-soft driving moccasins.

Emily's eyes left the moccasins and trav-
eled up the rest of Lulu. She wore jeans
seated so low on her hips that it seemed
that centrifugal force alone held them up,
and in her navel there was a tiny gold ring.
A cutoff T-shirt that just cleared her breasts
showed an expanse of silky, tanned skin.

She was thin; her ribs and collarbones and wrists were sharp. But her hips and breasts were sumptuous, and as tan as the rest of her.

"Holy shit," Emily heard Walt Junior whisper reverently. Her father's face turned a dark red, and he kept his gaze squarely on Rhett Foxworth. Emily looked down at her faux milkmaid outfit and shot him a glance of pure triumph. But he did not see.

"Well, I think the already-broke youngsters first, don't you, Emily? Show the Foxworths what Sweetwater Boykins can do."

Without a word, Emily went into the kennels and brought out three of her prize pupils, in various stages of their training, and put them through their paces. She had them sit, stand, heel, and go through their basic play-retrieving. After that she put Maggie, a full-grown, field-trained bitch, through her entire repertoire, including water retrieving and mock gunfire. Maggie performed flawlessly, returning the dummy to Emily with her soft mouth and leaping golden eyes alight. There was a spontaneous spatter of applause from the Foxworths, and Emily looked up and blushed. Even Lulu Foxworth was smiling and applauding. It was like seeing a statue come to life.

As she was taking the dogs back to the kennel, she heard her father say, "Yes, Emily is pretty handy with the dogs. She's a great little helper."

Before the flood of acid hurt and resentment could reach her throat, she heard her aunt say, sweetly and clearly, "Actually, Emily trained every one of those dogs. She has a kind of magic thing she does with them."

"I'd love to talk to her about that," Rhett Foxworth said. "I didn't see her give a single hand command, or hear one."

"I'm sure she'll be glad to talk to you," Walter Parmenter said. He sounded as if he was choking on the words.

When Emily returned to the group, Rhett Foxworth was deep in conversation with her father, and Maybelle Foxworth was chatting with her aunt, and the twins were shifting their too-big feet around and staring at Lulu.

Emily hesitated on the edge of the group, reluctant to be left with Lulu Foxworth and be expected to chat. But Lulu came toward her with a smile on her wide mouth and a flush of soft color on her cheeks, and eyes that seemed to spill out light.

"That was wonderful," she said in a soft, slow voice that seemed to have no breath behind it. "They were simply beautiful. So were you. I wish I could do that."

Emily stammered her thanks, and then they all went down to the kennel, where Daisy's puppies, three weeks old now, were tumbling around in the box and over their mother's curly bronze back, and trying valiantly to escape the high sides of the box.

"I don't know if I can pick," Rhett Foxworth said. "That's as pretty a batch of puppies as I've ever seen. Their mother—has she got any older ones I can see?"

"The oldest one that Emily showed is hers," Walter said. "The sire is in the far kennels. Buck is our nearest to breed standard. He has several ribbons for it. We'll see him on the way out."

They started out of the barn. Looking back, Emily saw that Lulu Foxworth was still crouched before the puppies, seemingly spellbound. She could hear her murmuring to the little dogs in a soft singsong.

Her father chuckled. "Haven't seen her

perk up like that since she got home from school. Mostly stays in her room playing that tribal music. Good to know something can get to her."

"For heaven's sake, Rhett," Maybelle said sharply, and Emily saw that two hectic red splotches flamed on her cheeks. "You know she's tired to death. She's done way, way too much at school, with her activities and keeping her grades up, and then the flu on top of that. No wonder she needs a little sleep. Maybe we could take home one of the puppies, though. . . ."

"Too young," her husband said. "Besides, I want this young lady to train them, if she will. It'll be a while before they can come to us."

"Well, maybe she can come and visit them?" Maybelle looked at Walter Parmenter.

"Of course," he said quickly. "We'd be glad to have her any time. Emily can show her around."

Lulu Foxworth did not come up to the group around the Land Rover until its engine was idling and her father had tapped the horn.

"They are the most beautiful things I have

ever seen," she said in her soft voice. At close range, Emily could see that her eyes were red and deeply circled. For a moment her face seemed as stark and bleached as a skull. The blue eyes were dark, all pupil. Emily stepped back involuntarily. Buddy had once told her about changelings, infants changed for another being at birth. For some reason the notion had frightened her badly. Now the word rang in the silent air. And then, Lulu was Lulu again.

When they had said their good-byes and the Land Rover had driven away, Walter Parmenter turned to his family.

"He bought three," he crowed. "We're on our way. They were nice people, didn't you think?"

"Very nice," they all agreed, the twins fervently. But as they followed her father into the house, Emily glanced at her aunt and saw a shadow of thoughtfulness in her eyes, a tiny frown between them.

Had she seen the changeling too?

They were midway through dinner that evening when the phone rang. Her father went to answer it. When he came back to the table, his stride was military and forceful, and he radiated excitement.

"You'll be pleased to know that I just had a call from Maybelle Foxworth," he said. "She said that she had a favor to ask of me, and of course I told her anything, and she said that they were worried about Lulu, that her fatigue was almost dangerous, and the flu was just hanging on and on, and all the pre-debutante hoopla was gearing up, and they were afraid that without a long period of total rest she just wouldn't be able to get through the big Christmas business. She said Lulu had been so restored, I think was her word, while she was with the dogs that it seemed almost a miracle, and they were wondering if there was any possible way she might board with us this summer and help with them. Her mother says she's good with animals. And I'd mentioned that there's an apartment over the barn, and if it wasn't occupied, might we consider it for Lulu? They would furnish it, of course, and she would get her own meals; they would bring what she needed for that. She said she doubted we'd even see her, except for her time with the dogs. She said it was the first thing Lulu had been enthusiastic about since she got home from school; it was her idea, in fact. She said Lulu could find some way to be helpful even if it was cleaning out the kennels, and it would literally be a life-saver for all of them. So I said of course, we'd be delighted."

There was a silence. The twins broke it with groans of joy. Jenny broke it in her quiet voice. "What a very strange thing for a tired debutante to want. Surely there are other, more upscale, retreats. Do you think it might ultimately be a bit much for you, Walter? The girl seemed pretty shaky to me."

Emily did not break in at all. From the moment her father had opened his mouth, she had known, as certainly as she had ever known anything, that this would be the summer of Lulu Foxworth. The summer of the changeling. It would happen no matter who opposed it, or for what reason. It was inevitable. It had been written in the air around Lulu. She felt cold and angry.

"I'm not going to let her hurt my dogs," she thought fiercely. "I'm not even going to let her touch Elvis."

For the rest of the meal her father exulted. His face, so often stony and abstracted, was literally illuminated.

"A Foxworth in our house for three months. We'll get her well. She'll get to be part of the family. Of course we're not going to let her sit out there all by herself all summer. We'll have her to dinner, and she can go with us to trials and shows. . . . And her friends will come to visit her, and her parents—it's the chance of a lifetime!"

"A chance for what?" her aunt Jenny asked, interestedly.

"A chance for this family to . . . finally be something, for us to be somebody. We'll be just as much a part of her world as she'll be of ours. And think of the things she can teach Emily, all that Charleston girl stuff she needs to know. Her friends will get to know her, too. Emily will be making her debut before we know it!"

"Aren't you jumping the gun a bit, Walter?" her aunt said. "Her mother said she needed rest and quiet and simplicity. Some time alone. If she wants our company, she'll ask for it. I think it would be kinder just to let her call the shots. And besides, it's going to cost the earth to redo that old apartment. It's a total mess."

"Maybelle said they'd gladly pay for renovating it," Walter Parmenter said. "And they'll pay board. Lulu doesn't want to be paid—simply to help work with the puppies,

to learn. That, and read, and sleep. Maybelle said we won't even know she's there."

"I'll know," Emily thought fiercely. "Oh, I'll
know."

Soon after dinner she took Elvis and went
up to her room. She snuggled him against
her on her bed while she watched TV. She
told him about the Foxworths, Maybelle and
Rhett, and Lulu, and what her father had
told them at dinner, and about the change in
Lulu, gone in an eyeblink, that she had
seen. Or thought she had. Now it seemed
ephemeral, like a fever dream. She shook
her head.

"But she's not getting her hands on you,"
she said to Elvis. He gave her his golden
stare and then nestled in against her ribs.
Soon his breathing, and then his dream-
twitching, told her that he was asleep.

But sleep did not come as easily to Emily.
She stayed awake as long as she could,
certain that her aunt would come up to say
good night, and she could tell her what she
had seen, or thought she had, and ask her
what she had thought about Lulu. But
Jenny did not come. Emily could hear her
aunt and her father talking for a very long
time downstairs, and at some point the talk

slid into the easy, desultory talk of long acquaintance. Soon they were laughing. Emily had seldom heard her father laugh. She lay listening. No matter how angry and disturbed she felt, it was somehow comforting to lie in bed listening to the adults in the house laughing together. Finally she slid into sleep on a gentle surf of laughter.

Maybelle Foxworth brought Lulu out to look at the apartment the following week.

For days, Walter and the twins and GW and, periodically, a sullen Kenny Rouse had been laboring in it, tossing out years of accumulated junk, scrubbing and polishing the old pine floor, painting the white stucco walls. The windows were still scummed and painted shut when the Foxworths arrived, and there was still a powerful odor of dust and dog hanging over it. The tiny kitchen had not been touched. Walter was displeased with the progress they had made. He had wanted to have everything ready for Foxworthian inspection.

He and Emily followed the Foxworths up the sagging stairs to see the lair proposed for Lulu. Emily had not been there for a day or so, and suddenly she saw it fresh, through Maybelle and Lulu's eyes. Her heart rose joyfully. The room was inalterably banal and shabby despite the new paint and polish; surely no Foxworth had ever spent a night in a room like this. Lulu was undoubtedly used to marble and mahogany and drifts of down pillows, and damask curtains and silky-cotton sheets. It seemed impossible that she would like it, or that her mother would approve.

There was a long, uncomfortable silence while they stood in the hot, bare room, dust motes dancing in the pallid rays of sun that penetrated the filthy windows.

Finally her father said, "We're not done with it, of course. New windows will go in, and we can do any kind of floor covering and paint that you want. The bath is being totally retiled, and we're putting in a shower in place of that old clawfooted tub. It can be really nice, I think."

"Well, I don't know," Maybelle Foxworth said slowly, clearly appalled but too well bred to say so. "I'd thought it might be a bit . . . more finished. And it's much smaller than I thought. And we'd have to have an air conditioner. Lulu would die in this heat up here."

"Oh, of course," Walter Parmenter said desperately. "We can do that in a day."

"Still, that kitchen . . ." Maybelle let her voice trail off. It had not trilled or fluted once today. This was a Maybelle down to business.

There was another little silence, and then Lulu said, "I love it. It looks clean and rough and stark, like a room in a Greek island house or a monastery. I don't want anything on the floor, and I want the walls white, like they are. If I could have just shutters in the windows like they have in Italy, I would. But I'll settle for plain windows. No air-conditioning, though. I've got a big floor fan; that will do fine. And I would *love* a clawfoot bathtub. And as for the kitchen, all I need is a microwave and running water in the sink. I have a little refrigerator that I had at school. It'll do fine."

"We're redoing the kitchen," Walter said. "Be done by the time you move in."

"Lulu," her mother began.

"I want it," Lulu said. Her voice was clearer and stronger than Emily had heard it.

"It's exactly what I imagined, and what I need, and I really, really want it."

She and her mother stared at each other for a moment, and then Maybelle lifted her hands and let them fall and smiled ruefully at Walter.

"Then we'll take it, and with thanks. I have some things that will soften it up a bit—a little French bed and a sofa and armchair and lots of pillows. And a wonderful Mexican rug. It could be quite charming."

"I don't want it charming," Lulu said almost under her breath. "I want it . . ." Emily could not really hear the rest, but she could have sworn that Lulu said "penitential."

"Maybe she's getting ready to go into a monastery, and is practicing on us," she thought meanly. "I hope it's one where they can't speak."

When they came out into the punishing noon sun, Lulu said, "I wonder if I might use someone's bathroom? I'd like to freshen up a little."

"Of course," Walter said. "Mrs. Fox-worth?"

"I'm fine, thank you," Maybelle said distantly.

"Pouting," Emily thought. "I'll bet this is

maybe the third time in her life she didn't get her way."

"Emily, take Miss Foxworth up to your bathroom. I don't think Cleta's gotten to the others yet," her father said. Emily knew that indeed Cleta hadn't, and that her father's and the boys' bathrooms looked like swampy gymnasium stalls.

"I'll show you," she said, and went into the house, with Lulu behind her. Inside it was very dark and silent. Neither said a word until they reached the door of Emily's room. Then she said, "It's through there, to the left. I'll wait for you here."

She sat down on a tattered brocade bench.

"Thank you," Lulu said, and went into Emily's room and closed the door. In a moment, Emily heard Lulu talking aloud, in the same soft croon she had used with the dogs the weekend before. Emily's heart flopped in her chest like a gaffed fish. Elvis. She had completely forgotten that Elvis was shut up in her room. Apparently her father had forgotten, too. She opened the bedroom door and went in.

Lulu Foxworth was kneeling beside Elvis, who was leaning into her and licking her face. Emily felt anger at both of them rise in her throat like bile.

"He's the most beautiful thing I have ever seen," Lulu breathed, turning to look up at Emily. "Tell me about him. What's his name?"

"His name is Elvis," Emily said sullenly. "He's my own personal dog. He usually stays with me. I forgot he was up here."

"I'd love to see him go through his paces," Lulu said. "If he's as good as he is beautiful, my father would move mountains to see him."

"He . . . he doesn't hunt," Emily said desperately. "He knows how; he's wonderful, but right at the last minute he just . . . won't. We don't know why. My father doesn't like me to let people see him."

"Then I won't tell," Lulu said, and gave Elvis another hug, and leaned over and whispered in his ear, loudly enough for Emily to hear. "I bet I know exactly why you won't hunt," she said. "I bet it's because you just plain don't want to."

Elvis licked her face again, and Emily sat down on her bed to wait. Presently Lulu came out of the bathroom, freshly scrubbed, and gave Elvis a kiss on the dome of his satiny head. His curly behind wriggled with pleasure. Jealousy chewed Emily's heart like a rat. She shut the door sharply and went back down the stairs, Lulu following her.

From behind, she heard Elvis whine. She could not remember him ever doing that when she left him. And deep into the night, she woke and heard the clicking of his nails on the cypress floor, pacing, pacing.

6

The third weekend in June, the Foxworths came to move Lulu in. There had been comings and goings all week, miscellaneous black men with trucks, unloading massive, shrouded burdens that might have been furniture or anything at all; Maybelle Foxworth herself, carrying up bolts of fabric and rolled rugs; once an unfamiliar electrician's truck, from which the unfamiliar electrician produced a window air-conditioning unit and wrestled it, cursing, up the stairs.

"Thought she said she didn't want any of that stuff," Emily muttered to her aunt, whenever a new load of provender came.

"I imagine it would be hard to argue with Maybelle Foxworth," Jenny said.

Lulu herself did not come, not until the final day.

"Sleeping," her mother said, shaking her head at the foibles of debutante daughters. "I never saw anybody sleep so much. Oh, well, she really has had a bad flu, and this last quarter at college almost finished her. I told her, I said, 'Sweetie pie, what's so important that you can't drop it until another quarter? What's more important than your health?' Half the time she was off campus in this meeting or that; she's Randolph Macon's representative to I don't know how many intercollegiate things. I finally had to write her a blanket permission to leave campus. I guess she's catching up."

The morning of the final diaspora was so hot and humid that the sky was flat and white with heat, and the river was oily and sluggish and black. Sullen, undulating heat distorted the distant hummocks and the woods; everything living on the marshes seemed stilled by it. The cordgrass did not ripple as it usually did, a running fan of gold-green; the Spanish moss on the great live oaks did not wave softly; none of the river's denizens were out and about. There were no plops, splashes, rustlings, trills, hummings, shrill chants from the cicadas, fizzing pops of shrimp in the shrimp holes. The river itself, at dead low tide, hardly seemed to move, and smelled powerfully of pluff mud. The little slappings it made against the dock pilings had subsided to a sullen wallowing.

Animals and humans were stunned. There was no yipping and scrabbling from the dog runs, as there almost always was, and the Parmenter family, assembled on the front drive to receive the Foxworths, mopped at necks and foreheads and did not speak. Even Walt Junior and Carter, preening and strutting in low-riding cutoffs and torn sleeveless T-shirts that read FOLLY IS A BITCHIN' BEACH—apparently the courting image of choice in their set—stopped their muttered innuendos and simply stood there, dumb with heat. Their powerfully developed biceps and chests gleamed. At first Emily thought they had oiled themselves like muscle builders in a contest, but now she wasn't sure if it was oil or sweat. Only her father, crisp in blue oxford cloth and pressed khaki twill, seemed untainted by the corrupting heat. His keen blue eyes were alert, fastened on the end of the driveway, where the caravansary would emerge from the woods.

They heard it first, the rumbling, grinding, crunching of many vehicles, and then it appeared, and the Parmenters simply stared. The line of SUVs, all-terrain vehicles, trucks, trailers, and conventional vehicles seemingly stretched out of sight. Rhett Foxworth came first, in the Land Rover, Lulu hunched down in the passenger seat. Maybelle Foxworth followed in, of all things, a cherry red BMW convertible. She was smiling and waving like a car advertisement, her flawless hair shining silver in the sun. Emily wondered why she had not had a heatstroke, if she'd driven far in a topless car. Walt and Carter resumed their whispering.

"Gon' need a chauffeur for that baby," one of them said. "Flip you," the other replied. Her father glared at them, and they fell silent.

Behind the first two cars, a shining green pickup with MAYBUD PLANTATION emblazoned on its gleaming side carried a spanking-new upright refrigerator, and the huge ATV trailer behind it, that usually carried hunting dogs, now bore standing lamps, a tall, scrolled mirror, towering green plants, and a large television set. Smaller vehicles behind them were freighted with boxes labeled books, china, microwave, sound system, computer.

Staring foolishly, Emily could not get camels and elephants out of her mind. She furrowed her brow, trying to think why, and from his place inside her Buddy whispered, *"The Jewel in the Crown.* Remember? We saw a rerun of it? The big raj processions, with elephants and camels. . . ."

Entirely without realizing that she did it, Emily laughed aloud. Her father shot her a withering look, but behind her eyes were only dreams of elephants and camels.

The black men who filed in and out of the upstairs apartment all wore forest green shirts and pants embroidered with capital M's on the pockets, and might have been picked for their uniformity of physical grandeur as well as their prowess as workers. They were absolutely silent, and when the last shrouded object had been taken upstairs, Lulu got out of the Land Rover where she had been napping and thanked them all softly, and by name.

"Miss Lulu," they responded, nodding their heads. One of them, older than the rest and grizzled gray around his sideburns, bent over and whispered something in her ear, and she hugged him fiercely.

"I'll see you before long, Leland," she said.

"You come on back home soon's you can," he said.

The line of vehicles filed away down the drive, empty.

Maybelle Foxworth came out of the barn and tripped toward them, smiling.

"You wouldn't believe your little apartment," she said to Walter. "It dressed up a lot better than I thought it would. If I were a single girl like Lulu I wouldn't at all mind living in it. If it was a bit closer to town, I mean. We plantation people," and she beamed at Walter, "have gotten used to living in the boondocks. But I think young girls need a bit more life around them. Well, anyway, you all come up and see it when we get it all straightened up. About another hour, I think. Lulu, aren't you the least bit curious? The air conditioner's going strong and it's cool as a cucumber up there. I need you to tell me where to put the last few things."

Lulu nodded her head to the Parmenters and followed her mother back into the barn and up the stairs. Emily strained to hear, but she did not think that a word passed between mother and daughter.

Rhett Foxworth had long since gone back to Maybud, pleading an appointment with a representative of the forestry service, to talk about the longleaf pines that were Maybud's cash crop.

"I expect you know how it is, Parmenter," he said, shaking Walter's hand. "If it ain't one thing, it's another."

The Parmenters sat in the shade of the front piazza for a while, drinking iced tea from sweating glasses that Cleta kept refilled. Of them all, Cleta seemed the only one not curious about Lulu and her family.

"What do you think of her?" Emily had asked her, after the Foxworths' first visit.

"She a pretty thing," Cleta said. "Got real pretty eyes and hair. But she too thin and way too jumpy. Like to jump out of her skin if you speaks to her. There's somethin' wrong with that child. Beyond bein' sick and tired, I mean. It ain't normal, a pretty rich girl like her hidin' out here all summer."

She would say no more, despite Emily's attempts to engage her in chat about Lulu Foxworth.

Maybelle Foxworth came back down the

stairs out into the corroding sunlight, fanning herself. Lulu was behind her. Despite the smothering heat, Lulu looked so dry as to be almost desiccated. There were even little dry lines around her astonishing eyes. Emily was annoyed that it did not mar her spectacular good looks. Even without makeup, even with the gilt hair down her back in a single pigtail, even with red rimming her eyes and a sprinkling of freckles visible across her nose and cheekbones, she still caught the eye like wildfire. Her white shorts and T-shirt were bone-dry, and her long, muscular legs were a silky matte tan, not glistening with sweat like everyone else's.

"Maybe she'll be okay up there in that air-conditioned little apartment of hers, but I'd like to see how long she lasts in the dog ring," Emily thought with sullen satisfaction.

"No, I can't stay," Maybelle trilled to Walter, who was offering iced tea and benné seed cookies. "Lulu says she needs a long nap and will shoot me if I hover over her, and I'm late for a bridge game. She'd love to show off her apartment later this afternoon; she promised me." She slewed her eyes around at Lulu, who nodded and smiled. It was like a smile drawn by a child in spilled flour.

Maybelle Foxworth hugged her daughter fiercely and said, "You call us tonight, remember? And you know you can come home whenever you want to."

"I'm fine, Mama," Lulu said in her soft, slightly dark voice. "Thanks so much for everything you've done. Tell Daddy, too."

And she smiled again all around, murmured "Excuse me," and vanished into the darkness of the barn stairwell. Her mother stood looking after her, a frown knitting her pale brows.

"You all look after her for me," she said, this time to Jenny. "She's not as grown-up as she thinks she is."

"Of course we will," Jenny said. "It will be a pleasure."

Maybelle Foxworth got into the little red BMW and purred away into the heat haze. The Parmenters all looked at each other. It was three o'clock Saturday, June sixteenth, and the world was entirely still.

Lulu did not, after all, appear in the late afternoon with an invitation to view her domain. But she did come to the front door and knock softly on the screen, and when Emily answered it, said politely, "I hope you'll forgive me for not giving you the grand tour just yet. I have some phone calls to make, and I want to edit things a little before you see it. Mama gets . . . overenthusiastic sometimes."

By that time Walter and Jenny had appeared at the door.

"I can't wait to see what it looks like," Jenny said, smiling.

"Right now," Lulu said, "it looks like a New Orleans cathouse."

Emily and her aunt laughed aloud; how could you not? Walter Parmenter frowned at them and once more invited Lulu to share their dinner. Emily stared at him. Where did "dinner" come from? Supper was what they had at six o'clock.

"You're very kind, but I'm going to make myself an omelette and go to bed and read. You don't know what a luxury that is. Just try doing it in my mother's house."

When she left to go back to the barn in the failing light, Elvis whined and looked up at Emily.

"Stay," she said, more sharply than she

intended. He sat, staring up at her with soft hurt in his golden eyes. She leaned down and hugged him.

"I'm sorry," she whispered. "I promise not to take it out on you."

Elvis had been given a reprieve from Walter insofar as Lulu was concerned, as she had already seen him in Emily's bathroom, and had given Emily her promise not to tell her father about him. So he had yard privileges. But he was still under house arrest when anyone else connected with the dogs visited.

Emily agreed. It was better than nothing.

When she and her father went out to the kennels and runs at eight o'clock the next morning to feed the dogs and puppies, Lulu was already there, sitting on a sack of Eukanuba puppy chow with an armful of Daisy's puppies. They were squirming and wagging their stumpy tails and licking her face, and she was smiling as blissfully as if she had had a vision of heaven. Her eyes were closed, and her face shone with soap and puppy spit. In the early-morning light she glowed golden, like a well-rubbed amulet, and a faint curl of English lavender soap hung about her. Even in frayed cutoffs and hollow of eye and cheek, she was just as beautiful as ever, and Emily wondered sourly what it would take to diminish that impact. She wondered, also, how it would feel to know that you were so wonderful-looking that you could just forget about it. Emily thought little about her own looks, but it was not because she knew she was beautiful. As long as her looks were out of her mind, her steady ripening did not frighten her.

"I hope I'm not doing anything wrong," Lulu said to Walter when he and Emily arrived. "I just couldn't resist."

"No," he said, beaming. "Actually, small puppies like these need to get used to people early. It socializes them. Play with them whenever you want to. It will give poor old Daisy a rest."

Emily simply looked at her father. He had never allowed the puppies who were to be trained to the gun to enter the house. It spoiled and confused them, he said. Instead of responding to just one person, as a good hunting dog should, they'd learn to respond to everybody—disastrous for a flushing spaniel.

He looked down at Emily and reddened slightly.

"I just finished that book by the monks of New Skete, that everybody says is so great," he said. "They train some of the best dogs in the world, and they've convinced me that a lot of contact is probably a good thing after all. I was going to suggest to you, Emily, and to the boys and Rouse if he ever turns up again, that you should all spend as much spare time as you've got just being with the very young ones. Pet them, groom them, play with them. They need to get used to being indoors, too. I can't have them all over the big house, but I'm thinking about making a sort of living room out of that big empty storage room in the barn. Sofas and rugs and lamps, a radio, stuff like that. Maybe a Mr. Coffee and an ice maker for you all. The pups could learn a lot about what not to do in there, like chewing electric cords and, ah, urinating on the rug. It would be a good early start to housebreaking. Maybe all of you could take turns spending an hour or so with them there after work."

"Oh," breathed Lulu Foxworth, "let me do that. The rest of you have other chores, I know, and I would *love* to have the puppies for a little while every day."

"We'll give it a try; see how it works out," Walter said. "Meanwhile, you could take one or two at a time up to your place, if you'd like to. Only I'd hate to think of what those little teeth could do to all your pretty things."

"I wouldn't," Lulu said.

Even on that first morning, Lulu proved to be a natural with the dogs. Emily was working with four ten-week-old puppies from Ginger, who was a sweet-tempered and patient mother, and whose puppies Emily had never had trouble communing with. She knew she would not tell Lulu Foxworth that most of the time she could just think with the dogs; Lulu would think her totally insane. She had decided she would show Lulu the conventional way that Sweetwater started their pups off, and see if she caught on. After thirty minutes, it was clear that she did. Emily had begun teaching Bandit, a big, happy male puppy, to sit by pushing his behind down gently and saying firmly, "Hup." Her father had once told her that it was the traditional spaniel sit command, but she had never had to use it. Also, she raised her right hand, so the puppy could get used to visual signals that would serve him well in advanced training. Lulu watched her every move.

"You need to do it this way while she's here," Emily thought to Bandit. "We'll go back to the other after she's gone."

Bandit looked at her gravely, and then faultlessly sat, grinning.

"Oh, that's wonderful," Lulu said. "The very first time. They're smarter than most people, aren't they?"

Emily gave her Molly, who, unlike her serene mother, was a first-class canine diva-in-the-making if Emily ever saw one.

"Now let's see Miss Perfect in action," she thought meanly.

Lulu sat down on the grass in front of Molly and looked at her. Molly looked back, whites showing around her yellow eyes. Presently Lulu rose and put Molly through her first "sit" paces as if she had been doing it all her life.

Molly sat after one try.

Lulu smiled up at Emily from the grass, where she was hugging Molly.

"She's so smart! They all are! Imagine two of them getting it on their first try," she said.

For the first time since Emily had met her, Lulu did not seem clenched or masked. Her smile lit her dry face like a candle. Wherever the changeling lurked, it was not here, not now.

"Well, sit is the easiest one," Emily said primly. "Most of them get it the first time. Wait until we get into the advanced parts."

"What are those?" Lulu asked. Emily saw that there was a flush along her cheek-bones, and the dry mustiness was gone from the fire-blue eyes.

"They'll learn 'stay' and 'heel' next. And 'down.' 'Heel' is usually not easy for most of them. Then 'come when called,' and next the tough stuff like basic dummy retrieving, introduction to gunfire, and introduction to water. The last ones will probably come up after you're gone, but we can start on the first ones."

"Gunfire," Lulu said thoughtfully. "Is that hard?"

"For them or you?"

"Them," Lulu said, looking coolly at Emily. "I've been shooting since I could hold a shotgun."

"Oh, so you hunt?"

"No. I never have. But other people are

going to, and their dogs should be trained
as well as possible. For the dog's sake."

It was so nearly what Emily thought herself that it made her even more resentful.

Silently, they put the other two puppies
through their first paces, and except for one
bobble with Molly on Lulu's part, it went
flawlessly.

"That's it for today," Emily said. "We'll
have as many sessions as it takes, but
they'll be short ones. Puppies have short attention spans."

"So what's next?" Lulu said, wiping the
puppy drool off her shorts with her long,
tanned hands.

"Next we exercise. Some of them in the
ring, but most of them on leash. The older
ones need a lot of it, but they have to stay
on their chains."

"And then?"

"Well," Emily said, "then lunch. And after
that, we clean the kennels and put down
fresh straw, and look in on the new mothers
to see if they need their tits massaged, and
feed them, and wash down the concrete
floors of the pens. And we check everybody
over to see if any of them might need the
vet."

"And then?"

"Then we go home for the day," Emily snapped, losing her temper with this shining paragon. "You'll be so ready for a bath and a nap you won't believe it. The boys take the intermediate and the upland retrievers in the afternoon. Daddy usually does the real finishing stuff."

"Could you teach me to do that, too?"

"I could, but I won't. That's Daddy's specialty. He'd go ballistic if he caught anybody messing with his superadvanced dogs. He doesn't even know I can do it."

"How did you learn?" There was only interest in the blue eyes.

"Hid and watched," Emily said shortly.

"I can't imagine your father going ballistic," Lulu said, smiling a little.

"Well, it's his version of ballistic. Believe me, you don't want to see it."

They said no more to each other while they exercised and fed the older dogs. When they parted for lunch, Emily into the house and Lulu up her stairs, they only nodded to each other. Emily heard the window air conditioner go on in the apartment, and slammed the front screen door sulkily. Nobody in the big house had an air conditioner. Even on the sweatiest, most sheet-rumpling nights, Emily endured heat as a necessary, if disagreeable, part of plantation life.

"The river gives us all the air conditioning we need," her father was fond of saying. But Emily thought for the first time what it must be like to come in out of the blinding noon heat and turn on a machine and feel cool dry air pour over your body.

"I bet she stands in front of it naked," she thought. And then, unwillingly, "But she's pretty good with the dogs. I wonder if she thinks with them too? It sort of looked like she did."

This would be the last blow to Emily's already bruised ego. She shoved the thought out of her mind and went upstairs to wash the doggy sweat off her face and bangs and hug Elvis before she went down to lunch.

Elvis was not in his spot on the rug beside her bed, and he was not in the bathroom where his water bowl was. Emily clumped down the stairs into the kitchen, where Cleta was serving lunch.

"Has anybody seen Elvis?" she said, sliding into her chair. It stuck unpleasantly to her bare thighs.

"Went trottin' through here an' out the dog do' a while ago," Cleta said. "Lookin' for a spot of shade, mos' likely."

Emily nodded. The cool, damp patch on the front lawn, where the hose was kept hooked up for watering, was a sometimes retreat for Elvis, and there was usually at least a breath of wind off the river.

But he was not there when she looked, before going back out to the kennels. When she reached the training ring, Lulu was just coming down the stairs from her apartment. There were two sleepy puppies in her arms, and Elvis trotted beside her left heel.

"I hope it's okay about the puppies," she said. And, catching Emily's look, "I really didn't kidnap him. He just appeared and scratched at my door, so I let him in. I expect he heard the puppies up there, and was checking on them."

"I expect so," Emily said. Elvis trotted up to her and thrust his nose into her hand as he did when he wanted attention.

"You mustn't bother Lulu," she said to him in a sweet, false voice. He looked at her intently, and then licked her hand. For the rest of the afternoon, while Emily and Lulu raked and swept and spread straw and

checked the nursing mothers and filled kibble and water bowls, they hardly spoke.
Elvis followed at Emily's heel and sat down
gravely when she began a new chore. Emily
and Lulu maintained their silence. The gap
between twelve and twenty is enormous,
and the one between downtown Charleston
and a spaniel breeding farm is even larger.
When they were done for the day, they
parted with polite good-byes. Elvis trotted,
grinning, beside Emily as they went into the
house to get ready for supper and flopped
down beside her on her bed when she
stretched out after her bath.

"I'll bet she called you up there, didn't
she?" she said to him. He grinned his doggy
grin and burrowed closer.

"Well, don't follow her around. It hurts my
feelings," Emily said, and Elvis whined and
licked her face.

The next day was a repeat of the first, except that great, bulbous purple-rimmed
clouds blew in from the ocean and piled up
over the river, and the smell of ozone and
fresh rain hung in the air.

"We'll skip the puppies for today," Emily
said. "It's going to pour, and we need to get

the older dogs checked and fed and watered. I think it'll storm before noon."

At lunchtime they went from the barn out
into the ring, where everything lay still and
charged before the breaking of the storm.
Kenny Rouse sat on the fender of his truck,
just outside the fence, legs crossed. He
grinned when he saw Emily and put his
hands up to cup his chest as if holding
breasts.

This time fury, not fear, reddened Emily's
face. Beside her Elvis began to growl softly.
When Lulu came out into the sun, Kenny
cupped his hands over his crotch and thrust
his pelvis forward, all teeth showing. Elvis's
growl deepened.

"Who is that moron?" Lulu said, in a cool,
carrying voice.

"Kenny Rouse," Emily muttered. "He
cleans and feeds sometimes when we're
not around. I don't know why Daddy keeps
him. He's always staring at you and grinning, and touching himself. I hate him."

"Hmmm," Lulu said, but she said no
more. She gathered up an armful of the
puppies she was keeping in her apartment
and nodded good-bye to Emily and went up
the stairs. This time Elvis did not follow her.

He went into the house with Emily, his eyes on Kenny Rouse, who still lounged on his truck looking after Lulu. Elvis's hair was a stiff ridge on his neck.

Just after lunch, as the first fat raindrops were starting to sizzle and splatter down on the parched earth, Kenny Rouse banged on the screen door. Walter Parmenter went to answer it. Elvis growled again, deeply. Emily got up and went out into the foyer and hid in her old spot under the stairs to listen. Elvis had never growled at knocks on the door before.

"I quit," she heard Kenny Rouse say in his lazy, nasal drawl. "You owe me for last week."

"You weren't here last week," Walter said. There was no affect in his voice. He had never, Emily knew, liked Kenny Rouse, but kennel workers were few and far between.

"Well, the week before," Kenny said sullenly.

"I don't owe you anything," Walter said, his voice flattening. "But it looks like somebody's already paid you what you deserved."

"Shit," Kenny spat, and Emily put her head around the stair railing and looked at

him. There was a perfect, small handprint
on his cheek, glowing redly in the storm
dusk.

He turned and swaggered off the porch,
and made an obscene gesture back at the
house, and stalked across the lawn and got
into his truck. As he was screeching out of
the turnaround, gravel flying, Emily looked
toward the barn and saw Lulu standing at
the bottom of the stairs, hands in pockets,
rocking back and forth on her heels. She
was smiling, a faint smile, and when she
saw Emily she gave her a little salute, then
turned and went back up her stairs.

"It's just you ladies from now on," Walter
Parmenter said when he joined Lulu and
Emily at the puppy ring early the next morning. The storm had scrubbed the earth and
sky clean, and everything glistened with
sunshine and coolness.

"Why is that?" Emily said innocently, not
looking at Lulu.

"Rouse quit yesterday. Just quit. Didn't
even wait around for his money."

He cocked his head at Lulu.

"Wonder why that was, now?" he said.

"What a pity," Lulu said mildly.

Emily grinned unwillingly at Lulu, who nodded slightly.

No more was said about the defection of Kenny Rouse, but after that it was as if a tiny fissure had appeared in the lacquered wall between Emily and Lulu Foxworth.

In the days that followed, Lulu captivated the Parmenters, with the exception of Emily, with her willingness, hard work, impeccable manners, and passion for the dogs. She was proving to be a talented and intuitive trainer, and she never went up to her apartment without a brace of Daisy's puppies. By now they were happy, cheerful pups, eager to please. It was just as Walter had said. No one saw her after she went up to the apartment at the end of the day, but sometimes they heard faint music, usually classical, and an occasional puppy squeal, and sometimes deep in the night, if Emily waked, she could see a light burning in the apartment window. Beside her, Elvis would whine, but he did not pace as he had at first, and he did not follow Lulu up her stairs again. Gradually, Lulu was weaving herself into the routine of Sweetwater, and she did it so quietly and matter-of-factly that even

Emily, though grudgingly, had to admit that the arrangement was working well.

Walter Parmenter had not ceased his attempts to lure her in to dinner with them, and the twins were still scuffling and preening, but the momentum finally faded, and the posturing slowed and stopped. When Walter made yet one more attempt to invite Lulu to dinner, and was just as pleasantly and politely rebuffed as always, Jenny took him aside.

"I wouldn't push her," she said. "She seems to need to keep things like they are, and if you push, she'll just leave, and then what will you do about the Hunt Club?"

So Walter gave up, and in the hot nights, the light in Lulu's window burned late, and sometimes Emily would wake and hear Elvis, pacing once more.

"It's none of your business," she said sleepily to him, and he jumped back into bed with her and snuggled into sleep.

7

On the first of July, Rhett and Maybelle Fox-worth came to visit Lulu. They had not come before; Emily wondered why, and once asked her aunt.

"I don't imagine it's their choice," Jenny said.

It was a Saturday afternoon, and for once the Lowcountry was behaving as it did in the dreams of people who had left it a long time before but never stopped aching for it. The air was soft and sweet with the scent of flowers both close by and borne in from far-away by the river wind. It was cool in the deep shade of the front porch, and not really hot when you went out onto the lawn and down to the river or back toward the kennels and barn. The sucking humidity had lifted temporarily and the sky and reflecting river were so blue that they almost hurt the eye. The wind that lifted with the incoming tide made the river, running full, glitter and dance, and off on the faraway hummocks, and even to the woodland beyond, you could see the sharp details of palmettos and soft webs of moss and resurrection ferns, the shivering of the small live oak leaves, and the ink black trunks of the forest trees.

Every citizen of the water and marsh and sky seemed to put in a courtesy appearance for the Foxworths: mullet jumped in the river, shrimps popped, turtles splashed into the water from mossy banks, ospreys dived and wheeled in the blue vault of the sky, and even the young eagle who lived across the river, on the edge of the wood, swept by, casting a prehistoric shadow. Off on the hummocks the ensigns of the white-tailed deer flashed in the deep shadows, and from Sweetwater Creek, the roar of a big bull alligator drifted across the peninsula.

"Why, it's lovely here, isn't it?" Maybelle Foxworth said. She wore a flowered shirt-waist, and a blue band held her helmet of gilded hair off her face. "It's the kind of day that makes you remember why you wanted a plantation in the first place. Yours is such a sweet place. It's very like Maybud, don't you think, Rhett?"

"I think it's got a lot of what I wish Maybud had," Rhett Foxworth said genially, his baby's face, snub as a .45 pistol, turned to the river and the woods beyond.

"It's got enough uncut field and pasture land, and the ridge back there we saw coming in, for some great upland hunting. We've got the wetland, but we don't have that. Like to hunt it sometime."

"Anytime," Walter Parmenter beamed. "Just say the word."

They sat in the old wicker armchairs and glider that had been on the porch as long as Emily could remember. They looked better, though. Walter had made the grumbling twins give it all a new coat of dark Charleston green, and Cleta had washed and ironed the cushion covers. Jenny had brought some of her prized green plants and hanging baskets from her small balcony, and somebody had dragged the molting rubber plant that mourned its life away in Walter's office, and trimmed it, and polished its leaves. Two or three days of sun and air had restored it to some of its former Victorian grandeur. Emily had a fleeting glimpse, in her mind's eye, of what this porch, and indeed the whole house, might have looked like in its glory days.

Cleta brought out mint iced tea and the cheese straws that Jenny had made earlier, and everyone but Emily and Lulu ate and drank and pronounced it all wonderful. Lulu was once again as still and white as when she had first come and Emily felt unsettled and apprehensive, though at what she did not know. She disliked the long flowered skirt and yellow sleeveless T-shirt Jenny had bought her, and she disliked the senior Foxworths. She wished that they would go away so that this perfect day could be given its due.

"Lulu," Maybelle said, putting down her iced tea with the air of someone getting down to business, "you're looking well, sweetie. I was afraid, you know, that maybe the isolation and all . . . but you do look rested, and I think you just may have gained a teeny bit of weight. Are you getting lots and lots of rest? Are you taking long walks and enjoying this pretty place? Have you had a swim yet?"

"Mostly I'm working with the dogs, Mother," Lulu said evenly. "But yes, I get plenty of rest when the day's over."

"Don't you just adore her little nest?" Maybelle burbled, looking fondly at her daughter, who did not return the look.

"Well. . . ." Jenny said hesitantly.

"I haven't had them up, Mother," Lulu said. Her voice tightened slightly. "Everybody's so tired at the end of the day that I hate to insist they come see my . . . nest."

"Lulu, that's really very rude of you," her mother said. "We'll go and have a peek before we leave."

"Maybe Lulu hasn't gotten it quite like she wants it," Jenny said hastily, and Lulu shot her a grateful look.

"Yes, I'm still moving things around," she said.

"I had it just perfect, sweetie," her mother said, pouting a bit. It would have been effective if her pink lipstick had not smeared on her front teeth. "I couldn't wait for you to show it off. Don't fiddle with it too much. I thought it was just *you.*"

Lulu said nothing.

"I guess you've noticed that we brought your car out for you," Maybelle went on. She nodded toward the little red BMW, whose top was down, red lacquer gleaming. "Your daddy had it repainted. Doesn't it look pretty?"

Pretty was not the word Emily would have used. The little car was perfect, jewel-like, like a fine netsuke carving or a Fabergé egg. Walt Junior and Carter were practically quivering with the desire to put down their glasses and dash out to inspect it. Even Cleta, coming in and out with refills, looked at it and shook her head and smiled. "MMMM *Mmmmm*! That some car," she said.

Still, Lulu said nothing. Emily noticed that the muscles beside her mouth were clenched and a small vein throbbed in her temple. Lulu's face was like the satiny mask of a geisha, but anger was breaking through, crumbling it. Emily had never seen anger on that face before. She stared, fascinated.

"Thank you, Mama, but you know I don't want the car out here," Lulu said. Her voice was perfectly level. "I told you that from the beginning, didn't I?"

"Yes, but everybody changes their mind, lovey. It's been a long time now. All your friends miss you. They're all talking about you, wondering why you've buried yourself out here in . . . ah, this pretty place. I thought you might not want to disturb these nice people by having visitors out here, but with the car you could run into town whenever you wanted to for a little lunch or something. Or you could meet halfway. Sister's at Jasmine, that's not far at all, and Missy Longstreet is having a house party in a couple of weeks for her roommate, the one from Virginia. Everybody you know will be there. I said I wouldn't be surprised if you didn't leave your little nun's cell—not that it isn't divine out here—and come. Surely your sweet doggies could spare you for a few hours a week."

She looked at Walter and smiled brilliantly.

"Of course," he said. "Emily can easily take over."

Yeah, right, Emily thought.

Lulu drew a deep breath. "Mother," she said, "I work very hard out here all day long. I'm doing a good job, I think. The puppies are coming along just wonderfully, and I don't want to break the momentum with them. I'm doing valuable work for a change. I'm not going to just leave and go into town on a whim for lunch with somebody I've known since Miss Hanahan's, and I'm not coming to Maybud, and I'm not going to Missy's stupid house party. I told you I wasn't going to leave here until at least September, or until they threw me out, and I meant it. I'm happier here than I've been in a long time." ("Happy?" Emily thought.) "So you'll just have to take the car back."

She stopped and looked around, and said, in her low voice, "I must sound ungrateful and very rude. I hope you'll forgive me."

The Parmenters all nodded vigorously.

"Lulu . . ." her mother began. Lulu stood up, suddenly and stiffly.

"Please excuse me," she said formally. "I haven't fed Giddy's puppies yet, and the big dogs need a run."

She turned as if to leave.

"Lulu!" Maybelle's voice was no longer lilting and teasing.

"Emily will be glad to do it for you if you want to visit with your parents a while longer," Walter said.

Emily glared at him. She had planned to take Elvis over to the dolphin slide that afternoon. They might be there, it had been so hot. . . .

"No," Lulu said. Her voice was steel. "I love doing it. Besides, I talk to Mama every day on my cell phone. Mama, I'll call you tonight. Excuse me."

And she was gone. But before she turned, Emily had seen tears on her smooth bisque cheeks. Unwilling pity twisted her heart. The Foxworths really were awful. Or at least, Maybelle was.

"I'd have left too," she said to herself.

There was a long, stinging silence, and then Maybelle Foxworth said sweetly, "She's such an impulsive thing. She always was, wasn't she, Rhett? I hope you don't think she was raised to behave like this. She's been so overtired. . . ."

"Don't give it another thought," Jenny said warmly. "She's really working very hard, and she's just a natural with the dogs. I can remember some truly spectacular scenes with my mother. Lulu couldn't hold a candle to me at that age."

Emily looked at her aunt; she could not

imagine Jenny Raiford making a spectacular scene with anyone.

Maybelle Foxworth half-rose from her chair, obviously ready to concede the field to her daughter and flee. But Walter said genially and loudly, "You can't go yet! Jenny and Emily made their special strawberry shortcake just for today. You have to have a piece before you go."

Emily looked wildly at her aunt. Strawberry shortcake? Jenny would not meet her eyes.

"Well, just a bite," Maybelle murmured, and sank back into her chair. Emily did not think she had ever seen anyone so anxious to be somewhere else.

Cleta brought the shortcake and the Foxworths sat nibbling it, poised on the edge of their seats. Emily's face and neck burned. Didn't he realize? Couldn't he see? The Foxworths had been slumming all along, and doing it so well that no one had noticed. Until now.

"Emily, come and join us," her father said, and she got up apprehensively out of her chair and went to sit beside her father on the glider.

"I've heard that you're very active in the

affairs of Charlotte Hall," he said to Maybelle Foxworth. Emily could feel her face
drain white, and then flame.

"Well, I'm an alumna," Maybelle said
stiffly. "As was my mother, and as is Lulu."

"I'm considering schools for Emily here,
and I wondered if you thought Charlotte Hall
would be suitable for her. Her grades are
top-notch, and of course she has long
Charleston ties, through her mother's family."

"Her mother. Yes," Maybelle said in the
tone that one would use in charming a co-
bra. "I think I was at a party or something
with her before I married," Maybelle went
on. "Very vivacious and so vivid, wasn't
she? We all wondered who she was. Oh,
and of course you would have been there,"
she turned her shark's smile on Jenny. "I
think your sister was still in school, but I remember that you had just graduated
from . . . was it North Charleston Community College?"

"It was the College of Charleston," Jenny
said sweetly.

"Oh, yes. Well, as to this pretty child's
suitability for Charlotte Hall, we'd just have
to see, wouldn't we? I could be of more help

if I knew your family better, but I'll have some literature sent to you."

"And maybe put a word or two in the right ear," Walter said.

"Walter," Jenny said, standing up. "It's getting late. I'm sure the Foxworths have things to do on an afternoon like this."

"Well, there *is* a garden party at Spartina," Maybelle said, managing finally to get to her feet. She looked like a parakeet poised for flight. "We really should hurry if we're going to get dressed. Rhett, will you drive the little car back? I've had enough sun for today."

They were gone into the shadow of the woods beyond the circular drive before anyone spoke.

"Well, Emmybug," her father said. "Now you've got a friend at court. Or Charlotte Hall, I should say."

Emily turned and ran.

Outside, away from the deep well of the porch, early afternoon blazed like a solar flare, like a terrible just-born sun. It was not hot, but the glare off the river beat down on Emily's head and shoulders as if a giant was trying to push her down into the earth. Off in the runs, the dogs were barking in a many-voiced chorale: Lunchtime! Did you all forget it's lunchtime? The noise and the sun melted into a supernova. Emily ran from it, terrified, unthinking. The earth and the sky had united to kill her.

She ran like a small animal with dogs after it, ran for shade and quiet and safety. She ran straight for the old barn, where it was twilight all the time, and silent. Where Elvis was. She had shut him in there herself before the Foxworths came, saying in her heart, "Just for a little while. They're horrible people and they'll go home soon. They don't want to stick around with the oh-so-not-elegant-Parmenters, even if Daddy thinks they do. I'll come get you and we'll go to the dolphin slide."

He had wagged his tail and lain down with his muzzle on his crossed paws in the small hollow where her grandfather had kept the salt blocks for his soon-to-be-gone horses, and looked up at her tranquilly.

"I know," his mind said to hers.

Emily ran through the sun, and as she did she found herself running in cadence to the Gullah song GW had sung for her:

Honey in the rock, got to feed God's
   children,
Honey in the rock, honey in the rock.
Honey in the rock, got to feed God's
   children
Feed every child of God.
Satan mad and I so glad
He missed the souls he thought he
   had.
Honey in the rock, honey in the rock.

Emily took care that her right foot always came down on the accented word, otherwise she would fall off the earth.

Under the song a flat, wailing voice kept up a dialogue with her: "He's never going to stop. He never is. He doesn't understand. He never will. As soon as I'm sixteen I'm going to run away. After all, my mother did. I can see why.

"Two daughters at Sweetwater running away from their parents today. That's funny. All that money and she's not any better off than I am. She's worse off. I've got Elvis. . . ."

("Oh, honey in the rock.")

She reached the barn and slammed the big double doors open and went in, blinking in the sudden musty darkness. It smelled of hay, even though no horses had lived in it for a very long time. Hay and dust and pungent smells of the medicines kept there for the dogs, and clean, dry pine straw for their beds. The only smell that was missing was the one she had come running for: the sweet smell of young dog with sun and dust caught in his blazing curly hair.

Emily walked slowly to the far end of the barn, where the old salt tray had been. Where she had left Elvis. In the mote-dancing slants of sunlight from the gap in the back door, she could see clearly. Elvis was not in the barn.

He would never leave where I left him, she thought numbly. She's got him. She came in here and got him and took him up to that fucking apartment, and she's locked him in with her.

"Fuck is not cute for almost-teenagers," Buddy said, far down.

"You laughed the first time I said it."

"Yeah, but you were eight years old."

"I don't care. I'm going up there and get him, and I'm going to tell her to leave my dog the hell alone. Let her buy herself a dog if she wants one. She could buy this whole damned kennel without blinking an eye."

"You're making a mistake."

"I DON'T CARE!"

She ran back out into the sunlight, borne on fury, and clumped up the steps to Lulu's apartment. The door was closed, but she did not care about that, either. She jerked it open.

She took a step into the room, and then stopped. She saw an insane kaleidoscope of images: drifting, filmy white hangings; a small forest of green plants; a bookcase wall full of books and sound equipment; a rolled-up rug and a pile of bright pillows tossed in a corner beside a small coral slipper chair, turned to the wall; a narrow, pretty painted bed. Lulu sat on the bed, her knees drawn up to her chin, rocking back and forth as though wounded in the stomach. Her eyes were squeezed shut, and her mouth was open in a square retching rictus of pain, like a crying child's. But she was not crying, merely rocking silently back and forth. Rocking, rocking—with her arms around Elvis. He sat still in her embrace, his muzzle pressed into her shoulder. When she rocked, he rocked with her. When Emily came into the room he raised his head and whined softly, but he did not move. Lulu didn't, either.

Emily went back down the stairs and out into the sunlight, walking slowly and stiffly so that she would not fall into the abyss that had opened in the earth. She was not surprised. She knew somehow that she had always known it was there, but she had never seen it because until now she had had companions to shield her. Buddy, for as long as he could. Elvis, always.

Nobody now. She could feel a rattling, too-cool breath on the back of her neck, and from the depth of the abyss, cold wind, blowing upward. From the sky above her, only endless, empty iron-blue space.

"This is what it is to be alone," Emily thought, putting one foot precisely in front of the other on the narrow bridge over blackness. Her heart slammed with terror, rang like a hollow bell with loss. "Buddy, where are you?" she whispered. He did not answer.

When she reached the front screened door, there was a note stuck on it with a Band-aid, from her aunt:

"Your father and I have gone over to

Edisto Beach to pick up the boys. Their car broke down, and nobody was around to give them a ride. I'm sorry not to be home when you get back. I thought I should take the opportunity to have another talk with your dad. I know he hurt you today. Take a nap and we'll work it out when I get home. Cut him whatever slack you can, Emily. He really does not understand."

"I will cut him no slack," Emily thought, going quietly up the stairs to her room. She walked steadily and mechanically, one foot in front of the other. "I will cut him no slack ever again. I will not cut Miss Gotrocks Foxworth any, either. I don't care what's the matter with her. They sure as hell don't cut me any. He's got my future all tied up neat, or thinks he has. And she's got my dog. So we will not work it out. Not this time. I'm not going through all that stupid hiding and preaching and he said, she said. He's not going to give me any more rules. I'm going to pretend it never happened. I won't talk about it even if he tries to, even if Aunt Jenny tries to make him. I'm going to be quiet and polite, and simply ignore him when I can. It's only for a few more years. If I have to be alone, I'll just learn to be. Lots of people do. And I'll get my dog back. And I'll get rid of Lulu. Nobody stays forever. Nobody."

Calm certainty and a feeling of strength and competence rose from some cell deep inside that she had never known she had, and walked with her into her room. It stayed with her while she pulled the long curtains against the glare off the river and skinned out of her loathsome lady clothes and put on the worn old GOD IS DOG SPELLED BACKWARD T-shirt. It sank with her onto her bed.

And then the calm whirled away into the abyss, and Emily fell after it. Turning and turning, falling and falling. Into darkness deeper and emptier than she could ever have imagined. Her mouth full of wind, her heart jolting slower and slower.

She grabbed her pillow in both arms and pressed her face into it and scrubbed it back and forth, smelling sweet soap and sunshine from the line outside. And she erupted into the hardest weeping she had ever known. It tore her throat and flooded her lungs with salt. For a long time she could not breathe, and when she finally could, she sobbed and gasped and wailed and howled aloud, but only the old down pillow received the grief.

"I want my mother," Emily cried over and over again. "I want my mother!"

It is true that you can literally cry yourself to sleep, and Emily did, into a sleep so profound and sucking that she did not move for more than two hours, and when she did, the muscles of her legs and arms ached. She lay, cradled in clinging drowsiness, feeling at her side and into her neck a soft, heavy warmth that soothed and comforted, promised safety, promised cherishing.

Half mired in sleep, Emily smiled.

"Mother . . ."

Elvis.

Emily woke fully, and reached for him. She felt his wet nose in her ear.

"Thank you for coming back," she whispered to him, her anger at him gone on the flood of tears.

An hour later, as the brilliance was seeping out of the day and a cool dusk was coming in, Emily stood at her bedroom door, bathed and dressed in soft, faded-to-white blue jeans and a new pink T-shirt, the damped-down fire of her hair pulled back into a ponytail. Elvis sat at her side, panting happily and thumping his stumpy tail on the floor.

"Remember," she whispered to him. "None of it happened. He doesn't matter to us anymore. We'll be very polite because it's the easiest thing to do, and in a few more summers we'll be gone. You think of a place you'd like to live, and I will, too."

And she went out into the twilit hall and down the stairs to dinner. They were standing on the last step, girl and dog, when there was a light rapping on the screen door. Walter Parmenter came out of the kitchen to answer it. Lulu Foxworth stood there, dressed in sleeveless white, her silver hair a waterfall straight to her bronze shoulders, her cheeks hectic with spots of color over the tan. Her eyes glittered and her lips, without lipstick, were curved up in a child's tentative smile. Her lavender scent curled through the screen into the foyer.

"Does the invitation to dinner still stand?" she said.

8

Later that year, Emily told Lulu that when she saw her walk into the foyer on that first night, in her candlelight white, her first thought had been, "Oh, great. The dinner from hell. Well, at least I can tell Elvis about it, and Buddy. And there don't have to be any more of them."

"I bet you hated me," Lulu said comfortably when Emily told her this.

"No, I just . . . yes. I did," Emily said.

"I don't blame you," Lulu smiled. She was smiling a lot more by then. "I must have seemed like a cuckoo in the nest."

Emily looked at her inquiringly.

"It's a nasty habit of cuckoos to lay their eggs in other birds' nests so they'll have to raise the babies. And when the eggs hatch, it's obvious that the babies are strange and alien, and don't belong. But the mother birds raise them, anyway. It's like . . . a stranger coming into the middle of your family and taking everything."

Emily shivered. It was, for some reason, an eerie thought. It made her think, for the first time in months, of changelings.

"You don't seem like that now," she said to Lulu. "You seem just like a big sister."

"You don't need a big sister," Lulu said. "Way too bossy and judgmental. You need a friend. I'd much rather be that."

"Okay," Emily muttered shyly. "Only I don't know why, when you have so many others. And they're all your age. I'm just a kid."

"You know things most adults don't ever even think of. You care about the same things I do. That's a lot of what a friend really is. And you're strong. I felt that the minute I met you. You don't know how much I've needed that this summer. And you share your world, and you don't judge. Those are very grown-up things, Emily. I can't name one of my so-called friends who has them all."

"I'm not strong," Emily thought. "I've

never been strong. Don't even say it. Don't expect it. It scares me."

But no matter what anyone else said about suitability and don't-bother-Lulu-all-the-time, she knew she had a friend in Lulu Foxworth. It did not matter why.

It began, tenuously and falteringly, at that first dinner that Lulu shared with them. Despite Walter's hovering heartiness, and the twins' preening (Lulu said long after that they were pumping testosterone out into the air, like fog) and her own sullen silence, a small, tough rootling was planted that night, and it clung tenaciously to its life. Before she left, Lulu had all the Parmenters laughing, even, unwillingly, Emily. Lulu in her storyteller mode was irresistible. She might have been the Sybil appointed by the tribe to sit by the fire in the mouth of the cave and tell them, without frightening them in the least, about the world outside the cave. Soon they were clamoring for more, for the Sybil's stories both explained the unexplainable and defanged it with laughter.

So it was with Lulu Foxworth.

When she first came in and sat down with them in the little breakfast room, she was hectically flushed, as if she might have a fever, and her eyes glittered, and she was trembling all over, a fine, almost unnoticeable tremor. But in a way it was all charming; no one had ever seen Lulu this animated and the tremor made it seem as if she was so eager to please them all that it made her anxious.

She sat by Jenny Raiford, with Walter on her left, and she lit the dim little room like a fire. Beside her, Jenny looked, as usual, elegant and as fine-drawn as a young doe, but oddly muted, as if she had been outlined in sepia.

Walter Parmenter, in his swelling pride and fatuity, looked like a balloon in the Macy's Thanksgiving Day parade. Or at least, he did in Emily's mortified eyes. The boys looked, simply, like squat cave drawings. Across the table from Lulu Foxworth, Emily suffered over her farcical family.

Aunt Jenny had made shrimp and grits because the twins had been down to the pier at Folly Beach and brought home a dripping croaker sack of the sweet brine shrimp of the Lowcountry. Walter Parmenter apologized for serving his guest such pedestrian fare, but Lulu, catching the swift arrow of hurt in Jenny's eyes, said, "There's nothing that says 'home' to me like shrimp and grits. Our old cook Lutetia made it every Saturday and holiday morning, at home and at Maybud, and if you didn't like it, that was just tough. I loved it, but it wasn't as good as yours is, Mrs. Raiford. What's different? I can't quite tell. . . ."

"Call me Jenny," Jenny Raiford said. "I start with fresh shrimp and John's Island tomatoes, when I can, and make a sauce instead of using ketchup, and I throw in a little of whatever's growing in my herb garden. Right now it's thyme and cilantro. I don't think anybody but me likes the cilantro, but the cook gets to choose."

"Well, I love it," Lulu said. "All I ever knew how to make it with was ketchup, because that's what Lutetia used. One winter when we were all about in the ninth grade at Charlotte Hall our mothers were playing bridge at the Yacht Club and decided that we should all learn to cook. I think we were all bored and driving them crazy. So they hired the cook from the Yacht Club whose shrimp and grits was widely admired and got her to meet in one or another of our kitchens after school one day a week all that winter, and she showed us how to make real Lowcountry dishes. Or so she said. Shrimp and grits was the first. We all had to make our own batch—I remember it was at our house on Legare—and we used every pot and pan in the kitchen, and it looked like a slaughter-house when we were through because of all the ketchup mess.

"The deal was that the Yacht Club would put our shrimp and grits on the menu for the next Sunday brunch, and so the cook went off with a potful on the Friday before that Sunday, and our mothers called everybody they knew to come and eat the shrimp and grits that their charming little Charlotte Hall girls had made. And since Charleston is nothing if not supportive of its clans, and since everybody is related to everybody else in town, the dining room was packed."

"I'll bet it was a great success," Walter said, nodding appreciatively. "I've been telling Emily right along she should learn some classic Charleston specialties. Maybe you could give her a little lesson."

Lulu smiled at him, and then at Emily, and, incredibly, winked. It was just the brush of a fan of gold-tipped lashes very briefly on her cheek, and Emily did not know if anyone else saw it, but she did.

"I'm not sure I'm quite the right person, Mr. Parmenter," Lulu smiled. "We'd swacked the sauce with as much gin as we could steal from our parents' liquor cabinets, and everybody commented on how unusual and tasty it was. Of course, half of them couldn't walk when they got up. Mrs. Burton Triplett Sr. fell down the front steps and lay there laughing like a hyena, and she was ninety-three at the time. All of us were under house arrest for the rest of the semester. The cooking lessons were hastily abandoned, and the next siege we underwent was bridge. On the whole, I liked the cooking better."

The Parmenters all burst into laughter, even Emily. Walter looked faintly scandalized, but he laughed, too. Apparently not all Charleston debutantes were perfect wives-in-training.

It was that night that Emily sensed that Lulu Foxworth might become an ally.

They stayed late at the table, later than Emily could ever remember. Usually they were up and away by seven o'clock for the mandatory hour of TV togetherness that Jenny had instituted. But on this night it was near nine before Jenny rose, interrupting another gale of laughter at one of Lulu's downtown dialogues, as she came to call them.

"Lulu, dear, this crowd could and would sit here and monopolize you all night, but I know how early you and Emily get up, and we must not keep you any longer," she said, smiling.

Lulu clapped a hand over her mouth.

"You know, the one thing I hate most about Southern women is how they run on, and here I am doing it," she said. "I am *so* embarrassed. I guess it's because you're all such good listeners, and nobody in my crowd pays any attention to me. They just say, 'Oh, well, that's just Lulu.' So I appreciate your indulgence and I promise not to hold you captive ever again."

"We're willing captives," Jenny said. "We'll do it again anytime you want to. We've all learned more about old Charleston in two hours than we have in all our lives. Next time we'll just start earlier."

"Oh," Lulu said ruefully. "I hope there is a next time."

A chorus of Parmenter voices assured her there would be.

"I hope we can make it a regular affair,"

Walter said, beaming at her. And then, turning to Emily, "You listen to Lulu. You can learn all you need to know about the kind of life I want for you from her. You can learn to be a lady."

Emily felt her cheeks heat. Anger flared up again. Anger at her father, anger at Lulu.

"I'm not a lady," she said, not looking at anyone. "I'm a river-swamp kid with dirty shoes."

"You've got the makings of something better than a lady," Lulu said seriously to Emily. "You've got the makings of a terrific woman. That's something I just know. But you're right about one thing. You sure have got dirty shoes. So have I, for that matter. Would you do me the honor of walking me home in your dirty shoes? I'd like to see what you think of my nest, as my mother insists on calling it."

The anger faded. Liking stood trembling off at the edge of Emily's consciousness, waiting to creep in.

"Sure," she said nonchalantly. "Can Elvis come?"

He was nowhere to be found. But when they had walked through the warm, mothy darkness to the pool of dim light that illumined the entrance to the barn's staircase, Elvis was waiting for them, thumping his tail and grinning.

"What are you doing here?" Emily asked him, not at all pleased to see him back at the fringe of Lulu's domain.

"He knows where you are all the time," Lulu said. "I've noticed that. I'll see him get up and start off in one direction or another, and in a minute, there you are. It's uncanny. Have you been casting spells on dogs, Emily?"

"He's always just kind of done that," Emily said, scratching Elvis's ears. "It's like he's sort of my brother or something."

"Good brother to have," Lulu said. "Elvis makes three; you're lucky. I'm an only child. I think I would have loved having a brother."

"I had four, counting Elvis. And you would have loved having Buddy. And he'd like you, too," she thought, to her surprise.

But she said nothing. She wasn't ready to share Buddy with Lulu Foxworth.

They groped their way up the old staircase. It needed a much stronger light, Emily noticed. For some reason, the knowledge shamed her. Lulu could not have been used to such negligence. She would tell Jenny; Jenny would see to it.

At the top of the staircase Lulu unlocked the newly glossy door and pushed it open.

"Ta-daaa!" she said.

Emily walked into the apartment and stood still, at first unable to process it. Under this strange new vision of fluttering white and shining bare wood and small flares of color and rioting green, she kept seeing the old apartment, weeping cobwebs over its decaying bones.

"Wow!" Emily said inadequately.

Lulu smiled at her. "Wow is right. At least it's better now that I've sort of edited my mother's version of it. Come on in."

They moved into the big room that served as a bed–sitting room. Behind them Elvis whined, but did not come in until Emily said, "Oh, come on in. You've already . . ."

She did not finish. She did not want Lulu to know that she had seen Elvis here earlier in the day, a willing receptacle for her unknowable anguish.

Elvis came in and lay down on the small white rug beside the bed and laid his head on his crossed paws. Home, his position said.

"No, it's not," Emily thought to him.

He thumped his tail again. *I know.*

Only one lamp was lit in the big room, on a low table beside the pretty little painted bed. The French one, Emily thought, remembering what Lulu's mother had said on the day she had first seen the room. It's like a kid's drawing of flowers and vines. I've seen better than that at Wal-Mart. I could do that.

The narrow bed had an iron canopy, and clouds of what looked to be mosquito netting puddled on the polished cypress floor. A plain white cotton bedspread covered it, and there was only one pillow, also white. At the foot was folded a quilt, so faded with age that you could hardly make out its pattern of tiny blue flowers. Beside it, on the floor, a sumptuous drift of white fleece served as a rug, sheepskin perhaps, Emily thought. She had never seen a sheepskin rug. Sheep and warmth were not Lowcountry prerequisites. The rug was the only thing in the room that spoke of privilege. Even with only a narrow circle of light from the lamp, you could see that the room was as plain as a nun's cell.

And yet . . . it was not. It drew you in like

quicksand, promising peace and rest and dreamless sleep. A bank of tall green plants forested the wall behind the bed, and with the netting, nights here must be like sleeping in a toothless jungle. Old embroidered pillows were piled on a low sofa, which was covered with what looked to be another age-bleached quilt. The deep, small-paned windows, open now, were uncurtained, letting in moonlight or sunlight or stormlight or whatever flooded the marshes. There were a few plants in rough terra cotta pots on the windowsills, herbs, Emily thought. Aunt Jenny had similar ones in her garden. A plain wooden bookshelf covered the wall opposite the bed, crammed untidily with books. Emily's chest tightened. Buddy had had one in his room that might have been this one's twin. There was a little radio, a small cassette player, and a battered laptop on one of the shelves. These, plus a deep armchair and ottoman under the window, partly covered by a length of batik the colors of desert sand and adobe walls, were the only other significant furnishings in the room. Emily wondered where the raj procession of furnishings had gone.

On the last unadorned wall a large painting burned like a wildfire, turning the nun's cell into something else entirely, something sensuous and half-hidden and throbbing with primal life. In it a jaguar unlike any that had ever padded the earth prowled through a fever dream of tropical foliage. Blood-red pyramids were silhouetted against an empty, murderous blue sky, and over them old, terrible birds wheeled and dove. A squat brown man held up a stone vessel to the sky, a vessel dripping red. Emily felt a surge of fear and heat and a fierce joy start deep in her stomach and spread out all over her. Overwhelming. Terrifying. Sweet. She turned to look at Lulu, almost expecting to see, instead of the thin golden blade of a girl she knew, a dark, half-naked priestess, chanting. The painting was totally unlike the trembling girl who had come to them, or this stark Mediterranean-washed room. And yet again . . . it was right. Emily thought of Lulu's whisper she had only half heard on that first day that the Foxworths came. "Penitential." If that was so, then here was the altar at which the penitent would kneel.

"Richard Hagerty," Lulu smiled at her. "A Charleston painter I've loved since I was a little girl. He's a doctor, too. I guess, if you hit people like this, you need to be able to heal them, too. Do you like it?"

"I don't know. It's not like anything else. You wouldn't ever want flowers or ancestors after you saw it, would you?"

Lulu laughed.

"No, you wouldn't. It outrages a lot of people. My mother absolutely hates it. She says it's pagan. Of course, that's the whole idea. Come in and I'll make us some iced tea and then I promise I'll let you go."

Emily came into the room and sat down tentatively on the sofa. Elvis leaped up to settle beside her. Lulu went into the kitchen to make the tea, and Emily and Elvis sat listening to the night sounds of the summer Lowcountry: the dissonant song of the katydids off in the live oaks, the stealthy scramblings of some small creature in the cordgrass on the marsh, the yip of a restless puppy in the kennels, the all-swallowing silence. There was no moon, but the stars burned hot and huge and near. The sky seemed lower than it usually did; it seemed to lean down to look into the windows of Lulu Foxworth's room. Emily almost squirmed under the weight of it. She did not know if she could live in this room. Even while it soothed you, it asked everything of you.

Lulu came out with iced tea on a tole tray.

"So what's the verdict?" she said. "Do you approve of my lair?"

"Yes. It's really unusual," Emily said politely. In point of fact, she had no idea if she liked the room or not, just that she would see it in her mind's eye forever.

There was a small silence as they drank their tea, and then Emily said, "Where's all that stuff your folks brought out here? It looked like enough to furnish a whole house."

"Most of it's downstairs in that space your father said he might make into a living room. I told my mother that I didn't want it, but she hears what she wants to hear, and that's that. So I just moved most of it down there. I'll get somebody to move it out when your dad needs the space."

"You moved all that stuff by yourself?"

"Yes. I'm a lot stronger than I look right now, Emily. I was on the varsity field hockey team at school my first two years there."

Debutantes could play rowdy sweaty contact sports, too. Emily snapped the knowledge into the grid of Lulu lore she was accumulating.

"I don't think your mother's going to like it very much," she said.

"I know damned well she isn't. But this is my place, not hers. It's the first one I've ever had that suited *me,* and not the vapory lady of some eighteenth-century manor."

"Wouldn't your mother have bought you new furniture if you wanted it?" Emily said. In her world, if you disliked what you had, you bought new—if you could afford it. That the Sweetwater Plantation house was sparsely furnished with peeling old things only meant that the Parmenters couldn't afford new. She had never questioned the veracity of that.

"Well, downtown you don't buy your furniture," Lulu said, grinning. "You *have* your furniture."

They drank tea again in silence, and then Lulu said, "Listen, Emily, I know you saw Elvis in here with me this afternoon. I just plain went and got him. I was hurting very badly, and I needed something to hold onto. The puppies aren't people enough yet, and I couldn't impose on you all. But Elvis just feels so . . . permanent."

"I know," Emily said. The absurdity of speaking of her dog as if he were a human being was not lost on her, but it did not seem to matter here.

"But I shouldn't have done it," Lulu said. "I hurt you, and I really didn't mean that. I want you to know that he's your dog to the core. He whined and looked at the door when you came up. He didn't leave me, but he wanted to. When I finally was . . . better again, he was out the door like a shot, back to you."

Emily scratched Elvis's ears, and he shifted position, but did not wake.

"Are you really sick?" she asked Lulu. She had never spoken to anyone as intimately as she was doing now, except Buddy, of course. This was something else to ponder when she was alone.

"In a way, yes, I am," Lulu said. Her face was in shadow, and she did not look at Emily.

"Then why aren't you at home with your folks? I don't think we can take care of you right if you're really, truly sick."

"Only you all can," Lulu said. "You all and the dogs and this room and this place. It's not like *sick* sick, with fever and germs. My folks would only make it worse. They wouldn't mean to, but they would. As I said, my mother hears only what she wants to hear. If I tried to tell her what was really wrong with me, she'd just say I was tired and needed a little rest. It's what she *did* say, as a matter of fact. So I knew I'd have to get myself well, and when I came here and saw the dogs, I knew that if I could just get here, I could maybe heal myself. And I think perhaps I can. Elvis was a big help today. You all were, tonight."

Emily said nothing. Huge questions hung in the air between them, but she could not bring herself to ask them. This was painful and frightening; adult territory. I am not ready to know this stuff, she thought resentfully. I'm not old enough.

As if she had read Emily's thoughts, Lulu sighed and scrubbed her face with her hands and straightened up on the sofa.

"This is not fair to you, and I'm not going to do it. Whatever is ailing me is my problem; I don't want any of you to feel like you have to do something about me. I promise I'm not nuts, or dangerous, or anything. I'm not going to come howling up your stairs with a butcher knife—"

The image was so awful that Emily winced and Lulu laughed and brushed the tangled red hair off her face.

"To put it in a nutshell, so you won't be scared of me, I just got myself too deep into things I couldn't do anything about," Lulu said. "I've never really felt like I belonged in the Charleston my family has lived in back to Adam, although it's so beautiful and seductive that it just takes your breath away sometimes. But I did the walk-through so well that nobody realized that, not even me, sometimes. And then I went off to Randolph Macon, but that was Mother's choice, too, and from the first it didn't fit. I'd wanted to go to Bennington, in Vermont; they let you pretty much choose your own structure, I'd heard. But of course my mother almost had a hissy-fit. It was just easier to go on to Randolph Macon. And there's a lot about it I loved, and still do, but it was like Charleston; it didn't fit me naturally. So I got myself into every activity I could find so I didn't have to think about it, and got so strung out and tired and felt so trapped in it all, that I couldn't seem to see one day ahead. And then, there was the famous debutante season looming out there, and . . . one day I just started crying and couldn't stop. My mother came and got me and took me to a discreet shrink the day after I got home, and he said basically that I had gotten myself into a no-win situation so I could avoid facing up to my life, instead of trying to take charge of it. God, I couldn't have changed a light bulb at that point, much less my life. He was just one more person who didn't *listen* to me."

"So what did you do?" Emily said, fascinated. Debutantes didn't always want to be that. Another chip of knowledge for the grid.

"I told him to go fuck himself, and went home and locked myself in my room, and wouldn't come out. That's when my parents finally saw that I wasn't just 'tired,' but they couldn't find anything else to call it, so they told everybody in town they'd been told I needed absolute quiet and rest, and that I'd come roaring back for the winter season, full of piss and vinegar. When she saw that the dogs got through to me when nothing else did, Mother had the idea about my boarding here for the summer. It solved everything. She told people that I'd gone to spend the summer with a nice plantation family and learn about their prize Boykins, a new passion of mine, and was happy as a dead pig in the sunshine. I just let her do it. I didn't care what she told them, as long as I could get here. I knew I'd die back home. And I knew that here, maybe I could learn to live."

She fell silent, and Emily simply looked at her. This was more than any adult in her life had ever offered her. More intimate, more complex. More demanding. She didn't know how she should respond. Everything Lulu said rang true, but somehow Emily thought there had to be more. Lulu's face when she had come upon her that afternoon had looked . . . shattered. Despairing. Terrified. That face did not seem to Emily to belong to someone saving herself. She thought of a reproduction of a painting Buddy had once showed her, in an art book. It was called *The Scream,* by some Scandinavian artist, and it had utterly terrified Emily. What if, one day, she herself would come to feel that way? She knew that it would kill her.

Lulu had looked like that.

"Well, I hope you get better soon," she said faintly and inanely, and Lulu laughed again and gave her a small hug around the shoulders.

"I will. Don't give all this babbling another thought. This is the best place I could possibly be right now, and you and Elvis are a big part of it. All of you are. It's going to work out fine. But maybe, if I get to feeling really low again, I could borrow Elvis for a few hours or a night?"

Suddenly Emily felt calm, centered, powerful—the recipient of mysteries, the granter of boons.

"Sure," she said. "Just let me know. Only sometimes I need him too, and we'd have to work out a schedule. In case you hadn't noticed, my father is just about killing me."

Lulu nodded. "They will do it, won't they? Your dad seems nice, though. Steady. Just so steady. . . ."

"He's steady all right," Emily snapped. Walter Parmenter was to be accorded no acclaim. "There's only one way, and that's his way, and he doesn't any more hear what I say than your parents do. There are two things that matter more to him than anything or anybody, and that's the dogs and his great ambition. More than anything in the world he wants to be a part of this fancy plantation society of y'all's, and he thinks the dogs are going to get him there. He's over the moon that you're here this summer; he thinks it means that he's gotten in."

"God, why does he want that?" Lulu said fervently. "This is so much *realer*—"

"He wants to make me a debutante, too," Emily rushed on. She was in full spate now. "Can you imagine anything worse?"

And then she stopped, mortified. That life was going to be Lulu's very soon.

"It's okay," Lulu said. "Not all debutantes are like . . . you think they are. I actually know some who work in the migrant camps and volunteer their summers in Haiti or some other place just as desperate and awful. Lots of things like that."

"You could do that," Emily said. "You really don't have to do the normal debutante thing, whatever that is. . . ."

"Emily, I'm just too fragile right now," Lulu said softly. "Puppies are about all I can manage. It feels really good to be working at something I care about, though. I was afraid I never would again."

There was more, of course, something terrible; Emily already knew this. She also knew she would never ask. No matter what

Lulu thought about her being strong, she could not bear the weight of whatever it was that pulled Lulu's mouth into that silent scream she had seen. Suddenly she was desperate to be back in her own room watching *Stargate* and eating potato chips and cuddling up to Elvis.

"So do you think you'll need Elvis tonight?" she said politely.

"No, I don't think so. Tonight has been good therapy for me. You all go on back and jump in bed and for goodness sake, don't *worry* about me. I shouldn't have dumped all this on you. Poor Elvis. He should hang out his shingle."

Emily did not turn off her bedside lamp until much later. She could see no lights burning in Lulu's apartment, and Elvis slept peacefully beside her, sighing and wriggling occasionally, snuggling closer. He smelled sweetly of sun and dog.

"What strange stuff," Emily whispered to him as she turned over to find the hollow where she would sleep that night.

She did not dream, and he did not move, and the next morning, cool and bright for once, nothing seemed strange and she felt grown-up and competent and not at all surprised that she had a new friend, as vivid and fabulous as a unicorn, or a roc, who had come willingly to stay for a while in her barn.

9

All through late July, Lulu came to the farmhouse frequently for dinner. There was no
set schedule, though Walter Parmenter at-
tempted to establish one. Whenever he did,
Lulu would smile politely and say that she
wouldn't dream of imposing such an inflex-
ible routine on the entire family, and that
sometimes she simply needed a very early
supper and bed.

"And you needn't worry about cooking
extra for me," she said. "It's treat enough for
me just to sit with you and swap stories. I
really don't eat very much."

She obviously didn't; though she was far
more animated now, and there was a wash
of healthy new color over her fading tan,
Lulu was still as slender as a willow switch.

Her cheekbones and collarbones still stood out like bas-relief under the silky skin, and when she wore cropped T-shirts you could still count her ribs. Her eyes still had their febrile fire-blue glitter sometimes, and wire-fine trembling, though abating, still occasionally gripped her hands.

Walter worried that she was not getting enough to eat, and had Cleta take out plates of hot biscuits and ham or, if it was lunchtime, hearty sandwiches on homemade bread, with Cleta's own rich mayonnaise. Hardly a day passed that pies or cakes from Cleta's kitchen did not find their way out to the barn. Finally Lulu sweetly declared a moratorium on the largesse.

"You're a better cook than anyone I've ever met," she said to Cleta, "but the doctor says it'll be a while yet before my appetite really comes back, and it's just a shame to waste all this. Save it for the day when I'll clean you out of the kitchen and beg for more."

"She don't need food," Cleta said darkly to Jenny one afternoon when she came in from summer school. "Somethin' eatin' that chile up from the inside. It ain't food she needs. She hungry for something else."

"I'll talk to Walter about letting up on the food," Jenny said. "She certainly eats enough when she comes to dinner. I agree with you that something else is chewing on her, though."

"Y'all don't need to go pokin' around to see what it is," Cleta said, jamming on the battered old man's straw fedora that was her summer signature. " 'Specially Emily don't. Lulu a sweet chile, but she carryin' around some kind of germ that look to me like it catchin'."

"It's not that kind of illness, I don't think," Jenny said. "I think she really is getting over being so tired, and having the flu, and then there's probably some kind of trauma we don't know about, maybe family. She needs the peace and quiet, and I think she's beginning to need some company, too. I like it when she comes to us for dinner. And it makes Emily happy."

"She need a lot more than that. She need almos' everything anybody got. We needs to look after Emily."

"Emily's happier than I've seen her in a long time, Cleta," Jenny Raiford said. "And besides, I do look after her. That's what I'm here for."

Cleta's bottom lip went out.

"Folks don't always see what under their noses," she said, shutting the screen door behind her. Jenny stood looking after her. In the afternoon stillness, she could hear the dogs being exercised barking joyfully from the ring, and over it the sound of Lulu and Emily laughing. The small frown between her brows, that had first come on the day that Lulu did, appeared again. It had its own groove now.

But it was hard to worry; when Lulu was at their table, laughter beat in the air like birds' wings. Lulu still spun her wry, glittering tales of downtown Charleston, but now, occasionally, Walter Parmenter would proffer, clumsily, a tale of his own, and everyone would laugh—dutifully, for he was not a natural spinner of tales and never would be, but at least he tried. Even Walt Junior and Carter would sometimes chime in with some highly embroidered account of their own Herculean journeys through adolescence, heavily freighted with allusions to conquests and sexual prowess. They were dropped before Lulu like dead rabbits, Emily thought in embarrassment, but Lulu only smiled and nodded with interest, and asked for more.

Debutantes have incredible manners, went into Emily's grid.

July at the Parmenter dinner table was a time out of time after Lulu Foxworth came.

August dropped down over the Lowcountry like a soaking wool blanket, without wind or rain, smothering, relentless. The puppies and their mothers had to be moved out of their nests in the barn and into makeshift kennels made of wire netting and canvas outside in the deep shade at the edge of the woods. Emily and Lulu got up at daybreak to train the older ones in what cool there might be, and went several times daily to freshen water and sometimes spray mothers and babies with a fine mist from the hose. The older dogs were exercised at sundown, and Walt Junior and Carter, grumbling and dripping sweat in cutoffs and sleeveless T-shirts, took the intermediate Boykins for training to a long, flat field just above the cordgrass beside the river, cleared and leveled for the purpose. Most afternoons boys and dogs came home damp and smelling of river water. Swimming with the dogs was strictly forbidden, but Walter did not chastise his sons. Emily and Lulu sometimes turned the hoses on themselves and Elvis before going in to bathe and dress, but they had not been swimming yet. Lulu always demurred, pleasantly. Emily thought that she probably did not want to appear half-naked on the dock with the twins panting after her.

A day came in the stunned white procession of days when the sun boiled down with such coppery savagery and the air thickened to such a lung-swamping soup that Walter told Lulu and Emily to take the day off.

"I think it would kill the puppies to move around in this heat," he said. "We'll pick up again when it cools off a little."

"I don't guess it occurred to him that it would kill us, too," Emily said sourly.

"What difference does it make? We're still off," Lulu said. "Want to spend the afternoon up at my place with some of the littlest ones and Elvis and the air conditioner on high? I've got a video of *Seabiscuit.*"

"I didn't know you had a TV," Emily said in surprise.

"It's in the closet. But I can roll it out," Lulu said. "Would you like that?"

"What's *Seabiscuit*?"

"Emily, you really are clueless," Lulu laughed. "It's a wonderful movie about this little loser horse who becomes a great champion. Everybody loves it."

Emily looked over at Elvis. He groaned and got up and slumped into the damp splotch the hose always left. Emily thought, not for the first time, that a thick, satiny coat of blazing curls would be anathema on a day like this. She grinned at Lulu.

"We could make a movie like that about Elvis, and call it *Dogbiscuit*."

Lulu laughed appreciatively.

"That's really funny," she said. "Now where did that come from?"

"I don't know," Emily said.

"Yes, you do," said Buddy from down deep. Emily smiled. Buddy had been silent for a long time.

"I've got a better idea," Emily said. "Let's get a picnic lunch and I'll take you over to Sweetwater Creek and we can swim there. There might be something really wonderful over there, too, depending on the tide. It needs to be lower than now."

"What?"

"Show you," Emily said, and went to beg

sandwiches and fresh peaches and iced tea from Cleta.

They cut away from the house and the river, across the peninsula on which Sweetwater Plantation rode. The open field that Walter let grow wild so that they could train some of the upland hunters was scorched to fawn stubble, so still that not even the great vaulting grasshoppers took off on their dizzying flights. Swarms of droning midges seemed the only other living things. Emily, leading the way, thought that they could just about reach the edge of the strip of maritime forest that bordered Sweetwater Creek before they simply dropped in their tracks and died. Beside her Elvis trotted steadily, but his head was down and his tongue dripped sweat. Emily could not remember a day like this.

"We should have brought hats," she said, looking back at Lulu. Lulu's face was flushed deep red, and her breath came in short gasps.

"Just ahead it will get better," Emily said, and it did. When they entered the fringe of the live oak and palmetto forest, the searing burn went abruptly out of the air, though the fathomless, sucking wetness remained. The little path that ran through the trees to the creek was slightly overgrown now with the matted ghosts of sweet grass, and the sodden leaf mold that bordered it looked undisturbed.

Emily had not been to the creek since when? Last Thanksgiving eve. A lifetime ago, she thought. The whole world had been different then. Then, she had stumbled home in fast-falling purple darkness, Elvis ahead of her, her heart flaming with anger and grief. She remembered how his coat had suddenly ignited to fire when he reached the moonlit field, and the fierce wash of love she had felt at the sight of his red curls. Then, she did not know why. Now she did. Her mother. Her mother's hair burning in the light of the chandelier as she left Sweetwater forever.

Was it better to know?

"Yes," said her mind.

"No," said her heart.

But now there was Lulu, and a different kind of knowing, and slowly, slowly it was buoying her heart back into life.

The path was thick with silence and heat. The creatures who came out to sing and warble and click and splash and chirr and pop were somnolent, buried deep in mud or silent in the deepest shade, or drifting at the bottom of the cool, deep holes. The tide was running toward low; Emily knew that in the afternoon when it turned, a little wind would come ghosting through the trees and the marsh and creek world would resume its orbit around the sun. But now forest and the little mud bluff that bordered the water were totally stopped and still, a spell-cast, sleeping world.

They came out of the canopy of oak and palmetto and stood on the bank and stared down at Sweetwater Creek. It hardly seemed to move, but Emily knew that down deep it did, following the heartbeat of the great tides from the distant Gulf Stream. It washed only halfway up its banks, so that the slick gray mud on either side was visible beneath the beginning of the great prairie of cordgrass that swept off to the horizon. At full tide the marsh was an unbroken sea of undulating green, broken only by glints of deep blue where small tributaries snaked, seeming to stretch to the end of the earth but in truth reaching only to the far-distant line of trees that meant the beginning of rural life, along Highway 17. At half-tide, like

this, you could see the homes of the creatures who lived here: the thousands of
small, inset holes where the fiddler crabs
lived; the sharp-fanged oyster beds on the
banks; the darker water that meant shrimp
holes; the low-hanging branches and fallen
trees where turtles sunned and great, thick
snakes half-slept, waiting. But the citizens
of the marsh and creek were nowhere to be
seen.

"Nobody's home," Lulu said, dropping
down onto the grassy edge of the near bank
and brushing sweat out of her eyes.

"They will be," Emily said. She sat down,
too, and Elvis flopped beside her. He looked
longingly at the water.

"In a minute," Emily said silently to him.

"If we're going to swim, we ought to do it
now," Emily said. "In a little while it'll be too
shallow."

"You swim in that?" Lulu said. "It looks
filthy. And you'd mire down in pluff mud to
your butt. I'm not wading in pluff mud; I
don't care if I die of heat right now. And I
may. Besides, you'd stink like the creek for
days."

Emily sniffed. She was used to the rich,
clotted, algae-thick smell, and that of all the

other creatures that had lived and died in Sweetwater Creek, and underneath it all the sweet stink of anaerobic mud three feet deep. It was the breath of the living creek.

"We can shower when we get home. And it's not all shallow; see that patch of darker water down the creek a little ways? It's a shrimp hole; I've never felt the bottom of it, even at low tide. It's a lot cooler than here, and it's pretty big. If you stay in the cool you'll never touch the mud."

"But what is that stuff in it?" Lulu said in true horror. "The water's so thick and gray you can't even see two inches into it. Who knows what's in there? And it looks so blue from a distance."

"It's not dirt," Emily said. "It's things alive. This marsh is the most alive place on earth, inch for inch. If you looked at a glassful of this water you'd see a million things wriggling around in it. If you looked at it under a microscope they'd look like dragons and monsters. None of them are big enough to hurt you, though. You'd never even feel them."

"How do you know?"

"Well, I've been swimming here a long

time. And I *have* looked at the water under a microscope. It's really something."

"Who showed you all that?" Lulu said.

"My . . . somebody I used to know," Emily said. She wasn't going to introduce Buddy to Lulu. Not yet. Maybe not ever. You had to have *something* that was all your own.

"How do you get in it without clumping through the mud?" Lulu said.

"I go out along that dead tree trunk; it reaches right out over the hole. You just slide on in from that."

The sides and bottom of the oak were thick with barnacles, dead and living. A handful of fiddlers waved their gigantic, cartoon-like red front claws at the very end of it.

"God," Lulu said faintly. "You can't tell me you couldn't feel those crabs."

Emily clapped her hands and the fiddlers faded away as if they had never been there.

"They're not about to come out until we're gone. Nothing else will, either. There's a pair of otters who play around this bank, but they're gone if you make a move. All you have to watch for is snakes, and I don't see any today. I've looked."

Lulu was silent for a long moment. Then

she said, grimly, "Okay. I'd rather die anyway than stay this hot another minute."

And she stood up and shucked off her
shorts and halter top and stood stark naked
on the bank, breathing deeply, and then
picked her way out the length of the oak
and dropped into the water. Emily stared after her. She had never seen a grown woman
naked before. The only breasts and pubic
hair she had ever seen were her own, and
then only through soapy, undulating bath-
water. Lulu Foxworth looked . . . nakeder,
somehow, than Emily had imagined any un-
clothed human could look. The narrow
white strips where her swimsuit had hidden
her body seemed to magnify the tight,
round buttocks and the silvery bush of hair
at the V of her legs, and her nipples were so
dark in the full whiteness of her breasts that
they were like eyes. Emily felt a red tide of
embarrassment surge into her cheeks and
neck.

Lulu's head popped out of the water, gilt
hair darkened and plastered to her narrow,
beautiful skull. Her eyes were closed in ec-
stasy.

"Oh, God, it's heaven," she called.

"You're right, it's wonderfully cool. I don't care what's in it. Aren't you coming in?"

Emily stepped out of her shorts and T-shirt, slowly and reluctantly. She wore her tank suit underneath it, faded red-gray with years and creek water. Still, she automatically shielded her breasts with her hands. They were, she knew, spilling out of the tank suit like overripe fruit.

"Oh, for God's sake, Emily, take that awful thing off and get on in here," Lulu snorted. "You think I've never seen a naked girl before? Nobody wears clothes at Randolph Macon, not when they don't have to. You've never seen so many women walking around naked after hours, when they get out of the showers."

Emily squeezed her eyes shut, and then, flushed all over with shame and daring, peeled down the tank suit and ran along the tree and jumped into the water so fast that it surged up her nose and she emerged coughing and sputtering. Lulu was right. Cool water on naked flesh was—transcendent.

"I bet you wear that thing even when you swim by yourself," Lulu teased her. "Throw it away, Emily. You have a wonderful body.

It's going to make you very happy one day. It's going to make several people happy, I'd bet. If you've got to have a bathing suit, get yourself a bikini and strut that stuff of yours. You'll be a beautiful woman. You already are. What good is that if you don't enjoy it?"

Emily was startled. So far her burgeoning body had gotten her nothing but Kenny Rouse touching himself, leering. She did not know how to think about it in any other context.

"Do you enjoy yours?" she wanted to ask Lulu. She would not, of course. Somehow she thought Lulu's thin, attenuated body had not made her happy in a long while. It looked . . . hungry. Starved.

From the bank, Elvis whined.

"Oh, poor baby," Emily said. "I should have told you you could."

To Lulu she said, "Watch."

Elvis broke into a joyous run and launched himself straight out from the bank, head up, legs folded, tail stiff, all his flags flying. He looked like a bronze torpedo cutting into the water. Once in with them, he paddled in circles and shook his head so that his curly ears flipped water and barked once, as if to say, "This is more like it."

"That was beautiful," Lulu breathed.

"That's how a good Boykin does it," Emily said proudly. "Not all spaniels can. Lots of them just flush, but some are born retrievers, too. Elvis is."

Presently they climbed out onto the tree and picked their way back to the little bluff. Lulu did not dress, simply spread her clothes out on the ground and flopped down on them. After a moment, Emily did, too. At first she was miserably aware of her nakedness, but before long the slumberous heat and the silence and the smell of the creek seeped into her body, cell by cell, and she turned over on her back and let the heat wash her down into rocking water sleep.

"So what's this great thing you were going to show me?" Lulu said. They had waked and dressed and eaten their lunch. The creek had fallen until it was only a ribbon of water, perhaps four feet wide and three deep, between gray, slick banks, with the stains of the holes still dark, deep.

"I think . . . right around that bend down there," Emily said, grinning. She knew today was the right day. The widening mud beach

beneath the bluff was wet and deeply furrowed.

"What . . . ?"

"Shhhh," Emily said. "Listen."

Under the profound afternoon silence
they became aware of a tiny, rhythmic
splashing, almost felt rather than heard, at
the very edges of the water. The last stalks
of the spartina were out of water now. The
splashing segued into a continual churning,
as pervasive and subliminal as the heat
song of the cicadas and midges. Elvis lifted
his head and cocked it toward the creek,
and Lulu looked at Emily.

"What's that?"

"Come see," Emily said, and they got to
their feet and went to peer over the edge of
the bluff, down onto the mud beach and
into the water.

"Lord, what's that?" Lulu breathed.

Tight schools of small silver fish clung to
the banks, churning at its edges as if trying
to crawl out onto it. The sun glinted crazily
off their backs. Several large gulls and a
snowy egret stood silently on the bank
above them, motionless.

"They're mullet," Emily said. "Bait fish."

"They sure do look nervous," Lulu said.

"So would you. Listen, now," Emily whispered.

They heard a strange, high clicking, almost inaudible, from around the bend of the
creek, and then a long, silver projectile
ghosted into sight. Two or three followed,
silent and stealthy as partly submerged
submarines. In an eyeblink there were half a
dozen. Sleek, wet, gray and white, large
eyes set wide and benign on either side of
slim, pointed noses, smiling sweet, playful
Disney smiles, the dolphins came into the
creek.

"What . . . ?" Lulu began again, but Emily
made a sharp gesture and she fell silent.

The lead dolphin circled back to the pod,
and a strange, sonic blast shattered the air,
and the pack began to compress the school
of mullet into tight balls, pinned firmly to the
shore. The dolphins bobbed their sleek
heads just above the surface of the water,
eyes on the squirming ball of silver on the
bank, and then, with precision timing,
rushed the mud shore, roiling up a large
wave that carried both bait fish and dolphins out of the water and onto the mud.
The thrashing chaos was enormous, dizzying; silver water flashed and flew. When the

wave receded, the mullet lay high on the mud bank, wriggling frantically, and the six dolphins, completely out of the water, tails and all, thrashed toward their prey. They lay packed together on the beach, on their right sides, as precise and choreographed as a chorus line, and snared their flapping prey in smiling jaws. Above them the birds swooped down for their free lunch. After the dolphins had fed, as if on signal, the pod thrashed its way back into the water with dorsal fins and tails and vanished around the bend from where they had come. What mullet they left fell to the birds. In another moment the creek was as silent as it had been before.

The whole ballet of hunters and hunted had lasted scarcely five minutes. Lulu and Emily did not move for several more minutes after the dolphins were gone. Then Lulu turned to Emily, her face luminous, lips parted, tear tracks on her brown cheeks.

"Oh, my God," she breathed. "That was just . . . magical. It was unearthly. What are they? How often do they do that? Who taught them? How did you know they were coming?"

"They come in the late summer and fall,"

Emily said, enjoying her new role as tutor to Lulu Foxworth. "They may do it once or twice a day, or sometimes a lot more. I guess it depends on how many mullet are around. They come back year after year to the same place on the creek; it's kind of a family thing. These same guys have probably been coming to Sweetwater all their lives, and their ancestors before them. There are other pods on other creeks along the coast, but they don't go out of the Lowcountry except maybe into Georgia, a little."

"They came right out of the water! Out of the ocean and up on a creek bank!"

"Yeah," Emily said. "At just this spot, and they'll do it almost every day for a couple of months, and then you won't see them again until next August. But they always come, and they're always the same pods. Sometimes I think it's a game they play."

"You knew they'd be here? How did you know that?"

"Well, I've been coming to watch them for a lot of years," Emily said. "And I knew they'd be here because the skids were smooth and shiny and fresh. And there are a lot of them. It means they've been doing this a lot this summer. Some years there are just a few skids, kind of dry and old. This is a good year."

"Will they come again today?"

"Probably. But I don't like to hang over the bank too long, watching. I think it must spook them. You wouldn't want people watching you eat all the time, would you?"

"No," Lulu said. "Let's go home. I think it's magic enough just to have seen them, and to know they're down here doing that . . . wonderful ballet, over and over. I wouldn't ever want to get used to that."

They turned away and walked slowly along the deep-shaded tunnel of the path through the palmettos and live oaks, toward the edge of the burning field and home.

After a long silence, Lulu, trudging behind Emily, said, "Elvis doesn't bark at them?"

"No. For some reason he never has."

"Elvis knows magic when he sees it," Lulu said. And then, "I wish I were Vivienne. The Lady of the Lake. Do you know who that is?"

"No. Should I?"

"Yes, you should. Vivienne was Merlin's lover in the stories about King Arthur. She beguiled him into an enchanted cave by the sea, or maybe it was a lake, and they never,

ever left again. I wish I never had to leave here, this creek, this river, this water. You're lucky. You are Vivienne, in a way. You don't have to leave it, not yet. And when you do, you can always come back. Though you'll do really well out there. You have a very good mind, Emily."

"Out there?"

Lulu gestured vaguely to the north, where the world lay, and chaos.

"Out in the world. You'll have to go some day; all of us do. It's the only way we get knowledge. You can have all the brains in the world and still not have knowledge."

"What if I don't like what I find out there?" Emily said, thinking but not saying that Lulu herself had opted out of the world and appeared to have no wish to go back.

"Well, as I said, you can always come back. But first you have to go."

"Well, I'm not going," Emily said mulishly. "I'm staying right here. I want to run this farm one day. Daddy won't always be around, and Carter and Walt aren't going to stick around one minute after graduation. Daddy may think they are, but they're not. I think they're hot to see the great world. I think they'll head straight for Myrtle Beach."

Lulu laughed.

"I hope they get a little farther than that. Believe it or not, there's a good bit of world beyond Myrtle Beach. But even if you do end up running the farm, you'll need the kind of knowledge that you can only get out there. In the world."

"What for? I already know almost all there is to know about dogs."

"Well, how to manage a farm like a business, for one thing. The economics of it. And . . . public relations, I guess. It's no good to have these fabulous dogs if nobody knows about them. And like it or not, how to move in the world downtown, because that's where you'll sell most of them. And English literature, above all. It gives you an unshakable sense of your place in the world. The bad of it, because you have to know how to avoid it or beat it. And the good. . . ."

She paused for a moment, and then said softly, "If love wants you; if you've been melted down to stars, / You will love with lungs and gills, with warm blood and cold . . ."

She did not speak again for a long moment. Watching her, Emily felt her skin burn and a great, warm tide of something secret start up in her.

"What's that?" she said. "Who said that?"

"A poet I love. A woman named Anne Michaels. I read her first at school, and I've carried her poems around with me ever since. She knows everything about being human in the world. You should read her, Emily. She's a great start for the knowing."

"My brother used to do that," Emily said, the words flowing unstoppably out of her like too-long-bound lava.

"Do what?" Lulu smiled at her.

"Quote poetry. We used to read it together." She stopped and bit her lip, but it was too late.

"Your brother? Really? Which one?"

Lulu sounded astonished. Emily grinned, unwillingly. She tried to imagine Carter or Walt reading poetry, or quoting it, and the grin became a giggle. Then the pain, long buried, pushed its way up.

"No. My brother Buddy. He . . . died. He was seven years older than me."

"Oh, Emily," Lulu whispered. "I'm so sorry. Was he sick?"

"Yes," Emily said, briefly and formally. In her mind's eye the glinting Purdey looped forever into the air and down the deep curve of the river. She knew she would never speak of it to Lulu.

"You must miss him very much. So what do you read now?"

"I don't read," Emily muttered.

"Why on earth not?"

"There just doesn't seem to be any reason to."

"That's one of the great things about reading," Lulu said. "You don't need a reason to do it. I'd die if I couldn't read."

"I'd die if I did," Emily thought.

A small breeze, just an exhalation, really, stirred the moss on the live oaks and the damp hair on the back of Emily's neck. The tide had turned. The walk back to the house would still be hot, but not the breath-sucking blast they had come to Sweetwater Creek in. Behind her, Emily heard Lulu give a small sigh.

They reached the fringe of the stubbled field, and Elvis stopped dead and stared into the deep shade of the oaks and the palmettos to their right. They stopped, too. Elvis did not growl; he merely waited, but Emily knew that something or someone was coming. She laid her hand lightly on his head.

Out of the black-green shade a man and a dog moved, so silently that you felt the slight displacement in the air before you heard or saw them. The man and dog stopped. Emily and Lulu and Elvis stopped, too.

He was old, a very old man, so thin and stooped and sun-darkened that he might have been a dead, twisted vine of Low-country wisteria or a gnarled live oak limb. His face was furrowed like dark plowed earth, but his eyes, sunk deep into the fur-rows, burned as bright as peat coals. He wore faded denim overalls and a long-sleeved work shirt. The shirt was not stained with sweat, even in the savage heat. Broken over his arm was a shotgun, obvi-ously old and cheap, but gleaming with wax and tung oil.

The old dog, a black Labrador with an apron of matronly fat and a pure white muz-zle, was damp and smelled powerfully of wet dog and creek. Emily wondered if the dog was strong enough to swim; before she sat down beside her master, Emily saw the limp of arthritis and the slight dragging of the back legs that meant hip displasia. There was nothing to fear from either of them, she knew, and yet her heart thumped faster. They might have been the desiccated, dying spirits of the parched marsh.

Elvis trotted up to the old dog and put his muzzle to her frosted one, and wagged his stumpy tail. The old dog grinned, putting out a lolling tongue, and let her face be scoured by Elvis's pink one. She groaned slightly with pleasure.

Behind her, Lulu said, "Having any luck? I see your dog's been in the creek. I hope she found something worth retrieving."

If they've been hunting, it's way out of season for anything but doves, and there sure aren't any on the creek. They're upland. And all our land is posted. I wonder if I should say something? Emily thought. And then, why? How many other hunts, in season or off, would this old man and his old dog have?

The old man looked past her at Lulu and cleared his throat, a sere, rasping sound.

"Naw. Ain't had no luck. Way too hot. I don't hunt no more, anyway. I just do this for the dog."

He tipped a nonexistent hat and they

crossed the path and faded into the woods on the other side. Elvis gave them a small yip of farewell and sat down and leaned his head against Emily's leg. Neither she nor Lulu spoke. When she looked back at Lulu, she saw that silent tears were rolling down her cheeks again. But she was smiling.

"You see why I never want to leave here? First ocean dolphins dancing on creek banks, and then this wonderful old man who cares more about his old dog than anything else on earth. How can you leave a place where people love dogs like that? What else in the world is as wonderful as that?"

"Well," Emily thought, suddenly and obscurely annoyed, "I do, too. What's so hot about that?"

But she said nothing. The old pair on the creek path in the dying of the day had moved her deeply, too.

"You will leave, though, won't you?" she said to Lulu as they approached the old house, shimmering in the still heat. "I mean, you said this was just for a while."

She wanted, suddenly, an answer from Lulu, but she was not sure what answer it was that she needed.

"Maybe I won't leave after all," Lulu said. "Maybe I'll just stay. And maybe I won't; maybe you'll leave, instead of running this farm. Maybe you'll marry and have the biggest house in Charleston. Maybe you'll live in Morocco and take lovers and be a legend. Maybe you'll run for president. People change, Emily. Other people change them."

"Nobody's going to change me," Emily said belligerently. Who the hell did Lulu Foxworth think she was, playing God with Emily's future?

"There's somebody you need to meet," Lulu said.

"Not if they think they're going to change me, I don't."

"She will. If she wants to, she will."

"Who?"

"My grandmother," Lulu said. She hugged Emily hard around the shoulders and went into the shabby cave of the barn stairs, and closed the door.

10

Walter was elated.

"Of course she'll go," he said to Lulu at dinner the next night. "Everybody in the Lowcountry knows about that party. I remember hearing about it even before I came to the farm. You're very nice to ask her. It's just the kind of thing I want her to know about."

Lulu smiled at him across the table. In the light from the tall ivory candles her face looked mysterious, totemic. They had begun to eat dinner in the big dining room sometime during the late summer. Emily had not thought to wonder why. It was surprisingly pleasant. Cleta and Jenny had polished and dusted and cleaned a century's worth of grime off the beautiful inlaid mantelpiece and the fireplace, and Jenny had brought out her silver plate and the candlesticks that Emily saw only at Thanksgiving and Christmas. She unpacked her mother's beautiful old Haviland china, too. Emily could hold it up to the light and see her fingers through it.

"It's beautiful," she said to Jenny when she first saw the china.

"It was your grandmother's, you know. I've always thought you should have it one day, but I had so few of Mother's things that I guess I was holding on to it. But it belongs here, in this room, I can see that. So it must stay here."

"That's more than generous of you, Jenny," Walter had said, smiling at her. "I've always wished Emily and the boys had more things like this around them. We set a fine table when Emily was very young, but I don't think she was old enough to remember. . . ."

His voice trailed off. Of the six people seated at Walter Parmenter's dinner table that evening, five knew that the silver and the china and most of the crystal had gone with beautiful Caroline Carter Parmenter to wherever it was that she went.

Jenny jumped in. "Tell us about the party, Lulu," she said, smiling across the table. "I think everybody has heard a different myth about it."

"Yeah," Walt Junior said, chewing fried chicken. "I heard somewhere that this old lady has an animal staked out—usually a deer—and blows its head off at midnight once a year. I'd hate to meet that old gal on a deer stand."

Walter looked at him darkly, and he reddened.

"Well, but there is an old lady, isn't there?" Carter chimed in. "And she does shoot the bejesus out of something. . . ."

Emily, mute with anger, saw her aunt wince in the candlelight, and thought briefly that Jenny Raiford was the only person on this plantation with whom she was not furious beyond words.

Lulu's smile widened.

"That old lady is my grandmother," she said, "and she's never shot a living thing in her life. Once a year, at midnight on her birthday, she gets out the old Purdey that's been in the family for a gazillion years and shoots straight up in the air. It's her birthday party."

"Why does she do that?" Walt said with interest. Emily, still silent, thought that the twins were perhaps the only members of the Parmenter family who did not shudder at the name "Purdey."

"Because it's her birthday. Because she loves the gun and the noise it makes. Because she can," Lulu said.

"And there's a big party to watch her do that?" Carter said, incredulously. In his world old ladies did not shoot off shotguns on their birthday, much less hold parties for them.

"There is a big party," Lulu said. "It's been held every year that I can remember, and way back before that. My grandfather Foxworth used to throw it for her, and when he died, my father kept on with it. Mother and Daddy do it at Maybud now. The only difference is that Grand doesn't come to her own party anymore. She stays out in the lodge where she lives and only lets a few people she especially likes come out and be with her when she shoots the gun. She says any fool can shoot off a shotgun in the Lowcountry and she's not about to be gawked at by five hundred of them when she does it. People listen for the gun, though, and when they hear it, there's a big toast and all the guests throw their glasses in the fireplace, just like at the Queen's birthday, and the party goes on until the wee hours, but Grand goes to bed. Some people are at Maybud the whole time without seeing her, if she doesn't choose to come out and say a few words."

"They throw the glasses at the fireplace?" Walt Junior obviously thought this was on a par with old ladies shooting shotguns at midnight—unimaginable. "How many do your folks have left?"

"Mama gets cheap ones from Wal-Mart," Lulu said, grinning broadly. She was obviously enjoying spinning this tale for them in the candlelight, one more shimmering offering for her hosts.

Emily was not enjoying any of it. She was furious with Lulu for asking her father in front of the whole table, before she had even asked Emily, if she might take Emily to the party. Emily could imagine pain or sadness from Lulu, but she had never imagined betrayal. And she was profoundly angry at her father and the boys, for their Uriah Heepish awe. She was determined not to go to the party, but now she would have to fight all of them, except Aunt Jenny. She kept her eyes on her plate, her stomach too twisted with rage to eat.

"She'll have to have a new dress, won't you, Emmybug?" her father chortled. He did not seem to notice her silence.

"Jenny will take you somewhere special to get a pretty one," he plowed on. "Maybe one of those big stores at the mall? Or, if you want to, I'll even spring for King Street. Maybe you'll go along, too, Lulu. You know better than anybody what a young girl should wear to her first big party."

"I'll be glad to," Lulu said, not looking at Emily. "But I'm sure Jenny would be better at that than me. I haven't been shopping in a coon's age."

Emily finally found her tongue, or the ghost of it.

"I'm not going to any mall and buy a new dress," she whispered. "I'm not going to any stupid party where an old lady shoots off a shotgun, either. I'm not going to any party, period. If anybody had bothered to ask me, I could have told them that."

She looked straight at Lulu, who smiled gently at her.

"You are going to the party, and you are

going to have a decent dress, and you are going to apologize to Lulu and thank her for her generosity," Walter Parmenter said in the tight voice he used when his children embarrassed him with their obstinance and ignorance, and threatened this new dream hovering just beyond his fingertips.

Emily got up and stumbled out of the room. Behind her she heard her father calling angrily after her, and Lulu saying, "It's okay. She's right. I should have asked her first. I know my grandmother would have a good deal to say to her, if she'd listen, and she'd love Emily, but I'm not going to push it. I'll talk to her in the morning. And if she means it about a new dress, I've got some stuff that would fit her, though it's not very fancy."

Emily stopped in the hallway outside the dining room and listened to the disposition of her fate. Her aunt Jenny said evenly, "It's a little much for a young girl who's never been to a big party. I don't think we should expect her to just move into a totally unfamiliar society at her age and with no notice. Maybe next year, if Lulu is still kind enough to ask her."

"Well, it's never too early to learn to be a

lady. She's going to go if I have to make her do it. She'll thank me afterward."

"How can you make her, if she's determined not to?" Jenny said softly.

"I'll think of something. I could always put that dog of hers in the kennels and leave him there until she changed her mind."

Emily ran up the stairs choking on sorrow and panic. She knew she would go to the party. She did not hear Jenny and Lulu both protesting fervently.

She climbed into bed, still in her cropped, flowered pants and matching tank top, and pulled the sheet over her head. She had thought she would cry, but the tears would not come. The pain in her heart was a dry one. Elvis got up off the rug beside her bed and jumped up beside her. He licked her hot, clenched face, and when she lifted the sheet, he crawled under and nestled against her side.

She did cry, then. "I had one friend, this summer," she wept into his curly neck, "and now I don't. I'll never speak to her again. I may have to work with her, but I don't have to talk to her. And she doesn't get to borrow you ever again. I need you now."

Against her cheek he groaned softly and

put his nose into her hair. When she woke the next morning, neither she nor Elvis had moved.

The first thing she saw was Lulu, sitting on the foot of her bed, hands dangling between her knees, head down, staring at the floor. Emily did not move, but somehow her wakening reached out to Lulu, and she turned her head and smiled at Emily. It was a small smile; tentative. Emily looked at her, but did not smile back.

"I guess you're pretty mad at me," Lulu said.

Emily said nothing.

"Well, I'd be mad, too," Lulu said. "I got you into something you'd rather die than do, and I didn't give you any choice in the matter. You can refuse to speak to me for a month, or whatever you need to do, but please hear me out."

Still, Emily said nothing and did not move. Beside her Elvis stretched mightily and yawned, and looked at Lulu and thumped his tail, but he did not leave Emily's side.

"Here's the thing," Lulu said, her voice so low that Emily had to strain to hear her words. "There's no way I can get out of going to that thing, and besides, I love Grand to death, and I wouldn't hurt her feelings for anything. I've spent every one of her birthdays with her since I can remember. But Emily, I cannot go to that house by myself. I *cannot.* Those people are the very ones who'd rather see a daughter or a son drown than admit there was anything wrong, like Mother, and I simply do not have it in me to make bright little excuses about where I am this summer, or when I'm coming home, or any of that. And alone, they'd swamp me, but if you were along, they'd back off, because none of them would think it was proper to interrogate me when a . . . someone they didn't know was with me, especially someone younger. So I ambushed you. I knew your father would make you go. And I really mean it when I said Grand could come to mean a lot to you. You ought to at least meet her."

She paused, and when Emily did not reply, she murmured, so quietly that Emily could hardly hear her, "Emily, please come. I need you."

"Why do you need me? Why not somebody who knows how to behave in a place like that, a big party like that? I don't want to meet all those fancy people. I don't even know how to talk to them. They'd think I was a swamp rat and you were slumming, and they'd be right. And I'm not going to any mall and buy any new society dress, either. Besides, how am I supposed to get to know your famous grandmother in the middle of a big hoohaw like that?"

Emily had started off heatedly, but by the time she was done talking her voice had faded. In her ears it was a childish whine. She shook her head angrily.

"I need you precisely because you're *not* like them," Lulu said urgently. "You're not like anybody I've known before. You're like . . . this place. You have the dogs in you, and the river, and the dolphins and . . . the way the wind sounds in the pines at night. And you've got those incredible stars in you, too. If you were with me it would be like carrying a piece of all this with me. A talisman. So I could remember what I have out here and not get caught up in all that again. I wouldn't survive that, Emily."

"If it's all that awful, I couldn't either," Emily shuddered. "How can you expect me to stand around in the middle of that all night if you can't?"

"Oh, God," Lulu said, leaning back and

smiling tiredly. "It's just a fucking party. That's all it is. Nobody will conjure up the living Satan or sacrifice a baby. In fact, they can be fun. I can remember that they were fun sometimes. Just not now."

"It's Elvis you need, not me," Emily said, but the white-hot anger was fading. How could you refuse to help this glorious crippled unicorn of a girl?

"I'd take him if I could," Lulu said. "If he'd promise to poop on the Aubusson. But it's you I need most. Will you just think about it? We don't even have to go to the big party, or at least you don't, and I could just drop in for a minute. Grand doesn't come to these things anymore. As I said, she only sees who she wants to see. I know she'd like you. We two could be the only people with her the whole time."

"Then why do we need to dress up?" Emily realized she was speaking as if the deed were done.

"I do it in case anybody from the party waylays me, and wonders why I look like a ragamuffin. And I do it for Grand. She says it's important to fly your flags no matter what. She likes to see me dressed up. And as for you, I think you'd just feel more com-

fortable in something a little dressier than
cutoffs. Besides, I'd like to give you a present. We'll find something that you really like,
and you can put it away for later, if you want
to, until you need it. Please let me do that.
Giving presents is one of the things I love
most in the world, and I haven't been able
to give any to you all this whole summer."

Emily could not seem to get her mind
around the notion of anyone wanting to give
her a present. No one ever had, except for
the obligatory offerings from her father and
Aunt Jenny at Christmas and her birthday.
Well, once Cleta had brought her a small
black baby doll with a kerchief around its
head; it was a long time ago, but Emily remembered. It was just after her mother had
left. Emily had loved the doll fiercely. She
did not know where it was now.

"Well . . . all right, then," she said ungra-
ciously, and then, at Lulu's smile, said,
"Thank you."

And the deed was, indeed, done.

In the week before the party Lulu burned,
crackled, shimmered, fizzed, radiated light
like a bonfire about to go out of control. At
dinner she spun such outrageous and scur-
rilous tales of downtown Charleston that

even Walter finally divined that she was making them up. By that time no one cared. There was more laughter in the old dining room in that one week, Emily thought, than there had been in this whole house in her lifetime. Watching Lulu across the table, face lit with candlelight and glee, hands weaving in and out of the shadows as she wove her stories, Emily suddenly remembered something Buddy had told her once, a tale about a woman . . . what was it?

"*A Thousand and One Nights*," Buddy said enigmatically, from deep inside Emily.

"Well, *that's* helpful," Emily thought back. "I don't know what you're talking about."

He was silent. Emily knew that once he was quiet, she could not lure him into a dialogue again. Buddy picked his moments.

She did remember though, finally. It was a night just before the party, and her nerves were strung tight. It had been one of Lulu's best nights; her pièce de rèsistance was the story of an impeccably groomed downtown matron who had sent out Christmas cards one year that featured herself buck naked, reclining on a chaise in the style of Goya's *Naked Maja*.

"Only she had waited a trifle too long,"

Lulu said. "If she was going to do it, she should have done it about five years earlier when her boobs—'scuse me, Walter—didn't rest on her stomach. Right after that she ran off and left her husband and children and joined a commune in Ohio. Nobody was really surprised. People just said, 'Oh, yes, her people were always a little funny.' Mother knew her at Charlotte Hall. She said she was always walking around the locker room after gym naked as a jaybird. Grand just says some people weren't born to wear clothes."

"What did the card say?" Emily asked.

"It said, 'God rest ye merry, gentlemen, let nothing you dismay,' " Lulu said grinning. "Half of Charleston figured they knew just which gentlemen she meant, but I doubt if anybody really did. People always say that."

Emily and Elvis were heading up to bed when Emily heard her aunt and Cleta, who had brought Robert and Wanda over to see Gloria's new puppies. In the kitchen the babies rolled on a folded quilt in a tangle of puppies, squealing blissfully. Jenny and Cleta stood at the bottom of the stairs, leaning on the banister, watching the babies and talking softly.

"Lulu was in rare form tonight, wasn't she?" Jenny said. "Did you hear that story about the lady who sent out the naked Christmas cards?"

"Naw. Heard everybody laughing all night, though. She sho' know how to tell a tale, don't she? She remind me of that Sherry woman who had to tell fancy stories every night or the king lop off her head."

"Who on earth . . . ? Oh, you mean Scheherazade. The wife of some Oriental king who was going to have her beheaded but kept her alive another night to hear the next one because her stories were so good. Why in the world would Lulu remind you of her?"

"Ain't you seen her face when she tell them stories, an' her eyes, lookin' around to see if y'all are laughin'? And them stories gets wilder and wilder every time she over here, almos' like something bad gon' happen to her if she don't please y'all."

"What bad thing could we possibly do to her even if we didn't like one of her stories?" Jenny Raiford said in honest puzzlement.

"Send her home," Cleta said briefly.

"Surely that's for her parents to decide," Jenny said. "Where did you hear about Scheherazade?"

"Buddy tol' me and Emily 'bout her one day. He said, 'Now there was a lady who knew how to look after herself.' "

She went into the kitchen to untangle the mass of puppies and babies, and Jenny stood looking after her. The small Lulu frown creased her forehead. At the top of the stairs Emily remembered.

It had been a gunmetal winter day; rain ticked against the windowpanes of Buddy's room, and the fire spat damply. It was not particularly cold, but it seemed so in the big, dim room, and Buddy and Emily and Elvis sat close by the fire. Buddy was wrapped in an old plaid blanket that he said was the proper tartan of Clan McClellan, to which he had deduced, after weeks of perusing a book called *The Clans and Plaids of Scotland,* the Parmenters rightly belonged. A cadet branch, but valid just the same, he said. After he died Emily had brought the filthy old blanket into her room and put it away in the top shelf of her closet. Sometimes, on the nights when Buddy had been silent for a long time and loneliness howled in her heart, she got the blanket out and wrapped herself in it and drifted off to sleep to the sound of skirling pipes and clashing claymores. She knew she would keep it always.

That day Cleta had come in with a pile of freshly folded laundry and stopped to listen to Buddy tell of Scheherazade and the tales of the Arabian Nights. Emily had forgotten, but now it came back: the rain and the fire and the empathetic terror and elation she felt with the young woman who knew that only her wit and imagination were keeping her alive.

What if you were just too tired one night? she had thought.

In her mind's eye she saw again Lulu at the dinner table, almost manic in her animation, totally absorbed in the tale she was spinning. Did she indeed look around at all of them to see if they were laughing? Emily had never noticed. Now she would. The notion of Lulu as Scheherazade was both unsettling and pitiable.

"What do you think? Does she remind you of Scheherazade?" she said to Buddy.

"Well, you thought of it first," he said. "Earlier tonight, when you couldn't quite remember who she reminded you of. Where do you think that came from? Jeez, Emily, do I have to spell everything out for you? Of course she's Scheherazade."

"Of course," Emily thought grumpily to him. "Of course you said it first. Like always. But what awful thing will happen to her if we don't like one of her stories?"

"You'd have to ask *her*," he said, and faded away down deep. Emily knew the conversation was over. But she thought about it for a long time after she and Elvis piled into her bed and turned off the light, and when she finally slept, the bizarre image of Lulu performing for her life followed her down.

Emily stood at the top of the staircase the next night, afraid to go down. At the bottom, Lulu and Walter and Jenny and the twins were ranged, waiting to see Cinderella off to the ball. Lulu had spent hours with her earlier, fussing with the dress and piling her hair this way and that, and brushing something rosy out of a little pot onto her cheeks with a soft, fat brush. Now there was nothing left but to take her quailing alien self downstairs for the first of the scrutinies she would face this night. The unaccustomed flush of makeup on her face, the strange weight of her piled-up curls felt as though they would both slide off if she moved her head suddenly. The tiny kitten heels on the new sandals threatened to topple her. If she could have turned and run, she would have done so. Elvis, for once, had pattered on down the stairs ahead of her, and she could not feel Buddy anywhere.

But in the ranks of upturned faces Lulu's shone with pleasure and approval. Emily knew that if she kept her eyes focused on Lulu's luminous face and Elvis's happy grin, she just might make it to the bottom without disgracing herself. She could worry about the actual party later. She could even, if she absolutely had to, simply refuse to go. In a state of white pique and terror, Emily started down.

There was a series of drawn breaths as she reached the landing, but no other sounds. Intent as she was on not stumbling in the new heels, she did not look up, but the silence smote her. She had expected at least some comment from someone, a few compliments even if they were forced. But not this breath-held silence. Never this. On the last step she froze and raised her head.

Lulu was smiling radiantly and nodding. The twins, Aunt Jenny, and her father were staring as if they had been turned to stone. Emily felt her hastily gulped dinner come up into her throat, and tears sting in her nose. What was the matter? Was Emily Parmenter dressed up for a party simply grotesque after all?

Walter wheeled and walked out of the foyer. After he left there was a small, ringing silence, and then Aunt Jenny breathed, "My God," and the twins chimed in with "God-damn!" and "Holy shit!" Lulu looked at them all perplexedly, and then back at Emily, whose eyes were shimmering with tears.

"You look absolutely beautiful," she said to Emily. "Just gorgeous." And to the others, "What is the matter with you all?"

"You look so much like your mother it's uncanny," Jenny Raiford said, smiling at last. "And you do look beautiful. Just . . . beautiful."

The twins smiled, too, tentatively.

"Shit, you might have been Mama coming down those stairs," Walt said. "I've seen her do it a thousand times. I never thought you looked like her, Emily, but you just . . . could be her."

"Yeah," Carter said. "She used to look like that on her way to parties and stuff. God, Emily, it's almost scary. Pretty, though," he added quickly. Emily had never had a compliment from either of the twins before. It added to the palpable strangeness of the night. She felt the tears begin to track down her cheeks through the peachy blush.

Emily turned to go back up the stairs. She felt Elvis close beside her, thrusting his muzzle into her hand. She heard the thumping of footsteps that meant the twins were retreating to the television den where their father had fled, scattering like hawk-chased chickens before her tears. She heard Aunt Jenny's voice, soft with pain for her pain.

"Emily," she said, "please don't run back up there. You look wonderful, beautiful. This is your night. I'll talk to your father. It's just that you look so much like your mother, and it's hard for him . . ."

Emily whirled around to look at her, blinded with tears.

"Well, then, he'll just have to trade me in for another model," she said, her voice thick. "Or put me in a convent or something. Because if I look like her now, what will I look like when I'm older? Will he still be leaving rooms and closing doors when he sees me?"

"Of course not," Jenny Raiford began. "He'll get used . . ."

But Emily had turned again and started up the stairs.

"NO!"

It was Lulu's voice, sharper and more commanding than she had ever heard it. She paused, but did not turn again.

"Don't you *dare* go sneaking off up there like a scared rabbit! You've got nothing to run from. If he thinks he does, that's his problem, not yours. Now get back down here and let me fix your face, and then we'll get out of here. And high time."

Lulu stood straight and tall, her hands clenched into fists, hanging straight down beside her. Her face was still, but two red spots flamed on her high cheekbones. Her eyes, narrowed, burned like a falcon's from under her straight brows. Emily came down the stairs and walked into Lulu's arms. Beside them, Jenny Raiford dropped her own outstretched arms. Elvis, wriggling with love, tried to nose his way between the two girls. There was not a sound in the foyer but the ticking of the old grandfather clock in the corner and Emily and Lulu's breathing.

Presently Lulu held Emily away from her and looked at her critically.

"Mascara's run and blush is streaked. Red nose, too. This is a job for Superdiva."

And she took Emily into the downstairs powder room and set about her with puff pots and brushes.

"Now," she said. "All fixed. Take a look."

Emily had refused to look in the mirror while she was dressing. Now, in the wavering, dark-flecked old shell-rimmed mirror she saw a girl she did not know, a girl with a tumble of gold-red curls piled high on her head, tendrils curling around her face. A girl with cheeks flushed bronze-pink from blush and tears, a girl with tilted cat's eyes and a soft mouth blooming with coral lip-gloss. A girl with a pointed chin and a long neck and smooth bare shoulders, her only adornment small pearl earrings and a single strand of creamy pearls. A girl who was going to a party.

She turned back to Lulu.

"I don't know who I am," she whispered. "I'm not me and I'm not her. I don't feel real."

"Get used to it," Lulu smiled behind her in the mirror. "That very pretty girl is your future. Now let's blow this taco joint."

They went out into the foyer again. Emily's heart was pounding with the inevitability of this night. Jenny still stood there, smiling slightly, and gave Emily a brief hug.

"You both look smashing," she said. "Now go and have a good time and remember everything so you can tell me about it."

Elvis whined, but stayed still, sitting beside Jenny.

Emily and Lulu went out into the warm, cricket-singing night.

Lulu had borrowed the truck for the trip to Maybud.

"Can't you get somebody to bring your car out here?" Emily had said, when the arrangement was made. "Or at least let the boys clean their car up and take it. The truck smells like dog and dog food."

"That's the point," Lulu had said. "If I've got to go to this thing, I'm taking the dogs with me for good luck."

And so they ground and rattled down the driveway and onto the pitted road through the oak and palmetto forest toward the highway that would ultimately take them to Lulu's family's plantation. Lulu drove the cumbersome truck as well as she did everything else, wrestling it through ruts and over roots with elegant assurance.

"Where'd you learn to drive a truck?" Emily said.

"There are a million of them at Maybud," Lulu said. "I always loved them. And a friend of mine had one that I used to drive a lot."

They reached the crumbling blacktop that would lead them to Highway 174 and thence deep into Edisto Island to the south of Sweetwater, where Maybud Plantation had stood in its sprawling gentility on a deep tidal tributary of the Dawhoo River since 1798. As the crow flew it seemed only a long stone's throw from Sweetwater, which looked across the water from Wadmalaw Island to Maybud's site on Edisto. But like so many Lowcountry venues, you had to drive many miles and wend your way down many back roads before you got there. Bridges were not a priority in this wild old backyard of the Ace Basin.

They said little as they drove through the deep velvet darkness of the August Lowcountry. Occasionally an insect committed spattering suicide on the windshield, and the red-eyed, dark shapes of who knew what wild night things scurried or loped across the road in front of them. But not until they turned onto the overgrown dirt road that led down to the water and Maybud did Emily speak.

"I'd have thought a big place like y'all's would have some kind of gate or sign," she said. "How do people know how to get here?"

"The people who come here know," Lulu said. There was something in her voice that Emily could not quite catch, a kind of cool flatness that could have been anything at all except pleasure at coming home.

The rutted road narrowed to a track that wound its way through vegetation so dense that it became a tunnel of black-green. Moss from great oaks brushed the truck; branches of shrubs and saplings whipped at it. The tunnel was lightless except where the headlights caught leaves. "Black as Egypt," Cleta would have said.

Emily fell silent again, her heart dragging heavily with apprehension. Presently she said, in a strangled voice that sounded thin and mewling in her own ears, "I don't want to do this, Lulu. I want to go home."

"Too late," Lulu said, and they rattled around a moss-shawled hummock and into a great cave of light.

11

Always afterward, Emily remembered the end of that journey as you would an epiphany, a revelation, a lasting dream.

The dirt track widened into a graveled allée of giant old live oaks, heavily shawled with moss, some of their branches resting on the ground. About halfway down strings of small white lights had been wound into the moss on each tree, making an otherworldly cocoon of light-misted moss that enveloped the truck as they rode on. Even farther down, the tree lights became tall torchières on either side of the drive, flickering in the small, soft wind. Behind them all lay the plantation house, shining in the dark of the woods like a great ship. Every window blazed with light; votive candles outlined the circular drive, and the formally trimmed boxwood around the house glowed like miniature Christmas trees. Lights traced strict, linear paths behind the house and the garden balustrades and terraces, leading, no doubt, to the river. Close around the house, paper lanterns had been hung in the lower branches of the sheltering oaks. Maybud Plantation was, on this night, a house made of light, shimmering in the dark woods like an enchanted castle out of Sir Thomas Malory, seeming to float in space.

Emily drew in an involuntary breath, and Lulu smiled.

"It cleans up pretty good, doesn't it?" she said. "On an ordinary day you can see the patches of brown in the grass, and the mud in the turnaround, and the shutters that are shedding paint like fish scales. But when Mother goes all out, it's a magical place. From the outside, anyway."

They pulled onto the circular drive that looped around to the twin wrought-iron staircases leading up to the portico. The portico rose two stories high, on slender white columns that shone against the mellow old brick. Atop it rode a graceful gable, breaking the line of the roof, with a white oval medallion at its center.

Lulu pointed to an explosion of soft light spilling from behind the second-story portico balcony.

"That's the ballroom," she said, grinning. "Considered one of the finest in the Lowcountry and a great place to stay away from, in my book."

Sweetwater had only an attic.

"Did you stay away from it?" Emily mumbled. It was not possible for her to raise her voice in this luminous place. If she did, who knew what cracks in the enchanted eggshell would snake swiftly from top to bottom? Who knew what creatures would come out of the yolk inside?

"Nope," Lulu said, slowing the truck. "It got me once, for a Sweet Sixteen ball that was as ghastly an affair as I have ever attended. Did you ever read Edgar Allan Poe's *The Masque of the Red Death*?"

Emily shook her head. Buddy had considered Poe an overwrought pulp-fiction writer.

"It's about these people at a grand ball in a castle in the woods," Lulu said. "They've taken refuge there to escape a great plague that is decimating the countryside. They're carousing while the populace dies. It's a masquerade ball, so nobody knows who they've been dancing with. Well, they drink harder and dance longer and laugh louder, until midnight, when everybody unmasks. And when they do, they see that one of the dancers is Death himself, and they know that they've escaped nothing; they will die. My party was a little better than that, but not much. To me, at least."

"That's horrible," Emily said. "Didn't you ever like parties? Weren't there some you enjoyed?"

She knew she was chattering, to put off the moment when Lulu would stop the truck and she would have to step out into all that swirling, pouring light. She knew that she would drown in it.

"No," Lulu said. "There was never a party in this house that I enjoyed. There weren't many anywhere, that I can remember. Maybe birthday parties at Miss Hanahan's Little School, but I'm told I was a strange, unsociable child even then."

She pulled the truck onto the grass bordering the drive and hauled the hand brake

on. They were well into the curve of the circular drive, but not near the front portico,
where young men in white shirts and black
ties were politely decanting guests and taking their keys, and driving their shining, clifflike SUVs away. Emily did not see a single
regular automobile in the lot. Maybe these
guests had struggled through wild jungles
and savannas and veldts to reach this blazing haven. Maybe they had bashed through
herds of stampeding elephants and prides
of snarling lions. Maybe they had outrun
cheetahs and charging rhinos.

Lulu caught her thought.

"You'd think they'd come from the Ama-
zon rain forest, wouldn't you? But most of
them came out from downtown Charleston.
I guess you need those things to plow
through the tourists."

She sat still in the darkness of the cab,
taking slow, deep breaths. Emily noticed
that the fine, birdlike tremor was back in her
hands. Lulu did not want to go into her ancestral home any more than she did. The
thought cheered her slightly, and then she
felt a stab of guilt. How awful to be terrified
of your own house.

"Where is everybody?" she said.

"In the ballroom. In the dining room. Out on the terrace and in the gardens, down by the river. Everywhere there's food and liquor. Come on, Emily. Let's go."

Emily had turned to stone.

"I can't go in there," she whispered. "I can't talk about anything but dogs."

"We're not going in there. We're going around to Grand's house. There's a path around the house and back into the woods that leads to it. It's dark, but I know the way."

"Are you just going to leave the truck?"

"Yep," Lulu said. "Give the place a little class."

Emily got out of the car on wings of relief. Outside, she could hear faint music from the terrace behind the house, and laughter. She stood beside Lulu, staring at the conflagration of white light, and then Lulu turned and plunged off the grass into the deep shadows of the bearded live oaks.

"Follow me," she said. "And watch these damned camellia bushes. They're thick as a jungle now, but Grand planted them when she was first married, and she won't let Mother have them cut."

The little path was pitch black. The dissonant songs of katydids and crickets and the sweet slap of faraway water were the only links to the world she had left behind on the blacktop road when Lulu had turned toward Maybud. Dew-heavy leaves slapped her face, and more than once the ridiculous heels of her shoes caught in the gravel and she stumbled. She fixed her eyes on Lulu, a shimmering column of white silk ahead of her. It was like following a will-o'-the-wisp with no notion of what eerie place you might fetch up in. Emily liked this whole thing less and less.

"Are you sure this is the right way?" she called to Lulu, and flinched at the sound of her own voice cracking the silence. What sort of old lady was this who lived alone out in this black, haunted wood?

"Yep. And here we are," Lulu said, and the path sloped abruptly down into a hollow ringed with live oaks and palmettos. In the center of the hollow stood a small stone house half-covered with vines, the crooked chimney on its steep slate roof sighing out sweet wood smoke, its deep-set, small-paned windows glowing with yellow light.

Around it was a low piled-stone wall that enclosed a rioting cottage garden. Bowls of dried dog or cat food were set out in a ring at the edge of the tiny, neat lawn. Behind the house, just over the far lip of the hollow, the river gurgled and ran. It was the same sound Emily's river made when the tide was full in. Something in her chest that had been cold and clenched loosened just a trifle.

"It's just like Hansel and Gretel," she breathed.

"It is, and aptly so," Lulu said. "Everybody in these parts knows Grand is a witch."

She knocked on the heavy, iron-bound wooden door and called out "Grand? You got room for two tired and hungry pilgrims?"

"Come on in this house," called a tiny, silvery voice, that sounded like it might belong to a very old-fashioned china doll. "If I'd had to wait any longer I'd have eaten all this stuff myself."

Lulu pushed the door open and ran into a big, low-beamed room to hug a tiny, silvery elfin creature who sat beside a blazing fire in a morris chair so large that it almost swallowed her. The hug lifted the elf half out of her chair, and Emily saw that her legs were withered and matchstick-thin, though she wore smart black satin slippers on her tiny, gnarled feet.

She hovered in the doorway, unsure of what she should do, until the old woman called out, "Come here into the light and let me get a look at you, young lady. I've wanted to meet you for a very long time."

Emily wobbled slowly forward, teetering on the renegade heels. She would have given anything to be back in her own bed eating popcorn and watching *Stargate* with Elvis. When she reached the paper-thin oriental rug in front of the fire where the old woman sat, Lulu kneeling at her side, she stopped and simply waited.

Strange, light-blue eyes, so like Lulu's, peered at her out of pouches and webs of wrinkles. She seemed to be made of wrinkles; her fine, thin skin was pleated with them. She had silver white hair piled high on her head, showing spots of pink scalp, and her nose was that of a Roman emperor. When she smiled her teeth were fine and white, set off by a gash of brilliant red lipstick. She was very tanned.

She held out both her hands to Emily, and Emily bent over her and took them, unsure what to do with them. There were rings on both the old hands, huge, dirty old diamonds set in gold; massive rubies and emeralds, threatening to slide off the fine-boned fingers. There were diamond teardrops in her tiny, webbed ears, and she wore a long black satin dress cut low enough to show a terrifying swath of spotted, wrinkled skin behind a necklace of diamonds that matched the earrings.

"This is Grand," Lulu said from the arm of the old woman's chair. "I told you she was a witch. Grand, this is my friend Emily Parmenter."

"Yes," the old lady said, still holding Emily's hands. "She certainly is a Parmenter. Or a Carter, I should say. Child, you are the very image of your mother when she was a young girl, although I imagine you are tired of hearing that. When I first met her, she had her hair up just like that. A Renoir, just as you are."

"Did you know my mother?" Emily breathed out of flaccid lungs. There was nothing about this night that was not alien to her. Down deep, very faintly, Buddy said, "Nothing of him that doth fade / But doth suffer a sea-change / Into something rich and strange."

She smiled involuntarily, and the old lady smiled back.

"Sit down beside me and after a while I'll tell you how I knew her," she said. "Lulu, bring the tea tray. I had Rusky bring out a little of everything they're having at the house. It's enough to stun an elephant."

Lulu brought a heavy old silver tray and set it on a small table next to her grandmother's chair. She poured out three cups of tea into thin white porcelain cups and handed them to Emily and her grandmother, and made up three plates of food and handed them around, also. She handled the tea things as if she had been born doing it. Well, Emily thought, she had.

She looked at her plate. There were enormous pink pickled shrimp; tiny biscuits with rosy ham in them; a minute, glossy brown bird she identified as a dove, sauced in something thick and purple; candied, sugared fruit; cheese straws; benné biscuits; a slice of just-pink roast beef; slender stalks of white asparagus dripping velvety gold sauce. On another tray waited elaborately carved pastries filled with swirls of creamy yellow and deep red and ivory, slices of seed cake, and something she had never seen before, tiny puffs filled with whipped cream and covered with chocolate.

"Profiteroles," Lulu said. "Rusky makes them better than anybody in three counties. Every bakery in Charleston has tried to hire her. Lemon and sugar, Emily?"

"Yes," Emily mumbled. "Please."

She looked around her for somewhere to put the cup and plate down; the spindly mahogany chair the old lady had indicated for her had no arms, and there were no small tables near.

"Lulu, the lap trays," the old lady said. "Have you forgotten all your manners in a measly three months?"

Lulu brought beautiful, thin, gold-and-ivory inlaid trays of some very dark wood and slipped one onto Emily's lap.

"This ought to do it," she said.

They ate in silence for a few minutes, old Mrs. Foxworth with gusto, Lulu nibbling at this and that, Emily watching Lulu and only taking bites of what Lulu did. She finished some of the beef tenderloin and several benné biscuits and cheese straws, but the rest was unfamiliar to her, and she was absurdly frightened that she would spit it out on her plate.

"What in God's name is this on the doves?" Lulu said querulously. "It tastes like cough syrup."

"It's port and prune sauce," her grandmother said gleefully. "Your mother and I made a deal: she gets to try out new things on each of my birthdays without my permission, and in exchange she doesn't just pop in with this person or that who 'just couldn't bear to leave without saying hello.' I'd never even met the last batch of pop-ins."

"Well, she should have stuck to the champagne sauce. This is terrifying," Lulu said, pushing her plate away.

"Actually, I'd have liked it better if she'd stuck to a quail stew and venison chili, like I had for the first few birthday parties, before they turned into obligatory audiences with the Queen Mother."

"You haven't given anybody an audience in years, unless you specifically asked them, and you know it," Lulu said comfortably, stretching her long legs in toward the fire.

"Well, the parties aren't about me anymore. They're about Maybelle's obsessive need for her friends to come and listen to a crazy old lady shoot off a shotgun at midnight. I understand it's considered a great coup to be invited to stand on the terrace and listen for the shots and drink champagne. Lots of people say they were actually here with me when I did it, I'm told. I'm a Lowcountry legend. Maybelle wouldn't give up one of those for a membership in the Colonial Dames. Only the very oldest and best Lowcountry families have living legends. People write me up in tour guide books, I think. It's been almost ten years since I actually came to the party at the big house."

Emily grinned. She couldn't help it. This was power; not the trappings of plantations and Christmas hunts and debutante balls and the Saint Cecilia Society. This was the power to refuse the lot of it and live as you pleased. She thought old Mrs. Foxworth had been born with that power. She thought Lulu might be reaching for it now, with her refusal to come home to Maybud for her season. She'd make it, too; Emily would bet on that. She'd bet that Lulu would ultimately do anything she wanted, and pay no price at all.

After they had finished, Mrs. Foxworth looked keenly at Emily and then Lulu.

"Stand up and let me look at you both," she said, and they stood obediently before her. Maybe, Emily thought, she's going to give us the signal for the long down.

"Lulu, you look well," the old lady said. "Far better than you did when you got home in June. You've got color, and those awful shoulder blades have filled in some. Are you eating well? People who cook for themselves often don't."

"I *am* eating well," Lulu smiled. "I have dinner most nights now with the Parmenters, and Emily's Aunt Jenny is a fabulous cook, and I'm sleeping well and loving every minute with the dogs. Emily's teaching me; she's so good that all she has to do is think a command to a dog and he does it. It's uncanny. So don't fuss, Grand."

Sleeping well? Emily thought. All those nights when her lights burned till dawn, all those nights when she needed Elvis?

"Well, I won't fuss then. According to your mother you're being held captive on a dog farm hundreds of miles away from home and can't manage to escape. I'm glad to know the truth."

"You knew it anyway," Lulu said. "I told Mother and Daddy I wasn't coming home until I was good and ready, and . . . I'm not. I'd stay at Sweetwater forever if they'd have me. Anyway, I talk to Mother every day, practically. I just tell her I'm going to hang up if she starts in on coming home for the season. After a couple of times, she quit bugging me."

"So *are* you coming home? At all?" The old woman looked intently at Lulu.

"Oh, probably. Sometime. But not for the goddamned season. I really do know what's best for me now, Grand."

"So you do," her grandmother said. "At any rate, you both look terribly glamorous tonight. It's a shame to waste those dresses on an old lady with a shotgun. Lulu, don't I recognize that one you're wearing?"

The dress was a long, slim column of white silk satin that fell to the floor in folds around Lulu's shoes. It had a pleated bodice and only one thin shoulder strap, and in it, with the golden tan and her gilt hair falling straight and shiny and only small diamond earrings, Emily thought that she should be living on Olympus instead of a dog farm.

"Yep," Lulu said. "Steuben's on King Street made it for me for my eighteenth birthday party. You're the first person besides the Parmenters who's seen me in it."

"That's right, you didn't go to that party," Mrs. Foxworth smiled. "I heard you went out to Booter's bait shack off Folly Creek and drank beer and ate oysters and shagged with the locals till dawn. You must have been a sensation."

"Oh, I was," Lulu said.

"Now, Emily," the old woman said, turning her blue pagan eyes on her. "Let's see. Hair, perfect. Pearls just right for a young girl. And the white piqué is just lovely on you; it's plain and modest, and yet it shows what you'll be when you grow up. You're a very pretty girl, you know. As your mother was. You could walk into any ball anywhere in the Lowcountry and cause a commotion. As your mother did."

"My mother . . ." Emily began.

"Later," Mrs. Foxworth smiled. "I promise. Now, Lulu, don't I know Emily's dress, too?"

"My graduation dress from Charlotte Hall," Lulu said. "It fits Emily far better than it ever did me. It might have been made for

her, that tiny waist and those nice boobs.
I'm trying to give it to her."

Emily felt scarlet heat climb her neck to
her face.

"Well, they are nice," the old woman said.
"You'll be quite glad of them one day, my
dear. I had to stuff stockings in my bras all
my life. But how on earth did you get hold of
the dresses, Lulu? Did you stage a com-
mando raid on the house in the dark of the
moon?"

"I called the kitchen line and got Moselle,
and she went and found them and the jewelry and Leland smuggled them out to me.
The shoes we got at Target."

She held out one narrow brown foot,
nearly naked in strappy silver. The very high
heels were caked with mud. Emily put one
foot behind the other and tried to hide her
ruined white satin kitten-heeled sandals.
They would not bear close scrutiny.

"Don't be embarrassed, my dear," Mrs.
Foxworth smiled. "Lulu and I get all our
shoes at Target. I don't mind paying a king's
ransom for a really good dress, but shoes
are just—shoes. They wear out. They get
scuffed and muddy. Feet are ugly anyway. I
never saw the sense in those Manolo Blah-

nik things. These are Target's finest. Cost me twenty-four dollars."

She held out a twisted old foot so Emily could see the gleaming black satin pump.

Some debutantes are cheap. Yet another truth snapped into the grid inside Emily.

"All right, you've earned the story about how I met your mother," Mrs. Foxworth said. "Get comfortable on that couch. Lulu, see if you can find my cigarettes. I think I left them on my dressing table."

"Those things are going to kill you one day, Grand," Lulu said, getting up and leaving the room.

The absurdity of that struck Emily at the same time it did the old lady. They smiled at each other. Suddenly Emily very much liked this cigarette-smoking, Target-wearing, shotgun-toting, diamond-encrusted, chili-eating old woman. To her surprise, she felt comfortable in the deep old sofa in front of the fire. The fire lulled, and the rich eccentricity of the big room warmed, and the surety of safety from party-going eyes soothed. She tucked her feet up under her with a small sigh of relief.

"I don't know if Lulu's told you, but at one time I taught at Charlotte Hall. English. I was just married and the house was about as furnished as it was going to get, so I needed something to do and they were kind enough to take me on. But then the children came along and there was no thought of going back to work. Not in Charleston, even if you could have afforded nannies and such. Not even I thought of it, not then. But I did have all the help in the world, and I just couldn't make myself do the bridge club-garden club-Junior League business. So I thought I might do some tutoring at home, and Charlotte Hall referred some of its students to me. Pretty soon mothers from all over the place were bringing their children to me, children of all ages, and it got so I could only take just so many. I was really full up when your mother called and asked if I could take her son. Buddy, she said his name was. I don't think I ever knew his full name."

She stopped and looked at Emily. Emily merely stared. Buddy here. Her mother, here. She could not make it compute, so she said nothing, merely looked.

"He was ten when she brought him to me," Mrs. Foxworth said. "He had been in public school on Edisto, I think, but his dis-

ease was beginning to make him clumsy,
and the children were pretty cruel to him.
Caroline brought him in, holding his hand,
and he stopped and looked around the
room and said, 'If Merlyn had gotten to pick
his cave, this would be it.'

"I loved him instantly. And I think he saw
a friend in me. From the beginning, he was
the quickest child I have ever taught, and
his hour-long sessions turned into two and
sometimes three. When we were not reading we were talking—about everything.
Everything under the sun interested him.
And this room just enchanted him. We spent
a lot of time just looking at the things in
here, and I'd tell him stories about how this
or that got here."

She paused again, and took a deep drag
off her crimson-smeared cigarette. Emily
looked around the room. She could see why
Buddy loved it. Every wall had shelves
bursting untidily with books. Window seats
and tables were piled with them. Here and
there paintings were propped against the
shelves, rich, savage things, along with luminous landscapes of the Lowcountry. Photographs crowded tables and desks. Her
eye stopped on one. It was silver-framed, a

photograph of a youngish, very blond woman standing at the foot of a bridge. Crowds milled in the background. A black man stood beside the woman with his arm around her shoulder. They were talking earnestly. The black man was unmistakably Martin Luther King Jr. The young woman might have been Lulu, but it was old Mrs. Foxworth in her youth. Emily looked at her, and then over at Lulu, who was lounging in a deep chair with her legs stretched out, smiling.

"Your eyes do not deceive you," Lulu said. "That is indeed Dr. King with Grand. And that's the Edmund Pettus Bridge, in Selma, Alabama. Grand marched with Dr. King that day. In fact, she marched a good bit, around the South. If she hadn't been a Coltrane who married a Foxworth, she would have been shunned like the Amish do to their rebels. As it was, everybody just shook their heads and said, 'The Coltranes never did keep their girls on a tight enough leash,' and 'The Foxworths got just what they deserve, sending all their boys to Princeton and Yale.' Granddaddy's back there in the crowd, waiting for the march to start. He had a scar on his arm all his life from a police dog."

Old Mrs. Foxworth smiled.

"Yep," she said. "Brad and I were Charleston's original hippies. Only hippies, in fact, so far as I know. Your brother loved that photograph. He made me tell him the story over and over. The first time he saw it, he said, 'I would have marched, too.' And he would have. Even if he had had to do it in a wheelchair. Your brother was one of the bravest people I have ever met, Emily."

"You should have seen his room at home," Emily said through a tight throat. "It looked just like this. Did you get to know my mother?"

Mrs. Foxworth shook her head. "Not really. Just to exchange pleasantries with when she brought Buddy. She was a beautiful thing; looking at you is like looking at a photograph of her. So intense and effervescent. She was always in a hurry to be somewhere. I always imagined the places she was going were glamorous in the extreme. She would kiss Buddy on the forehead and say, 'Don't get too smart, sweetie,' and be gone out the door like a hummingbird. Buddy would dive into a pile of books and hardly look up until she came back for him. He absorbed more in three years than an ordinary boy could in twelve. We got drunk on books, Buddy and I did."

"Did you like her? My mother?" Emily asked. It was an important question.

The old lady considered. Then she shook her head. "No."

There was another silence. The fire snickered behind its screen.

"Three years . . ." Emily whispered.

"Well, he didn't come back much after your mother . . . was gone. Once in a while your aunt would bring him, if she had some time off from school, and once your father did. I could see a lot of your father in Buddy. I missed him terribly, but we talked on the phone several times a week, up until . . . he was maybe seventeen."

"Did he ever talk about me?" Emily said in a small voice. It seemed a very self-centered thing to say, but she was desperate to know this other undreamed-of part of Buddy's life.

"Indeed he did," the old woman said. "You were just three when he first came here, and he was very excited about you. 'I'm going to have somebody to read with me,' he said. 'When she gets a little older we're going to read everything in the world.' And I believe you did, didn't you? When we talked he'd always tell me about what you were reading, and what you thought about it. He said that you were very smart. Very . . . intuitive, I think he said."

"I'm not smart," Emily said, looking into the fire. "I don't know how to do anything but train dogs."

"But you read, don't you?" Mrs. Foxworth said.

"No," Emily said briefly. She was not going to go into this, not even with this fabulous old witch. Not even with Lulu.

"That's a shame," Mrs. Foxworth said, but she did not say it reprovingly.

Out over the river the sky suddenly burst into bloom, in arcs of silver and blue and red and green.

"Oh, God, it's the damned fireworks," Mrs. Foxworth said. "I must be a year older. I really let it slip by this time. Lulu, fetch me the gun, please."

Lulu got up and went out of the room and came back carrying a shotgun. Emily felt her stomach heave and bile rise up toward her throat. She could not speak and she did not move. The gun was old and polished, silver-clad, carved, very beautiful. When Mrs. Foxworth took it from Lulu, Emily flinched, and made an involuntary sound of pain and revulsion.

Holding the gun broken over her thin arm, Mrs. Foxworth turned and studied Emily.

"It was a Purdey, wasn't it?" she said gently.

Emily nodded, her eyes squeezed shut, both against tears and the sight of the shotgun.

"Oh, child. I'm so sorry. Come and sit by me and let me tell you about Purdeys. They are beautiful pieces of art and work, and I would hate for you to carry all that fear and horror around with you all your life. You'll surely see other Purdeys if you train gun dogs. You can't run from every one of them."

She patted the arm of her chair. Emily did not move.

"I can't," she whispered, tears starting. "You can't make me. I want to go home. Lulu, I want to go home now."

"Grand, do you really think . . . ?" Lulu began, and then stopped. She looked from Emily to her grandmother and back again. It was clear that she did not understand the exchange, but clear also that she knew it was causing Emily pain.

"I really do," Mrs. Foxworth said. "I really do. But it must be Emily's decision, of course."

Emily half rose to go out of the room; she would wait for Lulu in the truck. And she would never come back into this insane doll's house again. This old woman, this young one—why were they trying to make her do things that were so clearly beyond her? Couldn't they see that she was not yet thirteen years old? She felt that their clawing expectations would kill her.

From deep down, Buddy said, very clearly, "I need you to do this for me, Emily. So you'll understand."

Almost robotically, Emily turned and walked stiffly over to Mrs. Foxworth's chair and sat down on the arm. She was trembling so hard that she could see the stiff white folds of her dress quiver.

Old Mrs. Foxworth put one arm around her, and held the gun loosely on her lap with the other.

"These are the guns of royalty," she said. "There is no other piece of equipment so perfectly suited for its purpose than a Purdey shotgun. The London firm that makes them is very old, and most of them are built especially for their owners, perfectly fitted to them. They are rarely sold; most of them go down through generations of the same family. This one was made for my father in 1929. See here on the stock? His name is engraved into the design so that it becomes a part of it, and the gunsmith who made it has signed his initials just below. See?"

She took Emily's stiff fingers and guided them lightly over the beautiful silver stock engraving. Emily had thought that it would feel cold, but it did not. An almost-living warmth came from it.

Mrs. Foxworth moved Emily's hand down the barrel. "These are 30-inch barrels," she said. "Over/unders. A barrel-maker is an artist in the truest sense of the word. There aren't many of them. When this gun was made, there were only a few in England. The top two made Purdey barrels."

Under the withered old fingers, Emily's fingers felt the satiny steel. It, too, was warm.

Mrs. Foxworth sat back and Emily did too, folding her hands, simply waiting.

"The worth of a near-perfect work of art is entirely in how it is used," the old woman said. "If it is used with clear purpose and a kind of gratitude, it becomes a very fine thing indeed. Only misused are they in any sense evil. Buddy was as purposeful and courageous a person as I have ever known, even at seventeen, and he used the Purdey exactly as he wished, on his own terms, to best a mortal enemy. And I truly believe that he did that."

Emily thought of the scrawled line on the bottom of the poem by John Donne that he had left her: "I got him, Emily." She bowed her head and let the tears come. They, too, were warm and steady and did not choke her. They merely fell. A few of them fell onto the gun in Mrs. Foxworth's lap. The old lady sat still, simply letting her weep. When Emily finally lifted her head, Mrs. Foxworth said, "Now come on outside with me. It's time to celebrate my birthday or that lot in the house will be out here like a pack of hounds to see what's wrong. I'm going to take the first shot. And I want you to take the second. To celebrate Buddy."

The three of them walked out into the still, moon-flooded garden, old Mrs. Foxworth leaning heavily on her granddaughter. The silence was profound; only the swift, deep song of the river beyond the high bank broke it. No creatures stirred or scuffled; none sang or chirred or bellowed. The stillness of the night seemed a part of the magic of the house and the old woman. Emily was breathing very lightly. There seemed no force in her lungs.

Mrs. Foxworth steadied herself against the stone garden wall and lifted the gun and shot into the empty air out over the river. The noise seemed to roll on and on and on; it would surely not stop until it had lost itself in the Atlantic Ocean, far to the south. Emily had thought the kick of the gun would knock the old woman backward, but she stood erect, braced and still.

"Happy birthday to me," she said, and handed the gun to Emily. Emily took it, trembling again, deeply frightened. Who knew what she might kill if she shot it into the air? Who knew what the shot would rouse?

"Can you shoot a shotgun, Emily?" Mrs. Foxworth said.

"Yes," Emily said through stiff lips.

"Then brace yourself like I did, and hold the stock very firmly into your shoulder. Here, let me buffer you a bit with my shawl. And ease the trigger back. Just ease it."

Emily put the gun to her shoulder as her father had taught her to do when she was eight or so, lifted the barrels into the black air over the river, squeezed her eyes shut.

"Open your eyes," Buddy said softly. "Don't close your eyes on anything."

Emily opened them, saw starlight, and pulled the trigger. The roar deafened her, shook her, broke the world apart. She lowered the gun over her arm and looked at Mrs. Foxworth. The world slid back together as seamlessly as it had been before. Faint and faraway, from the house, came the sounds of cheers.

Mrs. Foxworth put her arm around Emily's shoulder and let her take the slight weight of her body as they walked back to the house. In the light from the front-door lamps, she smiled at Emily. Lulu, only half comprehending, smiled, too, a tentative smile.

"Courage runs in your family, I see, Emily," said Mrs. Foxworth. "Now let's get back in the house before a passle of tackpots show up with champagne. I'll make us some hot chocolate. How does that sound?"

"It sounds wonderful," Emily said and began, silently, to cry again.

"Thanks, Emmy," Buddy said.

12

After that, Emily felt as though she had just come from the dentist's, giddy with relief. She sat in the deep embrace of the sofa and talked and talked and talked. She chattered as if someone had wound her up. She knew it was ridiculous but she could not stop the words. She felt her cheeks flush with the silliness of it, but everything that came into her head came out of her mouth in a bubbling flow like a spring. Across from her, in one of the chairs beside the fireplace, Lulu smiled at her in silence. On the other side of the fireplace, in the morris chair, old Mrs. Foxworth simply sat still, smiling faintly, a receptacle, letting Emily fill her up with words.

"This is the best hot chocolate I ever

had," Emily sang gaily. "I bet it's not that powdered stuff Aunt Jenny buys. It reminds me of Christmas and skiing and things. Only, it's not even September, is it? I didn't think about that until now. The fire is just so perfect. And it's not a bit hot in here. If I lived here I'd have a fire like this every night."

"Grand does," Lulu said, licking chocolate off her mouth. "In cool weather it's just right. In hot weather she just turns the air conditioning up to high and lets it blast. It drives Mother insane, but there's nothing she can do about it. Grand owns every inch of Maybud, the air conditioning included."

"I don't, really," Mrs. Foxworth said. "I deeded it over to your father when I moved out here, except for this cottage and garden. The only provisions were that he could not sell any part of it and the whole estate would come to you. Maybelle has never forgiven me, but what is a McClellanville Cutler going to say to a Coltrane and a Foxworth? It works out pretty well. Maybud stays in the family, Maybelle gets to be lady of the manor all she wants, and I get the run of the place without having to wait for an invitation. And, best of all, her daughter inherits. So nobody's going to run her off the place if Rhett goes first, and she can queen it up over there all she likes. She knows I'm not going to pop in. I always did think it was too big and drafty for human beings to live in, and when Bradley died I simply couldn't stay in the place, so I had the mangy stuffed trophy heads and the photographs of eight generations of gun dogs tossed out of this little house and moved out here. I always loved it, and the river, and all the wild things around, but I couldn't stand all those dead dogs and antelopes and elk and whatnot staring mournfully down at me. There was even a lion. He was a beautiful thing; I had him sent to the museum. They couldn't refuse him because we've endowed it for generations. I don't know what happened to the rest of them. And I filled it up with all the books I'd been collecting for years, and all the photographs of people who were dear to me, and all the paintings that I bought for myself and loved, and had a great kitchen put in, and a piazza out back where I sit and catch the breeze when the tide turns, and I feed all the stray dogs and cats and raccoons and possums and skunks in a fifty-mile radius, and nobody can say a word. It was here that I had my private students come. Buddy was one of the first to see this room."

"I used to spend as much time as I could sneak away from the big house out here," Lulu said, smiling at her grandmother. "Sometimes I'd tell Mother I was going to play tennis or bridge with somebody, or go into Charleston for lunch, and just come out here and hang out with Grand. She never threw me out. And she taught me some things every proper Charleston debutante ought to know and almost none of them do."

"Like what?" Emily said. The adrenaline was ebbing, and her eyelids were growing heavy. She looked at the little ormolu clock on the mantelpiece. Almost one o'clock. She felt as if she had been awake and on point like a finely tuned bird dog for longer than she could remember. But she could not bear to lose this magical night.

"Like James Joyce and Henry Miller and the Kama Sutra," Lulu grinned.

"Oh, Lulu, I did not," her grandmother said. "Well, maybe some of the Joyce. But it didn't seem to me that there was much I could teach you in that department, even when you were much younger. You have always had the soul of a courtesan, my dear. Although a very nice one."

Lulu laughed, a delighted belly laugh, and her grandmother did, too. Emily smiled politely. Buddy had told her about James Joyce, though they had not read from him, but she had no idea who Henry Miller was, or the Kama Sutra. Nevertheless, the laughter that knit them together was an irresistible part of this place, and they were sharing it with her as if she were grown-up, no age at all. The feeling was as heady as wine.

"Who's Kama Sutra?" she said. "Another one of those courtesans?" She did not know what a courtesan was, but if Lulu's grandmother thought she had the soul of one, it must be a fine thing. And she liked the rich way it rolled off her tongue.

"It's a what," Lulu said. "It teaches you how to be a courtesan and a lot of other things, too. Like . . . oh, belly dancing. Bumps and grinds . . ."

"Lulu," her grandmother said in a warning tone, but Lulu was on her feet, facing them. She kicked off her sandals and tucked her silky white skirts into her bikini underpants and held her arms out, and thrust her pelvis forward, and threw her head back. Her blond hair streamed down her back and her eyes were closed, and she snapped her fingers and moved her hips to inaudible music. She was a different woman entirely from the one who had come to live in Emily's barn, a woman who threw off sexuality and heat like a kiln. There was absolutely no doubt in Emily's mind what Lulu was pantomiming, even if she had never seen it and could not, even in her most private moments, imagine it. Now she knew, not only what it looked like but how it felt. A small, hot trembling started up deep in the pit of her stomach. It made her wriggle on her chair and her face and chest flush.

When Lulu began to make soft, breathy sounds and rotate her hips faster and faster, Mrs. Foxworth sat up straight and frowned at her.

"Sit down, for God's sake, Lulu," she said. "I never taught you that."

"No," Lulu said, dropping back into her chair and smoothing her gilt hair. Her cheeks and chest were flushed, and her breath came fast and shallow. She grinned evilly at her grandmother, and was Lulu again. Emily gave a sigh of relief. That other woman had been taking her to a place she desperately did not want to go.

"You can't teach it," Lulu said to Emily. "You don't learn it. It's in your hands and your hips and your DNA. Bet you had it, Grand. Bet Emily will, too."

"No, I won't," Emily thought mutinously. "Not ever, not that stuff."

For some reason it made her think of Kenny Rouse and his scouring eyes, and the day he had touched himself while he stared at her and Lulu. She shivered. All of a sudden she wanted more than anything to go home and climb into bed with Elvis and burrow deep under the covers, even though the night was as hot and still as high summer.

"You must admit, Grand, that I taught you some things, too," Lulu said to her grandmother.

"My dear, you still do," Mrs. Foxworth said. "But so far as that stuff goes, I knew it before you were a gleam in anybody's eye. And, if I may say so, did it a sight better."

"Grand!" Lulu pretended to be shocked. The old woman and the girl burst into laughter. Emily joined in, hoping hers sounded adult and indulgent, and praying that no one would ask her anything that required an educated answer.

The laughter faded. Old Mrs. Foxworth looked at Emily thoughtfully.

"Buddy left me a book to give you, just before he stopped coming here. He said, 'What would be a good age for a girl to start reading poetry?' And I said, 'Almost any time. But about twelve would be good to have a whole book of poetry of her own.' And he asked me what I thought you would like most, and I said I thought you would like Yeats, because he'd been reading bits of it to you, and you seemed to respond to it. So we picked out a collected works and he wrote a little message in it for you and asked me to give it to you if for some reason he wasn't able to. I still have it. I'll give it to you before you go."

"I don't want it," Emily said fiercely. "I'm not going to read it."

"That's up to you," said Mrs. Foxworth. "But you're going to take it with you when you leave tonight. I promised him."

Emily felt the stinging in her throat move up behind her eyes. It was all too much. A whole world of Buddy's that she had known nothing about had been given her. She did not know how to receive it. She wanted desperately not to know about it. The world she had shared with him had been world enough.

A quick, light knocking tattooed the door. It was unmistakably feminine, almost flirtatious, and the three in the cottage fell silent.

"Oh, shit, it's Mother," Lulu whispered. "Grand, I really can*not* do this right now. She'll be on me like a duck on a June bug, and if I have to do this when-are-you-coming-home dance again, I'll wring her neck. I will."

Her grandmother looked at her for a moment and nodded.

"Just keep quiet," she said. "She doesn't come in if I don't invite her."

Looking from one of them to the other, Emily fell silent, too. An odd sense of itching unease began in her stomach.

"What is it, Maybelle?" Mrs. Foxworth called in an exaggerated polite voice.

"I just wanted to say happy birthday, Mama F," Maybelle Foxworth trilled. "Everybody missed you. And I need to see Lulu for a sec. Just a tiny sec. Can I come in?"

Lulu screwed her eyes shut and shook

her head so violently that her hair whipped her face. She looked now like a beautiful child in a tantrum, not the hip-rolling Siren she had been a few moments ago. On the whole, Emily liked the tantrum better.

Mrs. Foxworth nodded at her grand-daughter again and called out, "And what makes you think Lulu is here, Maybelle? For goodness sake, it's after one. I was headed for bed."

"Well, I heard her voice, of course. Don't you think I know my own child's voice? Listen, I have a wonderful surprise for her. Lulu, can you hear me? A surprise all the way from Charlottesville, Virginia. Now isn't that nice?"

Lulu made a small, strangled sound and they looked at her. She stood absolutely still, as if stricken to stone. Her face was blank and paper-white; even her lips were bleached, and her breath came so fast and shallow that she sounded to Emily like a small animal that one of the dogs held at bay, perhaps a rabbit. Her blue eyes were unfocused and as dead as a winter root. Mrs. Foxworth stared at her, and, without turning, called out to the woman pecking at the door. "You heard that idiot Conan

O'Brien's voice and nobody else's, Maybelle," she said sharply, without moving her
eyes from her granddaughter's blanched
face.

"Then just let me pop in and say happy
birthday . . ."

"You just pop back to the house and take
your surprise with you," Mrs. Foxworth said.
"I'm not dressed and I'm going to bed."

"I really need to talk to her, Mama F . . ."

"So call her tomorrow at the farm. Go
home, Maybelle. I'll come over tomorrow if
it's so important, and you can tell me."

"Mama F—"

"GO HOME!" Mrs. Foxworth snapped in a
tone that Emily would not have disobeyed if
her life depended on it. She doubted that
many people would. There was an indistinct
murmur of voices outside, one fretful and
one slow and deep, and finally the sound of
footsteps on the rolling stones of the path,
going away.

Mrs. Foxworth opened the heavy drapes
an inch and peered out. Then she turned to
Lulu, who still had not moved or spoken.
She was even whiter, and Emily could not
see her breathing.

"You can go out the kitchen door and

back down the path from there," Mrs. Foxworth said. "Your mother surely is not going
to risk her Blahniks out there. Lulu, what on
earth is going on? Is there someone with
your mother?"

Lulu's eyes flew open then, and Emily
saw the breath start in her chest with an almost audible thump. Her eyes were white-
ringed, wild with terror. Emily stood frozen.
If there was something abroad in the thick,
still night that inspired that sort of terror in
Lulu, she did not think she could put a foot
outside.

"Grand, I can't . . ." Lulu whispered.

"All right, baby. You all go on now. I'll wait
and head her off if she comes back. But
Lulu, if it's all this bad, you need to tell me.
You know I've always looked out for you.
You know I can handle your mother . . ."

"You can't help me with this, Grand," Lulu
said, in a tiny voice that was almost a
wheeze. "Nobody can but me. And I'm han-
dling it. Or I was, until Mother stuck her
nose into it."

The old woman stared at her granddaughter again for a long moment, in the
shadowless white kitchen light. Then she

limped over and kissed them both on the cheek, Lulu first, and then Emily.

"Then go on. But I'm always home, and I *can* help, no matter what you think. You call me tomorrow."

She moved to the kitchen door and held it open. Outside, the damp, hot, river-breathing darkness had swallowed the world. The moon was down. A cloud of iridescent moths bumbling at the dim yellow porch light was the only life Emily could feel in all that vast space of water and earth and sky. Still, Lulu did not move, and presently, her grandmother pushed her very gently out into the night. Emily hung back. She did not want to go out into that consuming, secret-hiding blackness. More than anything in the world, she did not want to do that. There was no one now who could protect her.

"Take care of her, Emily," Mrs. Foxworth said to her softly. "She's by no means as cool a cookie as she thinks she is. Call me if this business keeps up. Call me anyway. It's in the book under B. Foxworth Sr."

She took Emily's cold hands in her own. Hers were as fragile as bird's bones, but surprisingly strong and warm. Emily felt competence flood back. I am in charge now, she thought. Lulu has to do what I say.

She nodded and took Lulu's cold hands and moved her out of the circle of light and onto the dark path.

"Oh, wait, your book," Mrs. Foxworth called from behind her.

"I don't want it!" Emily called back. Anxiety came flooding back. She had taken in and absorbed a strange and luminous old woman, and the familiar Lulu Foxworth in two violently different and unimaginable new personas. She did not think she could bear to have to see Buddy in a new light. Something that she could cling to had to remain unchanged.

"You take this book and you read it. It's one thing you can still do for your brother!" Mrs. Foxworth said sharply, holding the book of Yeats's poetry out into the light, and Emily mumbled chastened thanks and took it from her. She planned to toss it into the muttering river or simply let it fall into the thorny, ferny underbrush on the path. She went back to where Lulu stood motionless on the path and took her arm.

"Come on," she said. "We'll be home before you know it."

The tide was full out and the pluff mud stank richly. The trip back to the truck was accomplished in utter silence. The small rustlings and chirps and deeper beast-songs seemed to have faded with the moon.

Their feet stumbling over roots and through tufts of brier and grasses were the only sound. Emily could hear her own breathing, but she could not hear Lulu's. The girl who had laughed so richly and pantomimed sex so joyfully now moved like a zombie through the dark ahead of her. Twice she stumbled, and Emily reached forward and caught her shoulders. But she did not speak at all, and Emily did not, either. When the fading aureole of light from the big house came into view, and the truck rose up in black relief against it, Emily felt her chest rise and fall with a great sigh of relief, and heard Lulu breathe, taking the thick, black night into her lungs like pure ether.

"It's okay now," she said in a tight, small voice to Emily. "I can drive us back."

And she could. Even though her fine profile never turned from the rutted road and she seemed stricken dumb, Lulu drove the truck with a careless familiarity seemingly born in a Lowcountry farm or trailer park. She was still white to the roots of her hair, and there was still a fine, piano-wire tremor in her hands, but the truck ate up the miles steadily to the paved road home.

When they reached the first of the lights along Highway 174, Emily stretched and looked sidewise at Lulu. Out of her heady new adulthood, she said, "I can't imagine why you let your mother scare you like that. Just tell her to butt out. You've done that all summer. What can she do to you? Geez, anybody would think . . ."

Lulu's head whipped around toward her.

"Shut up, Emily!" she hissed. "Just shut up! You don't have any idea what you're talking about. You sound just like the baby you are!"

And Emily, swung crazily too often this night between childhood and adulthood, took refuge in familiar, impotent childhood. She scrunched herself against the door and dropped her head to her chest, and felt hot tears lacquer her face. She sniffed loudly.

The familiar landmarks that signaled Sweetwater and home had rolled into view before Lulu spoke again.

"I'm sorry," she said, the words borne on a deep sigh. "I shouldn't take it out on you. It's just something that's so . . . complicated, and so painful that I can't talk about it. I didn't mean you were a baby. I just meant that you hadn't . . . been where I've been yet. It's not my mother, not directly. I can handle my mother most of the time. You're right, I've done it all summer with one hand tied behind me. But she has the power to destroy me, even if she doesn't know it, and I can't let her do that. I've worked too hard. . . ."

She leaned back against the seat and stretched her arms out straight, loosening her shoulders.

"I don't hate my mother, even if I act like it sometimes. I wish you'd known her like she was when she was much younger, when I was small. She'd laugh and play the piano and dance around with me and dress me up in her clothes, and she took me out on the river in our Boston whaler sometimes and we took sandwiches and Coca-Colas, and had picnics at one of the hummocks. I thought she was the most beautiful person in the world. She sort of gave off her own light. I wanted more than anything to be like her. It wasn't until I was in my teens that she changed. It was as if every ambition she'd ever had for herself got turned on me, as if she had to connive and posture and claw to get me all the things she'd never had until she married Daddy. Like the invitations, and the right little cliques within cliques, and friendships with all the girls who grew up on the big plantations around Charleston, and the right schools and dancing classes and little finishing classes, and of course the Junior League and the right college. She was so proud of everything I did at school, all the so-called honors and things, that I thought she was going to have a pamphlet about them published and pass it out at the Garden Club and the Yacht Club. And when it came time for this so-called season of mine, this debut business, she turned into somebody I didn't even know, and didn't like at all. I learned to get around her from age thirteen on. I pretty much went my own way. It was as if all the things she wanted for me made her vulnerable and ineffectual. And of course, Daddy never cared where I was or who I was with. He just assumed his daughter knew the proper drill. The sad thing is, Mother didn't have to do any of that. I already had all that stuff automatically. The Foxworth-Coltrane names got it for me. She never did quite understand that, even after she married into it. Grand's right. A McClellanville Cutler doesn't automatically make the cut in our crowd. It's all in the names."

"Well, I guess I'll never have all that Charlotte Hall la-di-da stuff Daddy wants for me then, because the Parmenter name wouldn't make any kind of cut," Emily said. For the first time in her life she felt the smallest wing-brush of loss and envy for that unimaginable world.

"You'll have something better than all that, if you want it," Lulu said. "It's all there in you. I can see it, even if you can't. Grand sees it. You could even have the Charlotte Hall la-di-da stuff if you really wanted it. There are ways. Charlotte Hall's not what you think it is, Emily. I loved a lot of my time there. Maybe part of it is 'society stuff,' as you call it, but a lot of it is as good an education as there is in the Lowcountry. And whatever you end up doing with your life, you're going to need that."

"So how do you get around all that other stuff?" Emily said. "All that . . . frou-frou?"

"You take what you want and need and just ignore the rest. It's possible. I did it. I know a lot of girls who did. We got the kind of educations you can't get just anywhere. And for some of us, like me, the first frilly society thing we ever put on was our graduation dress. And you look as pretty in mine as I ever did."

"I don't need all that education just to run a dog farm," Emily said mulishly.

"Yeah, you do," Lulu said. "We've been over that. And life is pretty minimal and gray without that kind of education. Your brother knew that. He was doing his best to give it to you."

There was a small, stinging silence, and then Lulu said, "Emily, I'm sorry about Buddy. I never knew he had died that way. If Grand thinks it was an act of supreme courage and grace, it must have been. But it must have been awful for you. I guess it was the shotgun. . . ."

"You shut up!" Emily choked. This ease of Buddy's name on Lulu's tongue was suddenly unendurable. She would not share Buddy, either his life or his death. "If I have to shut up about your mother, you have to shut up about my brother!"

"Fair enough," Lulu said presently, and reached over and gave Emily's stiff shoulders a small hug.

They said no more until they pulled up on the dark circular driveway at Sweetwater. After the blazing Kubla Khan splendor of Maybud, it looked scant and flimsy against the blackness over the river. A light burned downstairs; Aunt Jenny would be waiting up for her. That, too, made Emily obscurely angry. She would share none of this night with anyone.

They got out of the truck in their long skirts and muddy heels. Off at the barn, under the sickly yellow bug light that always burned there at night, they saw the beautiful, bronze shape of a dog: Elvis. Waiting for them. But why at the barn? For Lulu? Pain added itself to resentment in Emily's stomach.

Elvis trotted toward them, tongue lolling out, stubby tail arcing joyously. He came first to Emily and put his paws up against her waist and licked her outstretched hands. He made a small sound, a breathy little bark. And then he went over to Lulu and sat down beside her, as if it was she who had his heart.

Lulu looked at Emily. "Could I have him tonight?" she whispered. "I really, really need him. I think he knows I do. But if you'd rather not . . ."

"No. By all means, take him," Emily said. It was ungracious, she knew. As if he sensed her hurt, Elvis whined softly.

"Go with Lulu, Elvis," Emily said. But she need not have spoken. She knew that he would.

There were two new litters of puppies in the barn, far too small to begin their training, just beginning to tumble out of their boxes and toddle about the hay-strewn floor. Everything in their world was new and exciting, and was to be heralded. Their treble yips shattered the still night like glass. The yipping went on and on.

Elvis turned toward the barn door and gave one bark. It was a sound Emily had never heard: short, deep, authoritative. The yipping stopped abruptly.

Emily and Lulu looked at each other.

"Why am I not surprised?" Lulu said, smiling. It was a small, tremulous smile, and her face was still blanched, and her hands still shook slightly, but somehow Sweetwater had begun to heal her. She opened the door and went up the stairs to her apartment. Elvis trotted behind her.

"Are you going to be okay?" Emily called up after her.

"I think so. Sleep well, Emily," Lulu called back. "Thanks, more than you know."

Elvis whined again. The door shut. Emily turned and went across the dark yard, fatigue suddenly so heavy upon her that she could hardly put one teetering foot in front of the other.

When she opened the screen door, she heard Aunt Jenny's voice, lilting from the sitting room.

"Come in here and tell me all about it, Cinderella," she called. "Was it wonderful? Were you the belle of the ball? Did the old lady shoot her shotgun at midnight? I can't wait to hear."

Emily did not go into the sitting room. "It was a nice party," she said shortly, not turning her head toward her aunt's voice. "Yeah, the old lady shot the shotgun. I'm really tired, Aunt Jenny. I'll tell you about it in the morning."

There was a small silence, and then her

aunt said, "You go on up, then, honey. Tell me about it later. Your father promised to let you both sleep in."

"Good," Emily said, and went up the stairs and into her room and closed the door, the place where Elvis should have been aching like a wound. She shed her clothes and tossed them away, dived into bed, and turned off the light. Downstairs she could hear her aunt moving around slowly, turning off lights and then climbing the stairs and going into her room. The room down the hall that had been Buddy's.

Emily lay there for a moment, her body pounding with tiredness, and then remembered the book of poetry old Mrs. Foxworth had given her. She turned the light back on and got out of bed and found it under the wrinkled drift of Lulu's white graduation dress. She got back into bed and opened it, slowly.

On the flyleaf, in Buddy's careless, slanted backhand that went through her like a dagger, she read: "For Emily, in her thirteenth year. 'One man loved the Pilgrim soul in you.' " It was signed, simply, Buddy.

She turned off the light and scrubbed her face into the pillow, and once again that night, cried for her brother. It was not until much later that she realized that the message had been, even then, written in the past tense.

13

Down through the slow, tea-brown water of Sweetwater Creek, just off the dolphin slide, Emily sinks. Down and down, circling slowly in the fretful little wash that meant near-low tide: down to where the great, silent black rays lie half-hidden in the corrugated bottom sand; down into the cold of the until-now bottomless shrimp hole where she and Lulu had swum, clouds of transparent, nibbling shrimp picking her flesh now until she is near essence; down through the death-cold at the hole's bottom; down, finally, into the two feet of velvety, anaerobic mud that harbors so much invisible life that it is, people say, the most life-rich place on the face of the earth. Here, in the warm, silky, teeming, stinking pluff mud of the Lowcountry,

Emily finally stops, reduced now to a mere atom, a living point of light, an invisible awareness. It is wonderful here, succoring, amniotic, endlessly warm. Emily is finally home; she sinks no further than this, and does not want to. Here is forever.

The sound must have been going on for some time when it finally reached her in the womb of the salt marsh, the slowly pulsing uterus of the creek. She tried to shut it out of her consciousness, but it was too insistent. It pinched and tugged and tore at her until she was sucked up out of the silky mud; up through the icy shrimp hole to the blood-warm water at the top of it; up past the ray-shielding creek bottom, growing larger and more corporeal and clumsy until she burst up into thin, harsh air. The sense of loss was so profound that for a moment she could not move her limbs or open her eyes, and then she did, and was sitting up in her bed in the farmhouse, tangled in sheets and sweating in the hot night. Finally she opened her eyes, and there was Elvis, next to her face on the pillow, barking, barking.

For a moment, marsh-drunk and stupid, Emily could not place this red dog on her pillow who bayed steadily into her ear, and she tried to push him away in fright. And then the world gave a slight shift on its axis and she was fully home again, and her dog was telling her something dreadful. Her heart began to pound with fright.

"Elvis, shhhh, you'll wake up the whole house," she whispered, trying to gather him into her arms. He pulled free, barking, barking.

"What's the matter?" Emily could hardly get the words out past the lump of fright in her chest. "What's the matter?"

For something was. It was written in his golden eyes; it had followed them home from the party; its breath had found her fathoms deep in the safety of the creek floor.

The spaniel jumped off her bed and ran to the door and looked back. When she did not rise, he ran back to her and took the edge of her cotton nightgown in his teeth and pulled. He was growling softly in his throat, a sound Emily had never heard him make.

She got out of bed. He ran back to the door and sat beside it, staring at her with his great golden eyes, as stiff and still as if he was on point. She looked around in confusion for her clothes; not the crumpled white dress of the past evening, but the wrinkled shorts and T-shirt she had taken off much earlier. Elvis barked again, sharply, insistently. Hurry up, he said.

Emily skinned into her clothes and looked at him.

"Is it Lulu?" she said in her mind. "Is there something the matter with Lulu? Do you want me to go out to the barn?"

He barked one last time and flew out of her bedroom and down the stairs to his dog flap in the back screen. There he sat and waited for her, whining, as she groped and stumbled down the stairs in the darkness, not wanting to wake the house if his barking had not already done so.

He dashed through his flap and out into the darkness, and she followed, running lightly and in dread, sliding in the dew-slippery grass, stumbling over clods and loose pebbles and once a dropped dog biscuit. Ahead of her, in the barn, Lulu's light still burned. Elvis was waiting for her at the top of the stairs to Lulu's apartment when she got there, gasping for breath and shaking with fear.

The door to the apartment was standing half-open. More than anything she could ever remember, Emily wanted not to go into the room. But Elvis took her arm gently in his teeth and tugged softly, and at last she went in.

She did not see Lulu at first. The normally chaste, spare room was a whirlwind of tossed clothes, books, CDs. It was like looking into a crazy kaleidoscope. There was no sound except a CD, obviously stuck: Etta James singing over and over again, "At last my love has come along. . . ."

But there was a smell. A sick-sweet, overpowering stench of whiskey and human vomit, and it was that that Emily followed, stomach heaving, heart threatening to leap out of her mouth, around to the other side of the little painted French bed.

Lulu lay on her back on the skewed white sheepskin rug, a rug stained now with the fluids of despair. She wore nothing but white silk bikini panties, those, too, stained. Her eyes were closed and she was the white of dirty paper and she was still vomiting. It ran in dribbles from her mouth over her chin and down to her slight, gold-burnished breasts. She was choking, too.

Deep, terrible strangling noises rattled in her chest and throat. If it had not been for the noise and the steady, thin stream of vomit, Emily would have thought that she was dead. Beside her on the rug a quart bottle of Maker's Mark bourbon lay open. It was empty.

By the time Emily had galvanized herself into action, Elvis had put both paws on Lulu's shoulders and was licking at the vomit on her face.

A child raised on an animal farm knows instinctively and immediately what to do about dying. Death may be beyond him, but life, even if fading, is not. Emily lunged at Lulu and rolled her onto her side. The vomiting continued, as steadily as if pumped, but the choking stopped. Afterward Emily did not remember what she did during that time, but she did remember Elvis had sat still and at attention beside Lulu's matted head.

The vomiting slowed and stopped, and Lulu rolled over on her back once more. She was breathing in slow, shallow, wheezing gasps, but she was not conscious.

"No, you don't," Emily murmured, furiously, and pulled her to a sitting position, and then dragged her by her arms into the bathroom and heaved her into the tub. She turned on the shower full force. The caked stains of vomit and whiskey soon whirled down the drain, and Lulu's hair was clean once more, and her face and body shone with water. Beneath it, she was still a decayed, bruised white. Her eyes were still closed.

"Wake up, Lulu," Emily said fiercely, over and over, shaking Lulu's shoulders, not knowing she was doing it. "Goddamnit, wake up and sit up! This isn't fair. I don't know what to do about this. Don't you *dare* die!"

She did not consider getting help from the house. Somewhere deep inside she knew that to do so she might save Lulu's life, but would kill her soul. She was still savagely shaking Lulu's shoulders when Lulu made a small, strangled sound and opened her eyes and looked up at Emily. For a long moment they simply stared at one another, and then Lulu looked down at herself and the dirty water, and up at Emily's spattered clothes, and closed her eyes again.

"Go away, Emily," she whispered in a

cracked old woman's voice. "Leave me alone."

"I will not," Emily said, beginning to cry with fright and relief. "You were choking. You almost died!"

"I wish I had," Lulu said, beginning to cry, too. "I wish I had."

Lulu woke at first light, just as the dogs were beginning to stir out in the kennels, and the puppies were starting to yip frantically for their mothers' teats. On a branch of the huge old crape myrtle that pressed at Lulu's open window, a cardinal tuned up his first rusty Pretty-Pretty Pretty Cheer! Cheer! Cheer!

Nodding stiff-necked in the slipper chair beside the little bed, Emily heard Buddy whisper, "The bird of dawning singeth all night long: And then, they say, no spirit dares stir abroad."

She came fully awake, heart jolting, mouth sour and dry, bladder bursting. She had been sitting in the chair ever since Lulu had fallen asleep in the deep hours of the night. She was as uncomfortable as she could ever remember being, but she had been afraid to leave the chair. Lulu's sleep was cold and total, like death. Wrapped still in the damp bath sheet and towel Emily had found and wrapped her body and hair in, she had lain ever since on her back, covered only with a lace-edged linen sheet. She was so white and still that more than once Emily had gotten up and leaned over to see if she was still breathing. Beside Emily's chair, Elvis sat motionless, alert eyes on Lulu, guarding.

Hours had passed in this quasi-death watch, but Emily had felt, profoundly and without doubt, that if she left the bedroom even for an instant, Lulu would simply stop her slow, shallow breathing. When she heard Buddy's words she jerked out of the half-sleep she had fallen into. She looked wildly around the shadowy room, uncertain where she was for an instant, and aware only of the painful need to urinate. When she looked at the bed, Lulu was awake, though still motionless, and as white as a boiled onion. Her electric blue eyes were dulled to gray, but she was smiling ever so slightly, a ghastly death's-head rictus.

"Shakespeare always got it right, didn't he?" she whispered in a voice that sounded as if it must scar her throat. Emily realized then that it had been Lulu who had spoken, not Buddy.

"Only spirits did walk, didn't they? I'm so ashamed, Emily. I can't even imagine what I've put you through. I keep doing that, don't I? When I should be taking care of you."

She sighed, a rasping, phlegmy sound, and closed her eyes again.

"I don't know why you stayed," she said, "but I guess I'm glad you did. I would have died, I know I would have. And maybe I should have. How did you know?"

Emily nodded mutely at Elvio, who jumped up on Lulu's bed and settled down in the crook of her arm.

"I'm sorry," his face said to Emily. "I need to be here. I'll be back with you soon."

"I should have known," Lulu said, tears starting again. "I owe the Parmenters, dogs and all, for more than my life. It can't be re-paid."

Back from the bathroom, Emily's fear was turning to anger.

"I didn't know you drank like that," she said coldly. "I don't think Daddy would have let you come if he'd known. But maybe he would have. He wants to get me in Charlotte Hall awfully bad."

Lulu turned her head away on the pillow, tears sliding silently down her sallow cheeks.

"Please don't tell Walter," Lulu whispered. "Please don't. I don't drink like this, not anymore. It's the first time I've had a drink in I don't know how long. I've been trying my best to stop doing a lot of things that were wrecking me, and I was doing okay, being out here and all, until last night. I should never have brought the bottle here with me, but I thought it would be a good test, to know it was here and be able to ignore it."

Emily said nothing.

Lulu opened her eyes again and said, "Will you bring me a glass of water? I want to tell you about all this, and I'm just too dry to talk much."

"You don't have to tell me anything," Emily said tightly. "I wish you wouldn't tell me. I don't want to know any more about it. I won't tell Daddy. Let's just forget about it."

"No," said Lulu. "I care more about your understanding than I do anybody else's in the world. Mother and Daddy could never in a million years understand, and I wouldn't ask it of Grand. I don't think she could take it."

"Why do you think I can?" Emily said.

"Because you've taken in so much that was new and hard for you this summer. I've watched you do it. I think you can take in this, too. I've lost almost everything, Emily. I don't want to lose you. Young as you are, you're as good a friend as I've ever had."

Emily felt her throat close up, but she would not show Lulu her face. She went to the sink and got the water, and gave it to Lulu. She wanted none of this pain, whatever it was; it had the smell of something that would change her forever. She had had enough of that this summer. But she sat down again.

Lulu drank water in grateful gulps and then sighed again, and waited.

"You haven't really known me," she said after a long moment. "Not like I used to be. I used to be the strong one, the free one, the one who went her own way and didn't give a flip what people thought. I was alive in every cell in my body. My friends didn't understand me, but they put up with me. My parents tried their best to civilize it all out of me. Only Grand understood. She always said that I was a great deal like her when she was young. Grand thinks I hung the moon—that I can do no wrong. I guess I lived a sort of wild, kiss-off life for Charleston, but I loved it and it worked for me.

"And then, almost exactly two years ago, I met somebody at a house party on Wadmalaw, and it all went to hell."

"The person who was with your mother last night," Emily said, her mind making the leap with ease. "I knew it wasn't just her that scared you so."

"That's right. The person who was with my mother. The man. I don't know how he got to the party; he lives in Virginia and I haven't seen him for four months. I didn't even think he knew where I was; I hoped to hell that he didn't. I never thought he would find me out here. I guess my mother invited him to the party. She knew I'd probably be there, and she's been absolutely wild for me to get back together with him since I told her I wouldn't see him again. He's exactly what every Charleston mother wants for her daughter. He's charming and handsome and funny; he's so well-born that he practically stinks of First Family of Virginia. And he stands to inherit about a gazillion dollars and the biggest plantation in Virginia. It's on the James River, and it's five times as big as ours. And he's sweet and polite with my mother and father, and first in his class at Virginia Law, and there's just no doubt that he's going to be one of the South's great men of the law, to quote my mother. Governor. Senator. Who knows? And he seemed to absolutely adore me. If I told them how it really was with him and me, they simply would not believe me."

"So how was it?" Emily said. She was terrified. She wanted to grab Elvis and run, back to her room, back to the way things had been before Lulu Foxworth. But still, she sat.

Lulu turned her head back toward Emily. She seemed to really see her for the first time since she had wakened. The swimming blue eyes focused.

"For God's sake, what am I thinking of? I can't tell you this stuff. You're not even thirteen years old. I shouldn't tell anybody, but especially not you. With any luck you may never have to know about stuff like this. I ought to just get out of here and take my dirt with me, before I ruin you. I've done enough to you this summer."

"I know about things like that," Emily said. "There's stuff written on the walls in the bathrooms at school that you wouldn't believe. Pictures, too. I know what it means. And I've heard the boys talking when they didn't know I was around. I know what people do—"

"No, you don't," Lulu said. Her voice had a little more energy now; the fishlike gasping had gone from her throat. Fresh tears started in her eyes.

"You don't have any idea on earth about what we did, he and I. I didn't know about it until I met him. I didn't know stuff like that existed. There wasn't anything he didn't do to me, and I went back for more, and sometimes I begged him for it. At first I was so ashamed that I thought I would die, and then it got so that nothing mattered except that I see him again, be with him again. I knew what I had turned into and I didn't care."

Emily sat motionless, not speaking. She was nauseated. This was beyond embarrassment. This was a look into the terrible blackness that she had always known lay beyond the everyday world, but so far had never really surfaced, like a great black mal-

formed shark that hovered always just below consciousness. She had never spoken
of it, not even to Buddy. It shamed her in
some obscure way that it hung inside her.
She had always thought she was the only
one in the world who harbored such a
shark, but now Lulu was pulling another up
from her own depths for Emily to see.

"I want somebody to take care of me,"
Emily thought, the thought leaden with grief.
"I want Buddy. I want my mother."

Neither would come, of course, so she
simply sat still and waited for Lulu to boat
her monstrous fish.

"His family kept a little apartment in Char
lottesville for when they visited him," Lulu
went on, her voice dead. "We'd go there.
Every Friday I'd sign out and he'd pick me
up just off campus and we'd go straight
there. Most of the time we didn't come out
until early Monday morning, in time for me
to make my first class. He kept a little food
there, and a lot of liquor. Other things, too.
He made me try them all. But it was only the
liquor that took hold of me, that became an
addiction. The liquor and him. During the
week, while I went about my business like I
always had, I was burning inside, dying for

the minute that he would open the car door so I could climb in. The minute that he would look at me and touch me. The miraculous thing was that neither of us let our schoolwork go. I was hanging on by my teeth and nails, bleeding to death inside trying to maintain that normalcy. But what we were doing didn't seem to affect him at all, not the liquor, not the drugs, not the . . . other stuff. He could go right back to UVA and ace another law exam, write another brilliant paper, visit other girls in their big river houses, charm their parents just like he did mine. I knew about the other girls. Southern schools are linked up like jungle drums. It didn't matter, as long as I had those weekends. Later we started just staying on, two or three days longer after the weekend. I don't know what he told his parents, or how he handled it with school. I told mine I was involved with so many extracurricular things that I really needed a blanket permission for all the times I had to go off campus. I think if I hadn't just . . . stopped it, I would eventually have never left that horrible little apartment. I would have died there."

"But you didn't," Emily said, just to toss

something into the deadly silence. It seemed important that Lulu not sense her revulsion.

"No. I didn't. One morning after we had been there for four days and had drunk I don't know how much liquor and taken God knows how much of what, he got dressed and went out to class without even looking back at me, and I dragged myself to the bathroom and looked at myself in the mirror. It was like seeing what I had become for the first time. I saw this degraded, dehydrated, yellow-pale, bruised and starved zombie woman whose eyes even then burned for the time he would come back, and behind her I could barely see what I had been when I met him. All that health and vitality and laughter and up-yours attitude. All that intelligence. That was what had gone out of me the first night I met him. The intelligence.

"And I knew that if I saw him even one more time I would die. I hitched a ride back to school and told everybody that I had the flu and to leave me alone, and I locked myself in and I sweated it out. It was beyond horrible. I wouldn't put a rabid animal through that. I couldn't do it again. It would kill me; it nearly did. I can hardly talk about it, even now. But one morning I looked in the mirror again and saw the ghost of that other girl, plainer this time, and I knew that I had to get totally away from him or he would find me and it would start all over again. So I called Mother and said I had been sick so long, and was so run down, that I needed to come home, and she came and got me, and the whole time I was home I was locked in my bedroom trying not to sneak a drink or pick up the phone and call him. She thought I was 'resting up for the season.' The goddamned Charleston season at Christmas, with all these balls and parties and luncheons and teas and house-parties. All the liquor. Endless, endless. I knew he would be at a lot of those parties, because the South is a tiny little world and he was a prince of it.

"I don't know what would have happened to me if I hadn't come out here with them and seen the dogs, and seen that maybe out here I could get back my sense of self-worth again. It was just such a clean, sweet, slow world. And it was good; if I worked as hard as I could all day with you and the dogs, and spent what time I could with you all at night so I wouldn't be alone with that bottle sitting out here, I could remember how it felt to be me and start to find my way back."

"Scheherazade," Emily thought. "Cleta was right. She saw it first. Aunt Jenny saw it, too. She was doing a performance for us every night, so that we'd want her back the next night. So she wouldn't have to die. And all the time we thought it was us she liked so much. I'll never listen to her tell one of those stupid Charleston stories again. I'll never sit at a table with her again. And she sure as hell will never borrow Elvis again. Let her find somebody else to clutch on to."

As if she caught the thought, Lulu reached a trembling hand out to Emily.

"You all taught me how to start living again," she whispered. "You all saved me in as real a way as there is. I've come to love you for that. All of you, and you most of all. You and the dogs are the best thing in my life now. If I have to go I'll die very soon. I'm not strong enough yet. When it comes to him, I may never be. It's as sick an addiction as there is in the world. Way worse than the liquor, though that's bad enough."

Emily made no move to take her hand, and Lulu dropped it and looked away again.

"I've ruined it all now, haven't I?" she said faintly. "I can't stay and take the chance of putting you through this again. I can't look at Walter and know that he knows. But I can't go home either; Mother would have him at the house before I could blink an eye. I thought I was safe here. But now he knows where I am. You aren't ever really safe, are you?"

Emily knew this fear; the black terror of a freefall into nothing. It had been born in her with the sound of the door closing behind her mother. Tears burned her nose.

She reached over and picked Lulu's hand up in hers. The girl in the bed seemed a wasted child.

"We just won't let him come, then," she said. "If he shows up, Daddy and the boys will just run him off—"

"They can't know!" Lulu's face contorted with anguish.

"Then the dogs and I won't let him," Emily said. "I'll be with you all day when we work the dogs, and I'll stay with you at night. Elvis and I will just spend the nights out here. We can tell everybody we're reading late. Or you can tell them that you're teaching me to be a lady . . ."

A specter of Lulu's old smile flitted across her corpse's face.

"Even Yancey couldn't get past you and the dogs," she said.

"Yancey? What kind of name is that?" Emily said belligerently. That sick, spoiled prince was not going to get by her.

"Yancey Byrd. It's the kind of name that opens doors all over the United States."

"Well, it's not going to open this one," Emily said, and went over to sit on the side of Lulu's bed. Elvis grinned at her and licked her arm.

"Oh, God, I'm hiding behind a twelve-year-old girl and a spaniel," Lulu said, beginning to cry again. "I can't do this to you. I can't let you do this for me . . ."

"Hush," Emily said, brushing the wet gilt hair off Lulu's wasted face. "Hush. It's going to be all right."

Deep down in her memory the words surfaced, glinting: someone had said that to her once, someone with a soft, slow voice. She could not remember if things had been all right, but the words had been a powerful amulet ever since.

"Everything's going to be all right," she said, making a gift of the words to Lulu.

In the brightening day, Lulu turned over in the linen sheets and slid back into sleep.

14

Lulu came out to the dog ring late that afternoon while Emily was finishing up the "sits" and "stays" for a new class of youngsters. They were a beautiful lot, born of pretty-faced Phoebe and sired by Elijah, Elvis's father, known at Sweetwater as "The Hunk." Elvis invariably sat quietly at the gate to the ring, watching as the young spaniels received the rules of their calling. He seldom moved, but once in a while, when a fractious baby romped away from the group, or a timid one hung back, he gave a short, gruff bark. The miscreants usually fell sweetly into line.

"I don't need to be here at all," Emily was saying to Elvis, who grinned and cocked his red head. "Why don't you just take over?"

"He'd put us both out of a job in no time," Lulu said, coming into the ring to stand beside Emily.

Emily looked at Lulu obliquely from under her lashes, dreading what she might see. The dread morphed swiftly into amazement and relief. Lulu stood smiling in the slanting sunlight, fresh in pressed white shorts and clean T-shirt, her skin scrubbed and shining. Her gilt hair was still damp, and she smelled of shampoo and the French lavender soap she used. Her eyes were clear and there seemed to be no more tremor in her hands. Elvis left his post by the gate and trotted over to her and bumped her leg with his head, looking up at her, tail flailing. The puppies, sensing release from their duties, swarmed over her shoes and worried the laces of her sneakers with their little needle teeth.

"Hi, guys," she said, stooping to pick up an armful of wriggling puppy. "I hope you behave better than this for your aunt Emily. Otherwise you'll turn into bench dogs and never see a marsh or a boat."

Emily smiled at her in simple relief. Lulu had set the tone of the afternoon, and it was, after all, okay. More than okay. Her smile widened. Bench dogs, in a hunting dog's world, were the pampered, effete creatures of the show ring, objects of scorn among the breeders and hunters of the Lowcountry.

"Not a chance," she said. "If I don't beat manners into them, Elvis will."

The sun slanted lower now, in the dying of the summer, but it still bit into forearms and bare legs and dampened collars and under-arms with sweat. After they had cleaned the dust from the puppies and deposited them back with their mothers, Lulu looked at Emily, wiping sweat from her forehead with the back of her hand.

"Let's go see the dolphins," she said. "There's time before dinner."

"It's too late for them," Emily said. "I've never seen them this late."

"I think they'll be there," Lulu said, smiling at her. "I dreamed they were."

They cut across the field and into the creek woods, which lay hot and still and silent at this hour, only a few autumn-stunned bees droning, a few grasshoppers burring in the tall grass. The air smelled of dust and drying pluff mud. The mud hardly ever worked up a really lush, rich stench in this dreaming, suspended time between seasons. Everything would sleep, dry and warm, until nightfall.

When they reached Sweetwater Creek and the dolphin slide, Emily was surprised to see that the grooves in the little beach's mud were still slick and damp.

"You dreamed right," she said, and Lulu smiled.

They lay on their stomachs in the heat-curled ferns on the little bluff, not speaking, almost drowsing, waiting for the tide to retreat a bit further. Already the green cord-grass at the creek's edge loomed high over the emptying sand bed, and the sea of green stretching to the western horizon was gilded with the dying light. When the dolphins burst into the creek they started up out of a drifting half-sleep. Lulu sat up straight, eyes spilling light. In a heartbeat the somnolent creek was full of splashing and murky storms of creek water. The big, shining fish made their usual choreographed wave, which surged onto the beach, but this time only a few frantic mullet were cast up before them. It was too late in the season for mullet. Most had left their holes and gone back to the sea.

But the dolphins followed the thrashing few up onto the sand, lying close-packed on their sides, as they always did, and picked off the fish one by one, in a lightning carnage. The one huge, cold black eye that was visible on all of them seemed to stare up at Emily and Lulu. The mandarin grins stayed in place even as mullet slid through them and vanished.

In a few seconds the wild, boiling water subsided and the dolphins ghosted away. But one stayed behind, lying on its side in the sand, its silvery duct-tape hide flashing with sunlight. It lay still, looking at them, smiling.

"Is he hurt, do you think?" Emily said. "I never saw one do that before."

Lulu got up very slowly from the creek bank and climbed, nearly soundlessly, down to the beach. Still the dolphin lay there on its side. Without the rest of its ballet around it, in the transparent brown water, it looked enormous, as big as a whale. Slowly, slowly Lulu knelt on the sand beside it and reached out and touched the shining hide. The dolphin stayed still, grinning up at her, and then gave a huge heave and writhed backward into the creek and slid away. They stared after it in silence. From the bank, Elvis, who had been watching as motionless as a spaniel in a breed book, erupted off the bluff and down to the beach barking joyfully and launched himself in his beautiful copper arc into the water. Wet head up, he paddled strongly after the retreating fish until it had slipped deep into the dark, running depths and disappeared toward the sea. He grinned his doggy grin and swam back and scrambled up to them. He shook creek water in a glinting spray, and then sat down beside Emily, smiling up at her, panting.

"I was born for this," the golden eyes said to her.

Emily hugged him and looked over at Lulu. She sat still, staring at the empty creek, tears on her tanned cheeks, smiling.

"It really is going to be all right, isn't it?" she said softly. "First you said it would, and then the dolphins did, and now Elvis. Who could want more assurance than that?"

"Well, of course it is," Emily said briskly. "I wonder why they came? Most of the mullet left a week ago."

"To say good-bye," Lulu said. "They

came to see if we needed them anymore, and if we didn't, to say good-bye."

After that, they never spoke of the terrible night, not even obliquely. Emily thought about it, though. It was not that either one of them was embarrassed, it was just . . . over. It was as if some huge tectonic shift had taken place in the long dark, and Sweetwater was now an island of safety, moated around with magic. It's going to be all right—As if, somewhere in that warm night, a great and formal shifting had taken place, and Emily had come into her power. Emily, the keeper of the moat. Emily the abbess, and Lulu the supplicant.

If Lulu sensed this, she never indicated it to Emily. Lying half-asleep late that night of the dolphins, Emily thought, "I didn't know you could grow up in one night, but I did. And it wasn't hard at all."

At dinner that night, in the circle of Aunt Jenny's candlelight, Emily picked at chicken and dumplings and probed her new grown-up thoughts. She seethed with impatience. Her father and brothers and aunt seemed silly children. She did not talk about the party the night before, even though Jenny Raiford urged her.

"Come on, Emmybug," she said, smiling. "It's the closest I'm ever likely to get to a to-do like that. Tell us about it."

Around the table Walter and the boys looked at her, waiting. Tonight she might be just Emily, in jeans and clogs, her hair skinned back in its ponytail. But last night she had been something else altogether, a changeling in their nest, a strange, exotic girl who looked like a painting of their beautiful mother and went to parties in the legendary great houses of the Lowcountry. It was that girl they wanted to speak.

But Emily would not. It was too big and too life-changing, and she had no words for it and no wish to share it with anyone but Lulu.

"It was okay. It was nice," she said, not looking up from her plate.

"It was more than that," Lulu said. She sat in her usual place on Walter's left, and she wore her usual cotton skirt and tank top, but to Emily she seemed to burn with an eerie swamp light. She wondered if the others saw it.

"It was a wonderful party and she was the belle of the ball," Lulu went on. "She looked just gorgeous, and Grand adored her. She wants Emily to come and visit her again as often as she can. She says I can come along if I'll be quiet and let Emily and her talk."

Emily did not raise her head, but across the table she felt her aunt Jenny's long, appraising look and the force of her father's beaming pleasure.

"Well, at least I know what turns him on," she thought. "All I've got to do is dress up like Mother and go to a damned party. Just like she did."

"I've asked Emily to spend the nights with me for a while," Lulu said. "There's plenty of room—the bed's a trundle—and I've got tons of books I want her to read and lots of music I think she should listen to. She's been letting all that go for too long. We'll probably be up late most nights, so I thought it would be easier if she stays there."

There was a small silence. Emily looked sidewise at her father.

"Maybe I'll even let her give me lady lessons," she said.

"Well, I think it's a fine idea," Walter said heartily. "Just don't let her get in your way, Lulu."

"No problem with that," Lulu said.

There was another silence, and then Lulu said, "Let us do the dishes tonight, Mrs. Raiford. We haven't done them in ages. You put your feet up and watch TV with Walter."

"Not tonight," Jenny said. "You both had a late night last night. You can help another time."

She got up and went into the kitchen. No one looked after her but Lulu. Lulu looked for a long moment. Then she looked back at the table and the talk swirled on. In the candlelight, she talked and talked and talked and they listened.

That night Emily slept in her bedroom for the last time. She would move her things to Lulu's apartment the next day. For a long time she could not sleep, whether from the residue of the night before or from the sense of great change pressing her down, she could not tell. Elvis lay snugged tightly into the curve of her side, twitching every now and then in some doggy dream, and once whining. When Emily stroked him softly he sighed and subsided, wriggling a little to find a comfortable place. After that he hardly moved.

Outside her curtained window the moon

hung huge and white and swollen with the coming autumn, and made the familiar shapes of Emily's bedroom furniture stand out in bas-relief. Emily stared at them for a long time. Ever since she could remember they had been the landscape and boundaries of her nights; she could have found her way around the room if all her senses except touch were gone. Tonight they folded her in like a blanket. She moved restlessly in her bed and wondered what the night world in Lulu's apartment would be like. Drifting white with moonlight and the gauzy drapings and the whitewashed walls, of course, but there were bound to be other things that would become her dark-time totems, her polestars. The wall of books, of course, so like the one in Buddy's room, and the delicate camel's back of the little sofa, and the spidery French writing desk under one window. They would, she thought, become comforting friends to share her nights, as her own things were. And then she thought of the great, savage painting that at once discomforted her and drew her eyes like wildfire. She hoped that her bed faced away from those wheeling black birds, and the great pyramid and the cold cobalt bowl of the sky. From the brown man with his red hands uplifted. She thought that if she got up in the nights those hands might reach for her.

"Don't be silly," she thought. "You loved that painting from the first time you saw it. Lulu loves it. Her grandmother does, too."

But not at night, a deeper part of herself said. As cloistered as they were in the little apartment above the barn, they would not be protected from the red-armed priest and the diving birds. These were part of the room itself. They were shut in with them by the moat.

Then she thought of the familiar sounds of the kennels, and the droning cicadas off in the woods, and the ticking of warm rain on the barn roof, and Lulu's soft, even breathing, and most of all, Elvis's warmth against her. Elvis would let nothing touch her in the night.

Nevertheless, she felt a sudden stab of anxiety. She wanted to stay in this haven that was the only one she remembered.

"Do I have to give her everything?" she thought. And then: "Buddy?" reaching down to him, as she often had over the past summer. "Where are you? I need to talk to you."

He did not answer. She had the sudden thought that perhaps he might not like Lulu's apartment, would not come to her there; that the violence in which the past night had ended, and the new assurance that filled her, had stopped his voice.

"Maybe he thinks I don't need him anymore," she thought. "But I do. He keeps me safe, just like Elvis does. If he doesn't come back I'm not going to stay out there. I'm not giving her Buddy, too."

In the moony dark Elvis licked her hand drowsily. The childish doubts receded like the creek at dead low tide, and the new, grown-up Emily stretched her arms and legs under the familiar flowered top sheet.

"She needs me," the new Emily thought. "Only I am helping her. Only I can. I can come back here later, if I want to."

Turning into sleep, she did not, as she usually did at this time of night, hear her father and her aunt talking. There was no sound whatsoever. Emily listened for another minute, and then, finally, slept.

She moved a few things out to the apartment the next morning, but did not go there when their last session with the puppies was over. She went back to her house, waiting dimly to see if anyone was going to say good-bye to her. But there was no one about. Her father and the boys had taken four of the new puppies to be neutered, and though she could hear her aunt moving around the kitchen, she did not go in search of her and Jenny did not come out. Emily stumped upstairs pettishly, thinking that everyone had just assumed she was gone from the house and moved on about their business. This hour after the day's work, when she had showered and changed, had always been her time with Jenny Raiford.

Lulu came for supper that night flushed and smiling and bearing a steaming casserole.

"Supper's on me," she said a little shyly, and everyone smiled. Lulu, wreathed in fragrant steam and smiling bashfully, was totally charming.

"But you shouldn't," Jenny said. "You work all day in that heat. I'm accustomed to cooking, and I really like to do it."

"Well, I just thought all of a sudden that

I'd like to try it," Lulu said. "It's my famous shrimp and grits. You know, the recipe that closed down the Carolina Yacht Club. I'm afraid the shrimp was frozen, but the grits are honest to goodness Carolina Gold. My mother sent a bag of them with me when I came. I think she believes that Carolina Gold will ward off evil spirits."

The shrimp dish was a great success. Everyone exclaimed over it and had seconds, and Lulu sat in an aureole of her own light, pleased and flustered as a small child at the praise.

After dinner, she said to the table at large, "Listen, I have a proposal to make. I'd like to get supper most nights. I've got all the things I need in the apartment, and Emily can help me. Charleston ladies should be able to hold their own in a kitchen, whether or not they ever actually cook. Everybody's cook has nights off, and no Lowcountry lady ever ordered in pizza in her life. Mrs. Raiford has slaved all summer in the kitchen in this heat, and I'd love to wait on her for a while. Please let me. I really, really want to do this."

Walter smiled at Lulu.

"I think it's a fine idea," he said. "You're

certainly a good cook. I've never had better shrimp and grits. But only if you promise to stop if it tires you. And between the dogs and supper you're not going to have much time for that reading and music you and Emily were going to do."

"We don't need much sleep," Lulu smiled. In the candlelight, she seemed a creature who would never need sleep or food or drink: an eternal creature living on light.

"Well, we'll try it then," Walter said. "If Jenny is agreeable?" He looked at Jenny Raiford for the first time.

She nodded slowly.

"But the first time you look droopy, I'm going to insist that you stop," he went on. "After all, it's what Jenny's here for."

Lulu's eyes flew to Jenny Raiford, sitting at her end of the table. Emily's did, too. Jenny's face was still and expressionless.

"Nice to have some help," she said.

As she and Lulu walked across the grass to the apartment after dinner, Emily said, "Do you really want to cook? You never said anything about liking to cook."

"I really do," Lulu said, smiling. "I used to do a lot of it out at Grand's. She was teaching me."

"Well, I don't know if I want to help," Emily sniffed.

"You don't have to if you don't want to," Lulu said. "But it's a lot of fun, really. I think we'd make a good team."

They did not, after all, stay up talking that night as Emily had thought they might. Lulu pulled the little trundle from under her bed and made it up for Emily, and said, "You take the first turn in the bathroom. I'll set the alarm for seven."

So Emily dutifully went into the bathroom and scrubbed her face and teeth, and pulled on a new batiste nightgown her aunt had given her, that she had never worn, and came back and climbed into the little low bed. She thought that, after the soft sea of her big bed, it would feel narrow and con-stricting, but the silky, lavender-smelling linens were delicious, and Elvis's weight against her side was sweet and familiar. She did not, after all, face the painting, and the nighttime sounds from outside soothed in a way that the breath of the river never had. By the time Lulu came back into the room in short white pajamas, Emily was fast asleep, and she did not stir until the unfamiliar chime from the little bedside clock woke her.

They had a breakfast of toast and fresh peaches and coffee, and while they ate, Lulu played a slow, dreaming little CD that, oddly, made Emily want to cry.

"I like that," she said. "What is it?"

"Pavane pour une Infante Défunte," Lulu said. " 'Pavane for a Dead Princess.' An elegy played at the death of a little royal princess. Maurice Ravel wrote it. Funeral music at breakfast is a specialty of mine."

"That was French you spoke, wasn't it?" Emily said. "At first? Do you speak French?"

"You don't get out of Charlotte Hall without speaking something besides English, and French is considered the language of diplomats and ladies," Lulu grinned. "I'll teach you some."

"I'd rather stick to pig Latin," Emily said, and they laughed, and the day began.

15

Often, in the hot days of that early fall, Emily would look at Lulu, lithe and golden as always, in the sunlight of the dog ring or the table's candlelight, and would feel for the first time the fierce, obliterating love of a parent for a child.

If she had examined it, she would have seen that it was a mocking sham of an emotion, and the moated Sweetwater an ersatz world, shimmering in the mists of unreality like a bewitched castle out of *Le Mort d'Arthur.* But she did not and could not examine it. She dimly knew that to lose that world would be to watch Lulu wither and die.

And so all of Sweetwater—house, river, marshes, creek—and all living things in it—

people, dogs, dolphins, even the nameless, one-celled creatures deep in the cradling mud—were protected by the circle of Emily's power. "It's going to be all right," burned in the thickening September air like a great hovering planet.

The next day was the Saturday before school started, and Emily and Lulu had the weekend off. Lulu slept late and mooched around the morning-cool little apartment in her nightgown, drinking coffee and absently straightening up the counters of the small kitchen. She was distant in the mornings, Emily would learn, and not to be chattered at or engaged in plans for the day.

"Chill out, Emily," she said on this first morning. "This is the only absolutely down time I have. The rest of the day will find itself."

And Emily, who could not sit still, took Elvis and a peach across the yard to the river and down to the dock, where they sat watching the tide churn into the river from the distant sea and soaked in the sights and sounds and smells of a larger marsh and wider water. There was a salt taste and smell to the air that you did not get on the creek, and the rustlings in the cordgrass were made by larger creatures than the creek harbored. Emily had not been to the river much that summer. It cast its net of living light over her once more, and it was nearly eleven o'clock when the blatting of a horn in the driveway pulled her back into the world.

She heard Lulu calling her, faintly, and she and Elvis went back up the dock and around the house to the driveway. The red BMW convertible glimmered in the sun like a cauldron, its grillwork throwing off lances of light. Lulu stood beside it, dressed in white pants and a black T-shirt, hair freshly washed and shining eyes shielded by dark aviator glasses. She was grinning. Emily thought she looked like an Italian movie star, though she couldn't have said why. She couldn't remember ever seeing one.

"Where did that come from?" Emily said, prowling around the car. Elvis sat in coppery dignity beside it, as if he was a doorman. He stared at the car and then up at Emily.

"Are we going somewhere in this?" the yellow eyes asked. Elvis knew about trucks fitted with dog crates, and SUVs, and high-bouncing old cars, but he had never seen

transport into which sunlight poured down on buttery smooth leather like syrup.

"I don't know," Emily told him. "Would you like it?"

He thumped his tail and lolled his tongue, grinning.

"Leland just brought it out with some books and things Grand sent us. I asked him to when I called yesterday. Austerity is over. From now on you ride around like a south of Broad princess."

"Ride where?" Emily said suspiciously. She had hardly left the farm the entire summer, and as far as she knew, except for her grandmother's party, Lulu had not left it at all.

"For starters, to the grocery store. And then to the oyster place on Bowen's Island for some fresh ones. And then, who knows? Have you ever been to Kiawah?"

"No, and I don't want to," Emily sniffed. "I heard they had a gate and security people who wouldn't let you in if you didn't live there, and houses bigger than the ones on the Battery. It sounds awful."

"Well, I guess it is, sort of," Lulu smiled. "I don't think of it that way because Grand's family had a big old wooden house on the beach for years down there, before the resort bought it. Grand can remember when the beaches were empty and white and beautiful. She used to run loose on them all day as naked as a jaybird and not see another soul except family. Okay. No Kiawah. How about Folly Beach?"

Emily had been to Folly often. Its careless, sandy-rumped ambience and close-leaning beach shacks on stilts did not intimidate her the way a gated community would.

"Okay," she said. "But I don't want to swim or anything. Just ride over there."

"Good. Hop in. We'll eat shrimp at Sandy Don's and be home by midafternoon. We've got to unpack books; Grand sent boxes and boxes of them."

They slid into the car. Beside the door, Elvis whined.

"He's coming with us, isn't he?" Emily said. "He always comes with me and the boys, or Aunt Jenny. I'm not going off and leaving him."

"Will he stay still and not try to jump out?"

"What do you think? Of course he will."

Lulu nodded and Emily patted the hot leather seat. Elvis soared over the closed door and settled into the space between the two seats.

Lulu started the car and it purred out of the driveway and down the dirt road toward the highway. The wind was cool on their faces, and the sun was warm on shoulders and forearms. Riding so low was like being a part of the road. Elvis sat perfectly still in the circle of Emily's arm, head up, ears streaming joyfully in the wind, golden eyes closed. When they reached the blacktop Lulu pushed her foot down on the accelerator. After that the countryside was a blur and the wind was as intoxicating as alcohol, and there was no sound but velvety, growling engine and wind. Emily leaned back and stretched, drunk on air. Lulu smiled at her.

"Beats a Toyota all to hell, doesn't it?" she said.

In the big, cool Publix on the outskirts of Hollywood, Emily tagged along as Lulu filled a cart with food. When it was fully loaded, they put the food into the trunk of the BMW, laid a mylar blanket over it, and roared out of the parking lot. Heads turned to see the sleek little beast of a car and the three pretty heads in it, one gilt-blond, two burning red, blowing in the wind. Catcalls and whistles

followed them from pickups and motorcy-
cles.

"A red BMW convertible is the ultimate
sex toy," Lulu grinned.

They swept over to Highway 171 and
down toward the sea, stopping at Bowen's
Island for a sack of still-dripping oysters just
out of the wide creek, and then bowled into
Folly Beach. Elvis nodded sleepily while
they went into the scabrous, cool waterfront
restaurant and had fresh boiled shrimp to
peel and eat with red sauce. They brought
him back a plain hamburger, which he ate
sedately after consulting Emily with his yellow eyes. They stopped for hot boiled
peanuts, and by three o'clock they were
home, the groceries stashed away, the
boxes of books surrounding them on the
shining bare-wood floor of the apartment.
Elvis lay stretched full-length on the sheepskin rug, watching them. It was only then
that Emily realized that they had ventured
far beyond the moat and she had never
once thought about it. Perhaps there was a
kind of magical protection in the two of
them together. Strange. She would have to
think about this.

On the first of the boxes was a Post-it

note with "Enjoy!" written on it in a sprawling backhand.

"Grand," Lulu said. "When I asked for
some books, she said okay, as long as I let
her pick them out. It's fine with me. She
knows what I love, and probably what you
would, from knowing your brother."

The first box was entirely poetry, more
volumes of poetry than Emily had ever seen.
Most were old and dusty; Buddy had many
like them. He had read a lot of it aloud, but
had discouraged her from reading it alone.

"Poetry is for when your mind catches up
with your heart," he had said. "Wait till
you're thirteen or so."

Emily was suddenly fiercely reluctant to
hear any poetry in a voice other than his. "I
don't know if I want to plow through all that
poetry," she said, watching Lulu decant the
books in towering, untidy piles. "I don't
much like poetry."

"You will when we get started," Lulu said.
"There's some new stuff here, but most of
them are old favorites. Grand and I used to
read them together. Every now and then
she'd stop and ask me what I thought, or
she'd read me something she thought was
especially wonderful. I still remember whole

chunks of poems, and I can still hear her voice, as clear as day."

"Buddy and I used to do that," Emily said, remembering. Her throat closed. "I can still hear him, too."

"I think he picked that up from Grand," Lulu said. "She taught like that. And she knew all about you; he must have told her at the lessons. She specifically asked me to bring you to her party. What great memories you must have of your brother and the reading."

"No. I mean I really hear him," Emily said. "From somewhere inside. We talk."

Hearing her own words, Emily stopped.

"I guess it sounds crazy," she said.

"No, it sounds wonderful," Lulu said. "I wish somebody talked to me from inside. I think I would have loved your brother."

"Yes," Emily said. "You would have."

But it was just me that he loved, she thought.

"Oh, here it is," Lulu said, taking a little notebook with brittle yellow pages from the box. The script on the front, spidery and elegant, read *My Mother's Receipts.*

"My great-grandmother's favorite recipes," Lulu said. "Only they called them 'receipts' in those days. We're going to eat like nineteenth-century Lowcountry ladies."

School started the next Monday. From the first day of her last year in middle school, Emily was bored and restless. Anxieties simmered, always just under the surface of the days. They were not feelings she had ever had at school—well, except for the boredom—and she did not examine them. She sat in stale air-conditioning and listened to droning lectures or giggling, insinuating talk of sex during lunchtime and between classes, hardly sharing either. School this year did not seem real. She only felt reality flow back in, and life resume, when she was back inside the moat, safe again at Sweetwater.

On that first Monday after school, she changed into capris and a halter top and went out to the apartment. Lulu wore a long flowered voile skirt and tank top and looked older and more elegant with her shining hair pinned up in a knot at the back of her neck. She picked up a covered dish and a long, thin loaf of French bread.

"It's called a baguette," she told Emily. "It's really good with most casserole things."

"We usually have corn bread or biscuits," Emily said.

"Well, give it a try. You might just like it."

That night they ate Lulu's great-grand-mother's brown oyster stew with bennó seeds, over grits.

"Or hominy, as they called it back then," Lulu smiled.

The exclamations of pleasure from Walter and Jenny and even the twins could be read on her face.

"We can get you even better oysters than these," Walt Junior said. "There are beds of them all up and down Sweetwater Creek. Or you can get them yourself. It's cool. Finlly knows how to pick and shuck oysters."

"We'll do that next time," Lulu said. "I hadn't even thought of that. Imagine—our own oysters."

Emily looked around the table to see who had caught the "our." Walter and the boys beamed. Jenny Raiford smiled, a strange, remote little smile. It made Emily uneasy. Usually her aunt's smile crinkled her eyes and lit her face.

On Tuesday, Lulu brought a shrimp pie. She and Emily had worked together on it in the tiny kitchen. Even though there was not much space, Lulu's mother had equipped it with handsome, matte-black cookware and an array of implements that Emily had never seen in Cleta's kitchen.

"Oyster forks," Lulu explained. "And these are asparagus tongs. And grape shears. Mother was just showing off. Nobody uses that stuff anymore except maybe at a real formal banquet. And I haven't been to one of those in years."

On Wednesday, the Parmenters exclaimed over shrimp pilau, pronounced, Lulu said, "purloo."

On Thursday, there were Aunt Maudie's scalloped oysters. This time the oysters came from an overhanging bank just down from the dolphin slide on the creek. Emily had showed Lulu how to harvest and shuck them, and they had done it together in the little kitchen.

"I think Aunt Maudie was an ex-slave," Lulu said. "I don't remember her, of course, but Grand remembers when her mother had some ex-slaves in the house."

On Friday they brought fresh pompano stuffed with just-caught Bowen's Island shrimp. That night, after seconds and praise and groans of contentment, Lulu asked

Jenny Raiford if she might cook some of the meals in the big kitchen in the house.

"Emily and I bump into each other," she said. "And of course we'll clean up afterward. Mrs. Raiford can go most evenings without even seeing the inside of that kitchen."

Aunt Jenny smiled the strange smile and inclined her head, yes. For the last few evenings she had said very little. Emily did not note her silence directly, but somewhere inside her was a void where her aunt's light, laughing voice had been.

The first night in the big kitchen she produced creamed sweetbreads, which everyone loved until she told them the provenance of the dish. There were gasps and eye-rollings from Walter and the boys, but they were expected caricatures, Emily knew. By now she thought that the three Parmenter males would happily eat hyena offal if Lulu prepared it.

For Sunday dinner, at midday, there was Country Captain over hominy.

"I remember my mother making this," Walter said, "but I hadn't thought about it for years. Yours is much better than hers."

"And it's a great way to get rid of a stringy

old rooster if you have one," Lulu said. The table dissolved in laughter. The plantation kept no chickens, and Emily was fairly sure you could not buy roosters at a grocery store. Later, Lulu told her it was a capon, male, but not at all the same thing as a rooster.

"But with a little of the same strong flavor," she said. "The fruit and spices would overpower anything else."

After a pickup supper that evening, Walter got up from his chair and went to stand behind Jenny Raiford, and said with a smile, "Well, you've put Jenny out of a job. Tell them, Jenny."

She smiled at them. In the candlelight she was suddenly as beautiful as a madonna. Emily remembered that Buddy had said she had a natural elegance.

"I've been offered a job at Saint Francis Hospital in Charleston," she said. "And I've accepted it. It's in the public relations office and the pay is really good. I'd have enough to travel like I've wanted to, and to maybe one day buy a little house. A friend from college has asked me to share her house in West Ashley, and since we've always gotten along wonderfully, I think that's what I'll do."

She fell silent. The table was silent, too. Emily stared at her. For just a moment, the bridge crumbled and the moat ran dry. She heard in her head the companionable talk between Jenny and Cleta in the kitchen, Jenny and Walter's laughter floating up the stairs into her bedroom at night. She looked at Jenny Raiford's silver candlesticks gleaming on the table, and felt again her aunt's arms firmly around her on the day she had gotten her first period and had thought she was dying. For a moment the world went black and howled. Jenny Raiford had always been a buffer between her and her father.

Jenny looked around the table, still smiling. "You really don't need me now," she said. "You girls are both grown-up and doing a fine job of looking after things, and Cleta will come in the mornings just like she always has to straighten up and get lunch, and her niece will come in after dinner and wash up. It's all I could have wanted, a really good job and finally getting to travel, and seeing Emily so happy and busy. Everybody's happy, now, it seems to me. We owe Lulu a lot."

Lulu bent her head, accepting the words,

but she was not smiling. Emily looked at her, seated as always on her father's left. She was frowning, a small, puzzled frown.

"I'll miss you," Emily said, throat and nose beginning to burn. "I really will."

Behind Jenny's chair, Walter squeezed her slim shoulders.

"Well, for a long time we surely couldn't have done without her," he said. "She deserves her own life now. We'll be just fine."

For a moment Jenny Raiford's eyes closed, and then they opened and she was smiling around the table once more. In a burst of clarity, Emily read behind her aunt's closed eyes. She looked up at her father. His face in the candlelight was suddenly younger, warm and softened with a tenderness Emily had never seen, really quite beautiful. She saw, in a sort of swift epiphany, how he must have looked when he met her mother, saw with astonishment that he was a man a woman could love.

"We're going to be just fine," he repeated. His eyes were on Lulu, who looked down at her plate. The burning in Emily's throat grew into a lump she could scarcely swallow around.

Oddly, she and Lulu did not discuss her

aunt's leaving when they got back to the apartment.

"Back to school for you and back to work for me," Lulu said, and they both simply got into bed and Lulu turned off the light. But it was a long time before Emily slept.

When she got home from school the next afternoon, Jenny Raiford was gone. There was no one in the big, dim house, and the silence echoed louder than shouting would have done. Emily went up to her hot, closed room to get another armful of clothes to move out to Lulu's. Beside her, Elvis whined.

They stopped by her aunt's bedroom before going down the stairs. Buddy's room. It was locked, as it had been for so long before Jenny Raiford had come to Sweetwater. Elvis paced nervously in the silent hall, ears back, toenails clicking.

Turning away, Emily noticed for the first time the yellow Post-it on her own closed bedroom door. It was from her aunt.

"Here's my address and phone number, both at work and at home. If you don't get me, there's an answering machine. I'll call back as soon as possible. You call me *any time,* if you need anything at all, or if you just want to talk. I'll be pretty busy at first, but I'll check in with you at least once a week. Be happy, Emmybug. And be careful. I love you. Always have. Always will. Aunt Jenny."

Emily sat down slowly on the top step of the dusty staircase in the empty house and buried her face in Elvis's curly neck and cried.

16

For what seemed to Emily a long time, they did not speak of Jenny Raiford. Occasionally, at dinner, Walter would say, "Have you heard from Jenny? I haven't heard a word. Give her a call, why don't you?"

But somehow they did not. Obscurely, Emily felt that to do so would open the door into that great, echoing interior cavern she kept tightly shut since Jenny had left. Lulu had been silent and abstracted. But even unevoked, Jenny Raiford's presence hung in the air like a toothache.

One evening in late September as they were riffling idly through Lulu's battered old English textbook, *Contemporary Poetry,* Lulu laid the book aside and looked at Emily.

"Is there something between your aunt and your father?" she said.

Emily was caught off guard, and for a moment could not think of a reply. It was a far more complicated question than it seemed on the surface.

"Well, there was once, I think," she said carefully. "He was dating Aunt Jenny before he ever met my mother. He came out here to visit her sometimes; there's a photo of them together in the library. But I don't think they saw each other anymore after Mother came along."

"But I think she's still in love with him," Emily thought but did not say. To speak the words would be to edge far too close to the mouth of the cavern.

Lulu turned her head away, but not before Emily had seen a sheen of tears in her eyes.

"You better go on down to bed," she said. "I want to read a while more, and you've got school tomorrow."

Emily was unaccustomed to being downright dismissed from Lulu's presence, and shifted awkwardly on the sofa, looking at her. Then she got up and went silently down the barn stairs to her bedroom. Elvis followed, clicking behind her and bumping her legs with his cold nose. Emily did not think she would sleep for a long time that night.

In the second week of their shared occupancy, it had become clear that the apartment was too small in some ways for both of them. When they fiddled about getting dressed or read and listened to music after dinner everything was fine; they laughed a lot, and Emily was beginning to love the sound of Lulu's rich, light voice speaking words that had come to resonate in the deepest parts of her. But when it was time for bed, or occasionally even at the beginning of the evening, old routines collided and neither seemed to be able to accommodate them. Emily was accustomed to watching television in bed, often late into the night, and Lulu loathed the TV. She kept hers in a closet, and Emily had to ask if she especially wanted to see something. Lulu said nothing, but tapped her foot restlessly while the screen flickered, and pointedly tried to read, without success. Often Emily was tired and wanted just to sink into the lavender-scented sheets with Elvis and sleep, but was kept awake by Lulu's CDs and her reading light. For a few days neither said anything, but the evenings were soon strained, and finally Lulu said, "This isn't working. I love being with you most of the time, and I need to know you're near, but we're going to end up having a fight one of these nights, and I couldn't stand that. I have an idea."

The next evening she asked Walter if she and Emily might fix up the little feed room to the left of the staircase up to the apartment in the barn.

"I know there's a water line, because it leads into that big trough, and there's electricity. I thought we could sort of spruce it up and make a little bedroom of it. I'm keeping Emily awake on school nights, and I don't want her to have to come back to the house just to get some sleep. I've got almost enough things stored in the stable to furnish it."

Within the week, Walter and the twins and Cleta's son GW had paneled the dreary little room in cypress and laid down a hardwood floor over the cold concrete, and installed a tiny bathroom with a fiberglass shower in one corner, shielded by a red Chinese screen that Lulu had banished from the apartment, and a wall of shelves. The gas line that fed the winter puppy kennels next door was run into it, and a hot water tank and small furnace installed just outside. Emily found an old maple twin bed in the barn attic that she thought she remembered from early childhood, along with a birds'-eye maple rocking chair and a spavined sofa from who knew where. Dusted and polished and dragged downstairs, they shone sweetly in the light from the lamps Lulu's mother had brought early in the summer. An exotic, faintly Persian bedspread with matching poufy drapes and bright throw pillows and Mexican scatter rugs, all rejected by Lulu, lit the low-ceilinged dusk of the room into enfolding warmth.

Emily's bureau and mirror and desk from her old room were the only things she brought to her new bedroom—those and armloads of books from Buddy's shelves. She had not delved into them yet. It was enough for the moment to have so much of Buddy close by.

She had thought she might find some prints or paintings for the walls, but she did not want to take Buddy's from his room, and the rest of the house yielded little but hunting prints and photographs of long-deceased champion Boykins. She would have loved the painting of the plantation over the dining room mantelpiece, but it seemed irrevocably wedded to its spot, and so she settled for photographs of Elvis taken at different stages of his life, from earliest puppyhood to beautiful maturity. In some he held a perfect point, in others he leaped forever out into the river in his glorious copper arc, and in still others he lay on Emily's bed looking up at the camera and grinning.

The one small, high window looked out into the little stand of trees whose branches kissed Lulu's upstairs windows, and under it stood an ornate carved Mexican chest, destined for Lulu's apartment and banished early on. Elvis often slept there, curled into a Greek throw in the daytimes, but he slept at night tucked as closely into Emily's side as he could manage. It was comforting to wake in the cooling nights not quite knowing where she was, and feel his warm weight, and know that wherever she slept, with him beside her, it was home.

Emily loved the cavelike little room, and though she still spent the bulk of her waking time upstairs with Lulu, it was often with real gratitude that she slipped downstairs to her lair at evening's end with Elvis and reruns of

Stargate SG and *The X Files.* Lulu laughed at her choices and lobbied for *Masterpiece Theatre* and old movies. But Emily was not yet ready to give up the swaddling world of science fiction that had been such a safe haven for her in the cold, flat time after Buddy died and before Lulu came.

The next morning Lulu's shine had been restored, and she sang as she drove Emily to school in the red convertible. At the top of her lungs she sang, "I didn't know God made honky-tonk angels. I might have known you'd never make a wife. You gave up the only one that ever loved you, and went back to the wild side of life."

Her rich molasses voice slid up into a perfect hillbilly twang, and Emily laughed helplessly as they roared into the school parking lot. Heads snapped around and slouching cool was abandoned at the sight of the little red lance of a car and Lulu, gilt hair streaming, eyes shielded by enormous black sunglasses, singing Hank Williams so loudly that it carried over the silken noise of the engine.

"Everybody's going to be talking about me," Emily said, getting out of the car. People were still staring. Her cheeks and neck reddened.

"High time," Lulu said, and squealed out of the parking lot.

No one mentioned the car directly to Emily, but a couple of the older boys sidled up to her at lunchtime and said, "Who's the babe?" and one of the varsity cheerleaders asked her to sit with her crowd at lunch. But Emily was suddenly stricken mute by the unearned attention, and muttered a refusal and had her sandwich sitting on the steps with a copy of Tennyson's *Idylls of the King,* which Lulu thought a good vessel for launching her into poetry.

Lulu took Emily to school most mornings, and soon the BMW became a part of the landscape and the conspicuous admiration abated. But Emily knew that she had advanced several giant steps in the game of Middle School, even if it was in a red BMW convertible.

Lulu's high spirits lasted the whole week; at the dinners she and Emily cooked she was once again the magical, gesturing spinner of tales and fables, and the general laughter largely banished the thin ghost of

Jenny Raiford that hovered at ceiling level in the dining room.

Emily's school had altered their training routine, so now they trained the older puppies and dogs ready for finishing in the afternoons. In the mornings while Emily was away, Lulu took over the schooling of the youngest puppies, and often Walter worked with her. He did not have to; Lulu was almost as good as Emily now with the babies, but it pleased her father to see the new crops coming along so smoothly, and Emily suspected that he hugely enjoyed the time spent with Lulu. His awe at her social cachet had largely been replaced with something easier, almost lighthearted. But the Foxworth name still lit his eyes. The twins still lingered around Lulu as long as they decently could, but they had long ago relinquished any hopes of impressing her, and had to be content with warming themselves at a distance at her fire. GW came in the mornings to help with the kennel work, and the boys and Walter took the late-afternoon advanced training. Cleta still came in the early mornings to make breakfast and clean, but she did not stay long into the afternoons now. Her niece Tijuan, the feckless mother of small Robert, now in one of her domestic phases, came to do the dishes and tidy up after dinner while Cleta sat with Robert. All in all, it was a comfortable arrangement, and life at Sweetwater continued on largely as it always had.

The one exception was that Emily seldom saw Cleta anymore. She and Lulu got their own breakfast in the early morning, before they left for school, and Cleta was gone when Emily got home. Caught up in the spell of dogs and Lulu and the slow bronze Lowcountry fall, she seldom thought of Cleta's absence from her life. But sometimes, on the back of her neck, a cool little wind blew, as if from a vast empty space somewhere behind her. And then sometimes she would see or hear something that pleased her and would think, "Oh, I have to remember to tell Cleta that," and just as quickly she would forget it. Still, there was that sense of wind at her back often that fall. Jenny and Cleta had displaced a lot of air.

One evening in mid-October Walter said at the table, "I hear that Jenny has a new beau. Have you all heard anything about that?"

"No," Emily said. "How do you know?"

"Cleta told me this morning. Apparently Jenny calls her occasionally just to check in. I'm surprised she hasn't called you, Emily, but then you're not in very much. You could catch her on weekends at home, though."

"I will," Emily said. "Who's this boyfriend?"

"A hospital administrator, or something," Walter said. "I'm glad to hear it. She's a pretty woman, and she's buried herself in other people's lives too much. She needs to have some fun."

Obscure resentment stabbed Emily. Present or not, Jenny Raiford was a part of the cloth of this family. Emily wanted no strange hospital administrators introduced into the tapestry. She looked across the table at Lulu, but the girl sat with her eyes on her plate, long gold-tipped lashes shuttering her eyes.

The next morning before school, Emily crossed the dew-frosted lawn to seek out Cleta in the warm kitchen.

"Hey," she said, hooking a hot biscuit from the tray Cleta was carrying in to the breakfast room.

"Hey yourself," Cleta said. "You honoring us with your presence this morning?"

"I miss your biscuits," Emily said, taking another one. "I miss you. Why didn't you tell me about Aunt Jenny's new boyfriend?"

"When I ever see you?" Cleta said, smacking dishes around in the sink. "I'm always in here, and you're livin' out in the feed room now. I guess Lulu kicked you out of her apartment?"

"No. I'm there most of the time. We read together and listen to music. We both just needed separate sleeping places so we wouldn't bother each other."

"Well, you got a separate place right here, a big, pretty room upstairs. Seem to me like it be a lot more comfortable than an old dog food room."

"You ought to come see it; it's really pretty," Emily said defensively.

"I bet," Cleta said. There was a long silence. It was obvious to Emily that she was not going to chat, so she turned and went slowly out into the pale sunlight, calling behind her, "Tell Aunt Jenny I'd like to talk to her when she calls again."

Cleta said nothing.

"Cleta's acting really funny, all quiet and

grumpy," she told Lulu that evening. "Do you think she's sick?"

"Not in the way you mean," Lulu said, and was quiet again herself for the rest of the night. Vaguely uneasy and weary of nuances she could not quite grasp, Emily put it out of her mind, and the golden autumn rolled on.

On a Sunday afternoon so washed with muted gold and green and warmed with sun from a high, clarion blue sky that it seemed to have at its heart the entire essence of a Lowcountry autumn, Emily and Lulu were stretched out on a blanket in the shade at the edge of the puppy ring, playing with an armful of puppies and reading Keats.

"Listen, Emily, isn't this perfect?" Lulu said. " 'Season of mists and mellow fruitfulness.' He could be talking about fall on these marshes and this river."

"Mmmmm," Emily murmured, drifting in half-sleep while the puppies tugged at her shoelaces with their little briar teeth and Elvis, his red coat burning and smelling of sun and dust, sighed and shifted against her outstretched leg.

Autumn insects—cicadas, crickets, and grasshoppers—droned and burred in the soft pluff-smelling air. The crunch of approaching footsteps on the gravel of the drive broke into the silence, and a slow, throaty voice said, "I might have known I'd find the two of you here, covered in puppies and sleeping in the sun."

"Grand!" Lulu cried, sitting up straight and shielding her eyes to look at her grandmother. The old woman stood in the edge of the shade, looking to Emily frailer than ever, though wonderfully dressed in a smart tweed suit with leather shooting patches on the elbows and shoulder, and polished brown oxfords, and a tweed fedora pulled down over one blue eye. To Emily, coming up out of sleep, she looked like something come to preposterous life out of a book about English country houses such as the one Lulu had been reading to her.

"You look like you're about to head out to shoot grouse," Lulu said, grinning. "Where in the name of God did you get that outfit?"

"As a matter of fact, I did wear it out to shoot grouse once upon a time," her grandmother said. "It's what a lady used to wear on one of the big autumn hunts. You should have seen the getup your grandfather wore. He had shooting knickers, no less. I thought this would be appropriate for an afternoon in the country with the world's best hunting dogs. Or so Rhett tells me."

She gestured to Leland, whose arm she had been holding and he unfolded a little camp chair and set it on the blanket, and lowered her into it. She nodded and he went back across the driveway and lawn to sit in a bulbous black car that shone in the sun like ebony.

"I see you came in the Rolls," Lulu grinned. "I think a simple Mercedes SUV might have sufficed."

"Why have it if you don't use it?" her grandmother said. "Nobody else does but me. I love feeling like the old Queen Mum opening a parish fair. Is that gorgeous creature beside Emily one of the Boykins? I hope these babies will grow up to look just like him."

She gestured at Elvis and the puppies. Elvis cocked his head and looked at her, and then broke into a tongue-lolling grin and came over and laid his head on her knees.

"That's Elvis," Emily said, pride surging through her at her dog in the sun. "He's my own dog. He doesn't hunt, but he's out of the same stock as all our Boykins, and they're a dream to train and hunt with. We think Elvis is smarter than any of the rest of them, though."

"Well, he sure knows how to butter up an old lady," Mrs. Foxworth said, stroking Elvis's curly ears. "Oh, Lord, but Bradley would have loved this dog. He always said spaniels made the best flushing dogs. He always had English water spaniels, but I think he'd have changed his mind if he'd seen these."

"What on earth are you doing out here?" Lulu said. "Not that I don't love having you. But it's been how long since you left Maybud? Ten, fifteen years?"

"Don't be silly. I go shopping and get my hair done regularly," Mrs. Foxworth said. "I came to see what's up with you. You haven't called in weeks, and when I call you I only get that chirping answering machine."

Lulu did not reply, and Emily looked at her. Hadn't she said that she called her mother and grandmother regularly? Why would she lie about it?

"Come on up and see the apartment," Lulu said, taking her grandmother's arm. "I'll make us some tea. I still have some of the

Jacksons of Piccadilly stuff Mother brought, and a tin of those English tea biscuits that taste like toilet paper."

In the afternoon-dim cave of the little apartment Mrs. Foxworth took off the hat and sailed it onto Lulu's bed and settled herself onto the sofa. The thick silver hair that might have been, in the gloom, Lulu's hair, was swept back into a chignon this afternoon to accommodate the hat, but the tissue-paper wrinkles of her tanned skin and the lance of the blue eyes and the scarlet gash of lipstick were the same as they had been the night of her birthday party. She looked around the room and nodded in approval.

"It's very nice," she said. "Very Mediterranean, very . . . ascetic. When your father said you were going to live over a barn my heart sank, and when your mother left leading a caravan of chic, I feared the worst. But this is . . . very like you. I'll like remembering you here."

"Well, I hope it's not the last time you visit," Lulu said, pouring out tea, with the same grace she had done at the old lady's party.

"It probably will be," Mrs. Foxworth said.

"You know how I dislike social visits. But as you will not visit me or answer phone calls, I had little choice. Really, Lulu. Your mother says you're not talking to her, either, nor to your father. She's driving me crazy with it: 'What about Thanksgiving? Or Christmas? What about the Season? What will I tell people?'

"Tell them she's become a novitiate at a convent, I told her. Or that she's contracted Hansen's disease and is in need of seclusion. Maybelle has no idea on earth what Hansen's disease is, but you'd think I'd suggested she tell people you have gonorrhea."

"What is it?" Emily said, fascinated.

"Leprosy. I can't think people really get it anymore. But lepers used to hide away because it disfigured them so. Anyway, Lulu, I told her I'd find out if anything was wrong, just to get her out of my hair—and here I am. So you may as well level, toots. I won't tattle on you, and I won't nag you anymore, but I do have to know if anything is wrong. Surely you can see that."

Lulu was silent a long time, stirring her tea but not tasting it. She looked, not at her grandmother, but into middle distance. Finally she sighed and put the teacup down.

"I should have called. I'm sorry," she said. "There really isn't anything wrong. Just the opposite, in fact. I'm just so *happy* to be here, Grand. The dogs, and the marshes and the river and the woods, and music, and reading, and Emily—it's been so long since I could just . . . *be*. I guess I felt that calling home would be to . . . I don't know, invoke that awful chaos I was in when I left school. I couldn't handle that now, Grand. I couldn't take the holidays at home; I couldn't take Mother right now. You know she'd have me out at all those parties before I could say boo, and I just cannot do it. The Season can wait. God knows there's always another one. Maybe I'll think about it after New Year's. . . ."

"I don't blame you about the accursed Season, or about your mother, either, though to be fair she isn't trying to be a butt. It just comes naturally. She has lived all her life in the shadow of the goddamned Seasons, and the thought that you might do her out of one—well, I'm being too harsh. She does love you, and your father does, too. They're terribly proud of you.

"But I'm worried too. It's almost as if you're hiding out here. I wish I knew from what. I miss you. I need at least to talk to you every now and then. If something is wrong I can help, you know; don't forget that. I'll make you a deal. I'll keep your mother off your back if you'll keep in touch. Try to sort yourself out, Lulu. You have to come home sometime."

After the old lady had kissed them both and been driven away, Lulu and Emily sat silently in the apartment, watching dusk put blue fingers across the lawn.

Lulu spoke first. Emily did not think she had ever heard such desolation in a voice.

"Grand's right, of course," she said dully. "I have to go home sometime. I can't just stay here forever."

"Maybe you ought to tell her, you know, about all that stuff," Emily said. "You know she wouldn't judge you. She probably could help, like she said."

"No," Lulu said fiercely. "There's got to be one person who thinks I'm perfect. I need that. And I'm not sure she'd believe me, anyway. I tried to tell Mother and Daddy that I'm an addict, that I have to stay away from any place there's drinking. Mother said I was just tired and that I'd be fine as soon as

I had some rest. I can't be in my family, and I sure can't worm my way into yours."

"Why not?" Emily said, tasting tears. "You *can* be in our family. You already are."

"Because it really isn't my world," Lulu said. "I've just been pretending that it was. I'd give anything to switch, but . . . I can't. People can't. If I stay here very long I'll end up hurting somebody. I always do. I've already hurt Jenny. . . ."

"No, you haven't! Daddy says she's happy as a lark, you heard him. Lulu, please at least stay through Thanksgiving and Christmas and New Year's. I can't do those by myself anymore. I really can't. And besides, New Year's Day is my birthday."

Lulu looked up at her, and smiled slowly.

"Okay," she said. "Not until then."

Emily would always remember the long, honeyed slide of that autumn into winter. If there had been Lowcountry falls as dreaming-perfect as this one, they had not occurred in her lifetime. Even the adults seemed to notice.

"Nicest fall I can remember," Walter said at dinner on an October night when the moon rode high like a white galleon over the river and the stars bloomed huge and hung low.

Each day was so perfect that it seemed there could never be another one, and then there was. The great seas of spartina sweeping away to the line of dark trees at the horizon, ordinarily the color of an old lion's hide, were still as green in the beneficent sun as the little emerald lizards of the Lowcountry. They rippled gently in the small tidal winds off the sea, smelling of warm salt and sea grapes and flowers from unknown faraway shores. The skies were a tender, cloudless blue, almost indigo at noon, and the small citizens of the marsh and river and creek lingered, splashing and swishing and chirping and rustling. None seemed in a hurry to winter down. The creek banks and low-lying branches of the live oaks were festooned with big, drowsy snakes and turtles; whitetails whisked in the far-off hummocks, wood ibises and wood storks and ospreys and an occasional eagle circled lazily, riding the warm thermals. Only the dolphins were gone, cleaving more firmly to their internal imperative than the lure of the still-rich creek water.

"What do they know?" Lulu said once, on a lazy afternoon with Emily and Elvis and apples and cheese beside Sweetwater Creek.

"Maybe they're just dumb," Emily said, poking a horribly snoring Elvis with her bare toe. He started up and looked reproachfully at her, then settled back down into sleep.

"They're the smartest things with fins I ever saw," Lulu said. "They know something we don't."

Both Walter and Cleta endorsed this theory.

"Last time I saw weather like this was the fall right after Hugo," Walter said. "Thank God we're past the hurricane season."

"This weather mean a bad winter coming," Cleta said ominously on one of the few mornings Emily saw her at the big house. "Tricks all the critters and the flowers into staying late and then whups 'em with black ice. I seen it before."

But to Emily, drunk on sweet air and sun, the autumn was simply magical. Within the moat, Sweetwater seemed to dream under a spell.

Even crossing the moat was easier in this weather, almost heady. To charge across it and out into the green world in the red BMW was to start out on crusades, harness jingling with gold and silver, pennons flying, still untattered. Two or three times a week Lulu took Elvis and her for sweeps across the marsh country, bouncing along pitted hardtop and dirt roads that were often empty of other traffic, going nowhere except where the road led them. They would come home around dusk, and only when they crossed the drawbridge back to Sweetwater did Emily realize that she had, ever so slightly, been clenching her muscles.

Toward the end of October Lulu took Emily into Charleston proper. Emily was only able to do this if Lulu put the top up. They rattled over the cobbles and bricks of the old neighborhoods south of Broad, and Emily could look up at the narrow, beautiful old single houses lining the streets, the colors of soft heat, without the hairs on her arms prickling with danger. Lulu knew all of them. She would tell Emily stories of the family that lived in this house or that, would point out where she had played in walled gardens and gone to kindergarten and gone to her first cotillion, and received her first kiss.

"Boy, did *that* start something," she said ruefully. "And to think it was only fat, freck-led Austin Cavanaugh, when we were play-ing spin the bottle."

Sometimes she tapped the horn and waved to people on the street, and they would stare and then wave back. Emily, scrunching down as far as she could into the leather seat, saw surprise and specula-tion bloom on their faces.

"Why do you honk at every single soul we pass?" she said pettishly. "They stare at us like we're ghosts or something."

"Well, I'm kin to most of them," Lulu said lazily. "And then I like to kind of show the flag every now and then, let everybody know I'm still alive and well. They'll tell Mother they saw me and I looked well, and that'll keep her off my back for another week or so."

"They'll wonder who I am," Emily said.

"Not when you're hunched down there on the floor, they won't. They can't see you," Lulu grinned. "But they'll wonder whose ab-solutely gorgeous dog that is with me, and sooner or later they'll be out at the farm wanting dogs of their own. These are not just idle trips, Emmybelle. They're PR."

On one of these excursions Lulu took Emily down King Street. For hours they wandered, Elvis heeling perfectly, staring into one fabled shop after another. All the shops seemed alike to Emily, gold and silver and thin, translucent porcelains gleaming in cavelike gloom. And except for the tourists, with their cameras and guidebooks and fatigue-dulled stares, all the people on the street looked like Lulu. It was a fairy-tale street. Emily thought she would never walk down it again. It intimidated at every turn.

Lulu dragged Emily into one of the small, dark shops, where rich fabrics glowed and fabulous shoes lined the walls and cases of jewelry smote the eye, and introduced her to a tall, thin woman who looked to Emily like an elegant wood stork.

"Helen, this is my friend Emily Parmenter," Lulu said. "Emily, Helen Mills. She's been keeping the Foxworth women glamorous for years. Helen, I want to get an evening dress for Emily, something she'll wear for years and still look elegant."

The stork's appraising eyes measured Emily, and she smiled.

"I think we can find something," she said. "She isn't very tall, but we can camouflage that. And her coloring is lovely. Let me see."

She disappeared into the back of the cave and came out with an armful of Arabian Nights formalwear. She hung them in a curtained dressing cubicle and said, "Try them on, dear, and let's see which works best for you."

Emily started to back away, but a level stare from Lulu stopped her. Meekly she slunk into the cubicle and wriggled into dress after dress. All were exquisite, as formidable as medieval armor. In the mirror Emily resembled no one she had ever seen in any of them.

Eventually they left the shop with a silky hanging bag holding a moss-green velvet sheath with long sleeves and a low-cut back. It fit Emily almost perfectly except for the length, and transformed her into one of the women she had imagined she would see at old Mrs. Foxworth's party. She disliked the dress; it had been Lulu's choice.

"Where on earth will I ever wear it?" she groused. "To a dog show? To the vet's? While I birth a litter of puppies?"

"You'll wear it," Lulu said comfortably. "A

442 Anne Rivers Siddons

dress like this will create its own occasions. Don't scowl so, Emily. You won't have to buy another party dress for years."

On still another afternoon they drove down yet another street lined with live oaks and palmettos and tall old dowager houses, and Lulu slowed and stopped before the largest of them. It was massive and beautiful, with slender columns. It sat amid smaller but equally graceful outbuildings, like a mother hen with chicks. The faultless green lawn was encircled with a handsome wrought-iron fence, and through it and the great double gates Emily could see young women, all of whom looked like younger Lulus, walking on the lawn or the paths, laughing, calling to one another. It was a scene out of a Victorian girls' storybook.

"Charlotte Hall," Lulu said, smiling. "Lord, how it brings back memories. I know every inch of that house and those buildings and that lawn. Look, see that little house made entirely of shells? Only seniors are allowed to go into it. And further on there's a stone den the first owner made for his pet bear. I can still smell the chalk and hear the teachers droning on in that sweet way Charleston teachers have. I bet I still know most of them. Listen, let's go in for a minute. I can give you a quick tour and introduce you to some of the faculty, and you can see for yourself that there are no torture dungeons. You might even like it."

"If you try to make me go in there I'll jump out of this car and hitchhike home," Emily hissed, her words trembling. "I will. I mean it, Lulu."

"Okay," Lulu said, smiling at her. "We'll save it for another time. But we're going to do it sooner or later, so be warned."

Emily was silent. All the way home the world outside the moat howled once more with danger. The very blue air throbbed with it. She kept her eyes on the ribbon of road unwinding beneath the little car. Only when they turned off the blacktop onto the dirt road that led to Sweetwater did she take a deep breath and feel her heart slow. Within the moat the dying day turned once more to gold.

Just before Thanksgiving Lulu's father came to Sweetwater. He came in one of the shining, clifflike SUVs with Maybud written on the door in a graceful script, and there were four other men with him. They all looked alike to Emily: heavy-shouldered, tanned, slow of speech, indolent of movement. Emily would have known they were plantation owners just like Rhett Foxworth if she had met them in a bazaar in Algiers. They commanded the air around them.

Walter had told them the night before that "some people were coming to look at the dogs," and that he would appreciate it if Lulu and Emily would meet them.

"And maybe bring some of those little seed things you make, Lulu. I'll get Cleta to leave us some iced tea. Looking at dogs is thirsty work."

If Emily had not been lulled by the afternoon sun on the creek and a long warm shower, she might have noticed that her father was wearing the smug, full-cheeked look he got when he thought he had scored a considerable coup. But she and Lulu were talking together, walking up the driveway from the barn, and did not look up until they were almost even with the SUV.

"Oh, shit," Lulu whispered. "It's Daddy. Oh, how *could* Walter? Now I'm going to get the whole nine yards about coming home and I just do not think I can stand it."

But after hugging her hard and nodding genially to Emily, Rhett Foxworth said only, "I've been telling these characters about Sweetwater Boykins ever since I brought mine home, and finally they got so tired of me that they wanted to come see for themselves. And when I told them that my girl and her friend Emily trained each and every one of them, they simply didn't believe me. So I'm going to show them."

He introduced the men around, and they all smiled and nodded, and then Walter said, "I hope it won't be too much trouble for you girls to put a few of the dogs through their paces. Start with the new puppies and work up. After that the boys and I will take everybody out to the river and show them the gun work and the retrievals. And then we'll come have some iced tea."

There was no way to refuse, so for the next hour Emily and Lulu showed the youngest Boykins in the puppy ring. The youngsters were faultless, and the men nodded and murmured among themselves. But it was Elvis, sitting sentinel at the gate to the ring, who elicited the most comment. It had been too late to shut him up in the barn, and so Emily had looked levelly at her father when Elvis trotted into the ring, and he looked back at her, and, finally, nodded.

"Goddamned beautiful dog," the men said, "and if he can hunt like he looks, you can put me down for five of the next litter."

"He doesn't hunt," Walter said. "We're saving him for breeding stock. But he's got the same bloodlines as our best. Learns faster than any dog I've ever seen."

"Emily trained him," Lulu said clearly. "She trains most of the puppies. She's a witch with them."

Emily blushed and dropped her head.

When the men went with Walter out to the river to watch the older dogs perform, Lulu's father stayed behind. Walter had urged him to join them, but he had said, "You'd just be preaching to the choir, Parmenter. I think I'll stay and have a chat with my prodigal daughter. I haven't seen her since summer."

So Walter and the plantation owners headed out toward the flat training field beside the river, and Rhett Foxworth went over to sit beside Lulu, who was hunkered down on the bottom step up to the porch.

"Emily, get us some of that iced tea, will you?" she said without raising her head, and Emily went swiftly into the dim kitchen, where she put her cheek to the open window out onto the porch and listened shamelessly. Her heart beat strongly. All-powerful Emily, protector, was back. She would let nothing frighten or harm Lulu, not even her father.

But as it turned out, her services were not needed.

"Well, can you run a kennel yet?" Rhett Foxworth said to his daughter, one arm draped loosely around her shoulder.

"Just about," Lulu said almost inaudibly, looking sidewise up at him. She looked to Emily to be suddenly shriveled, as frail as her grandmother, her essential fires out.

"I'll bet you could," he said. "Those dogs are nothing short of phenomenal, and the way you work with them is really nice to see. I never knew you had a gift for dogs."

"Neither did I," Lulu said. "But since I've been out here I've realized that there's nothing I'd rather do than what I'm doing now."

"No reason why you should," her father said. "Lots of Lowcountry women have kennels and train their own dogs. Almost every other wife I know does it to one extent or another. It's a nice accomplishment; beats bridge and garden clubs all to hell. This is as good a way as any to learn the ropes. But listen, baby, you've got to help me out. I need some way to calm your mother down. She's almost crazy to get you home. She's pushing me to find out if you're coming for Thanksgiving and Christmas. Your grandmother is pretty good at shutting her up, but all your friends are asking, too. Your mother says everybody thinks you're pregnant."

Lulu laughed, a laugh rich with relief.

"Farthest thing from it, Daddy," she said. "But I just can't come home yet. I simply cannot do those parties, and they really need me here. I want to stay a little while longer. The new puppies will be finished right after New Year's. I'll see then. There's always next year for the Season. They go on into eternity."

Her father laughed.

"Don't they though? Well, I can take her over to Yemassee in South Georgia for Beau Troutman's big hunt at Thanksgiving. Everybody from Pawley's to Savannah will be there. She's always wanted to go. And I guess I could take her to St. Thomas or Anguilla or somewhere for Christmas. I'd still save a bundle over what I'd spend for launching you. But you need to call her,

Lulu. I can tell her how well you're doing out here, but she still needs to hear for herself."

"I will, Daddy, I promise," Lulu said. Emily did not think she would.

Walter and the men came back from the field, talking and laughing. Even at her distance, Emily could see that her father was elated, almost flying. He slapped one and then another of the planters on the back, talking nonstop.

"All in all, they ordered sixteen puppies," he exulted at dinner that night. "And they'll tell the whole Lowcountry, and two or three of them said they'd like to come hunt our land and use the dogs. It would be the chance of a lifetime for us. We're going to have our own Christmas hunt, just like the big boys do. We'll invite everybody. We've got the contacts now."

Emily winced. She knew that by contacts he meant that Lulu Foxworth was in his house. He seemed to her in that moment like a child who has finally gotten a clear sense of himself, even if it is an overblown one.

Emily looked obliquely over at Lulu, expecting to see her own pain and dismay on

Lulu's face. But Lulu was smiling at Walter over the candles. Her face was serene.

"I'll be happy to be your hostess, if you'll have me," she said.

Walter laughed joyously.

"Let the games begin," he said.

Walking back to the barn with Lulu after dinner, Emily said despairingly, "Nobody will come. They have their own hunts. They've never invited him. Why would they come to his?"

Lulu smiled at her. In the eerie, shadow-less glow of the sodium lights her face looked exalted, archaic, pagan. Diana the Huntress by Dalí.

"They'll come," she said.

17

And they did. On New Year's Eve, just at dusk, the big SUVs began to rattle down the dirt road and between the gateposts into Sweetwater's circular driveway. Lulu and Emily and the twins had lined the long drive with luminarias in paper bags—nothing fancy, Lulu had said—and set outdoor torches around the circle in front of the house. Votives lit the steps up to the porch. Behind the long windows, massed candles flickered.

The tender fall had slid into a soft early winter, often silver-shrouded with mist from the river and creek. There was mist this night, and all of the lights wore opalescent halos. Just before their guests were due to arrive, Emily and Elvis had slipped out to the end of the dirt road and looked back at the house. Emily caught her breath. House and drive seemed to float in a nimbus of soft white light, shimmering slightly in the moving mist. It was a sight out of an old spell, lovelier in its diffused radiance than Lulu's blazing plantation had been the night of her grandmother's party. That had been, simply, glorious. This was, Emily thought, mysterious, almost holy. It made her want to kneel in the mist. She smiled to herself. She would never tell anyone how she felt; she could imagine what her father would say, and the boys. Well, maybe she would tell Lulu. Or maybe she would keep this vision of Sweetwater as her own, something to measure it against forever after.

Far down the dirt road she heard the crunch of the first vehicles, and picked up her skirts and ran back to the house. When their guests arrived they were met on the steps by Walter Parmenter in a new tuxedo, with Emily on one side in the long green velvet dress, and Lulu on the other, in simple floor-length black velvet and her great-grandmother's pearls. Elvis sat at grave coppery attention beside Emily. Walter was stiff and awkward, and Emily was tongue-tied, but Lulu was far from speechless. These were her family's lifelong friends. She welcomed them as such, with smiles and murmured greetings and little cheek kisses.

This night had begun just after Thanksgiving. That day had been a quiet one; Jenny Raiford had called to say that she and her new friend had tickets to the Clemson–South Carolina game and she was afraid she would have to miss Thanksgiving, but would make it up at Christmas. For the first time in Emily's memory, Cleta did not come to start the feast. With just the five of them, Walter had said that she might have the whole day with her family. Emily and Lulu could manage. And they had. They had put a fat wild turkey in to brine in a deep feed bucket the night before, a strange and suspect ritual to Emily. She had wrinkled her nose.

"Trust me," Lulu said. "It'll be the best turkey you ever had."

And it was. The imperial bird was brought out on the big Haviland platter in its glistening brown glory, surrounded with little crab-apples and kumquats and huge purple grapes. Oyster-and-pecan dressing steamed in a separate pan. Yams were not paved with gluey marshmallow, but whipped with raisins and nuts and sherry. Dessert was a regal Lady Baltimore cake that Lulu had spent an entire afternoon assembling. It was, she said, the Maybud cook's receipt. She could not imagine how old it was.

"All of it's out of Grand's receipt book," she said when the compliments began to flow. "A really old Charleston plantation Christmas, except for the brined turkey. Emily did half of it."

Two days after the holiday, Walter sat down to dinner with a list on a sheet of notebook paper.

"The hunt's all planned," he said. "The boys and I will sleep in the bunkhouse and there'll be enough rooms for everybody if some of them double up. A venison supper cooked by Cleta and her sister and niece. The band from Bowen's Island, and a hunt breakfast catered by the best barbecue place on the island. Then hunting all New Year's Day, and supper. Everybody will leave after breakfast the next day."

He looked around the table, beaming. Emily dropped her head in mortification. A band from Bowen's Island? Aristocratic planters doubling up in big, sagging beds like 10-year-olds at a sleepover or tossing on cots? Barbecue for breakfast?

She did not lift her head until she heard Lulu's voice, pleasant and matter-of-fact.

"Let us take over," she said. "You have enough to do getting the fields and the pastures in shape, and the dogs. Somebody will have to clean out the barn, in case anybody wants to bring their own dogs. The house needs some spiffing up. Emily and I will do the rest."

For the next three days, after finishing with the dogs and before cooking dinner, Lulu spent an hour or so on the telephone, with whom Emily never knew. She wrote invitations on thick ivory vellum notes she had brought with her, and mailed them. Within two days almost everyone had accepted.

"Gentlemen, start your engines," Walter crowed, with such exuberance that Emily had to grin, even though she did not understand the allusion.

The long march up to New Year's Eve began in earnest. Walter declared a moratorium on training until after the holidays, and Lulu and GW and, in the afternoons, Emily and the twins, put Lulu's battle plan into action. Emily had grave doubts about it; it was simple in the extreme, even spartan. Nothing about it could compete with the celebratory dress their guests' plantations would wear.

"Of course we can't compete with all that; we shouldn't try," Lulu said. "This house has its own personality, and it's just as valid and beautiful as any on the river or the creek. Even its bare bones are wonderful. It's one of the oldest plantation houses around Charleston, and those earliest ones weren't ornate and ostentatious. They were just what this one is—simple, functional, close to the woods and the river. In its own way it's a lot more distinguished than the later ones. And it has some wonderful touches that I've only seen in books; that beautiful old gougework in the dining room and library mantels, and that plain, perfect early Georgian staircase in the foyer. The open wraparound porch and the brick pilings under the house—and those are slave-made bricks, I guarantee you—and the thin, plain columns and the tin roof are textbook early river plantation. For decorations we should use what the earliest planters would have, greens from the woods, moss, shells, berries. It will be just as beautiful in its own way as any of the later, fancier ones, you just wait and see. Nobody will have seen anything like it."

And under her direction, the work began.

"We're going to put people in the bunkhouse to sleep," she said. "It's what bunkhouses are for. Trust me. Everyone will love it."

And the bunkhouse was turned out and scrubbed and polished and its walls newly stippled with creamy stucco, and the two great boarded-up fireplaces at either end were cleaned and readied, their brasses polished until they gave off their own rich light. The two big moribund communal baths were painted and retiled and their bulbous fixtures renewed. The sloping concrete floors were softened here and there with plushy sheepskin rugs, from where, no one asked. Every day a Maybud SUV appeared with Leland at the wheel, bearing another load of plunder.

"How on earth did you get your mother to lend you all this stuff?" Emily asked one day in early December, watching Leland and some of the Maybud hands wrestling an enormous, carved pine armoire out of the van. It wore a patina of centuries.

"Mother doesn't know about it," Lulu said, directing the placement of the armoire in the bunkhouse. "I cut a deal with Daddy. I'd come home, at least for a little while, right after New Year in exchange for borrowing some things from Maybud. Most of it is stuff Mother hasn't thought of for years, from the attic and the dependencies. She and Daddy have already left for the Caribbean. It'll be back in place before they get home. This monster will hold linens and blankets and pillows and comforters; you can get away with the simplest kind of beds if the linens are wonderful. This is just the beginning."

And it was. Every day another vanful of riches appeared.

"Everybody will know it's not our stuff," Emily said, watching boxes of tissue-swathed table linens and silver being carried into the house. "They've probably all seen it at your house."

"Who cares?" Lulu grinned. "Just the men are coming, and no man in this crowd ever noticed what he was eating off or sleeping in. They just notice that it's heavy and shining and old, if they notice it at all. They would, on the other hand, notice pa-

per plates and napkins and Wal-Mart platters, even though they wouldn't quite know
what was wrong."

"It's put-on," Emily sniffed. "I thought you
didn't like that."

"No, it's not," Lulu said seriously. "Put-on
is when you pretend to be something you're
not so people will think better of you. This is
making people comfortable, not pretending
Sweetwater is Maybud or any one of those
other big old piles. It's about other people.
Put-on is about you."

She was, in those last days of the year, as
incandescent and quicksilver as Emily had
ever seen her. Lulu in the puppy ring or at
her father's table was fine to watch; Lulu
moving smoothly among old linens and silver and laughing in joy as Sweetwater began to come alive under her hands was
mesmerizing. Emily had almost begun to
take her extraordinary looks for granted, but
in these still, lowering days before the hunt
she seemed to see her again as she had on
the first day she had come. Lulu dazzled in
the gloom of early winter.

Emily could see that her father noticed,
too. His eyes rested often on Lulu as she
moved around the plantation, and some-

times he simply followed her on her appointed rounds, silently and with his hands in his pockets. The twins dropped their after-school rendezvous with their cronies at the Harley place in Hollywood or the Qwik Stop Full Service convenience store in Meggett and came home to place themselves in her service. Only Cleta, watching the glittering provender slowly fill her kitchen and pantry and spill over onto the dining room table, was less than enchanted.

"Mules dressed up in buggy harness," she muttered once to Emily as Leland brought in piles of creamy, lavender-smelling damask. "Who gon' wash and iron all this stuff? Who gon' serve all them platters and trays? Who gon' cook enough stuff to fill 'em all up?"

Lulu, who, with Emily, was sorting napkins and tray cloths in the dining room, said, "Some of our folks from Maybud are going to come out and cook and do the heavy stuff. I promise they won't get in your way. They'll do exactly what you want them to do. You don't even have to stay if you don't want to. It'll be a long night."

"This my kitchen and I'm stayin' in it," Cleta said. "Ain't nothing leavin' it for that dining room I don' say can go."

"Fair enough," Lulu said. "Of course it's your kitchen."

"Huh," said Cleta. After that, she said little at all.

Early in December Lulu persuaded Walter to come with them into Charleston for the last fitting of Emily's dress. "Just to see the Christmas decorations," she said. "We'll drive down the Battery and then over to King Street. You don't even have to get out of the car. Come on. You never go anywhere with us."

But, "You all go on without me," he said on the appointed day. "I've got the intermediates starting to the gun."

"The intermediates can wait one day," Lulu said. "Walter, you promised. When else have I ever asked you to do anything?"

And so they drove, rattling, into Charleston and around the Battery and through the old streets south of Broad, and finally down to King Street. Walter stayed in the truck while Emily was fitted. ("My dear, stunning," the wood stork said.) After they were done, instead of heading out of Charleston for home, Emily had Walter park and marched him firmly into Ben Silver's legendary clothing store.

"They've been outfitting Foxworth men forever," Lulu said, smiling at the discreetly splendid young salesman who came to meet them. He was all over flannel and tattersall, and obviously knew her.

"Miss Foxworth," he said. "How can I help you? Little Christmas something for your dad?"

"No," Lulu said. "A tuxedo for Mr. Parmenter here, Armitage. Something plain and traditional, but maybe with a tartan cummerbund or something. He'll wear it mainly in the country."

"Of course," the young man said smoothly. "Would you step this way, sir? We have some nice things from England this year."

Walter's face was flushed red and his nostrils were pinched and white. Emily sidled away. She knew that look.

But all he said was "Thank you," and glared once at Lulu, and followed the young man back into the dim, wood-smelling reaches of the store. Lulu and Emily sat down in herringbone armchairs to wait. Another young man brought them tea in thin white cups, and shortbread.

"You must come here all the time," Emily said, feeling, in her jeans and barn jacket, like a farmhand in a palace. Lulu, who wore exactly the same clothes, looked just like what she was, a wealthy planter's daughter in her afternoon casualwear.

"Mother and I used to come a lot," she said. "Grand, too. None of the Foxworth men have ever willingly come down to King Street, even to be fitted. The store usually sends somebody out to Maybud and we corner them while he fits them."

"Daddy is going to just hate this," Emily said.

And perhaps he did, but when Walter Parmenter walked out of the fitting room in a tuxedo of thin lustrous wool, with a snowy, pleated front shirt and black bow tie and a cummerbund of discreet brick-and-moss plaid, they sat in silence. Then Lulu clapped her hands in mock applause and laughed aloud with glee.

"You look absolutely fabulous," she said. "You could be a model for Ralph Lauren, if you weren't so obviously a dog breeder. Nobody at this hunt is going to come anywhere near comparing to you. Have you looked at yourself?"

Emily simply stared. Walter Parmenter was transformed by fabric and alchemy into someone she had never seen, an elegant, attenuated man in evening clothes, his blond, silvering hair shining in the overhead light, his thin-featured face thrown into blade-fine half-shadow, his leathery countryman's tan as smooth and as golden as Lulu's. He turned to look at them and his eyes were the blue of a noon October sky in the store's flattering low light. Emily's breath stopped for a moment in her chest. She knew she was looking at the man young Caroline Carter had seen on a summer day long ago and promptly brought all her guns to bear on capturing him from her sister. For just that moment, she could see why. Beside her, Lulu made a small, happy sound in her throat.

"Now tell me I was wrong about this," she said.

He looked into the mirror for a moment, and then looked back at her almost bashfully.

"It's a nice suit," he said. "But I'm going to be way overdressed. It's the country, after all."

"They'll all be wearing them," she said. "For some reason, it's just what they do on the nights before hunts. The only difference is that their tuxes will be butt-sprung or slick on the elbows, or beginning to turn a little green. After they see you every one of them is going to go out and buy a new one."

Walter stood dutifully while a stoop-shouldered older man came to sketch patterns on the tuxedo with chalk. When he came back out of the dressing room in his field clothes, he said to the young salesman, "Will you take a check? I don't have my cards with me."

"It's taken care of," Lulu said. "It's my Christmas present to you. It's only fair, Walter. You've housed and fed me for the past six months. I'm not going to argue about this."

All the way back to Sweetwater, in the fast-falling winter twilight, Lulu and Walter talked of the plans for the looming hunt, laughing occasionally at some absurdity of hers. In the back seat Emily was silent. The image of the tall, elegant stranger would not remove itself from her mind. For some reason it made the back of her neck creep with unease.

That night, after dinner, she and Lulu sat up late listening to a CD of Dylan Thomas reading *A Child's Christmas in Wales.* Emily was enchanted.

"Buddy would have loved this," she said. "I wish he'd heard it just like this, with Thomas reading it."

"Maybe he did," Lulu said. "It's Grand's. I bought it for her when her recording wore out. She's had it for ages."

In bed that night, Elvis's dead weight warm against her side, Emily probed, carefully, deep inside herself.

"Where have you been?" she said. "You're missing all the good stuff. You ought to see this house, and Daddy in a tuxedo. And me, too. I've got this fabulous new long green dress. You wouldn't know me, Buddy."

He did not answer, but into her mind words came clearly: "I already don't."

They were not his words. Emily did not know whose they were.

"Did they come from me?" she whispered to Elvis in the still, quiet darkness. "If they did, I don't want them."

He whimpered softly, and slept again.

It was a long time before she slept.

18

The sweet, misted days held, a great slow wheel that climbed and passed and descended, through Christmas. Everyone went to the woods the weekend before, with a boiling honor guard of joyful Boykins, and brought back tractorloads of pine and magnolia leaves, smilax and holly and ivy, silvery Spanish moss and emerald green deer moss, dried ferns and feathery gray-gold spartina from the marshes. The twins found and cut two great, dense longleaf pines and dragged them back to Sweetwater, and put one up in the foyer and one in the bunkhouse.

Emily had never had a real Christmas tree. Each year that she could remember they had put up the aluminum one her father had brought home from Kmart when Emily was small. It was severely planed and edged, as if drawn with a ruler, and threw off glittering shards of silver. When it was decorated with red, blue, and green ornaments and tangles of colored lights in the barn, it always stood in the little morning room-turned-breakfast room where they spent most of their time and stabbed the winter gloom like a tree of knives. From outside, on a dark night, it was magical, a lightship on a dark sea. There were always a few presents under it, most of them wrapped by Aunt Jenny or Cleta. They were opened with murmurs of thanks and bright, stretched grins of appreciation and almost always put away soon after. Walter tended toward the doggy for the twins—bronze statuettes of champion spaniels, new field clothes, hunting boots—and the proper for Emily—shetland cardigan sweaters, knee socks, skirts. Once he gave her a kilt with a huge gilt safety pin on it.

"I think he gets them at a school uniform store." Buddy had smiled when she showed him the clothes, for they had been in his time. "Wear them just once, to Christmas

dinner, and make him happy. He'll never notice that he doesn't see them again."

In his time, Buddy gave books, wonderful
books. Cleta made tea cakes and iced them
with everybody's names, and fudge and di-
vinity. Jenny Raiford brought small things
for each of them, but they were unique and
personal: a tie knit with spaniels for Walter,
Dale Earnhart jackets for the twins, a coveted book for Buddy, little leather journals
and pretty fountain pens and stationery for
Emily, that made her feel grown-up, like
someone who had the sort of life you committed to journals, a life that many years
later would start a smile of recognition on an
unknown face.

This year, though, the house was truly
transformed. Cleaned and shined and
waxed down to its bare bones by Cleta and
Emily and Lulu, it bloomed with the largesse
of the woods and marshes and smelled, in
the chill twilights, like forest and marsh and
creek and river combined, a smell so evoca-
tive and piercing that Emily never entered
the house without a fresh welling of something close to tears in her throat. For the first
time, Sweetwater seemed a living part of
the world outside it. The life of the Low-

country marshes ran in its wide boards like the green life in vines and ferns and trees; like the dark blood of the tidal creeks, like the rich, living salt of the faroff seas.

Lulu decreed no decorations on the tree except Spanish moss and pinecones and clumps of dried deer moss, and small scarlet clusters of holly berries. From Maybud came a great box of fragile dried sand dollars, bleached moon-white and nested in cotton, that she and Emily spent an afternoon tying on the branches.

"I gathered them every summer of my life at Kiawah or Edisto Beach," Lulu said. "They've always been on our tree at home, but they got overshadowed by all the other stuff. They're perfect here."

And they were. They shone on the great tree like stars.

Forever after, Emily would remember that Christmas as one of dreamlike hushed stillness and soft light, of the cold, fresh breath of the marshes, of the strange, sweet minor music of another century. Lulu lit candles everywhere in the evenings: kitchen, dining room, breakfast room, windows, table. Fires burned in every fireplace, the pungent, clean-sour smell of dried driftwood curling into the air. Lulu's small CD player went everywhere they were, and on it she played thin, haunting music for a few strings, or a reed, or hushed voices with nothing at all behind them. They had puzzled and, oddly, disturbed Emily when she first heard them, but soon they were part and parcel of that Christmas out of time, and she came to breathe them in unconsciously, like air.

"Gregorian chants," Lulu smiled. "Plain-song. Festivals of carols and lights. Christmas music in this house's time was almost always sacred music, except for a few flighty reels and waltzes. 'I Saw Mommy Kissing Santa Claus' didn't come along un-til much later."

Emily did not know if her father and brothers ever truly made their peace with the music, but she thought that it somehow got under their skins. Their talk, in the evenings at dinner, was softer and slower and studded with pauses into which the music curled like smoke. Elvis did not ask to go out, but almost always remained at Emily's side. He sat contented, seeming to listen to the music, sometimes with his golden eyes closed, dozing, swaying a little to its tempo. He slept a good bit, in those days, under the tree or beside one of the whispering fire-places.

"He's a throwback to the eighteenth century," Lulu said. "Much prefers Bach to rock."

At twilight on Christmas Eve Lulu knocked on Emily's downstairs door. She stood on the threshold wearing a long rain-coat over velvet pants and a satin shirt and holding a large plastic Wal-Mart bag. It bulged oddly.

"Get your coat and follow me," she whispered dramatically.

Emily did.

"Where are we going?"

"You'll see. Hurry up. I've got scalloped oysters ready to go into the oven."

Emily and Elvis followed her through the yard and into the stand of forest that fringed Sweetwater Creek. Lulu said nothing, sweeping silently ahead of them on the path with ground fog curling up around the hem of her trailing coat. She had put the hood up against the mist, and might have been, in the pearly silence, a ghost, or a spirit of this place. Emily felt the need to tiptoe, and Elvis walked sedately beside her, eyes on Lulu, for once not forging ahead on the path.

When they reached the little cliff that overlooked the dolphin slide, Lulu turned and gestured into the underbrush. She was smiling.

At the edge of the bluff stood a small, wispy cedar that Emily had not noticed before, crowded around as it was by ferns and palmettos and seedling live oaks. It was perhaps waist high, and prettily shaped, round and soft and full. Lulu brushed a little path through the golden bracken to it with her foot, and put her sack down.

"Christmas for the critters," she said.

From the bag came clumps of peanut butter spread on bread and pinecones, strings of stale popcorn, small ears of dried golden corn, whole shriveled apples and oranges, handfuls of dried fruit and berries, small muslin bags of nuts and seeds of every sort. Emily clapped her hands in enchantment.

"I wish I'd thought of it," she said.

They set about festooning the little tree with the plunder of the Christmas fields and marshes. While they worked, Lulu said, "Did you know that there's an old legend that on Christmas Eve every kind of animal that was at the manger can speak aloud? Maybe this will give them something to chatter about. Meet around the water fountain."

"I wish we could come back at midnight and see," Emily said.

"I don't," Lulu smiled. "Too much like eavesdropping. Besides, we know they speak, don't we? I mean, look at Elvis."

He had lain down in front of the tree, stretched out with his head high, looking off into the misted distance. Guarding? Waiting?

"What do you see?" Emily thought at him.

"I see mysteries."

All through dinner and into the small hours of Christmas morning Emily kept seeing, in her mind, a little tree on the dark bank of a creek, surrounded by a small peaceable kingdom, giving off its own misted light.

On Christmas Day a weak, repentant sun came sliding out, and the earth and marshes and hummocks steamed as if still enshrouded in mist. Emily and Lulu woke early and trudged, yawning and scrubbing their eyes with their fists, into the big house to start Christmas dinner. Even early in the morning the house breathed life and light in and out; Walter and the boys had gotten up before they had, and had lit the fires and some of the white candles, and started a pot of the fragrant Kona coffee Lulu had brought with her from Maybud. With the sweet smell of the snickering fires and the clean odor of fresh greenery, it made the house smell ambrosial, a festival place.

For the first Christmas morning Emily could remember Walter and the boys had not gone out with the dogs to the river. Instead, dressed in fresh oxford cloth shirts and with damp comb tracks still in their hair, they sat contentedly around the breakfast table, drinking coffee and riffling through the *Post and Courier,* so obviously waiting for Lulu and just perhaps Emily that it gave Emily a lump in her throat. She could not remember her father and brothers ever waiting for her.

"What took you so long?" Walter Parmenter said. "Elves have already been and gone."

Lulu had made up batter for what she called Maybud Sally Lunn the night before, and put it in to bake while fresh coffee brewed.

"I always thought it tasted sort of like

polyester, but we always had it at breakfast at Christmas, and I think it's a very old receipt," she said, serving puffs of the steaming bread onto their plates. "Here, put some of this ribbon cane syrup over it. It's not bad that way."

And the Sally Lunn was not at all bad, merely strange and bland on tongues accustomed to Cleta's cinnamon-walloped sweet rolls or crisp, airy peach waffles. They finished the pan, leaving a substantial serving for Elvis, who sat patiently beside Emily's chair grinning up at her, tongue lolling in expectation. He sniffed and took a bite, and then laid it delicately on the floor beside Emily's shoe and turned ostentatiously around and lay down again.

"Dog's spoiled rotten," Lulu laughed. "Sally Lunn was the breakfast fare of nobler dogs than he is. I'm putting him on kibbles and water."

Elvis's stumpy tail thumped the floor twice, but he did not turn around or get up. The ghost of the marinated standing rib roast fingered its way out of the refrigerator. Elvis could wait.

Christmas dinner was at noon this year. Cleta had been in the day before to clean and polish, but she did not come back to cook. Lulu had told her she wouldn't dream of taking her away from her own Christmas dinner, and that she and Emily could certainly manage a simple roast. Grumbling to herself, Cleta left early on Christmas Eve. On her way out, she stopped beside Emily, who was fastening clusters of holly and berries onto a grapevine wreath and pricking herself often, and said, "You gets some spare time tomorrow, maybe you come on over to the house in the afternoon. GW has made a little something for you, and there's going to be plenty of turkey and dressing and sweet potato pie left over."

"Oh, Cleta, I will if I can," Emily said, smiling up at her. "We're eating early, so maybe after dinner . . . Tell GW thanks for me, and save me a drumstick. I've missed seeing you at the holidays. Aunt Jenny too."

And she found, suddenly and sharply at that moment, that she had. Missed the massive, humming warmth that was Cleta in the kitchen, missed the soft laughter and clean-cotton smell, and the swift little hugs that were Jenny Raiford.

"We be back anytime y'all asks, I 'spect," Cleta said darkly. "I will, anyway. Look to me like Miss Jenny got her a travelin' man for a boyfriend, and she travelin' as far away from here as she can. They in Canada skiing or some such, aren't they?"

"Yes," Emily said, not looking up. It had been her father who had told her that her aunt would not be with them at Christmas, not Jenny herself. Emily had not spoken to her since she left.

"She called last night after you all had gone to bed," Walter had said. "Didn't want to wake you. She said tell you that maybe you and she could go somewhere on your spring break. Hilton Head or somewhere. She'll talk to you before then."

Emily did not think that she would. Neither did she think she would go over to Cleta's little blue-doored house on Christmas afternoon. The moat around Sweetwater had deepened in the gray holidays, and she could not, for some reason, imagine crossing it again. But a very small part of her stood on the drawbridge and peered into the mist on the other side and ached for people who would not be coming back inside.

Dinner was a mahogany and pink standing rib roast, the first Emily had ever seen, with little puffs of Yorkshire pudding that Lulu swirled up at the last moment from flour and hot fat. They melted on the tongue, and were so fervently praised by everyone that Lulu made up batch after batch. After dinner, when the dishes had been cleared into the kitchen and Elvis ceremoniously presented with his roast beef trimmings, Lulu brought out stemmed glasses of a cold white milk drink that tasted so wonderful that Emily had another. But not another after that.

"It's got a good bit of whiskey in it," Lulu said, smiling at Emily's flushed face. "That and egg yolks and sugar and cinnamon and the milk. It's called flip. It came over from England with the Lords Proprietors. No wonder their noses are all so red in those old portraits. We always had it after Christmas dinner, and I thought you might like to try it. No more for you, though, Emily. Your eyes are rolling around in your head."

Everyone laughed. Emily would remember that day as one of laughter and firelight and exotic tastes on the tongue, and of a different Christmas music from what Lulu had played in the days before, this full of ringing brasses and bells and massed choruses, redolent with hosannas. Lulu and Walter sang along with some of it: "Hark! The Herald Angels Sing," "Joy to the World," "I Saw Three Ships Come Sailing In."

Emily, warm in her flip fog, simply stared. Never in her life had she known her father to sing.

Lulu's gifts to them were simple and small: a very old hunting print, yellowed and rolled up, for Walter; stainless steel divers' watches for the boys ("Rite Aid, but they'll be useful"); a red tartan collar with small gold bells for Elvis; a tiny crystal unicorn for Emily.

"This is just a little something," Lulu said, when Emily thanked her, caressing the little unicorn. Under her fingers it felt cool and alive. "You'll get your big present on your birthday."

On the day before New Year's Eve the weather finally broke. A frigid wind roared in from beyond the marshes and lashed the spartina into cold, rolling dun-colored waves. Ice rimmed the edges of Sweetwater Creek and threw up spikes in the mud and crackled in the dogs' watering troughs. The creek and river darkened. Out on the hummocks the palmetto fronds clattered. Walter suspended training. Emily and Lulu were distressed at the crushing wave of cold, but Walter and the boys were jubilant.

"Means there'll be ducks," Walter said. "Haven't seen a one on the river this year. They need the cold to force them down to feed. This should bring in plenty of them."

Wrapping herself in her down jacket and muffler for the dash from the house to the barn, Emily felt a shiver of pity and fear: the poor ducks. Dropping gratefully down onto smooth, hidden water to feed after a night's flying against the vicious ocean wind, and meeting, not duckweed but guns and dogs and death.

"I'm so glad I never let you hunt," she said to Elvis, as she slid into her bed that night. Beside her, he groaned happily and dug into her neck with his nose.

That night Emily dreamed that she stood on the drawbridge over the moat, looking out into darkness on the other side. Far away, down the dirt road that led to the highway, the little woodland tree glowed like a candle in the cold, moonless dark. Around it the animals of the Lowcountry stood as if in a tableaux. In their midst, Buddy stood, erect and whole and gleaming blond, like a gold-leaf statue. He smiled at her, but did not come to meet her at the far edge of the drawbridge.

"Come over here," Emily called, joy rising like a tide in her throat. "I know you can."

"No," he said. "I need to be over here right now."

"Well, then, will you help me come over there? I can't cross this drawbridge by myself."

"I can't do that, either," he said. "It's not allowed."

"When, then? I need to talk to you," Emily whispered, the joy thickening into tears. "I've tried and tried. Why won't you answer me?"

"I have been," he said, his voice, like the rest of him, golden and shimmering. "You haven't been hearing me."

"I'll listen harder . . ."

"It won't make any difference. Your ears are all stopped up. When you're really ready to hear me, you will."

"When will that be?" The tears slid down her cheeks.

"I don't know. Maybe never. I'll keep trying, though."

Darkness fell like a curtain on the road, and Buddy and the tree and the animals were gone. Emily woke in the dark of her room in the barn, sobbing aloud. Elvis was licking her face.

"Did you see him?" she whispered.

"I always do."

"Have you been crying?" Lulu said the next morning when she came downstairs to join Emily.

"No."

Late that afternoon they stood before the old cheval glass mirror in Lulu's room, finishing dressing. Besides the lamps, Lulu had lit candles, and in the wavy speckled old mirror she and Emily both looked like women out of an earlier time, in their long-sleeved velvet dresses, with their hair, copper and blond, piled on their heads. Lulu fastened her grandmother's pearls around her neck and then turned and studied Emily. She reached into a bureau drawer and took out a little twist of tissue paper and handed it to Emily.

"I was going to wait until your birthday

proper, but you need these tonight," she said.

Emily opened the twist. In the folds a pair of earrings lay, green and water-clear stones gleaming in mountings of old rose gold. Emily gasped and looked up at Lulu.

"Are they . . . ?"

"Emeralds and diamonds. They were Grand's grandmother's. She gave them to me on my eighteenth birthday, but I've never worn them and I never will. I hate emeralds."

"Why?"

"I read someplace they were bad luck," Lulu said. "I don't need any more of that."

"Does that mean I'll have it?" Emily said, turning her head this way and that to watch the teardrops swing and glitter against her bare neck.

"Not a chance. Nothing ahead for you but good luck. Anyway, I think they're only bad luck for blondes. Look at us, will you? Velvet and pearls and emeralds and candlelight. John Singer Sargent might have painted us."

Emily hugged Lulu fiercely, feeling her sharp bird's bones under the velvet, and

smelling silky-clean hair and the old-fashioned scent of tuberoses.

"I'll wear them always," she whispered
into Lulu's neck.

"Not exactly the thing for the puppy ring,"
Lulu said, and Emily felt her smile against
her cheek. "They look stunning on you,
though, as if they had been made for you.
Now aren't you glad I made you get your
ears pierced last fall? We'll have a proper
birthday party tomorrow, when everybody's
off on the hunt, with cake and confetti and
balloons and dogs—the works. Twelve to
thirteen is the biggest step there is."

"Why?" Emily said.

"Because thirteen is when you start to
know things."

"What things?"

"Just things. Things about the world and
people and yourself. About life. Things
you'll need to know the rest of your life but
that nobody will tell a child."

"Bad things?"

"Good and bad. Strange. Wonderful.
Scary. Beautiful. Sometimes things you hate
but can never un-know. And some things so
glorious that only a complex and aware

mind can comprehend. Thirteen is when you start getting complicated, Emily."

"I don't know if I want to know them then."

"You don't have any choice. But it all comes gradually. Nobody could stand knowing everything at once."

They went down the barn stairs and out into the grassy field around the dog ring. It was still early; an apocalyptic red sun was bloodying the marshes to the west, but in the east, high in the purpling arc of the sky, a great ghost moon hung, waiting to bloom into light.

"Wolf moon," Lulu said. "It'll be cold and clear as crystal in the morning, great for the hunt."

In her thin raincoat, Emily shivered. It was not just the stinging cold. Moon of the wolf. . . .

They were going to the big house early so that Lulu could show Emily where everything for the party was and what to do about it.

"Why do I need to know that?" Emily had grumped. "You're going to be there. It's your party."

"No, it's not," Lulu said firmly. "It's your

father's party, and that means it's yours, too. You're the lady of the house, Emily, like it or not. And the lady of the house is always the gentleman's hostess. Always. I can help plan it, but you have to know the entire drill."

"Those men know what to do. They go to things like this all the time. They can look after themselves. All those servants of yours know what to do. They can look after everybody. The only people who don't know are Daddy and me."

"Well, after tonight you will," Lulu said in exasperation. "Emily, if you're going to be part of this farm's future, or run it one day, you're going to be the hostess of Sweetwater. And you won't be entertaining folks from the VFW and the John's Island Lanes. This farm is going to be on another map entirely after tonight. Knowing how to run it gracefully goes with the territory."

"Did you have to learn all this stuff?"

"Every bit of it. How do you think I know?"

Earlier that afternoon they had walked through the bunkhouse. Fires blazed on the great stone hearths and the narrow bunks were deep with drifted featherbeds and old linens. Beside each stood a rough carved chest, and on each one Lulu had put a fat white candle in a hurricane glass and a small vase of holly and ivy. The stone floors were strewn with snowy fleeces, and between the fireplaces the other great pine stood, unadorned and lordly, breathing out the living essence of the woods. At either end of the room, in front of the fireplaces, tables had been set up and covered with green cloths, wooden chairs drawn up to them.

"There'll be a good bit of poker tonight," Lulu said.

Just behind them, narrower tables—sawhorses with planks, Emily thought—had been covered in white. A staggering array of liquors were arranged on them, and silver bowls already full of benné crackers and boiled peanuts. Two impassive black men in white jackets stood easily behind them, talking in low voices.

"Miss Lulu," they said when Lulu and Emily entered.

"Simon," Lulu said warmly. "Charles. I can't tell you how much I appreciate this."

"Glad to do it, Miss Lulu."

Before going to the bunkhouse, they had

looked briefly into the old stables, scrubbed and warm now, and piled deep with fresh straw, to see the old-fashioned buckboard wagons that had come over that afternoon from Maybud, and the four shining, impassive mules, also trucked over, who would pull the wagons in the morning.

"Mules?" Emily had looked up at Lulu.

"For some reason, the winter hunts always go out in mules and wagons with the men in one and the dogs in another. These are the same drivers we use at Maybud, and the same mules. The men will have had coffee and brandy, or neat whiskey, or whatever, and probably ham and biscuits. At noon a wagon will come out with Bloody Marys and a hot lunch. The drivers will set it up and serve it, and in the late afternoon everybody and the dogs will come back with the ducks, and while the men are cleaning up and changing, our men will clean and dress the ducks and have them ready in case anybody wants one cooked up at the last minute."

"My lord, what a to-do over a bunch of ducks," Emily said, inhaling the sweet smell of wood shavings and mule hide.

"Going to sell a lot of Boykins," Lulu said.

In the house, Lulu walked Emily around. Candles glowed everywhere; fires snickered behind their screens, and stair rails and mantels and sideboards were festooned with garlands of fresh greenery. The great tree in the foyer looked just as Lulu had said it would, a captured forest giant in the high-ceilinged gloom. They had made wreaths for every window, centered with a white taper, and on the front door they hung a great wreath of pine and cedar, studded with shells and moss and holly. The porch lights were already lit, so the wreath blazed out into the gathering darkness in a penumbra of light. In the library, small living holly trees in pots stood about the fireplace, and smilax and magnolia leaves gleamed. Small tables covered with white damask were scattered about in front of the old sofa, along with a phalanx of borrowed gilt Maybud chairs.

"People will probably bring their plates in here to eat," Lulu said. "There are too many to seat, and a buffet the night before a hunt is traditional, anyway."

In the dining room, the old oval table had been draped with silky, thin white damask and set with ornate silver platters and tureens and flatware. More white candles gleamed in tall silver candelabra, and a towering, beautiful old pierced silver bowl on a pedestal sat in the middle, heaped with holly and pomegranates and trailing ivy. An épergne, Lulu said. It had come over with the Lords Proprietors too. Emily thought it looked it.

On the sideboard a massive silver service and translucent porcelain cups and saucers rested, and cloudy old decanters of brandies and liqueurs. A full bar stood in the foyer, just to one side of the tree, snowy white and groaning under bottles of wine and liquor. Candles flickered here, too, and holly shone softly, and behind the bar a white-coated Maybud man stood at parade rest, studying the assortment of garnishes set out in small silver bowls.

"Miss Lulu," he said.

"Evening, Peter," Lulu said. "You look ready for action.

"Here's what happens," Lulu said after they had inspected the foyer and library and dining room.

"You'll stand beside your father at the door and greet everybody as they come in. I'll introduce you, and you repeat their names and smile and say you're glad they could come. The twins will take their coats and their overnight things and put them out in the bunkhouse, and your father will tell them to help themselves at the bar and join him in the library. After everybody's got a drink and is settled in, you walk through and ask if everybody has everything they need, or if you can get something for them. Smiling, Emily. Then you excuse yourself and go into the kitchen and get everything in there going."

Emily was panting with terror.

"You're not going to make me do all that by myself," she choked.

"Oh, don't be silly, of course not," Lulu said. "But you'd better pay attention, because next time you *will* have to do it by yourself. And do it right. Now for the kitchen."

The cavernous kitchen blazed with light and steamed with wonderful smells. More worktables had been brought in, and on them, and on the big old oak center table, pots and dishes and trays of food—Emily recognized little broiled quail, and tenderloin of beef and venison, and a plate of rosy sliced duck breast—stood ready to be

brought out into the dining room or put into
the great, wheezing oven. Pots on the stove
simmered, and the smell of shrimp and oysters and sherry and herbs and baking bread
made Emily's mouth water, dry with fright
though it was. Aproned black women from
Maybud whisked back and forth, doing un-
fathomable things to anonymous dishes,
chattering and laughing among themselves.
In the center of it all, like a great dark
mountain, Cleta loomed, unaccustomedly
aproned in white and holding a whisk like a
baton. She did not speak, but her eyes followed the Maybud workers' every move
and her lips were pursed with disapproval.

Emily ran to her and hugged her, grateful
for a familiar island in this sea of chaos, and
Cleta hugged her back and then held her off
and looked at her. Her face softened into a
smile.

"Look at you, Emily," she said. "Look right
out of *Gone With the Wind,* you do. Is those
new earrings?"

"They're emeralds," Emily said proudly.
"Lulu gave them to me for my birthday."

"Huh," Cleta said.

Lulu showed Emily how to inspect each
dish as it was put into its service piece and

then set on the table in the dining room. Emily should, the first few times she did this, keep a small list and check off the steps one by one.

"You don't," Emily pouted.

"I did."

On the threshold of the kitchen, Elvis sat tranquilly in his new plaid collar, eyes following every move.

"He's got his own list," Lulu said.

"When the table is laid and the hot dishes ready in their chafing dishes, you check the table once more for serving pieces and napkins and sauces and gravy boats and condiments, and then thank the kitchen staff and go to the library door and say, 'I believe we're ready for dinner, Daddy, if you'll tell everybody.' And he will, and they'll start in to the dining room, and you're on your way. After that it's just a matter of working the room, saying hello and refilling plates, if anyone wants them, and passing the dessert tray. I think it's profiteroles tonight. I remember you liked the ones we had at Grand's so I asked for them. Then you say, 'There's coffee and brandy on the sideboard, and the bar is still open. Please enjoy yourselves and I hope to see you in the morning before the hunt,' and you can cut out for bed. The kitchen staff does the rest."

"Jesus," Emily said profanely. "It's worse than the SATs. What about Elvis?"

"I think we can trust Elvis to pose quietly wherever he can best be seen," Lulu laughed. "He knows which side his bread is buttered on."

A faint, "Here they come" floated back from the far edge of the driveway, where the twins were stationed as outriders. They had flatly refused to wear tuxedos and mingle with the storied planters, so they had been allowed to dress in their good shetland sweaters and wool slacks, which they wore perhaps once every two years, and serve as scouts.

Inside, in the foyer, Walter and the two girls heard the hail. Walter smoothed the tuxedo coat and took a deep breath, looking white-eyed over at Lulu. Emily tried to breathe through lungs turned suddenly to cement. Lulu smiled at both of them.

"Here we go," she said, and opened the front door, and they went out into the clear cold dark of New Year's Eve to welcome the planters of three counties to Sweetwater.

19

At seven-thirty that evening Emily, bearing plates of crabmeat canapés and hot cheese puffs, paused in the doorway to the library and listened to the voice of the house.

It was not a voice she had heard before. Before tonight, the house had said nothing to her. Now, it spoke so closely and clearly into her ears that it might have been a great, living entity. For the first time, Emily saw that it was. She knew that the way she thought of Sweetwater had changed forever.

Its voice was almost entirely masculine, and very old. It was woven of the lazy, indistinct talk of men, punctuated by eruptions of raucous laughter; the creaking of wide, waxed old boards under men's feet; the tinkle of ice against crystal and the tink of silver against silver; the whispered roar of fires; and, as if from a great distance, the excited yips of dogs. It seemed to Emily that the voice had been speaking to her all along, speaking for centuries, even, and she was only just now hearing it. This, she knew without knowing how, was how the house was supposed to sound, and it opened and bloomed under its freedom to speak.

"I wonder if anybody else hears it," she thought. "If they do, they don't let on. I bet Buddy did, though. And Elvis."

She looked down at him, sitting at her left heel.

"Do you hear it?"

"Of course."

Emily smelled the breath of the house, too: rich tobacco, burning applewood, faint exhalations from damp old rugs and wet wool, the somehow old bronze smell of whiskey. And always, a constant undernote, clean and sweet to Emily, the smell of burnished spaniels.

Her mouth relaxed from the stiff social rictus bidden by Lulu into something softer, of a piece with the voice and breath of the old house: the smile of a daughter of the house.

Going into the room with her plates, Emily was, for the first time that night, able to perform her role with ease.

"Please try the cheese puffs," she said to one big, tuxedoed man after another. "They're a specialty of Cleta's. And we caught the crabs from off our dock. Lulu and I made these this afternoon."

And one by one the men took the appetizers and bit into them and nodded their heads appreciatively, and smiled at Emily the same easy smiles they bent upon Lulu.

"You the little girl who trained Rhett Foxworth's Boykins? He said he'd never seen anything like you. He didn't say you were so grown-up and pretty, though. Walter, where you been hiding this girl?"

"She's my secret weapon," Walter Parmenter said in a burst of unaccustomed grace, and smiled at Emily. Across the room, handing a fresh drink to a large, red-faced man indistinguishable to Emily from all the others, Lulu smiled too.

"Well, Missy, your daddy tells me you've spent the summer and fall out here learning about spaniels," the man said to Lulu. "Going to start your own kennel?"

"There's nothing I'd love more, Mr. Aiken," Lulu said.

"Well, you better get on back into town. Half the swains of Charleston are pining over your absence."

"Swains will keep," Lulu said. "Spaniels won't."

Everyone laughed.

Meeting Lulu back in the bustling kitchen, Emily let out a deep breath.

"How am I doing?"

"Good. Better than good. Didn't I tell you? I think it's in your genes."

"Well, it must be way back, then," Emily said, and then stopped. She thought of her beautiful, storied mother and her parties and dinners; she thought of Jenny Raiford's easy grace at their dinner table. Maybe not so far back after all.

"Now, that's the last of the chafing dishes," Lulu said. "You go in and ask your father to start everybody in to dinner while I do a last-minute check. After that we can go sit in the breakfast room and put our feet up and have a bite. They'll be occupied for a while."

Emily had started for the library when the big front-door knocker thundered. She looked around at Lulu. It was very late for anyone to be arriving.

"I'll get it," Lulu said. "You go on into the library."

Emily heard the big front door creak open, and a small silence, and then Lulu said, "Daddy! What on earth are you doing here? I thought you all were still on St. Bart's. Is Mother with you?"

Emily stopped to listen.

"No," Rhett Foxworth's big voice said. "She ran into three of her sorority sisters from Sweetbriar a couple of days ago, celebrating one of them's divorce, and the bridge and gossip show no signs of stopping, so I came on home. Didn't want to miss the hunt. You look beautiful, sugar. It sounds like everybody's having a good time."

"I think they are," Lulu said. "I'm glad to see you, Daddy. Come on in; there's time for a drink before dinner."

"Never turned one of those down," Rhett Foxworth said. And then, "I've brought you a surprise. Found him in the men's bar at the Yacht Club. Just got to town from UVA. He says it's been a coon's age since he's seen you. He's been trying to get ahold of you. I think he thinks you're hiding from him."

The silence rang. Emily edged out into the foyer. Rhett Foxworth, in a predictably elderly tuxedo, stood with his arm around Lulu, smiling down at her. Lulu stood as still as a statue, looking up at a young man in dinner clothes who was holding her hand lightly in his.

He was beautiful; there was no other word for it. Dark and fine-planed of face with startling blue eyes to match Lulu's own, and a cap of close-cropped black curls. His smile looked somehow archaic, the full-lipped V Emily had seen in pictures of heroic statues from the age of Theseus and Ariadne. He looked like a beautiful pagan, like a Greek god, or an Etruscan. Emily knew instantly who he was, and a fine, cold wire squeezed her heart.

After a moment, Lulu said, in a light, sweet voice, "How nice to see you. Yancey. Welcome to Sweetwater. Come into the library and meet my friend Emily and her father. They've been teaching me all there is to know about Boykin spaniels. I'll get you a drink."

"Thanks, Lu," Yancey Byrd said. His voice

was deep and lazy, as beautiful as the rest of him. His smile was quick and white and a little lopsided; endearing. Smile lines cut his cheeks, and his dark blue eyes twinkled. Something else lurked there, too, something that, Emily thought, could flash up suddenly out of its depths like a shark out of a dark ocean. The backs of his brown hands were furred with dark hair.

"I've had a hard time tracking you down, Lu," he smiled. "You're not going to get away again. I missed the biggest cotillion in Richmond to find you."

"Come this way," Lulu said evenly, and turned and glided away on her father's arm toward the library. Yancey Byrd noticed Emily frozen in the doorway and, incredibly, winked before he followed Rhett and Lulu.

Emily stood still in the doorway, sick and faint with fear.

But, after all, nothing happened. Lulu was as lightly and politely affectionate with Yancey Byrd as she was with her father's oldest friends, teasing and flattering and fetching refills and passing dessert. Emily, beside her, looked hard and often into her face, but Lulu just smiled and shook her head: "Okay. I'm okay."

After dinner, they sat for a while with the men by the fire, while brandy and cigars came out and laughter deepened and tales grew taller. Emily looked at her father, standing before the fire with one arm on the fabled gougework mantelpiece, holding a glass of Courvoisier and laughing. He looked unreal to her: young, handsomer by far than any man in the room but Yancey Byrd, totally at ease in his skin with these men who had intimidated him so long. Watching him, Emily felt Sweetwater's future shift before her eyes. She looked over at Lulu, the author of the change. Lulu was sitting beside her father, on the arm of his chair, telling a ridiculous little story about the first time she tried to get a Boykin puppy to sit and stay. She was hectic, radiant, as beautiful as fire unchecked. Every eye in the room was on her, and she smiled at each of these old family friends in turn. She did not look at Yancey Byrd, lounging in the comfortable old leather morris chair beside the fire. His eyes never left her, though.

She would not look at Emily, either. Beside Emily, pressed against her leg, so beautiful in his curly red coat and jaunty tartan collar that one man after another had

knelt before him as in obeisance, Elvis began to growl. Emily could not hear it, but
she could feel it, steady and throbbing
slowly like an inboard engine: inaudible,
eerie.

Emily was exhausted with apprehension
when Lulu finally rose and said, "Well, gentlemen, I think Emily and I will leave you to
your own evil devices. There's a bar out in
the bunkhouse, and poker tables, if anyone
is so inclined, and Peter will have Bloodies
and ham and biscuits before you go out in
the morning. Happy hunting. We'll see you
when you come in tomorrow."

Lulu went out of the room, with Emily behind her. The barbed bonds around her
heart eased slightly. They were leaving at
last. Nothing, after all, had happened. They
would get into their nightclothes and drink
hot chocolate and laugh and rehash the
evening. Lulu would have stories to tell
about the men who had come this night that
would rival any she told around the Parmenter dinner table. They would sleep late
in the morning.

In the foyer she reached for her down
coat, but Lulu laid a hand on her arm.

"I didn't realize everybody was going to

stay so late," she said. "Emily, you need to sleep here tonight. As long as your father has guests in the house, you really should be here, too."

"Lulu . . ." Emily began desperately, the fear uncoiling again and striking like a snake.

"It's the way it's done, Emily," Lulu said. She hugged Emily briefly and hard.

"You were absolutely magnificent tonight," she said. "Your father should be proud of you."

She turned and went out of the foyer into the silent cold. Before the door swung shut Emily could see her, whip-slim and erect on the icy stubble of the lawn, her long shadow preceding her, limned in light from the rising wolf moon.

In her dusty old room, deep under covers she had hidden in every winter of her life, Emily lay and listened until the last of the men's jovial voices faded from the foyer and the front door shut, firmly and finally. The house did not speak to her now.

Beside her, Elvis lay, rigid and still. Listening, too.

20

In the morning, stiff and sore, Emily dressed in her old jeans and a heavy sweater and went downstairs to the kitchen.

"Have you seen Lulu?" she asked Cleta, who was clattering dishes and humming once more. The kitchen was warm and spotless and empty of marauding Maybud servants.

"She stick her head in early this morning and say she going out with the hunt," Cleta said. "Said tell you she'll see you this afternoon when everybody gets in. Gon' have that birthday party before the oyster roast, she say. I hope she don't forget. I spent two hours at home last night making that carrot cake you like. See? Got your name and thirteen candles on it. Happy birthday, Emily. It seems like a hundred years since your last one."

"Out with the hunt . . ." Emily said slowly. "Lulu doesn't hunt. She hates hunting. She said she was going to sleep in this morning . . ."

"Well, she sho' ain't sleep good, then," Cleta said, looking sidewise at Emily. "She look like she been rode hard and put up wet. Shaky and white, with them funny blue eyes shining out—she look like she did when she come last summer."

"What does she want on the hunt?" Emily said miserably. "We were going to watch a movie this afternoon, before my party. She rented *Breakfast at Tiffany's*. She said it was time I got to know about Moon River."

"I don't think it's a what she want on that hunt," Cleta said. "I think it's a who. That big black-headed man what came in with Mr. Foxworth last night was standin' behind her on the porch. He was holding two shotguns, and they was both wearing them waxy coats folks hunt in. Boots, too. I'd say Miss Lulu gon' get her a good bag, and prob'ly not of ducks."

Emily swallowed a sob so hard that Cleta heard it and turned to her.

"She be back this evenin'," she said, pushing back Emily's tumbled hair. "And it ain't like we thought she never had a boyfriend. Bound to be a fox hangin' around the henhouse, pretty as she is. He be gone after breakfast tomorrow, and y'll be right back giggling and hustling dogs. Lord, Emily, you as hot as a firecracker. You got a fever?"

"No," Emily quavered, pulling away. It seemed to her that if she could just reach the safety of the little bedroom in the barn, crawl into her bed and pull Lulu's mother's pouffy covers over her head, she would fall asleep, and when she wakened Lulu would be there, teasing her and cutting cake and tossing tidbits to Elvis, and last night would have been a long dream, after all.

"Well, you sit down and have yourself some of this french toast, then. I made some for Elvis, too."

"I'll get something out at the barn," Emily mumbled. "There are some sweet rolls. Thank you for the cake, Cleta. It's beautiful. I'll save some for you to take home to GW and Robert."

She went out into pale, iron-cold sunlight. After the door closed behind her, Cleta folded her arms and stared without seeing at the cake with thirteen candles.

"Thirteen ain't old enough for another one to leave her," she said under her breath. "I knowed that girl got the dark in her when she first come. We needs for Miss Jenny to come on back."

But Jenny Raiford would not come back, Cleta knew. A golden cuckoo had pushed her out of the nest and was sitting her egg. Cleta bowed her head and said a small prayer that, when the cuckoo left, the egg would not be smashed beyond repair.

Lulu did not come back with the hunt that afternoon. Emily was watching from her window in the barn when the mules came in, pulling laughing men and milling dogs and canvas bags bulging with ducks. Lulu was not with them. Neither was Yancey Byrd.

She did not appear for the oyster roast on the dock that night, either. Leaden with dread, Emily went about her duties as daughter of the house, smiling dully at the planters and asking after their day's hunting, passing tin plates of steaming oysters

fresh from the beds on the banks of Sweetwater Creek, checking to see who might
need another drink.

How do I know how to do this? she
thought once, dully. Lulu was right. It must
be in my genes. Oh, Lulu.

Midway through the roast, Rhett Foxworth sought her out.

"Have you seen my wayward daughter
and that fellow of hers?" he asked. "Don't
like her leaving you to do all the work."

"No, sir," Emily said, looking down at her
feet in damp Wellingtons. Away from the fire
the air was frigid. Her breath lay silver on it.
The swollen moon seemed to hang just
above the river, spilling its cold radiance
down on the dock, so bright that she could
see his face clearly, and on it she saw only
amusement and mild annoyance.

"I thought maybe they might have gone
into town or somewhere. I haven't seen her
car since last night."

The "somewhere" was freighted with sly
import. None of the men missed what Rhett
Foxworth was saying. There was indulgent
laughter.

"Well, maybe they've made it up," a wiry
dun-colored man in oils said. "My girl was a

couple of years behind your girl in school. She says they were a hot item for a long time, until Miss Lulu dumped him and came home. This doesn't seem like no dumping to me."

"He that Byrd kid that's coming in with Comer Tarleton after he passes his bar exams? Is he those Virginia Byrds? If he is, I was at Princeton with his dad. Rolling in family and bucks. Your girl would be smart to marry him quick."

"You never can tell with Lulu," her father said. "For some reason she was dead set against even seeing him again when she got home. Well, if she doesn't marry him, I'm pretty sure Maybelle will. She fell without a shot the minute she met him."

The talk turned to other things. Emily stood still on the dock. It seemed to rock under her. She had never been so tired in her life. She looked across at her father. He was looking out over the river, his face mild and blank. Perhaps he had not heard.

He turned to face her then, and she knew that he had. Emily had watched fish die on the dock, drowning in air. The fish did not change, but something went out of the eyes and the scales. Something like that had gone out of Walter Parmenter.

"You go on up to the house, Emily," he said. "You look worn out. We'll clear up this mess in the morning. Cleta's coming. Thanks for . . . stepping in."

"Yessir," Emily mumbled. The genetic hostess seemed to drain out of her. She turned and trudged back to the house, Elvis clicking along beside her.

In the house, she wandered into the kitchen, still lit and warm, though empty now. The whole house was empty; you could feel it, like the emptiness of a cave. She looked over at the carrot cake, its icing hardened to a glossy shell. The inscription Cleta had piped onto it was beginning to soften and spread. The thirteen unlit candles looked like a cage. Emily walked over and stuck a finger into the icing and licked it off.

"Happy birthday to me," she said aloud. "I've been thirteen for a whole day and I don't know anything at all."

She went out of the kitchen and climbed the stairs to her bedroom. There was simply no way that she could sleep in that vast barn where Lulu was not.

"Lulu, where are you?" she whispered, knowing that there would be no answer.

Passing the window that looked out on the porch and yard and the barn beyond, she saw that the little red car was back. It was faded to sickly pink by the yellow sodium security lights and the bleaching moonlight. Joy came alive like the last ember in a dead fire. Emily opened the door and began to run, Elvis beside her, tongue lolling. She knew dimly that she was cold, but did not care. Lulu's apartment would be warm.

But when she pounded up the stairs to Lulu's door, she found it locked. Tentatively, she rattled the doorknob. Then she knocked.

"Lulu?"

No sound answered her. She knew that the apartment was, like the big house, empty. There was an old song Aunt Jenny sometimes sang, a song out of her time. "The Sound of Silence" it was called. This was what it meant.

Emily closed her eyes and leaned against the door. She did not think she had enough strength to get back to Sweetwater.

"Lulu, where are you?" she whispered again.

And suddenly, without the smallest shaving of a doubt, she knew. She was halfway across the stubbled, moon-silvered field that ended in the little maritime forest at Sweetwater Creek before she realized quite where she was. She was so bitterly cold that she would die of it if she thought about it.

Beside her, Elvis ran steadily, silently, his head down. Tracking.

She burst into the dark tunnel of the path through the woods, her breath sobbing in her throat. In the winter it was sparser, all stinging twigs and tearing vines. You could see farther than in summer. Looking ahead, Emily saw that there was a flickering yellow light where the little woodland tree would be, on the cliff over the dolphin slide. A fire; Lulu was there waiting beside a fire. What a lovely idea; how like Lulu . . .

She quickened her pace toward the far end of the path. Once or twice she stumbled and went down on one knee, but she felt no pain. Nor did she feel the cold. There would be warmth ahead.

Before her, Elvis stopped so suddenly that she literally jumped over him.

"Come on," she called, not stopping. But he did not come. Instead, he began to bark, furiously. Emily ran on.

And then she heard what he must have: a thin, guttural cry, and then another and another, closer together, higher, louder.

Lulu. Lulu in pain. She was with the corrupted pagan god and he was hurting her. All the roiling emotions that had torn Emily since that morning drained away, and it was Emily the Protector, the powerful bestower of "Everything is going to be all right," that pounded on the path toward the clearing and the light. Her fists were clenched, and her teeth, but she did not notice. Elvis dashed past her, still barking furiously; it was a feral sound, one she had never heard a Boykin make.

"We'll get him, Elvis," she said in her mind.

He stopped dead in front of her, blocking the path. She could see his teeth gleam white where his lips were drawn back, and this time heard the deep, continuing growl. It rose and fell softly, the sound of danger that came down from the first cave fires to which the wild dogs had come.

"Stop!" She heard him clearly.

And at the same time, in her ears so clearly that he might have been standing close beside her, Buddy said, *"Emily, stop!"*

She did, but momentum carried her the last few steps and she lurched into the clear space on the little cliff and fell to one knee.

She did not get up. The air in front of her wavered and thickened, as if she were seeing it through mist or a heat haze, and the entire clearing seemed bathed in a radiance far, far brighter than even the wolf moon could spill out. Later, she read somewhere that in times of extreme shock and fear the pupil of the eye contracts so profoundly that for a time the world seems almost unbearably bright.

The fire whose light she had seen was flickering beside the little tree they had decorated for the animals. Inanely, Emily noticed that most of the offerings were gone; good. The creatures had been here. They would hang up more. The fire had been made in a big aluminum washtub, and was near to wavering out. She looked out into the sea of spartina that rolled toward the

western horizon; it shone black and silver in
the moonlight, and was cut by the glittering
black tidal creeks, in each of which a tiny
moon shone. Tide must be almost full in,
she thought.

And then her eyes were pulled into the
middle of the clearing, and her legs crumpled under her, and she sat down hard in
tangles of briars on the cold earth. Elvis
edged backward to stand beside her, but he
did not stop growling.

In the center of the bare little cliff a black-
and-gold striped blanket had been thrown
down. Lulu lay on it, on her back, naked,
eyes closed, legs sprawled slack and far
apart, ribs heaving with breath. Her flesh
looked spongy and discolored, like bruised
fruit. There were red-black scratches on her
breasts and stomach. The entire clearing
stank so powerfully of whiskey and vomit
that Emily's stomach turned like a gaffed
fish.

The man who lay on top of her was not
naked, but his pants were down around his
ankles, as if he had been in a hurry. He
raised himself slightly from her body with
his forearms, which had pinned Lulu's arms
to the ground, and Emily saw that he was

still inside her. He looked slowly around at Emily in her supplicants' pose, and smiled. His penis slipped out of Lulu then, and lay flaccidly on her stomach, long and thin and white. As Emily stared it began to stir slightly against the spoiled flesh, and stiffen.

"Care to join us?" Yancey Byrd said.

Emily could not speak and she could not move. Elvis growled and growled. Yancey Byrd reached down and touched himself. "Plenty for everybody," he said.

"Emily, get out of here," Lulu said. Her voice was thin and frail, a sick child's. Her eyes did not open.

"GET OUT!" she screamed, when Emily did not move. There was nothing of affection or recognition or even of human life in the scream. Before it died away, Emily was on her feet and running back down the black path.

"*Run faster,*" Buddy said in her ear. "*Run harder!*"

Emily tried, but her feet were numb with cold and her legs trembled so that it seemed like running in waist-high water, running in one of those run-but-don't-get-anywhere dreams. She stumbled and fell and got up, and fell again. Behind her, Elvis barked and barked, his herding bark.

Midway back down the path the numbness wore off and Emily began to cry. Sickness and horror flooded her throat, and grief, and sheer revulsion. It almost doubled her over. She knew, suddenly, that something was coming after her down the path, something bound on consuming her, on doing her mortal harm. It was not Yancey Byrd; Emily heard the thin, lost wails start again from the banks of the dolphin slide and knew that he had what he wanted. But it was somehow *of* him. It rolled off him like smoke. It was dense and black and filled the world, stinking so of despair and sweat and sickness and fishy sex and utter corruption that she doubled over against the retching. Behind her, the darkness was boiling like smoke, thickening, moving inexorably, like a great autumn fog bank. If it overtook her she would drown in it, bobbling forever like a dead thing sunk to the ocean floor, slowly rotting, corrupted beyond reclamation. Doubled over, she faltered.

"RUN TO THE LIGHT, EMILY! GO INTO THE LIGHT!" Buddy shouted in her ear.

Elvis, running behind her now, nipping at her heels to prod her forward, looked back.

"Come on!"

Emily straightened up and saw, ahead, the mouth of the path that opened into the field. Beyond it, light spread like silver, like frost. Taking great, tearing breaths, she began to run again, oblivious of the tearing briars and jutting roots, her legs beginning to find a rhythm, her arms swinging with it. *"RUN, EMMY!"* Buddy shouted again, sounding farther away now.

"I'm running," she said back to him. "Can't you see that I'm running?"

"ONE MORE BIG PUSH, EMMY," he said, and she took a gigantic, dizzying breath and burst out into the light.

For a moment she stood still at the fringe of the woods, arms clutching her stomach, doubled over, gasping. And then she lifted her head and looked across the field toward the river. In the cold, pouring light of the moon Sweetwater stood black against the sky. A few of its windows still glowed yellow, and smoke came from the chimney that served the library fireplace. Her father. Her father was still awake. Whether he was mourning Lulu or waiting for Emily, it didn't matter. He was awake.

It was suddenly vital, imperative, life-or-death that he still be awake when she got home. Behind her, far back down the path, she smelled the black breath still coming on, though more slowly now.

"You're not quite there yet, Emmy," Buddy said. *"Run on, now."*

Straightening up again, she gulped freezing, burning air into her lungs and began to run once more. Elvis ran beside her, pacing her, perfectly silent, a ghost dog.

Under the huge, indifferent eye of the wolf moon, Emily Parmenter, thirteen years old and knowing things, ran for her life.

21

All that winter a great silence lay over Sweetwater. It had heft, mass, weight; enough weight to press Emily deep down into herself. She could hear the sounds of life and the world, but only faintly, as if through water. Buddy was silent. The house did not speak again. Only the dogs were clear. In the afternoons, when she trudged out to begin the puppies' training, their joyful treble voices washed her heart: "You're here! You came! Play with us! Teach us to be good dogs!"

"I'm here," Elvis said over and over. "I'm here." He said nothing else, but she asked nothing else of him in those numb, muffled days than that he be there.

Emily did not know if the others felt the

weight of the silence. She could see their lips moving at each other, see doors opening and closing, see dogs being loaded into their kennels in the truck bed, see guns being taken down from the rack to be taken to the river field for gun training. She could see the ghostly blue light from the TV set in the den every night, for her father and the boys had retreated back there quickly after dinner, as though they had never lingered in candlelight, laughing and captivated, at the dining room table.

But she did not hear, not really.

She had to assume that they did hear, for the life of the house went on, much as it had in the time before Lulu. Cleta came mornings as she always had, to get breakfast and tidy up, and her niece Anisha came now to cook dinner and do dishes at night. They all talked to her; she knew that they did, and every now and then she heard a fragment of their speech; "Emily, you lookin' weedy. Eat your breakfast." "Emily, did you take the choke chains out to the puppy ring? We need them for the big dogs." And from her father: "How is school this winter? Is the new litter doing okay? We've got four more coming up behind them, if you can handle them."

And she would strain and concentrate, and force their words to register in her brain.

To everything, she smiled widely and said, "Fine."

At school she could burrow into her books and not hear the words of her class-mates at all, but she saw them through thick air: "Where's that hot babe in the red beemer? You don't look half as good now as you did when you were cruising around in that car. She get tired of slumming? Your daddy and brothers put the moves on her?"

She would smile widely and move on to her next class. At lunch she stayed in her homeroom and ate the sandwiches Cleta had made for her, and read. Reading was real and fully engaging; she drowned herself in it. It was the only thing that was. Buddy had known that.

Every now and then she would think, "Is this what depression is? Or a nervous breakdown? I don't feel like either one, but I don't feel much of anything else, either. I wonder if I should tell anybody? But who would I tell?"

And then, "Lulu would know . . ." and

there would be a flash of pain so swift and keen and silvery that it only hurt a moment later, as a razor slash would have.

She could come and go without even noticing that a moat had ever been there, for Sweetwater was in a different country now, and if nothing seemed to particularly threaten, neither did anything particularly comfort. Going out from it was the same as coming home to it, only done at different times in the winter days. But still, after coming home, there were the puppies and Elvis, and their sweet cleanness and puppy silliness still engaged her, if less so than before.

"I'm back," she would think at a scramble of small just-released copper Boyklns. "You ready to rock and roll?"

And their frantic joy lifted her up, at least as long as she was with them.

Elvis was always there.

Sweetwater was busier than it had ever been. Lulu had been right; the word had spread swiftly after the hunt about Walter Parmenter and his remarkable Boykin spaniels, and orders for pups and training came in from all over the state. People came regularly to Sweetwater to see the paragons, and Emily and Walter and the boys put them through their paces, and the visitors invariably went home leaving orders behind. Many of them brought their own dogs to be started by Emily and brought along by the boys and the two new young trainers Walter had lured away from other South Carolina kennels. Walter was seldom at home; he took the dogs all over for field trials and exhibitions, and the mantel in the den grew crowded with dusty blue ribbons and tarnished silver bowls. Once there was a picture of Walter and a new litter in *The State,* Walter grinning at the camera and holding an armful of wriggling pups.

WALTER PARMENTER OF SWEETWATER FARM, WADMALAW ISLAND, AND HIS PRIZEWINNING BOYKIN SPANIELS, it was captioned.

Many of the weathered men who came to look at the puppies were from big plantations all over the Lowcountry, and many of them accepted with alacrity Walter's invitation to hunt at Sweetwater with the farm's spaniels.

But none of the planters asked him on their hunts. Everything had changed and yet nothing had. Walter had new trainers, new crates, a new SUV with "Sweetwater" scripted on the side, expanded quarters and a new ring for the older dogs, but he did not have the one thing his heart had thirsted for. If he wondered why, he never said. But Emily could have told him.

No one among the Lowcountry planters was going to give house room to the man who had lost Rhett Foxworth's daughter.

For Lulu did not come back. Not to Sweetwater, and not, apparently, to Maybud or Charleston or Randolph Macon, or anywhere else she might be expected to go. On the morning after the oyster roast, when she still had not appeared, Lulu's father, getting ready to go back to Maybud, asked Emily, scowling, if she knew where his daughter was.

"It's rude as hell," he fumed. "Not just to me. These guys are her family's oldest friends. Have you seen her, Emily?"

Crossing her fingers, Emily said, "Not since last night. I spent the night here, in the house, and she went out to her apartment. I think she might have been with that man from Virginia who came with you, though."

Annoyance and indulgence warred on Rhett Foxworth's bland babyface.

"Yancey Byrd. I might have known. He was hell-bent on finding her. No telling where those two might have gotten to. Well, I'm not going to worry about her, then, at least not for now. She's undoubtedly up to no good, but at least we know who she's up to it with. Maybelle will be thrilled. She'll be certain they ran off and got married. That would make up for all this flap about missing the goddamned Season. If she does show, send her home. We'll give her a few days before we start worrying."

"You should have started worrying months ago," Emily thought, grief and revulsion stopping her breath. She did not think the horrifying image of Lulu, flaccid and drunk and naked in the arms of that dark satyr of a man, would ever leave her. It felt burnt into her retinas, like the afterimage of a great red explosion. She thought that she would die before she told anyone about Lulu in that awful moment.

So she said nothing. After breakfast the planters left in their caravans of Land Rovers and custom Jeeps, scattering compliments and laughter, and Sweetwater was once again still and quiet. It was a quiet that echoed.

Walter did not mention Lulu to Emily, not then and not for a very long time afterward.

He simply said, "You did a good job this weekend, Emily. I'm proud of you," and vanished out to the field by the river with the older dogs. Watching him walk away across the lawn, Emily saw, not the vibrant golden man of the past few days, but her father again, abstracted as he had always been, emptied of the manic ambition and the strutting glee that had lit him throughout the fall. She wanted to cry for him, and then anger came sweeping in, anger at him for letting Lulu Foxworth become his polestar, anger at Lulu for tossing all of them away for the dark monster. There were things she could have done, Emily thought furiously. She could have left the party and locked herself in her apartment. She could have stayed overnight at the big house with Emily. She could have told her father that she was ill and had to go home.

In her heart of hearts, Emily knew that Lulu could have done none of those things, that her servitude to the dark man was absolute, and, this time, apt to kill her.

"I should have told her father," she thought, in an agony of guilt. "Or Cleta, or somebody. I let this happen to her. I swore I'd take care of her, and I just ran, and let it happen. And I didn't tell anybody. And I won't."

For a few days she moved in a miasma of guilt so thick and overpowering that she could barely stand under its weight. And then, as if summoned by her pain, white silence came, and she ran into it gratefully. It swallowed the guilt and everything else.

A few days later Maybelle Foxworth appeared at the farm, Caribbean-tanned and fur-coated and furious. She did not look like an older Lulu now. She looked like a harpy, a fury, a maenad.

"How could you let this happen?" she stormed at Walter. "She was under your roof! She was your guest! How could you let her just—vanish?"

Walter did not defend himself.

"I'm terribly sorry," he said. "She had gotten to be so much a part of the family that it never occurred to me to . . . watch her all the time. She never saw anybody but us, that I know of. She was with Emily constantly. I never even knew about this Byrd boy until he turned up."

Maybelle rounded on Emily.

"You must have known something!" she shrilled. "You lived with her; you slept downstairs from her, you were with her night and day for nearly seven months. She wouldn't have just . . . left without telling you."

Emily was silent, but her father spoke up. "Emily knows nothing more than the rest of us," he said, with an edge of iron in his voice that she had never heard. "If she did, she'd tell you. You might remember that it was you and your husband who asked if Lulu could come here, and said that you'd make sure she was no trouble at all. And she wasn't. But neither were any of us given any indication that we were expected to watch over her. Didn't she keep in touch with you? She said that she talked to you almost every day."

Emily saw in Maybelle Foxworth's face that Lulu had done no such thing.

"If you hear anything at all about her or from her, I expect you to call me instantly," she said coldly. "I'll have Leland come and get her things out of your barn this week-end. I never did think living upstairs in a dog barn was up to any decent standard, but . . ."

"But Lulu wanted it, and you let her," Emily thought. "And you were the one who tried every way you knew how to get her to come home and get swallowed up in all that drinking and partying, and you were the one who practically threw Yancey Byrd in her face. And if you didn't know about the liquor and the things that he did to her, you might wonder if a different kind of mother *would* have known. She tried to tell you."

But of course she said none of this, and Maybelle rocketed out of the driveway in her dusty Mercedes toward the highway and Maybud. No one at Sweetwater ever saw her again.

"That wasn't fair," Emily said, fighting tears.

Her father looked at her thoughtfully, seeming for once to see her.

"No," he said. "It wasn't."

Leland did indeed come, with a crew of Maybud workers, and moved Lulu's pretty things out of the barn, and drove away with them, and the barn was empty and echoing again, as if two girls had never laughed and preened and talked late into the nights in it.

Emily heard nothing more about Lulu Foxworth. She did not know if her father had, and did not ask. She had no idea whether Lulu had come home, or whether she was still lost and at large with Yancey

Byrd. She was not mentioned again at Sweetwater, not until much later, but the place where she was not howled with emptiness, and everyone walked softly, as if afraid they might step on her shadow.

And so Emily, dragging her great guilt, embraced the silence, when it came, like a mother or father. Like a lover.

In early March UPS brought two packages for Emily. They were waiting on the bed in her room when she got home from school. Cleta would have brought them up, she knew. Elvis lay beside them with his chin on his paws, looking up at her.

"Look. We got presents."

Emily opened the larger one first. It was very large, the size of a window, and fairly light. Ripping away the brown wrapping paper she saw, flaming out of the wrapping, the savage, blazing colors of empty steel blue sky, the black of wheeling winged predators, the red of bloody-handed men holding their terrible bowls up to the indifferent sun. The painting that Lulu so loved, by Richard Hagerty, that had lit her chaste nun's cell over the barn into a pagan priestess's temple. Lulu! Lulu was somewhere safe, at least safe enough to send this savage, beautiful message to her. Emily's heart hammered with joy.

The painting was a shout of power and strength. In its presence the guilt that hung about Emily was blown away.

"Look what Lulu sent us," she whispered to Elvis. "She remembers! She's okay, somewhere."

He did not reply.

She got up and carried the painting over to the wall of windows that overlooked the back verandah and the dock and the river. It looked right there, one with the great, spare elements of water and earth and sky. Only then did Emily come back to the pile of wrapping paper and scrabble for the note that she knew would be there. And it was.

It was written in bold black ink on an ivory vellum card, the kind that Lulu always used. At the top, Louisa Coltrane Foxworth was engraved in simple script. Her eyes dropped to the signature at the bottom.

"Grand," it read.

At first she did not comprehend what she was reading, and then it came clear and shock flooded her whole body. She sat stiffly, stock still, letting its surf break over her.

"Grand." Lulu's grandmother, old Mrs. Foxworth. Of course. Lulu's name was Louisa Cobb Foxworth, after some unremembered ancestor; Lulu had told her that. The painting was not, after all, a message from Lulu. Emily had not thought of Grand since Lulu had gone.

Numbly she began to read.

Emily, dear, I remember how much you liked this painting, and thought my granddaughter would like you to have it. Nobody else at Maybud will give it house room, and I don't know if I'm going to keep the cottage or not, so it needs a home. If you like, you can just look after it until, perhaps, you can return it to Lulu. That would be a happy day, wouldn't it?

So they don't know where she is, Emily thought dully. They didn't when Grand wrote this . . .

She read the rest of the note.

I've sent you a book of poetry that I found for Lulu, but on reading it over, I believe you might like it, too. These poems are raw and powerful and very sensual, but they speak so eloquently of love and loss and the sheer beauty of the world, things I imagine you are quite familiar with by now. Many people would think they are too adult for a thirteen-year-old—you had your birthday at New Year's, didn't you?—but I think they just might comfort you. You have had to grow up fast, I think, and believe some of the passages will have meaning for you. I marked many of them for Lulu, but there are some that call out especially to you; you will know them when you see them. I believe poetry is at its best when it gives you something that knows what you know, that will walk beside you always.

You have lost, one by one, many of the people you loved. I don't know how or if you can fill those empty places. But I've found that with poetry you are never truly alone. I hope you might find the same thing. Call me and let me know what you think.

And, below the signature:

I've sent you the old book of Foxworth family receipts Lulu brought to

Sweetwater. She said you'd loved cooking from them. Maybe you'll continue to make them for your family. Old-fashioned cooking, I've always thought, is very healing. And incidentally, did you ever read the entire poem Buddy's inscription to you in your Yeats book is from? It's called "When You Are Old." I think you will understand what he meant. Buddy had an uncanny way of knowing what people would need, and when.
—G.

Emily got up and put on her blue jeans and an old sweater of Buddy's that she had stolen from his closet after he died, and curled up on her bed with the book of poems. It was by a woman named Anne Michaels, called, simply, *Poems.*

She riffled through the book until she came to the first marked passage: "The dead leave us starving with mouths full of love."

She sat very still, feeling the line flower inside her until she could feel its heat out to the ends of her fingers, the roots of her hair. Mother. Buddy. Lulu.

She paged on until she found the next passage:

> *There are things that brothers and*
> *   sisters know—*
> *the kinds of detail a spy uses*
> *to prove his identity—*
> *fears that slide through childhood's*
> *   long grass,*
> *things that dart out later; and*
> *   pleasures like toucans,*
> *their brightness weighing down the*
> *   boughs.*
> *Who but a brother calls from*
> *   another hemisphere*
> *to read a passage describing the*
> *   strange*
> *blip in evolution, when reptiles*
> *   looked like*
> *"alligator-covered coffee tables."*

Buddy would do that, Emily thought. It's just what he would do. Comfort like hot chocolate began to uncurl in the pit of her stomach.

And the next:

Language is how ghosts enter the
  world.
They twist into awkward positions to
  squeeze through the black
  spaces.
The dead read backwards, as in a
  mirror.
They gather in the white field and
  look up, waiting for someone to
  write their names.

"I will write your names," she whispered to her mother and Buddy. But not to Lulu. Not yet.
The next:

Because the moon feels loved, she
  lets our eyes
follow her across the field, stepping
from her clothes, strewn silk
glinting in furrows. Feeling loved, the
  moon loves to be looked at,
  swimming all night across the
  river.

"Yes! I've loved the moon in the river and the creek all my life," Emily thought, smiling without knowing that she did. "From these very windows. From the dolphin slide at Sweetwater Creek. This woman can see inside my head."

And:

> Colette said, when one we love dies
> there's no reason to stop
> writing them letters.

"I've written you letters every day since you left," she said to Buddy, deep down.

And finally:

> If love wants you; if you've been
>   melted down to stars,
> you will love with lungs and gills,
>   with warm blood and cold.
> With feathers and scales.

Emily knew that this passage had been marked for Lulu. She closed her eyes, feeling tears burning behind her lids. Could Grand have known about the dark man after all?

She pulled her comforter up over her and read the entire book, face and heart burning. She did not go down to supper; she told Anisha that she thought she was catching a cold, and could she please have a plate in her bedroom. Anisha brought chicken pot pie and green peas and ice cream, and a bowl of Eukanuba for Elvis. Emily filled her ice cream bowl with water for him, and drew him close to her, and read on. She read and read and read.

She did not think that she slept, but she must have, for all of a sudden it was mid-morning on Saturday, and Elvis was whining to go out. Emily stumbled down the stairs and let him into the yard. Waiting for him, she listened to the house. It was silent. She remembered then: her father and brothers had gone early over to south Georgia, to some huge, famous plantation there, to deliver four finished Boykins to the owner. They would not be back until after dark. Neither Cleta nor Anisha came in on weekends. Anisha always left enough food to last, that could be eaten cold, or warmed up, and Cleta usually called each morning to check in with Walter or Emily. Emily stretched exultantly, her head swimming pleasantly with the lack of sleep and the burning poetry. A whole day. A whole day to read . . .

Elvis came clicking back in, and she took

a sandwich from the plate in the refrigerator and his kibble bag and went back upstairs. She was still in her jeans and Buddy's sweater; they felt warm and sticky and smelled faintly of her sweat. She took a quick shower and put on the long white flannel nightgown Aunt Jenny had bought her the year before, tied up her damp hair in a pony tail, and crawled back into the warm, tumbled bed. She picked up Anne Michaels' poems, and read on.

When she finished them it was nearly dark, and she called down to her father and brothers, who had come in stamping red spring Georgia mud from their boots, that she had a cold and would stay in bed, and there was cold ham and potato salad in the refrigerator.

Presently she heard the low, mindless voice of the television set in the library, and knew that they were settled for the night. She crept down and got cold ham and milk and took it back upstairs, and dived back into bed and into poetry. Beside her, Elvis slept. But he waked and looked up into her eyes occasionally, and whined.

"What are we doing? Why do we stay up here?"

"We're reading poetry. We need to do this. It's very, very important."

And he sighed, and turned around, and slept again.

That night, and early into the morning, and all the next day Emily read poetry and Elvis lay still beside her, not sleeping now, but head up, alert, looking up at her now and then. Guarding.

Her father and the boys were gone again, the boys to watch Bike Week in Daytona on the big plasma television set down at Sandy Don's on Folly Beach, her father to Columbia to talk to a breeder there about a new bitch. The house was dark and still and beginning to go dusty; Emily was crumpled and sweaty and dry-eyed from lack of sleep. But she did not go downstairs, except to get food from the kitchen and let Elvis out. Upstairs, poetry was burning life into her like a branding iron.

She read from Lulu's old *Contemporary Poetry* textbook: "Season of mists and mellow fruitfulness . . ." Keats, who might have been writing of every Lowcountry autumn Emily had ever seen. She found books of poetry in Buddy's dark, shuttered room, still smelling of old fires and dusty pages and, somehow him, and took them back to her bed. She found Thomas Hardy:

> *When the Present has latched its*
> *   postern behind my tremulous stay,*
> *And the May month flaps its glad*
> *   green leaves like wings,*
> *Delicate-filmed as new-spun silk, will*
> *   the neighbors say,*
> *"He was a man who used to notice*
> *   such things"?*

Written, surely, for and about Buddy.

And later, simply for the salt-burning, throat-filling loveliness of the language, Gerard Manly Hopkins:

> *Glory be to God for dappled*
> *   things—*
> *For skies of couple-colour as a*
> *   brinded cow;*
> *For rose-moles all in stipple upon*
> *   trout that swim . . .*

And Hart Crane:

> *And onward, as bells of San*
> *   Salvador*

Salute the crocus lustres of the
   stars,
in these poinsettia meadows of her
   tides,—
Adagios of islands . . .

The telephone rang and rang in the empty house.

Late that Sunday afternoon she found Lawrence Durrell, and read:

Something died out by this river,
but it seems less than a nightingale
   ago.

The dead, cold breath of the abyss stank suddenly in her nostrils.

"I can never go back there," she whispered to Elvis, and began to cry for Lulu.

She was still crying, silently, when she remembered Grand's question about the inscription in Buddy's birthday gift of Yeats to her, and found the book and riffled until she found *When You Are Old*. Tracing down the lines with her finger, she found it:

But one man loved the pilgrim soul
   in you,

And loved the sorrows of your
    changing face . . .

She put her face down into her pillow and sobbed. Beside her, Elvis licked her cheek frantically.

How could he have known that sorrow would write its words on her face so soon?

"I see," she whispered into the pillow.

"It's about time," Buddy said.

She slept then, slept until after nightfall, when Elvis's peremptory barking woke her. Her room was dark and stale, and her mouth so dry it cut her throat to swallow. She did not know quite where she was. As she lay there, her bedside lamp bloomed yellow, and a soft weight settled on the bed beside her, and her Aunt Jenny was there, pushing tumbled hair off her forehead with one hand and stroking Elvis with the other.

"I'm so glad you're here." Emily heard him distinctly. "I couldn't find anybody. Something's wrong. We've been up here way too long."

He spoke, Emily knew, not to her, but to her aunt.

"Emily," Jenny Raiford said, "what in the name of God are you doing up here? Cleta said nobody had answered the phone for two days. Are you sick, sweetie?"

Emily sat up and put her arms around her aunt's neck and her face into it. Not until she felt the remembered hollow there, where her cheek just fit, and smelled her aunt's lemony, clean-linen scent, did she realize that much of the dull ache inside her had been loneliness for Jenny.

"No," she quavered. "I've been reading poetry."

By ten o'clock her aunt had heard it all. She stood at Emily's dark windows, back to the room, looking out. She had been there for a long time.

"Can she see the river?" Emily wondered. "Can she see the moon on the river? Is there a moon? I don't remember. . . . 'Feeling loved, the moon loves to be looked at, swimming all night across the river.' "

Jenny had sent Emily to bathe and change into clean pajamas, and gone downstairs to let Elvis out and bring up Anisha's okra soup and cold milk. Emily ate the soup so fast it burned her throat all the way down into her stomach. She gulped cold milk; she had been starving. When had she last eaten? When had Elvis?

"All right," her aunt said, when Emily had scraped the bowl clean and set it aside. "Let's have it."

A dam broke inside Emily, and words burst out of her in a waterfall, tumbling over and over.

She could not have stopped if she had wanted to. Behind them was a force as elemental as the earth, the sea. On its crest pain rode. When the flow had abated, much of the pain had gone away from Emily, perhaps into her aunt's ears, perhaps into the very air. Emily knew only that she could begin to breathe deeply again.

Jenny had sat still beside her on the bed, her hand on Emily's forehead, for most of the story. Emily started with the ridiculous, brined-turkey Thanksgiving, went on through the soft, misted days that led to the magical Christmas, and on still through the spell-wrapped days just before the hunt: piled featherbeds on rough bunks; cold, fresh trees garlanded from the woods; the parade of china and crystal and silver and damask and servants from Maybud; dressing before Lulu's grandmother's old cheval mirror in green velvet and emeralds, black velvet and pearls. Her father, a different man, a golden one, in an English tuxedo, welcoming at last the planters of the Low-country to his home. Walking with Lulu through the readied house, learning how one came to be a daughter of the house. Then, the monstrous dark man, and the tossed-aside birthday party, and finally the goblin-haunted run through the dark woods to the dolphin slide on Sweetwater Creek, to the small tree they had decorated for the wood and marsh creatures, where Lulu lay, drunk and despoiled under the dark man's body. What he said to Emily, laughing, what Lulu cried to her, weakly. What Buddy said, urgently, into her ears. And the blind, terrible run back to the open field and, far in the distance, the lights of Sweetwater.

"There was something behind me," she said. Her voice was rough and rasped with talking and tears, and her throat was so dry that swallowing felt as though it was cutting her. Her lips trembled.

"It wasn't him, but I thought it sort of came *out* of him. It was like . . . black smoke boiling after me. I knew that if it touched me I would die."

Jenny Raiford had gotten up and gone to the windows when Emily got to the part about the dark man appearing in the door of Sweetwater behind Lulu's father. Emily did not think her aunt had moved since then.

Emily fell silent. The silence seemed to spin out for a very long time. Downstairs she could faintly hear the idiot muttering of the television set in the den. At last Jenny Raiford turned to look at her. Her face was bleached white, and her nose and mouth were pinched, and her voice shook with fury.

"What in the name of God was that girl *thinking*?" she whispered, as if she could not get enough air into her lungs. "How could she dump all that . . . *dirtiness,* that *ugliness,* on you. You were *twelve,* for Christ's sake! You don't tell a child that . . . filth. You don't tell *anybody,* unless there's something really wrong with you, something just left out of you . . ."

"I'm not a child," was all Emily could think to say. Somehow she had never imagined that the story could generate such anger. Pity, she had thought, pity for both her and Lulu.

"I'm sorry, Lulu," she whispered.

"No," her aunt said slowly. "No, you're not. In fact, you're far less of a child than you should be. But you're not grown-up, either. It should be years and years before you have to handle that kind of thing—if ever. Just hearing about it, not to mention seeing it—And then blowing off your birthday party. And begging you not to tell anybody about the drinking! I can't wish her ill, but I'm glad she's gone from here. There's no telling how badly she would have damaged you—and everybody else in this house if she'd stayed."

Emily began to shake her head, and Jenny came to sit once more on the side of her bed. This time she did not touch Emily, though. She simply sat, listening, an empty vessel to be filled up.

"It wasn't like that," Emily said heatedly. "She told me because she wanted me to understand why she got drunk. She needed me to help her not do it again. She'd been fighting it so hard, ever since she came. Her own folks wouldn't listen to her, and she didn't think she could tell her grandmother because she thought it would hurt her too badly to know. And I *did* help her, Aunt Jenny! I stayed with her every minute after

that, until that awful man came. If you'd
seen her when he came in, seen her face,
you'd understand. She couldn't help . . .
what he did to her."

   "Probably not," her aunt said after a long
moment. "She's not the first, and she won't
be the last. It's an obsession, sick and ad-
dictive. But she *could* help dragging you
into it. What did she think a twelve-year-old
could do to help her when she couldn't help
herself? That's what I'll never forgive,
never."

   "What was she supposed to do?" Emily
said desperately. She needed, above all
things, to make her aunt understand.

   "She'd have died if Elvis hadn't come and
gotten me. She was choking. I couldn't just
leave her. . . ."

   "No, baby. You did just the right thing. But
there were a lot of things she could have
done beside drag you into her mess. She
could have simply thanked you, when she
sobered up, and gone on about her business. She could have trained more dogs. Or
for God's sake, she could have gone home
and faced her parents and stopped be-
witching this family. You're all just so . . .
vulnerable to that kind of glitter and glamor.

You've never seen it, and your father hasn't in so long that he's forgotten how seductive it is. She played on that. I watched her do it. Cleta saw it, too. We should have done something."

"You make her sound like a witch of some kind. She wasn't—she isn't. She made us laugh, she cared about us, we were all together for the first time I can remember—and she needed me. We went everywhere together, we talked about everything. She never once treated me like a child."

"Well, she should have," Jenny Raiford snapped. "You were twelve years old, no matter how smart and supportive you were to her. You should be young for a long time yet. Nobody has the right to take that away from you. But then, nobody's ever really let you be young, have they? Not in this house. They just . . . leave you. Of course you adored her. Who else has ever really talked to you?"

"I talk to Cleta," Emily mumbled. "I talk to Buddy all the time; he talks to me, too. So does Elvis. . . ."

Her aunt reached out and pulled Emily to her. Emily could feel her lips making words on her cheek, her breath on her neck.

"Baby, what kind of life is it if your only friends are a dead boy and a dog?"

They were quiet. Jenny rocked her back and forth, back and forth. A slow warmth began to seep into Emily; she felt nearly boneless with it.

Then Jenny said, "Tell me about the poetry."

Emily did, feeling her face flame with joy, her voice thicken with it. The engulfing fever came back.

"Lulu's grandmother sent me the book," she said. "She said that poetry gives you something that knows who you are; she said if you have it you're never truly alone. And it's true, Aunt Jenny; I've read it and read it, all this weekend, and I haven't even known I was here by myself!"

"Let me see this book," Jenny said. Emily handed it to her. After a long time her aunt lifted her head from the pages and looked at her. The pinched whiteness was back.

"What kind of people *are* these Foxworths? It's shattering poetry, but Emily, all this dark, all this death, all this love melting you down business. This family has laid way too much on you. And that painting! It's stunning, of course, but in a thirteen-year-old's bedroom? My God. I really thought better of old Mrs. Foxworth."

"Do you know her?"

"Yes, a little. I heard all about her from Buddy; he adored her. I met her once, when I went to pick him up from his lesson. And I know you liked her, when you met her at her birthday party, but still . . ."

Emily started to tell her about firing the Purdey, but then she did not. She did not think there was any way she could make her aunt understand. And she thought that Buddy would want it to be just between them, their private covenant.

She showed Jenny the note that had come with the books and the painting. After she read it, Jenny laid it aside and smiled, slightly. "I guess she understands more than I thought," she said. "She knows you almost like she did Buddy. And she obviously loves her granddaughter. She must be hurting badly now. Why couldn't Lulu have told her all this? Surely she would have understood, even if the other Foxworths didn't."

"Lulu said it would kill her."

"So it would kill her grandmother, but not hurt you in the least. Good thinking."

Emily laid her head back on her aunt's shoulder, and Jenny held her lightly.

"Do you think she's dead?" Emily said finally.

"No," Jenny said. "But I don't think we'll ever know where she is unless the Foxworths tell us, and people like that don't talk about their failures."

"Do you think they know where she is?"

"Oh, yes. Somebody always knows where everybody is. There are a million ways to find people. If she was dead, everybody would know; you couldn't hide it. But I'll bet that's all anybody *would* know."

Emily whispered into the linen of her aunt's jacket, "Do you know where my mother is? Does Daddy?"

"I think he does, yes," her aunt said into Emily's hair. "But I truly don't. I only know that she's almost certainly alive."

Pain lanced through Emily. A dead mother couldn't come back to you. A live one could—if she wanted to.

"Have you ever asked Daddy?"

"No. He'd tell me, I think, but I just haven't. She left more than just you all when she walked out that door."

"Well, will you? Ask him, I mean? So I'd know . . ."

"No, love. That's for you to do."

"Aunt Jenny, I can't!"

"Probably not yet. You'll know when you can. Don't go asking for any more pain than you've already got, Emily. And your father doesn't need any more right now, either. He's lost the same three people you have."

"Do you think . . . that he loved her?"

It was a long time before her aunt answered. She rocked Emily absently, stroking her hair.

"No. I think he loved how she made him feel—a whole other person, one who could run with the big dogs. She gave him all that for a little while and then she took it away. You need to think about him now, Emily."

"Why? He doesn't think about me."

"Then reach out to him. You don't have to wait for him to do it. Make the first move. You're old enough to do that now, anyway."

"What if he doesn't answer?"

"Oh, Emily," Jenny Raiford sighed. "You'll never know if you don't try, will you?"

"What should I do?"

"You'll think of something. You'll think of just the right thing. Just let it come. You need to get to bed now. I want to talk to your father."

"Will you come back and see me?"

"Try and stop me," her aunt said.

"Aunt Jenny," Emily said. "Should I call her grandmother? She'd tell me about Lulu, if she knows. I know she would."

"No," Jenny Raiford said after a moment. "Let me do it. I suppose she's in the phone book. . . ."

"Yes, she is," Emily said. "She told me so the night of her party. She said to call her if I ever thought Lulu was in trouble."

She felt tears start in her dry, hot eyes.

"It's not your problem, baby," her aunt said, kissing her forehead. "It never was. Go to bed. Tomorrow's a school day."

She got up from Emily's bed and let herself softly out of the room.

The sheer, familiar banality of the words poured over Emily like warm water. She felt drowsy, soft throughout, only half-sentient, as a close-wrapped infant might. Safe.

"I'm thirteen years old, and tomorrow is a school day," she whispered, and sank back into her pillows.

Elvis bounded joyfully up the stairs and onto her bed, shaking it, smelling of wet

earth and kibble, turning around twice, bur-
rowing into her side. Girl and dog were
asleep before Jenny Raiford's footsteps had
faded down the stairs.

22

Jenny Raiford came back to stay at Sweet-water the next weekend. She would keep her job at the medical center, but would live in the room she had had before: Buddy's room.

"Will you miss your house and your room-mate?" Emily asked.

"No. The house backs up to the airport runway and my roommate leaves hair in the sink."

"What about your boyfriend?"

"He leaves hair in the sink, too."

"Are you going to leave again?"

"Not until you personally run me off," her aunt said.

Ever since the weekend before, when she had poured all of the debris of Lulu's time with them into her aunt's ears, Emily had felt light and fragile, hollowed out, as if she was getting over a long illness. It was not an unpleasant feeling. Often, out in the last of the March wind, she felt that she might simply be picked up on its green breast and borne out over the marshes, to the river and the sea.

On the Saturday that Jenny came, Emily got up early and put on her oldest jeans and took her oyster glove and knife and rowed the johnboat across the river to the high bank where millions upon millions of sweet, fat oysters clung. She brought them back and shucked them, and studied the book of receipts Lulu's grandmother had sent her, and carefully rolled out a rich pastry on the old marble board Cleta used. She stuffed the pie with layer after layer of oysters, adding butter and sherry and a little mace, and laid on the top crust, and set the pie to season on the porch. Cleta always did that. Emily had no idea why.

That night, as they had sherry before the fire in the library, she put the pie into the oven, and brought it, steaming and golden, to the table as they sat down to dinner. It was by no means a Lulu dinner; those were gone now from this house. But it was pleasant and serene, with Aunt Jenny's silver candlesticks holding white tapers, and, for the occasion, their grandmother's Haviland. Jenny brought white wine that tasted like flowers, and when the pie was cut, the fragrant steam clouded the breakfast room like warm, living breath.

Her father took a bite.

"This is wonderful," he said. "You've never made it before, have you, Jenny?"

"No, and I didn't this time," Jenny said. "Emily did the whole thing, from gathering and shucking the oysters to making the pastry. It's a very old receipt, I think."

Walter's eyes rested on his daughter. They were very blue in the candlelight gloom.

"It's beyond good, Emmy," he said. "Is this the girl who couldn't mix a batch of puppy kibble last year?"

"The same," Emily said, smiling at his smile. For one of the first times she could remember, it felt focused entirely on her.

"It's an old family receipt."

"Whose family?" he said grinning.

"Ours, of course," Emily said, and her father laughed aloud.

"Of course," he said.

The next morning, Sunday, Emily and Jenny Raiford walked down to the dock over the marshes, to the river. Spring had surged over the Lowcountry like a tidal wave during the past week, as it often did, and the entire world shone and sang with it. The sun was mellow still; the great heat would soon follow, but not yet. The greening marshes rippled like a silver-green sea, down to the water and off to the horizon beyond it. Every bird Emily could name and many she could not warbled and whisked in the undergrowth and live oaks. Leaves on every plant shone transparent, as if lit from behind by candles. The air smelled giddily of the sea and the marsh and the living creatures newly back, and powerfully of pluff mud. It was a day to make you silly; the new class of puppies had been manic with spring that morning, and for once Elvis did not chastise them, but rolled on his back in the new grass and let them tumble over him. Now he lay between Jenny and Emily, nose on paws, the sun burning his coat to red coals.

They sat in blissful silence for a while in the sun, and then Jenny said, "Emily, I have to tell you something sad. I called old Mrs. Foxworth at Maybud this week, and a woman answered and said that she had had a stroke and died just days before. It must have been right after she sent the book and painting to you. I asked if they had heard from Lulu, but she said she couldn't really say, and hung up. I'm sorry, sweetie."

Emily's eyes filled with tears, and she felt real grief. But it was a simple grief, a very young girl's grief. She thought that she had used up her small store of tearing complex anguish on Lulu. It was very like Grand not to require it of her.

Her father often watched her in those spring days, while she was training the newest puppies. He stood leaning on the fence to the puppy ring with his hands in his pockets. Often, Elvis sat beside him, leaning against his leg. Emily remembered how he had stood just like that at Christmas, watching Lulu as she bewitched his plantation into Camelot.

"How'm I doing?" she would call to him.
"Better than anybody," he called back.

Often, when she came home from school
that spring, her father and her aunt would
be sitting on the front porch, drinking iced
tea and rocking in the old chairs.

On one of those soft days, her father said,
"You've gotten really tall and skinny, haven't
you? When did that happen? You look a lot
like Jenny. Did you know that?"

"Sort of," Emily said. She knew she did.
She had only to look in her mirror.

"Yes, sort of," her father said. "I guess
you really look more like . . . you."

In those first days that her aunt was back,
Emily would lie in bed at night, listening for
the nearly forgotten sound of laughter from
downstairs. She heard it at the very end of
April, just before sleep, all of a piece with
the liquid gurgle of the quiet river and the
spring-teased tree frogs. In her sleep, she
smiled.

"I'm going to give the salutatorian's address
at graduation," she said shyly at dinner one

night in early May. It was still light outside, the green twilight of a Lowcountry spring, and the smell of mimosa and the breath of the river was intoxicating. Emily hardly knew how to talk about the address; it had surprised her profoundly when her student advisor gave her the news. She did not think her grades had been very good this quarter, and had absolutely no idea what a salutatorian saluted.

"It's not a very big deal," she said into the congratulatory outcry at the table. "Valedictorian is the big thing. You have to have sky-high grades for that."

"But this is because of your grades, too, isn't it?" her aunt said, looking candlelit herself in the light from the tapers.

"Well, Emmybug," her father said, leaning back and smiling hugely. "So far as I know, it's the first speech anybody in this family has ever given. We'll pack the house to hear you."

"Oh, don't," she said faintly. "I may refuse it and let it go on to the next person on the list. I don't know how to talk to anybody but dogs."

"You'll do no such thing," Jenny said. "We'll bring Elvis and you can talk to him.

But talk you're going to. Emily, we are so proud!"

"It's hard to believe you'll be starting high school," her father said later. They were sitting on the front porch, watching a great yellow moon slip shyly up the sky over the river. "Feeling loved, the moon loves to be looked at . . ."

"So will it be Hammond, or what? I don't even know where the high schools are around here. Some father of the graduate I am."

"Maybe," Emily said. "Or there's a new magnet school over on John's Island. My advisor says I could probably go there. I don't know. I don't have to decide yet."

"Nope," her father said, giving the swing a push and setting it creaking and soaring. "Got all summer."

A week after that, Walt Junior came in with news about Lulu.

"Spencer Hardin's older sister, the one that lives in New York, said she saw Lulu sitting in a lounge at Kennedy Airport. She was a wreck, Spencer said—thin as a skeleton, dirty and straggle-haired, and she was lying on the floor with her head on her luggage. She was asleep or drunk, or high—something anyway; she looked dead. It was in one of those lounges where you wait to go overseas; she was at a gate to some flight to Africa or Egypt or somewhere."

Tangier, Emily thought. Lulu had always wanted to go there. She said everything was the color of soft heat; you'd never be cold there.

She got up from the table and went upstairs to her room. Out her back windows she could see the lighted square of the apartment over the barn that had been Lulu's; a sallow young couple who were promising trainers had it now. Emily closed her eyes and thought of white walls and gauzy blowing bed curtains and Lulu's sheaf of fragrant gilt hair, falling across her tanned cheek; she smelled French lavender soap and sweet new wood shavings from the barn downstairs, and heard Lulu's lazy laughter.

Tears squeezed out from under her eyelashes.

"Oh, Lulu," she whispered. "Be warm."

Two days later, on an afternoon of thunderstorms rolling in from the west, and flying greenish clouds, Emily found a letter lying on her bed after school. It was heavy, a thick, creamy envelope with Charlotte Hall engraved on its upper left-hand corner. Emily's heart began to thud, violently. She put the envelope down and changed her clothes and went out to the puppy ring. When she got back it was, of course, still there.

"Dear Miss Parmenter," it began. After that the elegant roman typeface blurred in and out, but a few paragraphs came clear:

. . . the first recipient of the Louisa Cobb Foxworth scholarship. This is a full, four-year scholarship for English and language arts, recently established by one of Charlotte Hall's oldest and dearest friends, Mrs. Louisa Coltrane Foxworth, in honor of her granddaughter, who is a graduate herself. Ordinarily we would ask for transcripts from your middle school, and for preliminary testing and a meeting with you and your parents, and we will do so soon, but Mrs. Foxworth assured us that you were

*a proper, and indeed, in her mind, the
only possible recipient of this first
scholarship. We are pleased to honor her
wishes. As you may know, Mrs. Foxworth
passed away recently, and all of us here
will miss her strength and dedication and
her extraordinary rapport with young
people very much indeed. I believe that
establishing this scholarship was one of
her last acts before her death.*

*We hope to hear soon that you will
accept the scholarship, and we look
forward to meeting you and your family
as soon as possible. Please call me at
697-0000 so that we may arrange a time.
Welcome to the Charlotte Hall family.*

Sincerely,
Rose Curry Ashmead
Headmistress

Emily folded the letter into a very small
square. She did not tell her father or her
aunt about it. But she carried it with her
every day in her pocket or tucked into her
bra. It felt alternately burning hot and icy
cold there. The end of school approached,
and still Emily told no one about the letter

except Elvis, who said, "Will this change things?" and Buddy, who said nothing.

At night she slept with the letter under her pillow and had strange, endless dreams about water and docks and boats moored at docks. One of the boats was the beautiful schooner she had seen in a dream last fall, fully rigged and tugging at its moorings in the river wind. This time, though, there was no one on board. But a pile of tagged luggage stood on its shining teak deck. She could not read the tags on the luggage, and rolled over restlessly and fell deeper into sleep.

A week before graduation, with the commencement address still lying immense and unborn in Emily's head, the first wave of the huge, sapping heat fell down over the Lowcountry out of a whitened sky. Everything and everyone moved slowly and ponderously; even time seemed to seep away drop by infinitesimal drop. Walter Parmenter and the boys stopped work with the intermediate dogs down by the river at noon, and Walter came most afternoons to watch Emily with the new puppies. The ring was shaded by a giant live oak, and sometimes her father sat cross-legged on the grass under it or leaned back against its great baroque trunk. Almost always, now, Elvis sat or lay beside him, eyes quiet and steady on Emily.

On the second day of the heat Emily was just taking the puppies back into the barn to their mothers when Elvis began a staccato fusillade of barking. It was not admonitory or protective; Emily could only think that these were barks of joy.

She left the ring and went over to where Elvis and her father waited. Elvis was running forward for a small distance, and then back to them, looking up at Emily. Barking, barking.

"He wants us to follow him," Emily said to her father.

"Where?"

"I don't know. He always knows, though."

Her father got to his feet and wiped sweat from his forehead. In the full sun he was brown and lean, and the silver-blond hair blazed. Emily's heart contracted.

"He's not old," she thought. "Why did I used to think he was old?"

"Lead on," he said to Elvis, and the man

and the girl set out beside the Boykin, dancing like a dervish in his eagerness.

He bounded straight across the blinding
field and into the trees where the maritime
forest began, ending ultimately at the dolphin slide on Sweetwater Creek.

"I know where he's going," Emily said
suddenly, laughing aloud. "Come on,
Daddy. We'll be late!"

Walter Parmenter shook his head, but
lengthened his stride to match his daughter's. Soon they were deep in green
shadow, the air near-solid with heat and
steaming vegetation and the drone of insects. Elvis ran ahead like a bronze bullet,
his curly ears streaming back in his own
breeze.

They burst out of the forest and onto the
bluff that looked down into the creek. The
tide was near out, and the blue ribbon of
water cutting the great sea of cordgrass
hardly moved. Out over the creek, from the
branches of the fallen oak, something large
dropped into the water, and something else
croaked. Emily had a moment's sick, kalei-
doscopic image of spoiled-fruit flesh and
dying firelight; smelled the amniotic smell of
sex and the stench of vomit and the sour

breath of dying woodsmoke; felt the shape of the great blackness boiling behind her. And then all of it was gone. There was only heat and stillness and the little sullen lap of the retreating tide.

But there had been something. Down on the little beach there were fresh, deep, wet grooves in the sand, and the water still rocked a little, slapping at the banks. Far downstream a great thrashing died away.

"Oh, we missed them," Emily cried. "They came early; Elvis knew they were here. But we missed them! I wanted you to see . . ."

There was a swell and wash of creek water below them, just off the beach, and a large bullet-shaped silver head broke the water and hovered there. The huge, all-seeing black eye regarded them, and the closed, comic-strip smile saluted them, and then there was a great roll of rubbery silver flesh and the dolphin dove under and slid downstream, as silent as a ghost fish, to join his retreating pod.

"He waited for us!" Emily cried, tears and sweat stinging her eyes. "He did once before, when Lulu and I were here; Lulu said she thought they came when they knew you needed them."

Her father smiled down at her.

"My God," he said. "The river dolphins. I'd completely forgotten about them. I saw them when I first came here, right here on this bank."

"Did . . . my mother bring you here?"

Walter Parmenter laughed, an easy, almost boyish laugh.

"Your mother never willingly went outdoors in her life. It was your Aunt Jenny, before I ever met your mother. They're really something, aren't they?"

They sat down on the grass beneath the fringe of willows and small live oaks. His mission completed, Elvis lay down beside Emily, his pink tongue lolling sideways out of his grinning mouth. For a long time they sat in silence.

Then her father said, "Did you know that the ratio of salt to water in seawater is exactly the same as the ratio in human blood? I read that some place. No wonder so many people are addicted to the sea."

Emily smiled at him.

"Do you remember that time you had to come get me at camp in the mountains, and everybody thought I was just homesick and being a baby? It wasn't that at all. It was that I just couldn't breathe away from salt-water, from the river and the creek. I still can't, really."

"No," her father said. "I didn't know that." He put his arm around her shoulder and drew her toward him. Emily laid her head on his shoulder, very carefully and slowly, as though the shoulder would of itself heave her off.

"I didn't know much about you at all, did I?" he said. "I have a lot of catching up to do."

They sat in silence again. Emily did not lift her head. Beside her, Elvis snored rhythmically. She touched the breast pocket of her shirt and felt the stiff outline of folded paper.

"Tell me about my mother," she said.

EPILOGUE

On a blue September morning, the first one in a long time not to dawn white and thick and breathless, a pretty girl in a long flowered skirt and pink tank top stood before a pair of great wrought-iron gates, looking through them. Inside, on the clipped grass and the white paved paths crossing it, and alighting from a fleet of shining compact buses, other girls almost identical to her laughed and called out to one another.

Emily knew they were not like her, though. Their hearts did not drag; their blood did not fizz with the poison champagne of terror; their tongues were not cotton in their mouths.

Abruptly she turned and ran back to the green SUV parked at the curb, dusty from the rutted driveway of Sweetwater and dappled with the genteel shade of Rutledge Street downtown.

She put her head in the window on the driver's side and kissed her father's cheek. It was glassy-slick and pink with fresh razor burn, and his damp hair showed the tracks of a comb.

"You're going to be late, Emmybug," Walter Parmenter said. "Run on. Jenny or I'll pick you up here about four."

She went around to the other window and leaned in and kissed the dome of a shining coppery, curly head.

"I'll be back. And I'll still be me."

"I know."

She walked slowly back across the quiet street and up to the gates. Again, she stopped.

"You don't have to do it all," Lulu said clearly into her left ear. "Just take what you want and let the other stuff go."

"Go get 'em, Emmy," Buddy said into her right ear.

Emily squared her shoulders and spit on her fingers and slicked the unruly hair back off her forehead, and walked into Charlotte Hall.